**The six-man team emerged onto the tarmac at dusk.
The shadows they cast moved with
calculated precision.**

They passed under the idle blades of Black Hawk helicopters and crossed between the crates of supplies waiting to be shipped to hot spots around the world.

Any onlooker with even limited military knowledge would know the silhouettes did not belong to the average grunt. Their body armor was thinner and their muscles were sculpted in a way that reflected constant training and exercise. Further scrutiny would reveal that these men carried modified weapons.

But no matter how well trained the eye of an onlooker might have been, none would have known the shadows belonged to the Delta Force operator team code-named Ghost, because technically, they did not exist—technically, they *were* ghosts who were activated only when the most critical situations emerged.

Today was one of those days.

Books by Nicholas Sansbury Smith

THE EXTINCTION CYCLE

Extinction Horizon
Extinction Edge
Extinction Age
Extinction Evolution
Extinction End
Extinction Aftermath
"Extinction Lost" (An Extinction Cycle Short Story)
Extinction War (Fall 2017)

TRACKERS: A POST-APOCALYPTIC EMP SERIES

Trackers
Trackers 2: The Hunted (Spring 2017)
Trackers 3: The Storm (Winter 2017)

THE HELL DIVERS TRILOGY

Hell Divers
Hell Divers 2: Ghosts (Summer 2017)
Hell Divers 3: Deliverance (Summer 2018)

THE ORBS SERIES

"Solar Storms" (An Orbs Prequel)
"White Sands" (An Orbs Prequel)
"Red Sands" (An Orbs Prequel)
Orbs
Orbs 2: Stranded
Orbs 3: Redemption

EXTINCTION HORIZON

The Extinction Cycle
Book One

NICHOLAS SANSBURY SMITH

www.orbitbooks.net

Copyright © 2014 by Nicholas Sansbury Smith
Excerpt from *Extinction Edge* copyright © 2015 by Nicholas Sansbury Smith

Cover design by Lisa Marie Pompilio
Cover art by Blake Morrow
Cover copyright © 2017 by Hachette Book Group, Inc.

Orbit
Hachette Book Group
1290 Avenue of the Americas
New York, NY 10104
orbitbooks.net

Originally published in ebook by Orbit in February 2017
First Mass Market Edition: April 2017

Orbit is an imprint of Hachette Book Group.
The Orbit name and logo are trademarks of Little, Brown Book Group Limited.

The publisher is not responsible for websites (or their content) that are not owned by the publisher.

The Hachette Speakers Bureau provides a wide range of authors for speaking events. To find out more, go to www.hachettespeakersbureau.com or call (866) 376-6591.

ISBNs: 978-0-316-55799-3 (mass market), 978-0-316-55798-6 (ebook)

Printed in the United States of America

OPM

10 9 8 7 6 5 4 3

For my grandparents Lena and Angelo "Jake" Angaran. I wish there had been more time to get to know you, but in the short time I did, you taught me so much.

"Life on Earth is at the ever-increasing risk of being wiped out by a disaster, such as sudden global warming, nuclear war, a genetically engineered virus or other dangers we have not yet thought of..."

—*Stephen Hawking*

Prologue

July 10, 1968
Operation Burn Bright
Northwest Vietnam

Operation Burn Bright started off with a smooth insertion. Lieutenant Trevor Brett and thirty-one other marines jumped into the fray, fast-roping from the crew compartment of multiple UH-1 "Huey" choppers hovering fifty feet above the drop point.

The stink of the jungle filled Brett's lungs as soon as his boots hit the ground. They'd been dropped on the outskirts of a swamp, and the rot lingered in the sultry air.

Brett gagged at the smell and promptly clenched his jaw shut. He moved with his lips sealed and was careful not to swallow any bugs when he was forced to open his mouth and bark orders. Vietnam was the worst place for someone who suffered from a borderline case of obsessive-compulsive disorder. There was simply no way to maintain good hygiene in the jungle.

Breathing through his nostrils, Brett led his men slowly into the knee-deep water in a wedge formation. Every few steps he would pause, scan the area, and then flash a hand signal to advance. The men were experienced enough to know they should maintain combat intervals. Enough of them had seen buddies die from clustering together, forming double targets for the enemy.

If he didn't have his lips closed, Brett might have even smiled at the sight of his well-organized platoon. But smiling was reserved for peacetime, not war. In Brett's eyes, Vietnam was just a place for marines to go and die.

The farther they moved into the muck, the deeper the swamp became. Stagnant water crawled up his legs, sending a cold chill through his body.

Goddamn, he hated the fucking jungle and everything inside of it—the snakes, the bugs, and worst of all, the leeches. He stifled a curse when he saw a foot-long leech swimming in his direction. The last thing he wanted to do was notify Charlie they were coming. The sloshing water was already loud enough to tell every Vietcong in the area that a platoon full of fresh meat was on its way.

As he slopped through the water, Brett wondered how he had gotten so unlucky. The war had ruined everything. After graduating college, he had looked forward to a career in banking, with a nice little cookie-cutter house, a gorgeous wife, and a warm dinner waiting at home for him every night. Instead, his girlfriend had left him, and he was wading through water toward one of the most ruthless enemies the American military had ever faced. To make things worse, he and his men carried an experimental drug that they were supposed to take right before reaching their target. Command had said it would negate the effects of any chemicals lingering in the area, such as Agent Orange, but Brett had his doubts. It sounded more as if they were being used as guinea pigs.

"Shit," he muttered, as a fly the size of a peanut buzzed by his helmet. He swept the muzzle of his M16 over a clearing at the far end of the swamp. They weren't far from their target, a remote village that brass claimed was secretly supporting the local VC.

Brett wasn't so sure. He'd been down this road many times before. Most of the time, they didn't find shit.

When they reached the edge of the swamp, Brett balled his hand into a fist. He jerked his chin toward the platoon sergeant, a stocky Texan named Fern. The man was built like a football player, with wide shoulders and tree trunks for legs. He approached with a toothy grin, revealing a wad of chew that bled a brown trail of juice down his chin strap.

The two men were exact opposites. Fern cared nothing for hygiene and seemed to thrive in the disgusting jungle. The thicker the muck, the more he enjoyed himself.

"Lieutenant," Fern said, squinting, with a hand shielding his eyes.

"The village should be just beyond that ridgeline," Brett said, pointing toward an embankment across the field. "Tell everyone not holding security to pair up and take their doses of VX-99, and make sure they actually do it."

"Roger that, sir," Fern replied. He spat a chunk of tobacco into the soupy water, and Brett watched it vanish into the mouths of some small fish. His stomach churned at the sight.

Brett followed Fern onto solid ground. They stepped over rotting vegetation and slapped away sharp branches. When they got to the edge of the clearing, Brett dropped to his right knee and reached for his bag. He removed the small syringe of VX-99 and eyed it suspiciously. There was nothing he hated more than needles, except the jungle and everything inside of it. If sticking the needle in his arm meant he would get out of here quicker, well, then, fuck it.

He bit off the plastic tip and spat it out, found a bulging vein in his wrist, and jammed the point of the needle into his arm. Slowly, he pushed the mysterious cocktail into his bloodstream. A sharp pain instantly raced down his arm. Brett tossed the syringe into the brush and placed a finger over the spot. The other men were taking turns: one man on guard with weapon at the ready, the other with his weapon cradled while jabbing the chemicals into a vein.

Brett waited there, listening to the hum of oversized insects and the chirps of exotic birds, for several seconds, wondering if the platoon would notice any side effects.

After a minute, the tingling sensation in his veins passed. He stood, shouldering his rifle and leveling the muzzle over the field. So far there was no sign of the enemy, but that didn't mean they weren't out there. Charlie was always out there, waiting to strike like the drugs in his veins.

"Move out," Brett said. Fern nodded and flashed a blur of hand movements to the men on their right. The marines fanned out over the field at a brisk pace, their boots slurping through the mud.

Before they'd made it halfway, Brett felt a burning. At first he wondered if the wind had carried Agent Orange into the area, but this burning wasn't the same. It wasn't coming from outside of his skin—it was coming from inside his chest, as if he'd swallowed an entire bottle of Vietnamese hot sauce.

Small jolts of pain raced through his body with every heartbeat. The agonizing burn spread to his head and lingered there. He blinked, tears welling in his eyes. He felt as if he was being burned alive, only from within.

Out of the corner of his eye, he watched a PFC named Junko collapse to both knees, clawing madly at his skull. Then came the screaming. Wails of pain broke out as other marines fell.

What the fuck is happening to us?

The pain was so intense Brett could hardly think. Shimmering arcs of bright light broke across his vision. The oranges, reds, and yellows swam before his eyes. The jungle faded behind the colors.

Dropping his rifle on the ground, he cupped his hands over his ears to drown out the pained shrieks.

Whatever was happening to the platoon wasn't the effect of some chemical lingering over the field. Brett could hardly form a cohesive thought, but he knew the pain was a result of the VX-99.

A sudden surge of fire blasted through Brett's body. It was followed by a sharp tingling sensation, as if hundreds of bees were stinging him all at once.

He fell to his back, itching the bare parts of his skin violently. There was no relief, only more pain.

His mind responded by taking him away from the jungle, to a place where there were no massive bugs, rotting vegetation, or men trying to kill him.

A brick house, with a stone path leading up to it, emerged. At the front door, an attractive woman held a glass of ice water. She smiled. "Come in, honey. Dinner is almost ready."

Brett felt the pain diminish as he slipped deeper into this fantasy. He knew that the house and the woman weren't real, but he didn't care. He wanted to escape the godforsaken jungle. He *needed* to escape.

When he got to the door, the woman was gone. The door was closed. He tried the knob. It was locked. Then the house was gone too. The bright colors returned. He could feel his body again. Fear replaced the pain.

When his eyes popped open, he saw the cloudless sky and the brilliant white sun above.

Where was he?

He heard muffled voices, the rustling of gear, and the shriek of some exotic animal. There were other noises—distant noises.

The world became exceptionally vivid. Brett could hear the bugs crawling through the underbrush; he could smell the stink of sweat on his uniform. He could taste coffee he didn't remember drinking. His senses were heightened to a level he'd never experienced before.

It was terrifying, but at the same time it was oddly liberating. He clenched his fists, feeling his muscles contract.

He stared at his hands with grim fascination. He felt stronger than ever before, as if he could take on an entire army. He felt...

Invincible.

Dazed but alert, Brett leaped to his feet. Tilting the front of his helmet upward, he ran his sleeve across his face to clear the sweat dripping into his eyes.

When his vision cleared, he instantly stumbled backward, nearly tripping over his own feet as he sloshed through the mud. Brett spun to see two dozen men staggering across the moist dirt. They wore the same fatigues he wore and carried the same gear he did. They were marines, like him. Several of the men walked off aimlessly in different directions, cupping their heads in their hands. He felt there was something almost familiar in their faces, but he couldn't place it. Did he know these men?

He heard a woman's voice. "Kill them," she croaked. "Kill them all."

Brett spun again, his boots sinking in the mud as he searched for the woman. It was then he realized the voice was coming from inside his head.

"You must kill them," said the voice again. She snarled, "Do it before they kill you!"

Brett smacked the side of his helmet.

Who was this woman, and why did she want him to kill these men?

Brett focused on the marine in front of him. He was a short, stocky fella with a wad of chew jammed inside his lip. Brett could smell the tobacco juices dripping off the man's chin.

When he saw Brett he held up his hands and balled them into fists. The marine growled, "Get away from me, y-you"— he stuttered, swallowing a chunk of the tobacco—"you fuck!"

Brett experienced an abrupt wave of adrenaline. He reached for something to protect himself. His fingers found the warm metal handle of a blade on his belt. He pulled the knife from its sheath in one swift motion, as if he'd done this many times before.

The woman's voice returned, booming inside his mind. "Stab him. Stab him right in his fat little gut."

"Get away from me!" the man yelled, a vein bulging in his neck as spit flew from his mouth. Brett narrowed in on the vein. He could see it pulsating. He imagined the blood flowing through the thin passage.

The image sent a thrill through Brett's body. His own blood tingled inside of him. In one move, he jumped to the side with impressive speed. The stocky man moved quickly too, throwing a jab that whooshed through the air.

Brett ducked and plunged forward, sinking the blade deep into the man's stomach, just as the woman had told him to. The marine let out a scream of agony, blood gurgling from his mouth. Brett wasted no time. He withdrew the knife, took a step back, and then jammed the blade into the man's neck.

The stout man clutched both wounds and dropped to his knees before collapsing face first into the mud.

Taking a short, satisfying breath, Brett picked up a new scent. He could almost taste it.

It was the scent of death.

The sudden crack of automatic gunfire pulled Brett back to the rice field as if a switch had been flicked. His gaze roved across the embankment beyond the field, noting each flash.

An explosion went off a few hundred yards away. The deafening blast sent a red geyser of dirt and body parts into the sky. When the mist cleared, a bloody crater was all that remained of the marine who had been standing there seconds before.

"Run!" cried the woman's voice.

Shocked into motion, Brett gripped the knife tightly and took off at a dead sprint. The sound of his boots stomping through the muck faded against the sounds of war.

More explosions rocked the dirt around him. Mud, water, and vegetation rained down. He ignored the burning sediment that landed on his bare skin and ran faster.

The other marines ran too. Some of them dropped as bullets tore into them. He saw a man to his right disappear as a grenade detonated under his feet.

Brett felt nothing for the man. Nothing fazed him. There was only one thing that mattered...

Killing.

Something nicked him as he ran. He looked down, expecting to see a fly on his skin, but instead saw a quarter-sized hole where a bullet had torn into his bicep. A second round pierced his side. The impact slowed him momentarily. The coppery taste of blood filled his mouth. Licking his lips, he continued running.

He could see the faces of the men trying to kill him as he approached the embankment. They hid under straw hats and helmets, screaming in a language that he did not understand.

He could smell the sharp scent of gunpowder and the salty sweat on their uniforms.

When he was ten yards away from the bottom of the hill, he dropped to all fours, gripping his knife between his teeth, and galloped, using his back legs to spring forward. He leaped up in three rapid movements and landed on the chest of one of the Vietnamese soldiers. Pulling his knife from his teeth, he speared the unsuspecting man through the chest, penetrating his heart. The man's eyes rolled back in his head, and Brett moved on to the next soldier.

Every thrust sent a thrill through his body. A wide grin spread across his face. He felt insanely powerful.

Minutes later, the ridgeline was littered with the mangled corpses of the enemy soldiers. A growing river of red seeped down the hill.

Brett pulled his gaze away to scan his own body. Blood oozed from his wounds, but there was little pain. He ignored the injuries and stepped over one of the bodies.

The woman's voice boomed inside his mind. "You're not done!"

Glancing up from a nearby corpse, he saw a slender African American marine glaring at him with crazed eyes from the bottom of the embankment. The man licked his lips and tossed a knife from his left hand to his right. His green uniform was soaked with blood from a bullet that had clipped his neck. Behind him, Brett could see the field. Pockmarks littered the ground where grenades had exploded. Dozens of bodies lay in the shallow water around the craters.

Brett looked back and met the man's dark gaze. Gripping his own knife tightly, he swung the blade toward the skinny marine. The tip whooshed through the air, but it didn't deter the man. He dropped to all fours and climbed the hill quickly, his joints clicking with every motion.

Before Brett could move, the marine lunged toward him. They collided, tumbling across the bloodstained dirt. The air burst from Brett's lungs as he finally landed with a thud on the hard earth.

Brett sucked in a deep breath and then pushed himself to his feet with his knife still in his hand. He caught the other man off guard with an uppercut that lodged the blade inside his skull.

A strangled sound escaped the marine's mouth. He grabbed the knife's handle as he dropped to his knees. Brett kicked him in the chest and watched with grim fascination as the man hit the dirt on his back and choked on his own blood. He kicked against the ground violently, struggling for several minutes before finally going limp.

Gasping for air, Brett stumbled away. He dropped to both knees and squinted as a gust of wind swirled dust around him. Stars broke before his eyes. Dizziness set in. He was finally starting to feel the effects of blood loss, but there was still no pain.

As he looked over the field, a distant memory of a brick house and woman entered his thoughts. He quickly pushed them away. There was only one thing that he wanted now. Only one thing he desired.

To kill.

Forty-Seven Years Later
March 3, 2015
World Health Organization Field Hospital
Guinea

Doctor Chad Roberts popped a stimulant into his mouth and swallowed it without the aid of water. He was exhausted from traveling. In less than twenty-four hours, he'd left his office at the Centers for Disease Control and Prevention's headquarters in Atlanta, crossed the Atlantic Ocean, and landed in Conakry, Guinea. From there a chopper had taken him to a WHO field hospital on the outskirts of a remote village twenty miles west of the city of Dabola. The region, though isolated, had a population of approximately 114,000.

During his flights, he'd slogged through the reports of the new and deadly Ebola strain. Preliminary notes revealed the microbreak was severe. The virus was killing faster than ever before, and Chad suspected it had mutated. The mere thought had prevented him from sleeping while he traveled. Chad had arrived with deep bags under his eyes and a headache that made it difficult to think.

He slipped on his biohazard space suit. The white walls of the portable biohazard facility closed in around him as he pulled on his helmet. The narrow view through his visor always made everything seem smaller, but he also felt safe. Many scientists described feeling claustrophobic in the suits, but not Chad. The suit gave him the reassurance he needed to face the world's most lethal biological agents.

After hastily moving through the laundry list of protocols, Chad pulled back a plastic screen and moved into the next room, where Doctor Debra Jones, from the WHO, waited. She tapped her boot against the floor and glanced up with a scowl when she saw him.

"We're late," she said. "The rest of the team is already in the village."

"Sorry," Chad replied. "I have a hell of an awful headache."

"I presume it will get much worse when you arrive in the hot zone," Dr. Jones said coldly.

Chad's gut sank at the statement. This wasn't his first time in the field, but he'd never seen the effects of Ebola in person. He swallowed hard as they stepped into the blinding sunlight. The humidity instantly fogged Chad's visor as they left the cool interior of the biohazard facility. The door sealed behind them with a metallic click.

They moved briskly across a dirt path the color of clay. A Toyota pickup truck waited a hundred yards away, its aged muffler coughing smoke into the sky. Chad set his equipment on the tan bed of the truck and hoisted himself up. He spun and offered a hand to Dr. Jones. She took it reluctantly. They settled onto the metal bed with their backs against the cab as a slender Guinean man closed the tailgate behind them.

Squinting, Chad looked up at the ruthless midday sun. He'd been outside for only two minutes, but he was already suffocating within his suit. Salty drops of perspiration cascaded down his forehead.

It was going to be a brutally long day.

Typically they would have traveled in the morning to beat the midday heat, but a problem with his equipment back at the airport had caused a delay. Now they were heading out at the hottest time of day.

The Guinean man smacked the side of the truck, and the driver hit the gas. The Toyota lurched forward and pulled onto a brown frontage road leading away from the cluster of dome-shaped biohazard facilities. Chad stared in awe, realizing how foreign they looked against the lush green landscape. He could only imagine what the locals had thought when they were going up.

"How long until we get there?" Chad shouted.

Dr. Jones held up three fingers as she gazed out the window. The truck was racing toward a fort of trees in the distance. An oasis of green in an otherwise brown canvas.

The Faranah Region of Guinea was a beautiful place.

Thick forests claimed much of the terrain. The mixture of browns and greens formed a warm collage of colors. But somewhere amidst the dense trees they were driving toward, there was an ancient evil.

Chad focused on the forest and wondered where the Ebola virus was hiding. They still didn't know what the reservoir was—Mother Nature had harbored versions of the virus for millions of years, but it wasn't until the twentieth century that scientists had actually identified the Ebola strain.

Ebola wasn't the only virus Africa was hiding. The continent was home to some of the nastiest Level 4 contagions that Mother Nature had cooked up. Chad thought of some parts of Africa kind of like a modern-day Jurassic Park, without the dinosaurs. The diseases there were prehistoric.

The truck suddenly swerved to the right; dirt exploded from under the back tires and sent a cloud of dust into the sky. Chad flailed his arms and grabbed the side of the pickup. His head bounced up and down as the driver pulled the Toyota to the side of the road. Branches and twigs snapped under the weight of the truck's oversized tires. When the dust cleared, Chad saw trees barricading the road behind them.

"The locals did that!" Dr. Jones yelled. "They've done it for decades to stop the spread of infection. Smart, but it'll make it difficult for us to get back."

Chad nodded and tightened his grip on the side of the truck. He'd heard of villages isolating themselves in the past to prevent the spread of deadly viruses. It was probably one reason Ebola rarely showed up in major population centers. People tended to die at home, with their loved ones.

Several minutes later, the truck pulled back onto the road. Glancing through the glass of the cab window, Chad saw they were approaching their destination—a small village where the outbreak had started.

Dr. Jones had been deployed here a week ago, with the first team from WHO. Chad had read her most recent report. The population of the village was ninety-four. More than half of those residents had already been infected, with half of the infected already dead. Preliminary statistics pointed at a new strain, but Chad wasn't so sure. Not yet.

The truck eased to a stop about a hundred yards from two WHO doctors wearing biohazard suits.

The local driver jumped down and walked around the truck to let Dr. Jones and Chad out of the back.

"Thanks," Chad muttered. He followed Dr. Jones toward the other doctors, a short man named Howard Lacey and his taller colleague, Bill Fischer. After brief introductions, the two men led them toward the village at an urgent pace.

The buildings were mostly simple mud huts, built from the village's clay-rich dirt, with straw roofs. A few of the nicer houses were made of scrap metal and had tin roofs.

Chad listened to the buzz of insects echoing through the afternoon. A heat shimmer flickered in the distance, a reminder of the hell they had entered.

Howard paused outside one of the huts. Behind his visor, Chad could see an intelligent set of eyes—this was a man used to working in extreme conditions. For him, this was just another day in the office—but for Chad, it was much more than that. He was getting his Ebola cherry popped, losing his V card to yet another Level 4 virus.

"We have two patients inside. Both are in the late stages of infection. They may or may not respond to your presence. Please make your observations, take your samples, and leave them as quickly as possible," Howard said grimly.

Chad nodded. His job was simple: get samples for CDC, take his field notes, and observe. He wasn't there to provide medical support to any of the victims. He was there to see if this was a new strain and bring back a sample so CDC could get started on a cure.

Ducking inside the building, he blinked rapidly. The single-room hut was dimly lit by a few rays of sunlight bleeding through the wooden shades covering the only window. It took a few minutes for his eyes to adjust, but when they did, he saw a man and his wife curled up on straw beds in the center of the room. Blood and sweat-soaked blankets lay on the dusty floor next to them. Their skin was covered with blotches, bruises, and a thin layer of bloody sweat.

Flies buzzed over their skin, but both the man and his wife were too weak to shoo them away. Their glazed eyes stared blankly at the ceiling.

The sound of muffled breathing reminded Chad that Dr. Jones was with him. He moved to the right and then inched closer to the man's bedside. Placing a small box of supplies on the ground, he paused to scan the patient. Blood oozed from every visible orifice on the man's body. It trickled from his bloodshot eyes, his nose, his ears, and even his nipples. There was no mistaking it. This man had Ebola. Which strain of Ebola was the real question.

Blinking, Chad tried his best to remain calm. The sight was worse than he'd ever imagined. There was just *so* much blood. He looked to the man's wife. She too was hemorrhaging. Both victims were bleeding out as they lay helplessly in the scorching-hot hell. The bugs hummed inside the dark room like little engines, waiting to feed.

Chad remembered Howard's orders and felt Dr. Jones looming over him. Reaching inside his case, he pulled out a syringe and cautiously took hold of the man's limp right arm. He looked for a vein and found one hidden under a rash covering most of the patient's forearm. Clenching his teeth, Chad inserted the needle and quickly removed a sample of blood.

The man suddenly twisted his head and narrowed in on Chad's visor. Gasping for air, he choked out one word in broken English.

"Ha-llllp."

Chad froze, his stomach climbing into his throat. His heart kicked violently as he gripped the syringe. There wasn't time for empathy in situations like this, but it was difficult to suppress. He wanted to help this man and his wife.

A strong hand on his shoulder snapped Chad's gaze away from the dying man, reminding him of the truth. There wasn't anything he could do to help these people. Modern medicine couldn't save them, but the information he gathered from them could help save lives in the future.

"Let's go," Dr. Jones said.

Chad nodded and placed the sample inside his secure box, closing the lid with a click. Rising to his feet, he glanced down one more time at the man. His infected, bloodshot eyes followed Chad for a second and then rolled back up into his head.

"I'm sorry," Chad whispered as he rushed out into the blinding sunlight.

1

The six-man team emerged onto the tarmac at dusk. The shadows they cast moved with calculated precision. They passed under the idle blades of Black Hawk helicopters and crossed between the crates of supplies waiting to be shipped to hot spots around the world.

Any onlooker with even limited military knowledge would know the silhouettes did not belong to the average grunt. Their body armor was thinner and their muscles were sculpted in a way that reflected constant training and exercise. Further scrutiny would reveal that these men carried modified weapons.

But no matter how well trained the eye of an onlooker might have been, none would have known the shadows belonged to the Delta Force operator team code-named Ghost, because technically, they did not exist—technically, they *were* ghosts who were activated only when the most critical situations emerged.

Today was one of those days.

It was April, but Master Sergeant Reed Beckham hardly noticed the budding trees and vibrant colors around him. He was still trying to figure out why Command had canceled leave after a six-month tour of Afghanistan. He was supposed to be at a bar in Key West with his buddies, pounding beers and taking afternoon naps under the brilliant white sun. Instead of boarding a charter flight to the Keys, he found himself following his men into the belly of a V-22 Osprey at Fort Bragg.

When Colonel Clinton had told him the team would receive a full briefing on a flight to Edwards Air Force Base, Beckham hadn't been concerned. That wasn't unusual. On most missions, they were briefed on the fly before dropping into a hot zone. This was a source of great pride amongst his men.

Drop. Take out target. Repeat.

They had the process down, like a well-oiled machine. That machine never broke. The Delta Force operators on Team Ghost were so well trained they could prep for whatever bullshit the world had to throw at them in just minutes.

But that bullshit typically didn't involve what Clinton had said next: Beckham's team was to escort a CDC doctor to Edwards AFB, where they would rendezvous with two officers from the Medical Corps. From there they would receive more orders.

Beckham was team lead for a strike team composed of six men. They weren't in the business of escorting doctors. They weren't babysitters. They were operators who snuck in and out of dangerous places and took care of business the old-fashioned way. He led the type of missions the good old US of A loved to watch on the big screen.

Only Beckham wasn't Chuck Norris, and his men weren't actors. When they were shot, they bled real blood. They didn't get a second chance. He'd promised his team from day one that he would do everything in his power to keep them alive—that he would die before they did. For the average person, it was a promise that couldn't be kept. But for Beckham, it was sacred. It meant everything to him. He wore his promise like a phantom badge into every mission, right above the picture of his mom.

Patting his vest pocket, Beckham stared into the troop hold and watched his men board. Each and every one of them was capable of completing a mission single-handedly, and they were all responsible for making the same life-or-death decisions Beckham did. But he was their leader. He'd never lost a man under his command. Everyone on Team Ghost had come home in one piece. They'd been shot, stabbed, and hit with shrapnel, but they'd always survived. He'd felt every one of their injuries as if they were his own. Their pain was his pain.

The training bible had taught him that his men always came second to the mission, but in Beckham's book, the men surrounding him were just as important. His first squad leader had said, "My mission, my men, myself." Beckham had rearranged the order a bit.

This mission was no different, and the facts surrounding it gave him an uneasy feeling as he grabbed a handhold and climbed into the Osprey.

"Welcome aboard. I'm Chief Wright and this is my pilot, John Bush," said a voice from inside the dimly lit space. Beckham focused on a stocky crew chief standing with his hands on his hips and the slim pilot who stood beside him.

"Holy shit," the chief muttered. He took a moment to give Ghost Alpha and Bravo the reverse–elevator eyes look, starting with their black helmets and then scanning their clear shooting glasses, headsets, tan fatigues, vests stuffed with extra magazines, body armor, and finally, their boots. Then he moved on to their customized weapons, stopping on Beckham's own MP5 submachine gun with an advanced combat optical gunsight mount. The crew chief twisted his mouth to the side. "Damn, you all look like you're about to drop into a war zone."

"We just came from one," Beckham replied. He wasn't exactly in the mood for small talk. He was exhausted and had been looking forward to some R&R. On top of that, he was anxious to get moving. The sooner he knew what was going on, the sooner he could plan for the dangers—and, ultimately, victory.

The chief's features darkened. He narrowed his eyes and in a stern voice said, "We're still waiting for the CDC doctor."

Beckham took a seat across from Sergeant Will Tenor. This was Tenor's first mission at the helm of a strike team. He was a solid leader and quick thinker—the perfect pick to lead Bravo. Beckham scrutinized the man discreetly in the dimly lit section of the Osprey. The younger Delta operator held his helmet in his hand and cleaned the interior with a cloth, a pre-combat ritual. A modified M4 with an ACOG attachment rested next to him.

Tenor didn't give off any impression of being nervous. His stern face was framed by a solid jaw and topped with a strip of hair perfectly groomed into a Mohawk. He flashed Beckham a confident smirk, as if he knew he was being sized up. That was Tenor's way of saying he was ready to go.

The other men wore the same confident looks, but Beckham scanned each one of them to ensure none had shown up with a hangover. He started with Staff Sergeant Carlos "Panda" Spinoza, the team's demolitions expert. The thick man had a booming voice and the whitest teeth Beckham had ever seen. But he rarely smiled or spoke. Battle had hardened him years ago. He gripped an M249 Squad Automatic Weapon (SAW). The weapon had saved Team Ghost a dozen times.

To his right sat Staff Sergeant Parker Horn, also holding a SAW. The star college football player hailed from Texas. He'd earned the nickname Big Horn at Texas Tech, where he'd crushed the school's sack record. He was a staggering six feet two, with a thick skull and wide shoulders. He looked innocent enough at first glance, with his freckled face and strawberry-blond hair, but beneath his fatigues he was a hard man. Delta had made an exception by allowing Horn on the team. With a tumultuous background, history of a broken home, and arms covered in ink, Horn wasn't the model recruit, but Beckham had vetted the man himself. He'd read his file. He knew how Horn worked under pressure, when his life and those of his men were threatened. His valor in the early days of Operation Iraqi Freedom had earned him two Purple Hearts and a Bronze Star. Beckham knew instantly he wanted the man on Team Ghost, and he had never regretted the decision for a minute. Horn was one of the most talented operators he'd ever worked with.

Horn wasn't the only one. All of Beckham's operators were talented. Each of them had scored 95 percent accuracy or better in shooting tests at a thousand yards. They'd all survived the grueling endurance tests that would have left other men dead. They were the best of the best. Beckham's team was America's first line of defense that no one knew existed. Unseen and unheard, they were truly ghosts. He could count on every single one of them when the shit hit the fan.

A flash of movement from the tarmac distracted Beckham before he could examine the youngest members of his team, Staff Sergeant Alex Riley and Sergeant Jim Edwards. Both men carried Benelli M1014 twelve-gauge shotguns as their primary weapons.

Standing, Beckham watched a short man with an enthusiastic stride and slicked-back hair climb inside the compartment with the aid of a stern-looking African American MP. The soldier had the eyes of a hawk. Beckham stifled a snort. He knew the type. They took their jobs very seriously—sometimes too seriously.

Holding out his hand, Beckham said, "Welcome, Doctor..."

"Ellis. Doctor Pat Ellis," the man said, shaking Beckham's hand vigorously and turning to the rest of the team with a smile. "Most people just call me, uh, Ellis."

"Excuse me, sir," the MP said. "We will have time for proper introductions later. We need to get moving immediately." There was urgency in his voice.

"Just waiting on you guys," Beckham replied firmly.

The MP didn't look amused. He took a seat, and Chief Wright hit the button to close the cargo-bay door. The crew chief gave a thumbs-up and pounded the inside wall. "Good to go," he said. Groaning, the metal door crunched shut behind them.

Beckham watched Dr. Ellis like a coach sizing up a recruit. The civilian moved quickly down the troop hold, carrying a leather bag clutched against his chest. He searched the empty seats, stopping next to Horn. The operator ignored him, pulling his skull bandanna up to his nose as if to say, *This seat's taken.*

Ellis hugged the bag closer to his chest and moved toward Tenor. The man dropped his gear bag into the open seat next to him. "Sorry, taken."

Beckham chewed at the inside of his lip. Typically his men were better behaved, but they weren't used to babysitting.

"You can sit here," Beckham offered.

The doctor's face lit up when he saw the open seat, and he rushed over to it, plopping down just as the V-22's engines hummed to life.

"Thanks," Ellis said.

The roar of the aircraft's motors rippled through the walls. Ospreys were known for more than their speed and versatility; they were known for their noise. Beckham had always thought they sounded like a large lawn mower with too many ponies and a dire need for an oil change.

Beckham handed Ellis a pair of earplugs and said, "Better put these on."

"Thanks," Ellis remarked. He grabbed them and held them out in front of his face as if he'd never seen them before, then slowly slipped them into his ears. Then, with the utmost precision, he reached for his harness and buckled in with a click.

The whoosh from the rotors filled the cabin, sending vibrations through the craft. The doctor's eyes widened ever so slightly, but not from fear. He looked excited, like a kid riding on a roller coaster for the first time. The aircraft pulled to the right as the pilots maneuvered it onto the runway. The rumble of the engines intensified. Moments later they were ascending into the sky.

Beckham leaned over to look out his window. Below, the shadow of the aircraft glided across a vast, green field. They were still low enough that he could make out the shapes of several horses running freely through a pasture. The rolling hills and crystal clear creeks snaking through the terrain were serene, but Beckham still felt anxious.

The view quickly vanished, and the horses faded into tiny black dots moving slowly across the distant landscape.

"Which one of you is Master Sergeant Beckham?" asked a voice from the other end of the aircraft.

Beckham raised his knife hand. He craned his neck to see the MP pulling several tablets out of a bag.

"Take one of these, each of you," the man said. He walked down the aisle and handed the devices out in turn. "Once you submit your electronic signature and fingerprint, you will have access to a classified briefing from Colonel Gibson, commanding officer of the United States Army Medical Research Institute of Infectious Diseases. Mission details will be provided at the end of the briefing."

The MP stopped and handed Beckham his tablet.

"What about me?" Dr. Ellis asked, his voice more eager than before.

"I'm sorry, sir, but this briefing is for military personnel only. Master Sergeant Beckham will ensure you have all the information you need to help make this mission a success, but I should remind you that you are here *only* as a consultant." The MP returned to his seat at the other end of the craft and melted into the shadows.

Ellis spoke louder. "How can I consult if I don't know what's going on?"

Beckham glanced over at the doctor and gave him a reassuring nod as if to say, *Don't worry, I'll tell you everything I know.* But that would have been a lie. He didn't like the fact he had to drag a civilian along with them, and neither did his men. Even if Ellis did bring a medical opinion to the mission, civilians typically ended up becoming liabilities and only slowed his team down.

Beckham looked out the window to catch a final glimpse of the sun as it made one last valiant effort before disappearing over the horizon. Darkness filled the aircraft until a bank of lights blinked on above them.

With a quick flick of the touch screen, Beckham activated his tablet. He linked his headset to the device with a small cord, and a message appeared immediately.

CLASSIFIED—TOP SECRET

EYES ONLY—DELTA TEAM GHOST

Examination by unauthorized persons is an act of treason punishable by fines up to $100,000 and imprisonment up to fifteen years.

If you are Master Sergeant Reed Beckham, born 13 March 1978, please enter your electronic signature and then hover your index finger over the display for acceptance.

Beckham looked down the aisle at Horn and Carlos and then across the way at Edwards, Riley, and Tenor. Their faces were all illuminated by the same white glow radiating off their tablets. One by one they removed their gloves and signed the display.

It was odd being warned about the repercussions of sharing any classified information. In fact, it was downright patronizing, especially for a Delta Force operator. Beckham had given his entire life to his country. Chosen Her over a wife and kids and spent time away from the small bit of family he had fighting in faraway lands. But there was something else about the message that went far beyond insult. Its very existence made him uneasy; something didn't feel right about this mission.

Whatever *it* was.

Beckham considered what he already knew. The facts

were slowly coming together. Their leave had been canceled only a few days after returning to Fort Bragg from Afghanistan. That told him brass wanted a team that had been in the field recently and was sharp. The lack of a formal briefing from Command told him that someone higher up was in charge. The CIA instantly came to mind, but that didn't explain Ellis and the involvement of the CDC.

Without further hesitation, Beckham signed the display and pressed his index finger over the scanner. He was anxious to know what they were dealing with.

A video image of an older officer popped onto the display. The man was sitting in a large leather chair, his light blue eyes narrowed at the screen. He wiped a single bead of sweat off his forehead.

"As you already know, I'm Colonel Rick Gibson, commanding officer of the United States Army Medical Research Institute of Infectious Diseases. I'll make this briefing as quick as possible. Time is of the essence. At 1000 hours this morning, we lost contact with a top secret facility on San Nicolas Island, off the coast of California. This installation, which is known as Building Eight, is home to some of the most important medical research in the country. The scientists working inside deal with Level Four biohazards, the most severe contagions and chemical toxins known to man. Officially, this facility doesn't exist." He paused, throwing a glance over his shoulder, as if he didn't want anyone to hear him.

Beckham felt his muscles tightening, an involuntary reaction he experienced whenever he felt nervous. He waited for the officer to continue.

Looking back to the camera, Gibson said, "So what does this have to do with your team? Protocol is to activate an emergency operations team, contact CDC, and deploy a response. Along with Doctor Ellis, from CDC, and the assistance of two men from my division, you gentlemen are that response. I'm not taking any chances in this situation, and I'm told you can get the job done."

A lump formed in Beckham's throat. He didn't know what the job was yet, but he had a feeling it would take him inside Building 8. Level 4 contagions were his worst fear as an operator. He'd much rather face a building full of insurgents than walk into a viral hot zone.

"These next videos will give you an idea of what we are dealing with," Gibson continued, his image fading. "This was recorded on the twenty-fourth of March. Location is a WHO field hospital in remote Guinea. The patient tested positive for the Ebola virus."

Beckham tightened his grip on the tablet as the image enlarged. The body of a frail African man lay coiled on a cot. A pair of nurses protected only by masks stood by his side, one of them bending over to wipe a trail of blood leaking from his right eye. The thin blanket draped over the patient's bony body looked like the apron of a butcher, speckled with dark red blood.

Beckham had seen images of patients infected with Ebola before, but not this bad. This man hemorrhaged blood from every orifice. The nurses' attempts to dry his forehead with a red-soaked sponge ended when he lurched forward, black vomit streaming out of his mouth.

Beckham blinked and then focused on the man's ghostly stare. Something about his detached eyes reminded him that the enemy, in this case, wasn't human. It was a microscopic contagion, one that he couldn't simply shoot or blow up. The revelation scared the shit out of him.

"The second video was taken inside the isolation wing of a hospital in Guinea's capital city, Conakry. One hundred and four new cases were confirmed on the twenty-seventh of

March. Of those patients, ninety-eight have died since the recording."

Beckham watched men in white bio suits approach a pair of guards holding AK-47s. After checking for clearance, they opened the glass doors. Inside, the videographer panned the camera across the room, revealing dozens of beds, all of which contained the same scene: blood-soaked blankets and patients hemorrhaging out their insides. A doctor waved the camera away, yelling, "Get that thing out of here!"

The video fizzled, and Gibson reappeared on the screen. "I'm sure many of you heard about this outbreak in recent news. The virus is thought be a stronger version of the Zaire strain, the worst type known to man. It has spread to Sierra Leone, Liberia, and Mali. We have confirmed cases in Europe, the Middle East, and Asia. It's just a matter of time before this strain hits US soil."

Beckham's eyes shot up. He scanned the faces of his men. They all wore the same bold look, seemingly undeterred by the images.

Glancing back down at his tablet, Beckham saw Gibson's features had changed. The man checked his wristwatch. Then, with a new sense of urgency painted across his face, Gibson looked up. The creases on his forehead deepened.

"As you can probably guess, the researchers at Building Eight were working on a cure. Doctor Isaac Medford, the team lead, contacted me two days ago to say he had made a breakthrough. He'd extracted chemical samples from a weapon called VX-99. Many of you may have heard rumors of its use in Vietnam. Some of them are probably true. Anyone injected with a single dose is transformed into something that makes the criminally insane look like Girl Scouts. The weapon was designed to make supersoldiers. It was used in 1968 on a platoon of marines; they were to take a small but heavily defended village. Instead, the entire platoon turned on one another and turned the jungle red. They killed in the most barbaric ways. Most of the marines were found without their weapons, having used their bare hands to murder each other and the VC that ambushed them. The chemical was discontinued after its use was found to have irreversible effects, as you are about to see."

Beckham felt several pairs of eyes on him from across the aisle, but he did not look up. He focused on his tablet. The smiling image of a soldier dressed in uniform appeared. Gibson continued his narration. "This is Platoon Commander First Lieutenant Trevor Brett. He was awarded a posthumous Bronze Star for his actions during a classified mission in Vietnam. His family believed he died a hero. His file simply says KIA. But this is far from the truth. Ten years after his last mission, Lieutenant Brett showed up in a rural village outside Son La, over one hundred miles south of where his platoon had dropped in and injected VX-99."

A map appeared, with a red line leading from the upper mountain area to the city of Son La. Beckham recognized the area instantly. He'd spent several weeks of leave there when he first joined the military.

"Remember that red line," Gibson said.

Next, an image of a man in torn clothing emerged. Even though the picture was blurry, Beckham could tell there was no humanity left in him. He'd seen others like him in the slums of Mogadishu, the remote villages of the northern, tribal areas of Afghanistan, and the filthy alleys in Fallujah. War zones tended to produce the look quite often.

"This was a photograph of the lieutenant taken by a British journalist in 1980. Take note of his appearance. His lips, eyes, skin."

Using his fingers, Beckham enlarged the image. Brett

had been transformed into a monster, with hair clinging to his head in clumps. His skin was almost translucent; blue veins crisscrossed his exposed flesh. His eyes had developed some sort of second layer or membrane that was reminiscent of a reptilian eye. His irises were yellow, and his pupils had morphed into slits. But the most striking change was the man's lips. They had bulged into a grotesque sucker that reminded Beckham of a leech.

"And his necklace," Gibson continued.

A new image filled the display. Some sort of cord lay across the surface of a metal desk. Beckham thought he saw dried pieces of flesh. But was that possible?

As the image magnified further, his stomach lurched. He'd never seen anything like this. He'd heard of men keeping ears and other trophies, but there were more than just ears on the lieutenant's necklace. There were other things—unspeakable things. Now Beckham knew why Dr. Ellis wasn't allowed to watch the briefing. If anything got out about this chemical weapon, the military would not only be paying out large settlements to families but politicians would be hosting a barbeque on the Hill, grilling anyone connected to VX-99. Gibson would likely be the pig being slow roasted, with an apple in his mouth.

"What you saw are the effects of VX-99. Like I said earlier, the idea behind the serum was to create a supersoldier. What we got was Lieutenant Brett." Gibson paused again and then said, "That red line on the map of Vietnam I told you to remember? That was the path Brett followed for ten years. Murdering and eating anyone he came across. VX-99 didn't simply transform him into a monstrosity; it transformed him into a criminally insane soldier, one that stayed alive all of those years with a single goal: to kill."

Once again Gibson's tired face faded, replaced by a video

feed of the ocean. Beckham found himself wondering what Brett's fate had been. There was no way the marine ever saw the light of day again. He'd likely died a long time ago after enduring countless tests by the Medical Corps.

What a fucking way for a soldier to go out, Beckham thought as the camera panned to a beach.

"Your target is a sample of Doctor Medford's research. My men will know exactly what they are looking for." Gibson crinkled his nose. "I know what you're thinking. Why not just bomb the place? We would if we could, believe me, but I need to know what Medford created. It could be invaluable for future Ebola research. I *need* that sample."

Beckham mastered his anger with a deep breath, tuning Gibson out for a moment to think. This mission meant Team Ghost was cannon fodder. That wasn't new or unexpected. He'd signed the papers. He knew from the beginning what he was getting himself into. But this? His team was being sent into a potential hot zone with no real intel besides some shitty briefing about events that had happened nearly fifty years ago.

Ghost had dropped into remote locations with less information than they had now, but those missions had never dealt with Level 4 contagions. This was a different type of enemy.

The tension in the troop hold lingered like a thick fog of humidity. Beckham didn't need to scan his men again to know they all felt it. Never once had he questioned a mission before. Orders were always orders. And no matter how bad things were at Building 8, he still had a duty to his country.

Breathing deeply through his nose, he quelled another surge of anger.

"As I stated before," Gibson continued, "the target is on San Nicolas Island. Everyone working outside Building Eight has been evacuated. When you arrive, the only personnel left within a twenty-mile radius will be the scientists locked beneath the surface."

Beckham studied the screen. Sapphire waves crashed onto the shores of San Nicolas Island under the moonlight. The video, taken by a low-flying chopper, gave a full view of the terrain. Snaking across a background of brown sand was a landing strip with a cluster of buildings nestled around the perimeter.

Gibson continued, his voice growing more anxious. "My men will have a GPS locator with them. They will guide you to Building Eight. It's off the beaten path, away from the rest of the facilities. They have never been there, and neither have I, due to the sensitive nature of the research," he said with a slight pause. "It's one of our smaller labs, with a staff of only fifteen. Navy personnel on the island do not even know Building Eight exists. They've been told they were evacuated due to a toxic spill."

The video transitioned into a building layout. Beckham assumed the blueprints were of Building 8, but it was difficult to tell with the dim lighting in the cargo hold.

Gibson continued to narrate. "My men will give you access to the facility. Your mission is to protect them and retrieve the sample of Medford's work."

Protect his men? Beckham thought. *From what?*

Gibson coughed deeply into his hand and very politely said, "Excuse me. There are three levels in the lab. Your target will be somewhere on the lowest level, where Doctor Medford would have stored the samples. Level One is decontamination. You won't need to worry about activating the chambers because you will be equipped with CBRN suits, but keep in mind that if there is a loose contagion, you are only safe inside your suit. A single tear will compromise you."

Level Two popped onto the screen. "These are the personnel quarters. Navigate your way to the far end, where a final hallway will take you to Level Three. There are four labs on the final level. Each is color-coded and represents a different toxic level. You are looking for the red one. That is where Medford would have been performing his tests."

Gibson's profile reappeared. "Make no mistake, gentlemen—the likelihood of anyone inside being alive is slim to none. You may be walking into a morgue." He paused briefly and then added, "In approximately one hour from this briefing, you will land at Edwards Air Force Base. From there you will rendezvous with two men from our Emergency Operations Center: Major Walt Caster and Major Brian Noble. Major Noble is a virologist and a damn good one. You will then be fitted for your protective suits and further briefed. After securing your equipment, you will proceed to San Nicolas Island by helicopter. By this time tomorrow, I hope to be congratulating you all via conference call after you acquire the sample. Good luck."

The video fizzled out, and Beckham looked up to meet the intense stares of his team. Their eyes pleaded for reassurance, for Beckham to say something inspirational.

He sat there trying to think of something, but his mind raced. Suddenly, a single image froze there: He could see the black, detached eyes of Lieutenant Brett as vividly as if he was staring right at the man. He finally understood why they'd been activated. They were protecting Gibson's men from a possible Brett.

A distant voice snapped Beckham from his thoughts. The youngest and smallest member of Team Ghost, Sergeant Riley, stared at Beckham from across the aisle. An overhead light illuminated his youthful features, reminding Beckham why the man had earned the nickname "the Kid." With light blue eyes and an enthusiastic and contagious laugh, Riley was the team's little brother. He wore a constant cheerful grin.

"Guess we aren't going to the Keys after all?"

"No," Beckham replied grimly.

Riley pulled a bandanna with an illustration of a smiling joker's mouth over his own and let out a deep laugh. "Good. I didn't want to go anyways."

Several of the other men chuckled. Big Horn reached over and smacked the kid's armored knee. "Think of this like a game of football. That's what I do," he said, crossing his arms. "War is easier when you compare it to something you're good at."

Riley fidgeted with the bandanna. The kid was still new and he was probably nervous as all hell.

Beckham didn't blame him. Shit, he was nervous too. He considered telling Riley that everything would be fine, that the mission was just a routine recovery, but that would be a lie. Beckham had never lied to his men and wasn't about to start now.

Stiffening his back, he locked eyes with Tenor, his co-lead. "We're gonna get in, grab the sample, and get out." Turning to Riley, he said, "And *hopefully* we will have some leave left when this is all over."

Riley let out his infamous and reassuring chuckle. It reminded Beckham of the time Riley had climbed onstage at the Bing and danced in his underwear, which had actually been closer to a thong. At least they had the kid to lighten up the mood when it grew dark.

"So do you guys want to tell me what the hell is going on?" Ellis asked. He squirmed under his harness and looked toward Beckham.

The other men grew quiet, and the noise from the V-22's motors reclaimed the troop hold. They would let Beckham respond.

Closing his eyes, he took in a short, silent breath and rested his helmet on the metal wall behind him. *Need-to-know info only*, Beckham thought as he blinked and stared at the bank of LEDs above.

"You're on a reclamation mission, Doctor. Target is a sample of experimental work that the Medical Corps was doing at a secret location."

"What kind of sample?"

"Classified," Beckham replied.

"That's just great," Ellis huffed, settling back into his seat.

Satisfied with his cryptic answer, Beckham closed his eyes again. With any luck he would snag a nap before they landed. And if he was *really* lucky, he wouldn't dream of any hemorrhaging Ebola patients—or worse, of the monster that Lieutenant Brett had transformed into.

2

Beckham woke up suddenly, his neck straining as he lurched forward. The dim cabin lighting revealed the silhouettes of his team. Their heads bobbed up and down in the slight turbulence. Glancing down at his wristwatch, he saw he'd slept for half an hour. *Not bad, considering*, he thought.

"Catch some sleep?" an eager voice said.

He nodded and made brief eye contact with Dr. Ellis. He knew the doctor wanted to discuss the mission, but Beckham had no such plans. He reached for his bag and pretended to do a gear check, hoping the man would get the picture.

It didn't work.

"This is all pretty exciting. I've never been attached to a military unit before," Ellis said, leaning over in his seat as if he didn't want anyone to overhear their one-sided conversation.

Beckham pulled a magazine out of his vest and slapped it into his MP5 with a metallic snap. The sound echoed in the compartment. Helmets shot up instantly at the noise. Normally he wouldn't have charged his weapon on a flight, but he was hoping it would get the man to shut his trap.

"Never seen one of those before. I prefer a shotgun,

myself. You don't have to be as good a shot." Ellis paused and scrutinized Beckham. "I guess you don't really have to worry about aiming. You look like you could hit a target from a mile away."

Beckham caught a glimpse of the MP peeking his head around Horn at the far end of the aircraft to get a better look at the doctor.

"Listen, Doctor Ellis," Beckham began to say.

"Ellis—call me Ellis."

"Okay, *Ellis*. I'm not big on conversation. And even if I were, I wouldn't tell you anything I haven't already. Orders are orders. Nothin' personal," he said, ejecting the magazine out of his weapon with a loud click.

"I understand, sir," the man said.

"Master Sergeant, or just Sergeant. But not *sir*. I'm an NCO. I work for my rank," Beckham said. In his peripheral vision, he watched Ellis nod and run a hand through his jet-black hair, slicking it back.

They endured the rest of the flight in silence, the Osprey rocking back and forth as they traveled through a rainstorm. It gave Beckham time to contemplate the mission in more detail. He knew little of chemical and biological weapons besides the fact that their development had been banned decades ago. He knew even less about viruses such as Ebola or Marburg. Most of what he had picked up over the years had come from his training. If one thing was clear, it was that the average American civilian lived under constant threat of a chemical or biological attack. Even with the strides the government had made over the past two decades in organizing first-responder teams, they were all just one accident or attack away from Armageddon.

If Gibson had his way, the public would remain in the dark. That's why Beckham was sitting with a team of "ghosts" in an Osprey. They existed for the sole purpose of making sure the average civilian had no idea just how close they were to the apocalypse.

Ignorance is bliss, he mused. He shook his head, cursing his luck, just as one of the pilots said, "Prepare for landing. ETA fifteen minutes."

The sound of gear rustling filled the aircraft, and Beckham didn't hear the rap of the MP's footfalls.

"Master Sergeant," the soldier said, stopping in front of Beckham. "This is where I get off. Major Caster and Major Noble will brief your team further." He shot Ellis a glare and then said, "Good luck."

Beckham nodded. He didn't like the MP. There was just something about the man's stoic personality that ate at him. The feeling added to the sour sensation growing in the pit of his stomach. He'd learned a long time ago never to trust someone without a sense of humor. Beckham had known many men and women in his career that lacked this trait. He'd found it was a good way to judge character.

The Osprey lurched forward and then began to sway side to side as they descended. With an audible thud, the tires connected with tarmac, the chopper shaking before it settled.

As soon as they were stopped, Chief Wright stood and punched the button to operate the cargo-bay door. It groaned open, and the MP disappeared into the darkness.

"Good riddance," Ellis said under his breath. "Now can you tell me what's going on?"

"No, but I can," a new voice said.

Standing in the shadows of the aircraft were two men, both officers. The larger man, on the right, filled his uniform out with a thick set of arms and broad shoulders. The other officer took off a pair of black-rimmed glasses and said, "Welcome to Edwards Air Force Base. I'm Major Noble, and this is Major Caster. We're here on orders from Colonel Gibson. If you would, please come with us—time is of the essence."

Beckham stood and motioned his team out of the Osprey and onto the wet tarmac. They followed the two men toward a cluster of well-lit buildings. A warm breeze rustled across the runway, quite the change in weather from North Carolina. The air felt good. Not as good as Florida would have felt, but better than what they had just come from in Afghanistan.

They crossed the tarmac swiftly, making their way toward an unmarked metal building. Two guards wearing the insignia of the Medical Corps stood outside with M4s.

Noble approached a set of double doors and swung them open for the team. Inside, Beckham expected to find a room bustling with activity, but instead a dimly lit space greeted them. Four metal tables had been set up in the center of the room, gear stacked neatly on top of them. There were gloves, helmets, and hazard suits.

Beckham followed his men to the first table. Curious, he reached out and grabbed one of the suits. This one looked different from the ones he'd trained in before, thinner and more advanced.

Caster lowered his hand, motioning for Beckham to put the suit down. "We don't have much time," he said from the front of the room, looking down at his watch. "Our Black Hawk leaves in fifteen minutes. Major Noble will explain and help you into your gear. We can discuss the mission further on the flight to San Nicolas. Unfortunately, I don't have much new data beyond what Colonel Gibson's briefing already provided. We have made multiple attempts at communication with Building Eight. All have failed. If anyone is alive, they aren't answering."

Noble stepped forward. He scanned the faces of the team individually, locking eyes with every member, stopping at last on Beckham. Clearing his throat, he said, "Gentlemen, I never thought we would be in this situation. One of our most secure facilities has somehow been compromised. We don't know what we are dealing with, but we aren't ruling anything out. Could be an accident or could be an act of terror. We just don't know. That's why you are here. You are one of the best teams the US military has to offer." He paused and reached for one of the neatly stacked suits.

Beckham narrowed his eyes, focusing on Major Noble. "Sir, have you considered sabotage from within?"

The officer shrugged. "Like Major Caster said, nothing is off the table."

Unfolding the suit, Noble continued, "This is the most advanced chemical, biological, radiological, and nuclear suit available, designed with a new class of membrane. The manufacturer incorporated nanoparticles that are filled with novel ionic polymers. In short, it allows water vapor to pass through, so it isn't so hot. You may also notice there aren't oxygen tanks. The gas masks are state of the art. They filter out ninety-nine percent of any contagions you may encounter. They are a prototype, but..."

Riley wedged his way through the group. "Did you say prototype, sir?"

Noble nodded. "You heard right. Rest assured. You will be fine."

Beckham waited for Riley to say something stupid, but to his surprise, the younger operator backed away.

"So what exactly are we going to need those for?" Dr. Ellis asked from behind the team. He was still standing in front of the door, hidden by the large frames of Beckham's men.

"Ah, you must be Doctor Ellis, with the CDC. Glad to have you here. I know this has all been very last minute. I understand you are a virologist," Noble said. He pulled a notepad from a pocket and thumbed through it. "Yes, here we go," he said, narrowing his gaze. "You graduated at the top of your class from the University of California, Berkeley, in the infectious diseases program," he said, and then paused. "I was class of ninety-five."

"That's right. Crazy coincidence, but what I really want to know is, *why* am I here?"

"Some clause in a law written by politicians who have no idea about the nature of our business," Caster said.

"Checks and balances," Beckham added with a snort.

"Due to the top secret nature of this mission, there are certain things you aren't supposed to know, but…" Noble began to say.

Caster took over. "With time being a concern, I'm going to say fuck protocol, so listen up. Our mission is to retrieve the work of Doctor Medford, the lead assigned to Section Four of Building Eight, I believe…" He glanced at Noble and added, "We believe that this isn't a matter of sabotage or terrorism, but there may be hostages. A different type of hostage."

"The fuck does that mean?" Horn exclaimed. "I thought you said you didn't know what we are dealing with." He pulled his skull bandanna away from his mouth.

"We don't know anything for sure. It's only a theory, but if I'm right, it means we are dealing with a potential viral outbreak," Noble said.

Caster nodded. "As you know, Colonel Gibson received a message from Building Eight. Medford explained they were working with VX-99 in an attempt to destroy the new Zaire strain of Ebola. We think that when he attempted to kill the virus, the chemicals bonded with the virus shell, mutating the strain into something else."

Caster ran a finger over his right eyebrow. "Truth is, if things are as bad as I think they might be, then we are going to need more than your expertise and skill to retrieve Doctor Medford's work. We are going to need some luck."

"Wait a second," Dr. Ellis blurted. "Can you explain that last sentence?"

"I believe Doctor Medford may have inadvertently created a new virus in his attempt to destroy the Ebola virus. And I believe his team may be infected."

"Let's not jump to conclusions," Noble said with a hand raised.

Ellis ran a hand through his hair and blinked rapidly, like he was trying to make sense of the situation.

Caster seemed to notice the man's change in demeanor and said, "Can you handle this, Doctor Ellis? Legally, we are required to have you here, but you don't have to go with the team if you don't want to. We can't force you to do so."

"Yes," Ellis replied assertively. His posture said otherwise. His shoulders sagged, and his thin frame seemed to shrink inside his jacket, as if he was trying to hide.

Ten minutes later they were on the move again, with their gear in tow. The pale CDC virologist followed the rest of the team onto the tarmac. Like a child who had used up all of his energy, the doctor seemed defeated. Then Beckham caught a glimpse of the man's face and could see he didn't just look defeated—he looked terrified.

They climbed solemnly into the belly of the Black Hawk. Every man on the team knew this was no longer a routine mission. They were up against an unknown enemy, unlike any they had ever faced.

Beckham took the seat closest to the cockpit and saw

Chief Wright scrutinizing him for the second time. "Guess you aren't dropping into a war zone after all. Now the extra hazardous-duty pay makes sense."

This time Beckham didn't respond at all. He focused on a mental run-through of the briefing and began the mental prep for the mission. By the time they were airborne, it was finally all beginning to sink in, and he couldn't believe their luck.

Instead of paradise, he was preparing to enter hell—a hell that terrified him unlike any other he could think of. He remembered the first years of his training as a Delta Force operator back in the House of Horrors, the nickname for the training facility where he had become an operator.

It was there that he had attended a weeklong NBC course, in which experts had explained the effects of various nuclear, biological, and chemical weapons. He could still remember pulling that first gas mask over his face and the intense terror he'd experienced knowing he couldn't see his enemy. He'd pushed through and learned to adapt to the equipment, but he would never forget how it had made him feel—the tightness in his lungs, the shallow breathing.

Beckham fumbled with the helmet on his lap, staring intensely at the visor. If anyone had ever known of his fear, he would never have become an operator.

"Remember, those suits are state of the art, but they aren't indestructible. The tiniest tear will expose you to any contagions in the lab," Noble reminded the team. He shot a glance at Beckham's weapon. "I noticed you're not carrying suppressed weapons. Is there a reason why?"

Horn held up his rifle. "You ever fired a SAW with a silencer, Major? Trust me, it ain't as quiet as you probably think."

Noble shrugged. "Kind of defeats the purpose of Team Ghost, though."

The freckles on Horn's nose clustered together as he flared his nose. That was Hornspeak for *fuck you.*

"Should we be preparing for a firefight, Major?" Beckham asked before Horn could blow a gasket.

"No," Noble said. He went back to securing his suit.

"I thought nothing was off the table," Riley quipped.

"Gear up," Beckham ordered. He shot a glare down the aisle at Big Horn and Panda and then across the way at Edwards, the kid, and Tenor. They slipped into their suits, and a well-rehearsed chorus of pre-combat rituals echoed off the metal walls as they broke in their new gear.

Pulling back a handful of his thick brown hair, Beckham stuffed the helmet over his head, feeling the narrow sides squeeze his face. He cringed as he pulled it over his nose and mouth. No matter how much the military tried, they couldn't seem to acquire equipment that didn't smell like cheap plastic. For a suit that was supposed to protect him from the nastiest contagions, he was surprised it was part of the design. He sucked in one last breath of fresh air before securing the helmet with a click, and then he grabbed his night-vision goggles. They were the most advanced optics on the market, with four 16-millimeter image-intensifying tubes that had earned them the nickname "four eyes." He slipped the strap over the top of his helmet, positioning them over his visor.

Instead of headsets, the team was connected by a comm system built into their suits. By bumping his chin against a small pad, Beckham could open up a line to his men.

"Testing," he said. His voice sounded remarkably clear. Satisfied, he continued, "Listen up. I know you're all disappointed that we're not taking shots of Bacardi at the Bing right now, but remember, we have no idea what we are heading into. So stop feeling sorry for yourselves and suck it up.

We need to bring our A game to this one, Ghost. The Bing'll be waiting for us when we get back."

"Don't remind us of the Bing!" Riley laughed. "What's that dancer's name who said she wanted to marry you? She's going to be very disappointed."

The kid loved women. He loved them in all shapes and all sizes, and whenever they were granted leave, Riley made sure he experienced all the locals had to offer.

Spinoza chuckled. "Speaking of disappointment, Kid, remember that chick from Thailand? I mean, you *said* she was a chick."

Beckham laughed with his men and then grew serious. "All right, time to knock off the shit." They all needed to focus. Get with the program. Comedy was always good to calm nerves before a mission, but this was different. He wasn't sure what they were going to find in Building 8. And he didn't trust Noble or Caster. Both men seemed to be withholding vital intel. Their story had already changed once.

Beckham reached for a handhold as the chopper hit a pocket of turbulence that felt like driving over a speed bump. Typically, they'd be riding on the side of an MH-6 Little Bird, but looking over at Dr. Ellis, he could see why brass had opted for something a bit more stable.

Beckham patted the vest pocket that contained a photograph of his mom. The thirty-year-old image had been snapped in Rocky Mountain National Park, not far from Estes Park, Colorado, where he'd grown up. He didn't need to remove the picture to see her curly black hair blowing in the wind or her beautiful smile. He'd memorized it long ago and carried a copy on every mission.

The flood of memories always calmed his nerves, taking him back to a simpler time, when his biggest worry was making it home before dark. Closing his eyes, Beckham remembered. He remembered his father teaching him how to use a compass and how to rappel off cliffs. He remembered his mother coming home from work still dressed in her scrubs after a twelve-hour shift at the local clinic. No matter what time it was, she'd always slip into his room and kiss his forehead.

Cancer had taken her when he was a senior in high school, and his career had started with her loss. When he first joined the army he had felt invincible, naively believing that he would never be injured or watch his friends die. Now, fifteen years later, he'd seen too many of them arrive home in coffins draped with flags. For that reason, he had chosen not to marry or have a family. The only people he had to worry about were the men next to him.

After the chopper straightened, he caught the full profile of his team. The curved outlines of their CBRN suits made them look more like robots than soldiers, but he knew better. They were the brothers he'd never had growing up and more, Horn especially. Over the past few years, Horn and his wife had taken him in when Beckham's father too had passed away from cancer. They'd weathered some tough times together, like a mini family.

The rustling passed, and Beckham said, "Once we land, we will break into strike teams. Panda, Edwards, and Major Noble, you're assigned to Bravo, with Tenor as lead. Everyone else, including Major Caster, is with me. Doctor Ellis, you're to be my shadow at all times. Got it?"

A short nod from the doctor, and then Beckham continued. "We will enter the facility with the aid of Majors Caster and Noble. Primary objective is to secure Doctor Medford's research."

Caster cut in. "I should have made this clear earlier, but this is *not* a rescue mission. If we do come across anyone infected who is still alive, we leave them behind."

"Understood," Beckham said, with a hint of reservation. He didn't like the idea, but then again, he didn't like the idea of the mission in the first place. He wanted to get his men in and out as quickly as possible.

"Prepare to drop in sixty seconds," Chief Wright said.

Beckham lifted his helmet to see the primary pilot twisting the cyclic hard inside the cockpit. The chopper veered to the right. The Black Hawk rolled slightly onto its side, giving Beckham a quick view of dark waves crashing against the shoreline below. He pulled a magazine and palmed it into his weapon. "All right, Ghost. You know the drill."

The other men charged their rifles as the bird straightened out. They hovered over the beach as the pilot rotated the cyclic to a neutral position.

"This is where you get out," Chief Wright yelled over the whooshing of the blades.

Beckham flashed the pilots a thumbs-up and said, "Thanks for the ride." He caught a glimpse of something flickering on the horizon. He knew that somewhere out there, a squadron of F-22s waited with weapons systems hot, fully prepared to blow the Black Hawk out of the air if something went wrong.

Hazardous-duty pay indeed, Beckham thought. Shoving the thought aside, he moved into position at the door. It was go time.

Beckham flashed a quick hand motion to Tenor, who was crouched by the door. The operator nodded and secured the fast rope to a clip with a loud click. A sea of sand waited for them below. The mixture of sediment churned into a cloud, swirling around the chopper and making it nearly impossible to see.

Grabbing the nylon rope, Tenor handed it to Spinoza. With a slap, he said, "Go, go!" The man sprang into the darkness, with Horn close behind. Riley and Edwards went next, then Caster and Noble. Ellis hesitated, glancing over at Beckham.

"Why can't he just put us down on the tarmac?" the doctor yelled.

Tenor and Beckham laughed.

"Military protocol," Beckham said. "Now jump!" He gave the doctor a soft push.

Screaming, Ellis grabbed the rope and disappeared into the cloud of dust.

Then it was just the two leads. They exchanged a glance for a brief moment. They'd made enough jumps to know this one was different. Neither of them knew what awaited them on the island's surface.

Beckham suppressed the moment of fear and uncertainty. Grabbing the fast rope, he rappelled into the night, hoping—praying—that there was some rational explanation for Building 8's having gone dark.

Luck was on Ghost's side this night. The full moon provided a carpet of light across the island, illuminating the landscape with a radiant white glow. The team moved briskly across the beach with Beckham at their helm. They fanned out as they pressed on. Their movements were practiced. They'd done this a hundred times before. Waves slurped at the beach behind them, muffling the crunching sound of their stiff suits.

"So where is this place?" Horn asked, looking out over the sand as if the facility might appear in front of him.

A condescending laugh crackled over the comm. "Do you really think the government would have built a secret facility out in the open?" Riley said. "Haven't you ever heard of the Greenbrier, in West Virginia?"

"Doesn't ring a bell," replied Horn.

"The government built a massive bunker under the resort there. Kept it a secret for years. It wasn't until they declassified it that the public knew. If people were fucking in suites above a bunker built to house Congress in a time of war, I'm pretty sure they can hide a small facility out here from the public."

"Radio silence," Beckham said harshly, embarrassed his men had not acted with more discipline. He trotted over to Caster, who had retrieved a GPS locator from his pack. The facility's coordinates blinked on the display. Judging by their location, it looked as if they had about a quarter mile to trek. Beckham had been slightly surprised to learn neither of the men had been to the facility, but Riley's description of the Greenbrier reminded him the government had many secrets. Team Ghost was the perfect example.

Beckham moved first, climbing up the sandy hill. Over the ridgeline, a lightly traveled frontage road ran along the length of the beach. A loose power line whipped back and forth in the slight breeze. Besides the crashing of the waves, the island was eerily quiet.

With a few quick hand signals, Beckham broke the group into strike teams. Bravo fanned out across the road and into the ditch on the right, while Alpha trekked toward a series of sand dunes to the left. The landscape was stark and empty; nothing but underbrush and a few sporadic palm trees juxtaposed with the mostly barren terrain.

Overhead, the moon disappeared under sudden, dense cloud cover, and the teams halted to switch on their NVGs. Beckham had hoped they wouldn't have to use them until they entered Building 8, but with the moonlight gone, they had no choice.

With the optics active, he now had a 100-degree horizontal field of view and a 40-degree vertical field of view. The goggles revealed a landscape devoid of life. He slowly swept the optics to the right and then back to the left.

Nothing.

Did the animals know something he didn't? There had to be a reasonable explanation.

The more he scanned the area, the more he wondered. The optics normally picked up even the slightest movement, down to the smallest mouse.

Beckham tried to convince himself that they were hibernating or hiding. But it wasn't that cold—surely a few nocturnal creatures would be out scavenging for their next meal. Tightening his grip on his MP5, he shrugged the question away and started up the loose sand of the closest dune. At the top, he had his first good vantage on the entire island.

To the north, just beyond another cluster of hills, he could make out the airstrip and a collection of buildings. He scoped the area below, stopping on a sign at the bottom of the dune.

NO TRESPASSING—GOVERNMENT PROPERTY

Balling his fist, he took a knee and waved Caster forward. The man scrambled up the dune and pulled his GPS locator out, studying the screen intensely.

"We're close. Within five hundred feet of the facility," Caster said.

Beckham looked out over the landscape and saw nothing except for an empty road that looked as if it led to a dumping ground.

Chinning his comm pad, he said, "Tenor, you see anything?"

"Negative, just a large embankment," Tenor said. "I have a bad taste in my mouth. There's nothing out here."

Beckham listened to the sound of hissing sand. The area was freakishly quiet. He used the moment to think. There was simply no way they had the wrong coordinates. He was missing something.

"Regroup and show me this embankment," Beckham said. He stood and waved Riley and Horn forward. After a quick peek over his shoulder to check their six, Beckham followed them. They made their way past another series of sand dunes and came to a paved road. Collecting in the ditch were mounds of trash. The wind had scattered some of it across the road. Plastic bottles crunched beneath the weight of the team's boots. The sound didn't bother him. The sight of the trash did. It looked as if no one had used the street in days.

There was no sign of vehicles, no sign of Building 8, and no sign of animals of any kind. *What the fuck is going on?* Beckham thought. He was used to training Afghani forces or fighting insurgents whom he could zoom in on with a red-dot sight. This mysterious shit pissed him off.

Grunting, he followed the curved road through a series of hills and finally to what looked like a landfill.

"Over there," Caster said. He held up the GPS device and pointed to a metal building, aged with rust, that sat amidst the refuse. There were no windows, just a single steel door that had the same NO TRESPASSING sign.

Bravo had already taken up position on the west side of the building. All three men hid in the underbrush, the pointed outlines of their rifles aimed on the steel door.

"Tenor, get in there and see what the hell we're dealing with," Beckham ordered.

The four men were moving before the sound of Beckham's voice faded over the comm. Spinoza pressed his back against the building next to Tenor, while Edwards raised his shotgun.

Noble approached the door, but Tenor waved him back. The major made way for Edwards and Spinoza.

The larger operator shouldered his M249, and Edwards stepped up to grab the handle. He twisted the knob. It clicked, unlocked.

Tenor flashed a hand signal. Edwards opened the door, and Spinoza strode inside with his M249. Tenor followed his men inside.

Beckham checked his watch before motioning his team to follow.

0435 hours, 19 April 2015.

His gut told him it was a date he would never forget.

3

Doctor Kate Lovato paused to study the simulation of a brilliant sunrise filling the east wall of the lobby outside her lab. She'd called the facility home since the first case of Ebola had hit Guinea months earlier. The lab was buried deep beneath the surface of the Centers for Disease Control and Prevention's Arlen Specter Headquarters and Emergency Operations Center, or as its workers called it, Building 18.

The artificial rays were really starting to look like the real thing. At least that's what she kept telling herself.

Funny what working beneath the earth's surface for an extended amount of time can do to a mind, she thought. Kate knew she wasn't immune to the mental strain of isolation, but it could always be worse. She'd worked around the globe before accepting a position with CDC a year before, and she'd seen the worst the microscopic world of viruses had to offer: from children stricken with malaria during the dead of summer in Sri Lanka to a village in Uganda struck by an outbreak of yellow fever. What gave most people nightmares were part of her everyday life.

She found this part of her work ironic, knowing that several city blocks away the citizens of Atlanta went about their daily routines, most of them blissfully unaware that somewhere under their feet scientists were working with some of the deadliest diseases known to man.

Only a handful of those scientists were working with the Slate Wiper, as Ebola had been dubbed by the majority of the scientific community. Kate was one of them. She was part of a small team with two other virologists, isolated from the rest of CDC. They even had their own Level 4 biohazard laboratory. It took a special person to want to work on the Slate Wiper team.

Kate took a last swig of coffee and threw out her cup before approaching the glass doors. Even though the lab contained microscopic viruses that could kill her within hours, she'd always felt safe here. The faint hum of the advanced air-filtration system designed specifically for the facility reminded her how much the government had spent to ensure that what was on the other side of those doors never got out. They hadn't just spent money to keep things from getting out—they had also spent it to prevent the wrong people from getting in. The vestibule connecting the labs required voice and fingerprint recognition. Nothing short of a rocket-propelled grenade was going to bring down the glass wall.

Kate pressed her finger against the small pad and said, "Doctor Kate Lovato."

The door buzzed, the glass panels whispered open, and she stepped inside a room the size of a high school chemistry lab. Three lab stations were centered in the room.

Each stretched forty feet in one direction and fifteen in the other.

She smiled when she spied Doctor Michael Allen's bald head hunched over a microscope at the farthest station. He was more than the team lead—he was Kate's mentor and friend.

Michael was well known and respected in the international virology community for the advances he'd made in Ebola research. He had been around long enough to have an answer for virtually any question Kate could throw at him. His mind held a wealth of knowledge about the viruses that most scientists wanted nothing more than to stay away from.

"Good morning," she said, making her way to her station.

"Morning," he replied in his cool, clinical voice.

"Where's Doctor Ellis?"

"He's been outsourced."

"Outsourced where?"

"That's classified. I don't even know. Nothing to worry about, I'm sure. Typically these are just training missions."

"Oh?" Kate asked. "Just a training mission?"

Michael twisted away from his monitor. Dark purple bags rimmed his hazel eyes. They were deeper than normal, more pronounced. Had he been up all night?

"Like I said, I don't know much. The US Army Medical Research Institute of Infectious Diseases sent the request through late yesterday afternoon. Colonel Rick Gibson called me personally. He's an old friend, and he said they'd had to activate their EOC. As you know, protocol is to include CDC. So I sent Ellis."

His response didn't offend Kate. At thirty years old, she was just happy to be where she was in her career. Not to mention she'd only been working under Michael for a year. Sure, she had the credentials, but most of her career she'd spent traveling. Ellis was the obvious pick. What bothered her was the EOC activation. Michael had certainly downplayed it, but she couldn't help wondering if it had something to do with the recent Ebola outbreak.

"Any updates?" Kate asked, changing the subject and taking a seat on the lab stool at her own terminal. She flicked the touch screen and watched the display glow to life.

"Suit up," Michael replied eagerly.

Kate furrowed her brow and swiveled her chair to face him. She knew what this deviation from his sometimes frustratingly calm voice could mean.

He's made a breakthrough.

She didn't want to get her hopes up, but she could hardly contain her excitement as she prepared to enter the sterile environment of the BSL4 lab.

They entered the changing room—or as Kate liked to call it, the space suit room—together. Four of the special suits hung from the wall.

She stripped down to her underwear in the center of the room, and Michael did likewise. They'd seen each other this way a hundred times; modesty was not part of the process.

A few minutes later, Kate was inside her suit. Michael zipped her up from behind and made sure everything was secure. The hiss of cold air sent a chill down Kate's body as her suit was sealed off. The line swiftly pumped in oxygen. She took in a breath and checked on Michael. He gave her a thumbs-up and prepared to enter the lab.

As Michael keyed in his credentials, Kate felt her muscles tighten. She had handled Ebola samples a dozen times now, but the anxiety that preceded entering the lab never really seemed to go away. She'd seen the effects of the virus up close in Guinea. And even though she knew the chances of infection inside the lab were next to zero, she couldn't help but think about it each time.

The trick was not thinking about the virus itself and instead compartmentalizing the work, as an office worker would. She aligned each task in order and completed them one by one, carefully and slowly. There was urgency to their job, knowing that every minute they didn't find a cure was another minute the virus was spreading. But she never let herself think that way. Working with the thought of a gun to her head would only cause an accident.

Kate joined Michael at the workstation, where he was setting up a culture dish. He used a transfer pipette to squirt a sample into the small container. Moving to the microscope, he slid the dish underneath the lens.

"These are endothelial cells. Take a look," he said, gesturing her forward.

Kate hesitated. Was this the moment she had been waiting months for? She pressed her visor against the eyepiece. Microscopic strands of the Ebola virus moved about the sample. At first glance, she didn't see anything unusual. Nothing different from what she'd already studied before. Certainly nothing that told her this was a new strain.

Kate pulled her eye away, realizing with slight frustration that Michael was testing her. He stood a few feet away with his arms crossed.

"I don't get it," Kate said.

"That's because you haven't seen everything yet."

She opened her lips to speak but resisted the urge. Michael had spent forty years training and teaching scientists from around the world. He knew what he was doing. She reminded herself that he wasn't messing with her— he was simply showing her what to look for.

Kate transferred the image to the main monitor for a better look. She could see the large cobblestone pattern of the endothelial cells now. The spaghetti-like strains of the virus attacked the pattern as she expected they would. The cells began to separate, ball up, and die, but something was different. It was happening faster than normal.

"The virus has mutated," Kate whispered.

Michael nodded, his features darkening.

"That's why it's spreading so fast, and why the mortality

rate is higher. When the virus infects the endothelial cells, it causes a chain reaction that results in massive vascular damage, and ultimately ..."

"Hemorrhaging," Kate replied.

Michael nodded. "We are definitely dealing with a new strain here, Kate. And you are going to find us a cure."

4

Beckham moved into the hallway where the rest of the team waited with their backs to the wall and their weapons at the ready. Static broke over the net, and Caster said, "Noble found what he thinks is the entry to Level One of the laboratory. This way," he said, leading the group down the dark passage.

They found Noble standing outside a steel door. A sign bolted to the middle read AUTHORIZED PERSONNEL ONLY.

Next to the door's handle was the first indiscreet part of the entire setup, a glass scanner just large enough for a key card.

"They could have covered it with something," Riley said.

Noble pulled a card attached to a cord from a pouch on his belt. He held it in front of the operator's faceplate and said, "Wouldn't matter. No one gets into this facility without one of these."

A metallic click and a chirp rang out as Noble waved the card over the glass. The door creaked open, and the doctor took a step back to make room for Spinoza and his M249. The operator planted one boot firmly in front of the other and then inched the door open.

"Execute," Beckham whispered. He could hear the large Latino's nervous breaths as he eased the door open to allow

Riley inside. He raised his shotgun and strode through, with Spinoza right behind. They melted into the darkness beyond, leaving the rest of the team in silence.

The quiet was broken by a "Clear" over the comm from Riley. Beckham nodded, and the team proceeded down the staircase in a single-file line. Their new suits rustled as they entered the narrow space. It was a sound that made Beckham cringe.

Unseen and unheard, Beckham thought. They weren't exactly living up to their motto. He waited for Horn to move next. The six-foot-two operator turned sideways to squeeze through the opening.

Beckham followed his men into the dark stairwell. In the green hue cast by his NVGs were the small hubs of emergency lights on the low ceiling.

He followed the twisting stairs, checking his avenue of fire and shifting his gaze between front and rear, checking on Ellis every few seconds. The team moved with flawless precision, rotating from front to back.

By the time they reached the bottom of the stairs, a stream of adrenaline had spiked in Beckham's system. He felt powerful again. Invincible, even. He held back a grin. This was what he lived for.

An unmarked steel door separated them from Level 1. There was no warning sign or other indication that would imply there was anything significant on the other side.

Noble squeezed past Beckham, Horn, and Spinoza to use his key card. This time he pulled a sleek Beretta M9 from a holster before carefully opening the door.

Beckham saw Horn's bulky frame straighten in front of him, and then they were moving. The scuffle of footfalls filled the stairwell.

Even with his NVGs active, Beckham could see the floor

was spotless—so clean the concrete looked as if someone had just mopped it.

He swept the muzzle of his weapon over the space. The vivid green room was divided into two sections. To the right, a hallway led to the individual examination rooms where the scientists working in the facility would undergo health screenings.

The left passage connected three decontamination chambers. They were oddly shaped, like pods. Through the glass he could see the entrance to Level 2. Beyond that, there was only darkness.

With a quick flash of his hand, Beckham guided Alpha toward the decontamination chambers. Tenor broke off and led Bravo to clear the medical wing.

It became quite obvious right away that Level 1 was empty. There were no signs or evidence of recent life. That was a bit of a relief, but it deepened the mystery of what had happened.

"How you doing back there, Doctor Ellis?" Beckham asked.

"Fine," the doctor answered.

Beckham knew by the monosyllabic reply that the virologist was scared shitless, and he couldn't blame him.

White noise crackled over the comm, and Tenor's voice broke across the channel. "Area clear. No sign of Doctor Medford or his staff."

"Copy that," Beckham answered. He lowered his MP5 and waited for Bravo to make their way back to the lobby. Craning his head, he looked for Caster.

The officer was crouched next to one of the glass decontamination chambers, tapping the surface of his tablet with one of his thick gloves. Caster studied the display and then said, "Looks like access to the control room is just beyond the mess hall."

"Roger. Let's see if we can get the power back on," Beckham said. He motioned the team forward. The sound of boots pounding across the lobby echoed loudly through the sector as the two strike teams proceeded to the decontamination chambers. Beckham paused as the sudden feeling of being watched overwhelmed him. Horn had always suggested Beckham had a sixth sense. He wasn't sure if the man was right, but at that moment he felt the strong sensation of being observed. Someone was out there.

Beckham scanned the lobby.

Nothing.

He continued through the lobby to the front entrance of the first decontamination pod.

"How do we know that no one's escaped?" Horn asked while the team waited for Noble to open the first chamber.

"Those scanners," Caster said, pointing. "They have backup batteries in case of catastrophic power failure, in which case the lab is locked down. The system was designed so no one could get out if that happened. They would have to wait."

"Wait for us?" Spinoza asked.

"Anyone working in a lab like this knows if something catastrophic happens, they won't be rescued. If we didn't need the sample, we'd have already blown this place to hell," Caster replied.

The first cylinder hissed and the glass doors parted. When they were halfway open, they groaned to a stop.

"Shit," Noble said. "The hardware must have malfunctioned."

Beckham eyed the gap. It looked large enough for Spinoza and Horn, but if they had to back out quickly, it could bottleneck the team. "Big Horn, Panda, try to get those open."

Together the two men pulled the glass doors far enough apart that the team could get through. Beckham waved them forward. Noble moved quickly to the next scanner. This time the doors opened without resistance. The strike teams spilled into the final chamber in a single-file line, where they waited to enter Level 2.

Beckham stood next to Noble as he waved his key card over the last scanner. Through the glass he could see an empty hallway leading to the mess hall and personnel quarters, but it wasn't spotless like Level 1. A large, dark smear streaked across the floor beyond the door. He followed the trail to the wall, where it stopped.

Flipping up his NVGs, he risked using his head lamp. The beam cut through the darkness and illuminated a bloody handprint on the wall.

What the fuck? Beckham thought, taking a step away from the glass just as it cracked open. Balling his hand into a fist, he very sternly said, "Hold position." He then pointed at the wall and angled his light at the smear of blood.

The sight didn't seem to bother Noble. "Don't worry, that's why we have suits."

His response took Beckham by surprise. "That's not from a spilled test tube, sir. That's from an injury. A bad one."

"Turn off your light, Sergeant," Noble replied coldly, leveling his M9 into the darkness and moving through the door.

"Let's move," Caster said, patting Beckham on his shoulder.

Hesitating, Beckham clicked off his head lamp and flipped his NVGs back into position. He followed Noble's outline into the passage and scrutinized the trail of blood. He knew perfectly well how much blood a man could lose before dying. There was no mistaking it: Whoever had bled out here was severely injured. Any soldier would know this, but for some reason the sight hadn't fazed Noble or Caster at all. It was as if they were expecting it. Beckham was used to working with men he didn't trust—Afghani and Iraqi military forces were the perfect example—but US soldiers?

He reminded himself this wasn't a normal mission. In the past, he had been forced to keep key details of other missions secret when working with foreign troops. He had never been on the other side of it, however. He now realized how Dr. Ellis must have felt when he first boarded the Osprey hours ago. There wasn't anything Beckham could do about it either.

The end of the hall broke off in two directions. Beckham remembered that the corridor to the left led to the personnel quarters, while the other corridor led to the mess hall. With another quick hand gesture, he ordered Bravo to the right. Then he led his team toward the individual rooms.

The green outlines of several doors came into view as he rounded the corner. Placards identified the name of the scientist assigned to each room. The first one Beckham approached read *Dr. Jane Levoy.*

Placing his back against the wall, he waited for his team to move into position. Horn leveled his M249 at the nameplate while Riley took up a position on the opposite wall.

"Doctor Ellis, Riley, stay here," Beckham whispered. He put his hand on Horn's back and then tapped his shoulder. For the first time since the mission began, his suit felt tight around his chest. He waited for something to dart out at them when they opened the door, but the room was empty.

The living area was small, not much larger than a dorm room, and it seemed undisturbed, with a carefully made twin bed and a clean bedside table.

They backed out and switched positions. Beckham entered the next room, holding his breath, when the comm blared to life.

"Beckham, you…" Tenor's voice faded and then grew louder. "You better see this."

He knew by the sergeant's slight pause that he'd found something significant. Over the years they'd seen a lot together—mass graves, executed prisoners, war crimes of all types. Nothing *ever* spooked Tenor.

"Move," Beckham said, grabbing Ellis under his left arm and spinning him back the way they had come. "Riley, Horn, you clear the rest of these rooms. Major Caster, you're with me."

The officer grumbled, but fell in line. Thirty seconds later they entered the mess hall. Beckham immediately stopped in the entrance to survey the destruction. Flipped metal tables and chairs littered the ground like shrapnel from an explosion. On the floor he saw empty food trays, their contents having been splattered on the walls. There were more smudges on the ceiling. Clicking on his head lamp, he realized the red smears weren't Jell-O.

Blood.

It was everywhere. Like something done by a graffiti artist high on meth, the walls and ceilings were painted with the substance. Blood was splattered in every direction.

Beckham had never seen anything like it.

"What the hell happened here?" a voice said. He'd forgotten Ellis was still shadowing him. The doctor and Caster were slowly navigating the overturned tables.

The comm crackled, and Tenor came back online. "Beckham, where are you?" There was urgency in his voice, enough to kick Beckham into a full sprint. He raced toward the kitchen, where he could see the outlines of Bravo.

And then he stopped, his boots sliding across the smooth floor. He scrambled, nearly tripping over his own feet. Spinoza reached out and steadied him.

Inside the walk-in freezer were half a dozen bodies, most of them naked, their frames twisted and mangled beyond recognition. The one on top looked female, but the body was in such terrible condition it was hard to tell.

The woman had suffered extreme trauma to her skull. A gash ran all the way down to the tip of her nose, where her only remaining eyeball hung loosely from its socket.

"My God," Beckham said. He pivoted toward Caster. "Something you need to tell us, Major?" The man didn't reply, but Noble stepped into the freezer and crouched next to the female victim. He flipped over one of her arms. It snapped and broke at the wrist, revealing bulging blue veins. "Shit...She's infected."

"How do you know? Let me look," Ellis said, shoving his way into the room to examine the bodies. A few moments later he shook his head. "Hemorrhaging from multiple orifices. The jaundiced skin and bulging veins imply organ failure. Noble's right, this woman likely had Ebola. But that's not what killed her, is it, Major?"

Noble quickly shook his head. "No, it's not." He peered up at Beckham and very dryly said, "I'm sorry. This is much worse than I imagined." He looked back down at the bodies. "Medford must have accidentally created the monster virus I've always feared."

"What does that mean?" Riley, who had just entered the kitchen with Horn, blurted. "Monster virus?"

"Judging by the wounds on these bodies..." Noble paused and scanned the pile of corpses.

"It means that victims will display all the symptoms of Ebola, but also those associated with VX-99," Caster said.

"Meaning what, exactly?" Horn asked. His chest swelled as he stood staring over Noble's shoulder.

"Those exposed to VX-99 exhibit a range of violent

behaviors in addition to hallucinations," Noble said. "From the test files I've read, the subjects have all proven to be very cunning, with one overall purpose—"

"We saw the reports. We saw Lieutenant Brett," Beckham said, cutting the doctor off in midsentence. "They're killing machines."

"Precisely, but we don't know for how long. It's likely the victims die of the virus before they can do much harm," Noble finished.

"Not much harm? What the fuck do you call this?" Riley said, his voice rising just shy of a shout. "Someone was alive long enough to do this!"

"Riley, get a fucking grip," Beckham ordered.

"That one has bite marks on it," Spinoza remarked. He extended a massive arm and pointed at the bottom corpse. A swollen suction mark had formed a circle around shredded flesh and exposed muscle.

Ellis pulled on a leg protruding from the pile and quickly backed away. "What the hell . . ."

The stack toppled over, and the sound of limbs snapping under the weight of the pile reverberated through the room. The cracking sounded like a fork stuck in a garbage disposal.

When the bodies had finally settled on the floor, Beckham could see they all had bite marks. Someone or something had torn long patches of flesh from the victims. In other places the limbs were devoured to the bone. He stared in disbelief. Never in his career had he seen such an atrocity. It was in that moment he realized the freezer wasn't a grave site.

He leaned down and focused on the marks. Circular bruises surrounded the torn flesh, as if an oversized leech had clamped down to feed on the bodies. A flashback to the images of Lieutenant Brett's mouth made him flinch. They weren't dealing with some overgrown leech—they were dealing with a human monster, and he was looking at its leftovers.

"Fuck," he muttered. "This is a storage facility." He counted six corpses. Gibson had stated there were ten scientists and support staff working in the facility. So where were the others?

Beckham scanned the room, searching every corner and shadow. "Keep sharp. There must still be other scientists out there, and if my hunch is right, they are going to look a lot like Lieutenant Brett."

Riley gagged and choked.

"Don't puke in your mask!" Noble said, his voice just shy of a shout.

After he recovered, Riley looked up. "Whoever did this is some kind of vampire."

"More like a zombie, man," Edwards said in his perpetually calm voice. The man rarely spoke, and when he did, his words carried weight. The entire team grew silent for several beats.

"Not exactly," Noble said. "Whatever these scientists were infected with—"

A guttural, high-pitched shriek cut him off. Beckham spun along with the rest of the team to locate the sound.

"What the fuck was that?" Riley exclaimed, moving the barrel of his shotgun from wall to wall.

Beckham flashed several hand signals, and the team fanned out into the mess hall.

Another screech followed them into the larger room. This one didn't seem quite human. The sound was primal.

"Where's it coming from?" Horn said. He angled his M27 at the ceiling.

"Sounds like it's all around us," Riley replied.

Beckham knew that was impossible. They'd cleared Level 2, and there was no way the noise would carry from Level 3. The glass was soundproof.

He scanned the ceiling. There, in the left-hand corner just above their nine o'clock was a missing tile.

There was a blur of movement.

Beckham froze.

A man poked his head through the hole in the ceiling. His eyes were wild, vertical pupils darting back and forth as if they were adjusting to the darkness. A curtain of thin hair hung loosely around his face.

Beckham blinked, wondering if this was just an illusion. His focus cleared, and the face was still there staring back at him, studying him.

The man's mouth puckered and made a popping sound, snapping Beckham into motion.

"Contact at nine o'clock," he said into his mini-mic.

The beam from Beckham's head lamp caught the man in the eyes. The result was a long, deep, and painful scream as the sick man swatted at the light.

And then he was gone.

"Where? I don't see shit," Riley remarked.

"Got nothin', boss," Horn added.

Beckham blinked again, still wondering if what he had seen was real. His suit once again felt tight, pressing against his chest. Every breath seemed strained, almost as if his respirator was failing.

After a short, measured breath, Beckham concentrated. "You better find those lights, Doc," he said, gesturing with the muzzle of his weapon toward the missing tile. "I think your monster has found us."

5

Jim Pinkman awoke to an awful smell, a scent he couldn't quite place. It was reminiscent of rotting fruit, but more pungent and rancid.

He couldn't remember where he was. The room he found himself in shook violently. The sound of groaning metal echoed off the walls.

He tried to open his eyes.

Where the fuck was he?

Another small tremor rattled the walls. His ears popped from a sudden change in pressure.

He let out a moan and considered calling out for help, but he had no strength. He struggled to crack open his eyes. Stars crept before his vision. When his focus cleared, he saw the distorted reflection of his features inside a metal bowl.

The room shook again, harder this time, and then he remembered. He was on a plane heading to Maryland, with a stopover in Chicago. Dr. Medford was sending him to Fort Detrick for a secret briefing with some of the military brass there.

Blinking, he struggled to move. He was barely able to lift his face. More stars floated before his eyes. When they finally cleared, he realized that his metal pillow was actually a toilet bowl.

Shock gave him the energy to pull his face off the cold metal.

The terrible smell entered his nostrils again. His stomach growled. *What is that awful scent?*

Pushing himself upright, his hands slid across a gooey floor. He quivered when he saw the source of the rotting stink.

Covering the floor, the toilet, and even a portion of the wall was black-red vomit filled with specks of gore. He felt something drip from his lips and wiped it away, the substance leaving the same color smeared across his wrist.

"What the hell?" he choked. The words didn't sound like his own. Before he had a chance to think, a sudden and powerful hunger gripped him. The feeling was followed by a burst of energy that jolted him to his feet. He stumbled over to the mirror and blinked away the last of the stars.

What he saw caused him to flinch. This had to be some kind of sick joke. The man looking back at him was not Jim Pinkman. It couldn't be him. Clumps of thin hair hung loosely where just hours before he'd had thick brown hair that made other men his age jealous. Dark bruises lined his bloodshot eyes. He pulled up his right eyelid, revealing a bright red sclera. There wasn't a hint of white left, as if every blood vessel had simultaneously burst. Streaks of blood oozed from his nose and eyes. He twisted his face to the side and saw the same trickle of red coming from his ears. Blood leaked down his face and connected to a beard of dark red around his mouth.

And what the fuck was wrong with his lips? They were

pale and curved into an oval shape. He brought a finger to his numb and swollen flesh.

"Oh my God," he said, backing away from the mirror. His mouth looked like the sucker of a fucking leech.

He had to get control of himself, maintain control.

Slowly he inched back to the glass and cracked his lips, revealing curved and jagged teeth.

"No," he muttered. He had to be dreaming.

He forced himself to look away. It wasn't possible. He couldn't be the sick man in the mirror. A sudden spike of pain tore through his head, as if an instant migraine had settled right behind his eyeballs. He reached for the wall to brace himself as the plane began to descend.

Slowly, memories of Building 8 began to drift across his mind. He remembered the retractable robot arm breaking a vial of the virus that Dr. Medford had been working on for months.

The automatic containment system had kicked on inside the centrifuge, releasing a mist that destroyed the spilled sample. He'd suited up and entered the area, cleaning up the broken vial and recalibrating the robot manually.

When he'd gone to discard the glass, he'd cut his glove, but after examining his hand he'd seen no sign of a cut. And besides, the mist would have killed the sample—at least that's what he had thought at the time.

What if the chemical mist had only weakened the virus? What if that's why he hadn't shown any symptoms until now?

His eyes darted back to the mirror.

The man in front of him wasn't just sick; he was a monster.

"No," Jim groaned, shaking his head as the revelation sank in. He concentrated on his other memories. One of them was particularly vivid.

He had been in a hurry to leave Building 8 after Medford

had asked him go to Fort Detrick to brief Colonel Gibson on their work. Jane Levoy, a doctor he'd been having an affair with for months, had wanted to make love before he left. She'd insisted on it, saying he wouldn't be back for weeks. The image of their sweat-soaked bodies crossed his confused mind.

"My God," Jim muttered. Had he infected her?

A voice blared over the PA system and pulled him from his muddled thoughts.

"Prepare for landing. ETA thirty minutes."

Jim's stomach growled again, a deep hunger tearing at his gut. It was getting stronger now. And the itching. God, the itching. His skin felt as if it was being ravaged by hundreds of fire ants. He slowly raised his right arm and saw the rashes. Dark red blotches lined his bare flesh.

Could it be? Was he infected with Ebola? What about his lips? His teeth? Those weren't symptoms of Ebola.

A second surge of energy jolted Jim upright. It made no sense. If he was this sick, how was he so . . .

He doubled over in pain, clutching his stomach as the hunger ripped through him. The burning rippled across his skin. He felt possessed, as if some unseen force had suddenly taken hold of his body—a force beyond his control.

His tongue shot out of his mouth and flicked in a circle around his suction-cup-shaped lips. The metallic taste of dried blood seeped down his throat, bringing a short reprieve from the hunger. Thoughts of blood, flesh, and meat ripped across his mind. They were just images, but they were powerful. He began to chomp his sharp teeth together. They clacked noisily as he scanned the rashes on his arms.

Another wave of hunger slashed through him. He dropped to both knees in pain. His body shook as the sensation took hold. Seizing, he collapsed to the floor, his eyes locked onto the naked flesh of his wrist.

No—I can't, he thought.

A male voice snarled in his mind, "Feed! You must feed!"

Jim recognized the voice for what it was—a hallucination. He was sick and delusional.

But the force that had taken control of him tugged at his insides, at his mind, at his very core. The pain and the craving for flesh was simply too much to deny.

He latched his swollen lips onto his wrist. The numbness slowly faded as he fed. He could feel his mouth now. It was clamped to his arm, his lips forming a barrier over the skin. And he could feel his teeth. They shredded through his flesh like a garden tiller. The blood raced down his throat and he tore at the skin and muscle with a violent twist of his mouth.

A quick succession of raps on the metal bathroom door rang through the small space. He ignored it, swallowing a chunk of meat with a quick gulp.

"Sir, are you okay in there?" a male voice said. The man hammered at the door for several more beats.

Jim continued to tear into his wrist. The sound of his own flesh ripping filled him with delight. Oddly, he felt only the pain of hunger, and the more he fed, the more relief he found. After a few moments, his bloodstained eyes shot up to the door. The knocking was annoying him. He wanted it to stop.

The voice outside got louder. The man began yelling. "Are you taking a nap in there or what, man? I need to use the can before we land!"

Jim bolted up, his joints clicking and creaking as he moved. Crouching, he swung the door open to reveal a navy officer staring back at him. The man's eyes widened and he dropped the magazine he was holding when he saw Jim.

"What the fuck happened to your..." the man began to say, reaching out cautiously before yanking his hand away.

The craving inside him returned with ferocity. He tilted

his head, fixating on the bulging vein at the man's neck. Jim could almost see the blood pumping through it. He lunged. Unable to scream, the man collapsed to the ground. Clawing wildly, Jim fed.

His world became astonishingly vivid. He could taste every bit of the coppery blood and gamey flesh as it ran down his throat. He could hear the gurgling noises in the man's throat and could even smell the salty sweat on the officer's collar.

At the far end of the plane, another navy man turned in his seat, wiping the sleep from his eyes. "What the fuck?" he yelled. He unclipped his seat belt and raced down the aisle.

"Get off him, man, come on! Get off…" Then the second officer saw the blood. He spun to run, but Jim was much faster. He dove, caught one of the man's feet, and then climbed on top of the struggling officer, who lashed out with his hands, trying to hold back bulging lips and snarling teeth.

They rolled on the metal floor as the plane's wheels connected with tarmac, and when the plane finally came to a stop, the last hint of humanity disappeared from Jim Pinkman in one long, high-pitched primal scream.

Beckham and the strike teams gathered around a shredded electrical box in a storage room outside the mess hall. The metal sides were dented and smashed. Cords snaked out in all directions. By this point it was obvious that someone on Dr. Medford's staff—someone infected with the Ebola and VX-99 hybrid virus—had sabotaged the lab. But they hadn't stopped there. They had also murdered and eaten their coworkers.

Hours before, when Beckham was still en route to Edwards

Air Force Base, he had hoped that the lab had simply gone off-line, that when his team arrived they would be greeted by ten grateful scientists waiting for rescue. As he scrutinized the bloodstained walls of the mess hall, it all seemed like wishful thinking. Outside, in the disturbingly silent landscape, he'd known something catastrophic had happened, but he'd had no idea it would be this bad.

"Isn't there backup power?" Tenor asked.

"There is," Caster replied. "That's what's running the air ventilation and security systems."

"We need to get to Level Three," Noble said, his voice anxious and strained. "None of this changes anything."

Beckham took a moment to think. The victims in the freezer and the man he'd seen in the ceiling reminded him that they had more to worry about than just infection. They had a much more significant threat on their hands—a Lieutenant Brett was loose in the building.

"Keep sharp. Keep focused," he said over the channel. "You see anything, you shoot to kill."

Several helmets twisted in his direction, but no one said a word. Together the team moved forward in a cautious formation, their weapons sweeping across every shadow.

Beckham forced the mental pictures out of his mind as the doors to Level 3 cracked open. He entered first, leading the team into another atrium. From there, he did what he had been trained to do in isolated situations. He surveyed the area to ensure it was free of contacts, and then he analyzed potential routes. The ceiling tiles were all intact, and the lobby was clear. Like the previous level, this one had two hallways. A green sign on the right directed them to Labs 1 and 2. He recalled from the briefing that green meant those contained the least-severe contagions.

Beckham looked to the left. Through the darkness he

could see the outlines of Labs 3 and 4, red signs hanging above their doors. It was there they would likely find Dr. Medford's samples, but he wasn't taking any chances. They would clear all the labs.

"Bravo, you take Labs One and Two. Alpha, we're on Three and Four. Remember, your suit is your lifeline," he said. "Stay sharp, Ghost. I don't want any other surprises."

He took point, gripping his MP5 tightly. He could hear his heart pounding inside his helmet. The muffled noise of their suits echoed off the narrow hallway as they moved. Behind him he could hear Horn's labored breathing through the comm.

As they approached the first lab, a flash of movement darted across the hallway. Beckham froze and balled his hand into a fist.

"Boss," Horn whispered over the comm.

"I saw it," Beckham replied. He held his position, waiting for the contact to reemerge from the shadows. Whatever it was, it was gone now.

After several beats, Beckham flashed an advance signal and followed Horn down the rest of the passage. The door to Lab 3, on their left, was wide open, while the door to Lab 4 was sealed.

"The sample will probably be in Lab Four," Caster said.

"Roger, clearing Lab Three first, sir," Beckham replied.

The inside of the room had been trashed. Crushed vials were splattered across the floor, their contents still in puddles.

Beckham's heart kicked as he chinned his comm. "We have multiple contaminants," he said. "No sign of contacts." He stepped into the space carefully, avoiding the first pile of broken glass with a small hop. He sidestepped a puddle and kept his gaze on the shapes of several lab stations cordoned off by a plastic curtain at the edge of the room.

When he got to the first station, he realized he was holding his breath. Exhaling, he paused to scan the room, sweeping his muzzle over the ceiling for any sign of a breech.

Nothing.

Stepping around another pool of unidentified contaminants, he made his way toward the curtain. He poked the plastic with his rifle barrel and grabbed the lining with his right hand.

With clenched teeth, he pulled the curtain back, causing something limp and heavy to topple. Beckham scrambled, regaining his footing and shoving the thing into the glass wall.

Then, raising his MP5, he jammed the barrel into the soft flesh of a dead scientist. The body slumped to the floor and the head fell to the side at an odd angle, neck broken.

"Damn," Horn said, standing shoulder to shoulder with him. They looked down at the body together. This one, unlike the others, was fully clothed. Beckham saw a nameplate and crouched down to examine the man.

"Doctor Bob Welling," Horn muttered.

Beckham reached out with the barrel of his gun and raised the man's chin with it. He shut off his night vision and clicked on the tactical light at the end of his MP5 for a better look.

The victim's eyes were severely bloodshot. Dark trails of crusted blood trickled down his pale face, and his lips were bulging.

Beckham took a step backward.

"Infected?" Caster asked.

Beckham nodded and swept his light over the man's chest. The beam revealed a watermelon-sized hole in his midsection, the light shooting clear through to the floor under the dead scientist.

"Jesus," he said, forcing the light away from the revolting sight. He clicked off his tactical light and stood when a sudden burst of static broke over the comm. Beckham's own stomach tightened as he waited for Tenor to report.

His earpiece filled with a flurry of indecipherable shouts and then an agonizing scream so morphed by fear Beckham couldn't place it. The voices were followed by a loud sizzling sound, like melting plastic.

Gunfire broke out.

More screams followed.

Beckham's heart leaped with every pained scream of his men.

"Move!" he yelled. "Labs One and Two!"

He raced out of the room and into the corridor. Glass crunched under his boots, but the risk of infection was no longer on his mind. He had to get to his men—he had to save them.

There was another crack from a high-powered rifle that sounded like thunder over the comm. Beckham rushed out of Lab 3, navigating the minefield of broken vials as fast as he could. The entire time he was shouting, "Tenor, do you copy?" repeating the words to the sound of crackling static.

The noise meant something horrible had happened to Bravo. The sizzling, the screams, the gunfire, it could mean only one thing—Tenor had found the other scientists, and one or more of them had transformed into the monsters Noble described back in the mess hall.

What really terrified him was the quiet. When the firing stopped, Beckham waited for voices, shouts, anything.

There were none. Only silence.

By the time Alpha reached the corridor to Labs 1 and 2, the battle was over. It took only a few agonizing moments to see there had actually never been a battle. What Beckham was looking at was a massacre. The lumpy green outlines of four CBRN suits lay in wet puddles on the floor. Beckham felt his heart drop deep in his chest.

A voice from behind him yelled, "Wait!"

That was Major Caster. At least Beckham thought it was. He wasn't really listening. His eyes were focused on the bodies of his team. Ripping a flashlight from his belt, he flipped off his NVGs and angled the light over the outlines in front of him.

From somewhere inside Beckham, there came a sudden flare of anger, a feeling of pure rage. It consumed him, blinding him to the danger lurking in the darkness.

"Stop!" Caster yelled as Beckham rushed over to the first body. He swept the beam over the cheeseburger cheeks of Spinoza behind a broken faceplate. What looked like a human arm bone was lodged deep into the middle of his face, the impact area a bulge of broken skull and flesh.

The fury in Beckham grew.

This wasn't supposed to happen. He'd never lost a man under his command before. They were all supposed to go home as they always did, to celebrate another successful mission where the bad guys ended up in body bags, not the good guys.

Then he saw the next figure, his gaze falling on a helmet, or what was left of it. The visor was scorched, the glass melted onto the man's face; his eyes and nose were erased into a clump of blackened flesh. If it weren't for the M9 dangling from a gloved hand, he wouldn't have even known it was Major Noble.

The sizzling sound suddenly made sense. Someone had sprayed a chemical in the poor doctor's face. The situation had abruptly changed. This was no longer a recovery mission, it was a survival mission.

Beckham reared back when one of Noble's eyeballs burst, but the clear liquid still peppered his faceplate. He scraped it away and continued to the next body, knowing it would be Tenor or Edwards.

Another voice called out from behind him. "Beckham! Regroup. We need to find that sample!" This time he was sure it was Major Caster. The fucking asshole had led them into a trap.

He heard a second voice, Horn, calling from a corner, "We have contacts!"

"Cover me," Beckham shouted. He crouched down at the next body. The sample didn't matter if there wasn't anyone left to extract it from the building. Tenor's MP5 rested on the floor, spent bullet casings surrounding the weapon like a halo. But where were the bodies of the infected? Team Ghost didn't miss.

He moved back to Tenor. The operator lay on his back, his scorched helmet on the ground next to him. Leaning closer, Beckham saw a patch of darkened flesh where Tenor's perfectly groomed Mohawk had once been.

There were boots crunching behind him. Several boots, and voices, none that Beckham could make out. He hunched over Tenor and swept the light over his face. "Tenor, can you hear me, man?"

Tenor's eyes suddenly snapped open. He scrambled backwards, screaming, "Where is it? Where is it?"

"Boss, we have contacts heading your way!" Horn shouted again.

A high-pitched croak tore through the hallway, and Beckham spun to see two men in blood-drenched lab coats sprinting toward the team.

Gunfire erupted from Horn's M249. The rounds lit up the passage with bright muzzle flashes, just enough light to illuminate the blood-caked faces of both scientists and their swollen sucker lips. The head of the leader exploded into mist, but the other man leaped into an open ceiling panel.

Impossible, Beckham thought. *He was so fast.*

He moved back to Tenor, who now had his back against the wall, his eyes darting back and forth like a man possessed. "Where are they?" he kept repeating, his hands twisting in front of him.

"Snap out of it, Tenor!" Beckham yelled.

Tenor grew very silent. He looked toward Beckham, but not actually at him—it was as if the man was looking *through* him. Flashing his light across Tenor's face, Beckham realized his second in command was slipping into shock.

He had scooped an arm around Tenor to pick him up when the man jolted forward and projectile vomited onto the floor. Scrambling away, Beckham steadied his beam on the ground. What he saw didn't make any sense. The vomit was red and mixed with black, tarry granules of coagulated blood, but he had already scanned Tenor for injuries and hadn't seen any sign of wounds besides the burns. Internal bleeding might have explained it, but he couldn't confirm that until Tenor saw a doctor.

"Tenor, man, what the…" Beckham said.

"Stay away from him!" Caster yelled. "He's infected."

Beckham took a step back and held his flashlight on Tenor as the injured operator bent forward and hacked up another stream of the chunky fluid.

No, Beckham thought, shaking his head, *it's not possible. Tenor can't be showing symptoms that fast. Can he?* Even Beckham knew the incubation period for Ebola was days, or in some cases even a week—certainly not minutes.

"Leave me," Tenor choked. He wiped the blood from his

mouth, forming a red goatee around his lips. Then he scooted his back to the wall and yelled, "They're everywhere!"

Another voice exploded in the passage. "Master Sergeant fucking Beckham! We need that goddamn sample before they come back!" Caster shouted.

"We need to get the fuck out of here, sir, while we still can. Tenor is still alive!" Beckham replied.

Ellis crouched down next to Tenor. "My God," he said, gesturing for a flashlight. "Come on, someone give me a light." Riley quickly handed his to the doctor.

He swept the light across Tenor's face. Several red blotches and bruises were starting to appear. His eyes were crimson, and bloody tears trickled down his cheeks. A visible vibration suddenly rippled through the operator's body. Definitely not internal bleeding. He'd never seen anything like this.

"What the hell aren't you telling us?" Ellis asked suddenly, looking over at Caster.

"Shut up, Doctor Ellis, and turn off that light," the major said. He then very methodically raised his pistol and aimed it at Beckham's helmet. "I'm going to make this very simple. We are going to retrieve that sample, and then we are going to leave. Without him," he said, pointing with his free hand at Tenor.

Beckham gritted his teeth, his eyes darting to Riley and Horn, who had already aimed their weapons at Caster.

"Tell your men to stand down and get the sample," Caster repeated, shaking his pistol. "*Now!*"

"The mission is fucked, sir!" Beckham replied. "We're leaving while we still can." He was moving to pick up Tenor when he saw movement above Caster, on the exposed ceiling. Metal pipes from the air-filtration system snaked across the opening, and behind them were two crazed faces, their lips bulging in an *o* shape. Before Beckham had a chance to warn Caster, a mass of limbs reached down and plucked the major upward into the opening. The officer kicked, screaming for help. Beckham reached for a leg, but in two beats the man was gone. The comm channel filled with the dying man's agonized cries as he was pulled into the darkness.

Horn responded quickly, shouldering his M249 and unleashing three short bursts into the tiles. A white mist burst from the pipes, shrouding the hallway in a cloud of gas.

"We need to get out of here!" Ellis screamed. He disappeared into the haze in a mad dash back the way they had come.

Riley lowered his shotgun and yelled, "Wait, Doctor!"

The hallway quickly filled with the chemical fog, and Beckham snapped into action. He scooped Tenor up under an arm and began dragging him. "Help me, Horn," he shouted. "Riley, check Edwards."

Together they pulled Tenor down the passage. Riley quickly caught up. "He's gone, sir."

Beckham's heart skipped a beat again, even though he'd already known the operator was dead. There was no time to mourn the fallen men. He had to focus on getting the rest of his men out. Horn had a wife and two young daughters waiting for him at Fort Bragg. Beckham wasn't going to let those girls grow up without a father.

The team reached the cylindrical decontamination pods in less than a minute. Dr. Ellis was waiting for them, his gloved hands shaking violently. "We have to get the fuck out of here!"

"Move!" Beckham yelled. With Horn's assistance he dragged Tenor into the first cylinder. The injured man moaned and muttered, "I see them. *All* of them." His hands twisted and flicked through the air as if he was trying to shoo away a swarm of flies.

"What the fuck, man! What's wrong with you?" Horn asked.

"They're everywhere," Tenor choked. Then he screamed, "I see them!"

Before Beckham had a chance to react, Tenor lunged for Horn's suit, his teeth bared and his gloved hands mangled into claws.

Horn countered the attack quickly. With a strong shove, he sent Tenor flying back through the open doors to Level 2. The operator tumbled across the floor and slid to a stop. In one swift movement, he flipped from his back to his stomach and pushed himself up on all fours. Blood gurgling from his mouth, he lunged forward, bursting into a gallop like a wild animal.

A sudden gunshot behind Beckham made him flinch. This time it was from Riley's tactical shotgun. The first round hit Tenor in his collar, above his right shoulder. A loud crack sounded as fragments of flesh and bone exploded out of the exit wound. It echoed through the sector, but the blast only slowed him down. He continued on his left arm, utilizing his back legs to propel him forward in one long leap toward Horn.

"I'm sorry," Riley said over the comm.

Beckham resisted the urge to close his eyes. He had to watch; it was his responsibility. He had gambled with his men's lives, and now he had to pay the price.

A thunderous crack from Riley's shotgun took off the top of Tenor's skull. Tenor dropped to his knees and then his stomach, skidding to a stop a few feet away from the team.

"No!" Horn cried out, shielding his faceplate with one hand and holding his empty M27 in the other.

Forcing himself to look, Beckham stared at Tenor's faceless corpse. Like Spinoza, Edwards, and Noble, the man no longer looked human. Beckham's skin crawled, his suit seeming to close in around him. He tried to focus. He had to focus. He couldn't do anything for the dead, but he could still save the living.

The outlines of two figures in Level 2 yanked him out of his trance.

"Move!" Beckham shouted. He pushed Horn into the next pod and followed him into Level 1. From there they sprinted for the exit. Beckham watched his men and Dr. Ellis climb into the stairway before he stopped. He rotated in place, holding his breath. Standing in the lobby was a man wearing only trousers. Behind him, hiding in the shadows, was a female, still clothed in a blood-drenched lab coat. He couldn't be sure, but he thought the man fit Dr. Medford's profile.

For a moment they locked eyes, and he saw the true terror of the virus the scientist had created. Medford's face was covered in gore that looked like thick, chunky makeup. Cobwebs of bloody saliva webbed across his swollen lips. The man stared back with vertical pupils, and then tilted his chin toward the ceiling, releasing a deep, animalistic scream.

For the first time in his career, Beckham ran from the enemy. He didn't look back.

6

The late-morning sun glistened off the metal of the Black Hawk above them. What were the pilots waiting for? The chopper had hovered there for several minutes. Beckham took a deep breath, trying to suck in more air. Something was wrong with his respirator. He felt as if he was sipping air through a broken straw.

Gasping, he moved to a higher position and waved frantically at the craft. His arms burned. Every movement sent an agonizing surge of pain through his oxygen-deprived body.

Finally Beckham saw one of the pilots through the cockpit glass, yelling into his headset. Beckham knew then what was happening. The pilot was on an encrypted line with someone from Gibson's staff at Fort Detrick—someone who was deciding the fate of Beckham's team.

He craned his neck to see Dr. Ellis on his knees, pleading for rescue and yelling into the comm, "Get us out of here!"

Trash swirled around the doctor as the Black Hawk's blades whooshed overhead. Behind them, Riley and Horn had taken up positions outside the front of the facility, waiting for the infected to emerge from the bowels of the lab.

Beckham stopped waving and collapsed to his knees,

gasping for air. His breathing was beyond labored. He couldn't get enough oxygen. The respirator had malfunctioned, and with every torturous breath he resisted the urge to rip off his helmet. He knew the ramifications of removing the protection of the CBRN would be much worse than passing out inside of it.

But all he could think of were his men, of their corpses, and suddenly dying didn't seem like such an awful fate.

No, he thought, *you don't get to die yet; Horn and Riley still need you.*

Static finally crackled into Beckham's earpiece. The pilot spoke rapidly. "Beckham, HQ wants a sitrep. Do you have the sample? Is anyone infected?"

Beckham tried to respond, tried to speak, but the clunky words sounded slurred. "Negative. We..."

Fuzzy snowflake-shaped stars crawled before his eyes, transitioning into bright colors swimming across his vision. The thumping blades of the Black Hawk grew louder, and then he felt two strong arms under him, dragging him and lifting him onto a metal surface.

He tried to move, but his hands wouldn't respond. There was shouting over the comm channel, several voices. He made out a couple of the words.

"No sample..."

"Everyone else is dead..."

"Get us airborne!"

Then he felt the chopper lurch. Cracking an eye open, he saw the sandy ground below. He watched the facility become smaller and smaller as they pulled into the sky, but there was something else down there.

"Wait," he mumbled.

Was it Caster? Had he made it out, or was Beckham's oxygen-starved mind playing tricks on him?

Beckham forced his other eye open and saw a figure standing in the open front door of Building 8. He could swear the man was looking right at him. Then he heard a distant screech, faint but familiar against the whoosh of the blades. It was the same subhuman shriek they had heard below the surface.

"Hold on!" the pilot yelled. He pulled the bird hard to the right. Beckham slid across the metal surface. The wall stopped him as he smashed into it. A sharp pain raced through his chest.

The unmistakable rumble of F-22s rattled the Black Hawk as three of the jets zipped over them. Beckham struggled to keep his eyes open, the lack of oxygen finally taking hold of his body. He was completely immobile, his eyelids slowly shutting. His ribs felt as if they were about to burst. He knew he only had a few seconds of consciousness left—just enough time to watch the scientist and San Nicolas Island disappear in a carpet of flames.

Dr. Allen's raised voice startled Kate. He rushed into the lab, wearing a face creased with worry. "Something's happening in Chicago." He paused, his hazel eyes darting to the ground. "Preliminary reports are claiming symptoms of the Ebola virus."

Kate gasped. "What? How is that possible?" She pulled her eye away from her microscope, a sudden wave of anxiety rushing through her body. Her brother, Javier, worked as a professor at the University of Chicago, directly in the heart of the city. She hadn't seen him for weeks.

"I don't know. I just got a call from Jed Frank. CDC is hosting a conference call in an hour. I'll stream it in my office."

"What the hell is going on?" Kate asked. Had the outbreak somehow managed to cross the ocean? There were systematic procedures put in place to prevent anyone infected from carrying the virus aboard a flight. Still, she knew no matter what security measures were put in place, Mother Nature could find a way around them. The microscopic world of viruses didn't play by the same rules as other national security threats.

"Jed said that—" Michael paused. He looked confused. And after only a few hours of sleep, Kate could understand why. Still, she pressed harder.

"Michael," she said sternly. "Tell me what's happening."

The strategy worked. "Jed claims this is something worse than Ebola," he said. "Something much, much worse."

Beckham couldn't move. His body wouldn't respond. When he saw the clean white walls of the hospital room, he knew he had to be dreaming. Either that, or he was dead.

"You're so handsome," his mom said.

She was coiled up in her hospital bed, wincing from the pain as the cancer ate her body, the dark brown eyes he had inherited from her staring back at him. They were distant now, the pupils smaller. Her life force was fading. He was only seventeen, but he wasn't stupid. He knew she didn't have much time left.

He grabbed her hand. It was so thin, just bones covered in skin. For the first time, he saw just how weak, how fragile she was, lying there curled up in a fetal position shaking from the pain.

The cancer had eaten her insides. Starting in her stomach, the disease had worked its way through her entire body. It was a horrible disease. Like an invading army with no rules, no conscience, only the insatiable need to kill and consume.

"Reed," she said. "Please, promise me something."

"What, Mom?" He already knew what she was going to say.

"Promise me that you won't die on some battlefield in a far-off land. Promise me you won't throw away your life."

He looked at her, tightening his grip on her hand. "I promise you I won't throw away my life, Mom. But I want to make change in the world. I want to help people. I want to fight evil."

"There are plenty of ways to do that," she choked. "Become a doctor, not a soldier. I've worked with so many that have saved countless lives."

Reed looked at his feet. He knew he wasn't smart enough to become a doctor, and even if he was, he didn't want that life.

"Reed, promise me," she said. "Don't throw your life away, baby."

When he looked up, her eyes had glazed over. Her hand was limp in his own.

"Mom?" he said, shaking her wrist. A long beep from one of the machines she was connected to suddenly filled the room. His father and a doctor rushed inside, other medical staff swarming in behind them.

Reed backed away, tears forming in his eyes. He wiped them away swiftly and kept walking until his back hit the wall. He stared at his mother's bony frame. The cancer had taken everything from her and from their family. The disease was no different from any terrorist. It fought with no regard for the lives it afflicted.

It was then he knew he had to join the military. He had to fight evil. He would make good on half of his promise to his mom and not throw his life away. But he would also make good on his promise to make change in the world—he was going to kill the enemy, no matter where they hid. His mom would understand when they met again.

Distant voices called out to Beckham. The hospital room faded into darkness. He struggled to move, listening to the faint sounds.

Where were they coming from?

His body was a prison, suspended halfway between a dream and reality.

"Beckham!"

The voice was louder now. Closer.

There were other noises in the background, the whoosh of helicopter blades and grinding of metal. And there was light—slivers of crimson soaking through the darkness.

He finally awoke and peeled back an eyelid to see Riley staring down at him. The younger man fidgeted with Beckham's respirator, and at last Beckham sucked in a long, full breath.

"You're going to be okay, sir," Riley said.

"I told you not to call me that," Beckham choked.

"I know." The younger operator tapped Beckham's face-plate with a finger, *good to go*, and then hoisted himself onto the seat next to Horn.

Beckham slowly pushed himself off the metal floor and allowed himself several deep breaths. Within seconds the colors swimming across his vision vanished.

And then he remembered.

Tenor, Spinoza, Edwards—they were all dead, and so were the two Med Corps officers.

The revelation paralyzed Beckham with an agonizing surge of regret. His body went numb as he remembered, and he suddenly tasted blood. He'd bitten down hard on his lip and could feel a gash from where a tooth had sunk into the fragile flesh.

The pain was nothing compared to what he felt inside. Were his men really dead? Beckham couldn't bear the guilt and sorrow he felt. He'd served with Tenor, Spinoza, and Edwards for close to a decade. He couldn't even imagine how many thousands of hours they'd spent training, or how many deployments and battles they'd weathered together. It had all ended in a few minutes of horrifying madness.

A promise Beckham had made to each and every man on his team years ago boomed in his mind: "If you follow orders, I'll get you through this. I will get you home to your families."

Beckham shook his head, the memory haunting him. He took another deep breath and stared blankly out the window, the view nothing but a blur of hazy morning light.

Static crackled in his earpiece, snapping him momentarily from his daze. The familiar sound of Chief Wright's voice came online. "Master Sergeant Beckham, what the hell happened down there?" The crew chief's frantic voice no longer sounded friendly. His tone had changed; his words were systematic. When Beckham didn't respond, Chief Wright said, "I need a sitrep. HQ requests confirmation of the sample."

How was he supposed to respond? Would anyone even believe him if he told them what really happened? That Medford's staff had been transformed into monsters? That the doctor had been infected with a virus he had likely designed himself?

"Goddamnit, Beckham," Chief Wright said. His voice indicated he had lost every ounce of patience. He wanted an answer and wouldn't stop pressing Beckham until he got one.

But Beckham still did not respond. He peered over at Horn, who sat hunched over, his helmet dipped toward the floor. He looked like a statue under the faint overhead lights.

"Sir," Riley said over their private channel. "Do you want me to report?"

"No," Beckham said. He raised his hand to wipe off his faceplate and realized his hands were shaking.

Beckham looked toward Chief Wright and very sternly said, "Negative on the sample." He paused to consider his next words. He had abandoned the mission to save his men, but he reminded himself if he hadn't, then no one would have been around to even give a damn sitrep. "Tell them I hope those F-22s destroyed everything, because whatever we saw down there can't be allowed to see the light of day."

Chief Wright didn't immediately answer. The chopper pulled to the right and a mass of white clouds filled the skyline. Below, an infinite sea of sand stretched across the stark landscape.

"You can tell them yourself," Chief Wright finally replied. "We're landing in New Mexico in thirty minutes. Prepare for decon."

"Decon?" Riley asked.

Horn's helmet shot up. "You didn't think they were just going to send us back to Fort Bragg, did you?"

"We'll have to go through decontamination procedures," Beckham said. He double-tapped his comm so only Riley and Horn could hear his next message. "They're going to grill us. Ask us every detail of the mission. Don't try to protect me, guys," he said coldly. "I broke protocol. I abandoned the mission when I saw what we were dealing with."

"And you were fucking right to do so," Horn said. "Brass'll see that. They'll understand what happened. They can't—"

"They can do whatever they want," Beckham interjected. He directed his gaze at Horn. The operator was snorting like a raging bull. "Don't you fucking lose it when we land," Beckham warned. "I need you to stay focused. Remember your family, Big Horn."

Horn punched the side of the chopper wall and looked at the floor. Beside him, Riley fidgeted nervously. "That motherfucker Caster held a gun to your head!" he announced. "Don't worry, sir, we have your back."

Beckham shook his head. Neither of them understood. Colonel Gibson would place the blame on Beckham's shoulders and his alone. The loss of life, the failure to retrieve the sample—it would all be pinned on him.

"That sample is better off destroyed," another voice said. At first, Beckham didn't recognize it, but then he saw Ellis looking over at them from the corner of the compartment. His faceplate was covered with specks of gore. Sitting there stiffly in his blood-soaked CBRN suit, Ellis looked like a robot that had just gone on a killing spree.

"Thanks for getting me out of there," Ellis said, bowing his head.

"Prepare for landing," the pilot said over the main channel.

Beckham gave Ellis a nod and then turned to look out the window. He squinted and saw a glimpse of a landing strip at the edge of the sand dunes. The view was partially obscured by a few rays of sunlight peeking through the clouds, but there was no mistaking the three long white structures on the tarmac. The portable biohazard facilities were already prepped and ready for their arrival. Constructed side by side, a center passage connected all three. Near their entrances, he could vaguely make out several square boxes that he assumed were HVAC and negative-pressure isolation units.

They were state-of-the-art portable domes with controlled

environments, designed to deal with the most severe Level 4 contagions. The view reminded Beckham of the potential for infection, but as the chopper began to descend he wasn't worried about that, or even about a court-martial. All he could think about were the charred bodies of his men back at Building 8.

Tires squealed across the tarmac the moment their Black Hawk landed. Beckham watched a pair of Humvees screech to a halt a hundred yards away. Both vehicles had gunners in CBRN suits up top, one equipped with a TOW missile launcher and one with a .50-cal. They leveled their weapons at the chopper.

Beckham instinctively swung the bay door open. Weapons greeted him.

"We aren't infected!" he yelled.

"Don't move, Sergeant!" the man on the right yelled. His voice, muffled by the breathing apparatus, made him seem less human and more like a cold, calculating machine. Beckham wasn't used to being on the other end of a gun—not a friendly one, at least—and the sound of the soldier's stifled voice reminded him just how fast the tide could change.

"You will be given a set of directions shortly. We have orders to fire if you or your team fail to comply," the man in the other turret said.

Beckham watched the soldier grip the .50-cal even tighter.

"We aren't infected!" Ellis said, joining Beckham in the doorway. "I want to talk to someone from CDC!"

"Stay put, sir!" the right gunner repeated.

Beckham pushed the doctor back into the chopper.

The door to one of the Humvees swung open. Three men

wearing white biohazard suits, each bearing the insignia of USAMRIID, stepped onto the tarmac. They were trained to deal with the most infectious diseases in the world. And it showed. Their faces were emotionless behind their visors, devoid of worry or fear.

That's all about to change, Beckham thought as he awaited further instructions.

The men approached the chopper cautiously. One of them stepped out in front and said, "My name is Doctor Blake. I'm with USAMRIID. This is Doctor Fry," he said, gesturing to the man on the left. "And this is Doctor Ibsen," he said, pointing to the third man with a stiff arm. He paused for a second and then dropped his hands to his sides in a very nonthreatening manner. He continued in the same mechanical tone.

"I'm going to give you a set of very detailed instructions. Please follow them exactly. We will escort the members of Delta Force operator team Ghost and Doctor Ellis to the decon facilities first. Crew Chief Ted Wright and pilot John Bush will go last. Nod if you understand."

Beckham responded with a quick nod.

"Okay. Good. First, I'd like Team Ghost and Doctor Ellis to step out onto the concrete. Leave your weapons inside the Black Hawk. Then take five steps away from the helicopter, forming a line side by side."

"This is bullshit," Horn said over their private channel.

Beckham kept still, but said, "Just follow their orders."

They dropped their guns on the floor and climbed out of the chopper one by one. Then they paced five steps forward and stood shoulder to shoulder as instructed.

Blake kept his hands at his sides as he took two deliberate, slow steps toward the men, leaving only about fifty yards between them. Then he said, "Starting with the man on the left, I want you to answer the following question with a clear nod of your head if your answer is yes. If the answer is no, simply shake your head." He waited a moment and then continued, "Do you have any of the following symptoms: headache, fever, nausea, itching, or abdominal pain? Again, if the answer is yes to any of these symptoms, then simply nod. If it is no, then shake your head."

One by one, the four men shook their heads.

"That's good. Okay. Next I need to know if any of you have experienced tears in your suits. If you know your suit has been compromised, please tell us now."

Riley, Horn, and Beckham shook their heads, but Ellis hesitated. He looked down at his arm.

"Well, I," he stuttered. "I don't know. I can't tell with all of this blood." He began wiping the dark red gore off his suit with his gloves.

"Doctor Ellis, please don't do that," Blake said quickly. His voice was sterner than before, but still calm.

Beckham watched out of the corner of his eye as the .50-cal gunner trained his heavy weapon on Ellis. Beckham kept his gaze ahead, fixated on the group of doctors. His heart raced, the massacre inside Building 8 replaying over and over in his mind. He couldn't compartmentalize it.

"Yes or no," Blake entreated.

Ellis shook his head and slowly lowered his hands to his sides.

"Okay, good. Next, you will all follow Doctor Fry to Decon Facility One." He twisted his head in the same methodical manner and pointed a stiff arm at the first white dome, about five hundred yards away. "Walk in single file. No sudden movements."

"Let's go," Dr. Fry said.

Beckham led what was left of his team and Dr. Ellis

down the black tarmac in silence. He thought about using the private channel, but opted against it. There was no telling what USAMRIID would do if they thought someone in Ghost was infected, and he knew from firsthand experience what a .50-caliber round could do to the human body.

When they arrived outside the first plastic dome, a soldier in a full biohazard suit approached them with an M4. He kept the barrel aimed at the concrete, which helped Beckham relax a bit.

Doctor Fry punched a code into the keypad and waited for the door to buzz. "There are three compartments inside. A dirty room, where an assistant will help clean your suit and respirator. A decon shower, where you will be sprayed down with chemicals to further kill anything missed in the first area, and finally a shower, where you can get cleaned up and change into new clothes. Then you will be directed to the next dome for a debriefing. Please proceed one by…"

The sound of shouting caught the doctor off guard. He paused to see what was happening just as a sudden explosion boomed through the afternoon. An orange glow reflected off Fry's faceplate, and Beckham caught a glimpse of the Black Hawk disappearing in an enormous fireball.

Losing the battle to remain still, Beckham twisted to see the TOW gunner still aiming the launcher at the burning remains of the chopper. Huddling behind the safety of the Humvee were Doctors Blake and Ibsen. But where were Chief Wright and the pilot?

Beckham scanned the wreckage and stopped on two flaming lumps about five feet away from the chopper. He flinched as pieces of charred metal pinged off the concrete next to one of his boots.

It only took a moment for him to realize what had happened. Either Chief Wright or the pilot must have answered yes to one of Dr. Blake's questions, and one of the gunners had been a bit too trigger-happy. Beckham could tell by the look on Fry's face that things weren't supposed to go down like that.

"Shit," Fry muttered, shaking his head. He looked away from the smoking wreckage and scanned Beckham and his men. "Let's go," he said, gesturing for them to enter the dome.

7

Kate tapped her finger on the conference room table, staring at the wall-sized HD television screen. The display augmented the features of CDC Deputy Director for Infectious Diseases Jed Frank. He was middle-aged, with an intelligent and plain face. Deep grooves lined his forehead above arched brows. Kate had only met the man a handful of times but didn't remember him looking so old, or so worried.

No, she decided after scrutinizing him further. There was fear in his eyes. She'd seen the same look in Africa when she'd encountered scientists who'd come face-to-face with a Level 4 contagion. Ebola, Marburg, yellow fever, bacterial meningitis—they all had the same effect on even veteran doctors, transforming capable men and women into terrified shells of their former selves.

"Good afternoon, Doctors Allen and Lovato," Frank said, regarding them both with a nod. He brought a Styrofoam cup of coffee to his lips but did not take a drink. Instead, he looked down at it as if it was poison and set it aside. Without further delay, he said, "As you've already heard, we have a reported case of Ebola in Chicago. I've deployed Doctors Lucas and Roberts into the field. They are on their way to the Windy City as we speak. I've canceled my speaking engagement here in Los Angeles, and I'm boarding the first flight back to Atlanta."

Michael ignored the formalities and asked the most obvious question first. "Is it contained?"

"In short, yes. But—"

Kate felt like chewing her fingernails, an old habit she had developed as a kid. She waited anxiously for Frank to gather his thoughts. He was a freaking deputy director of CDC! Was it really that bad in Chicago?

"It's been difficult to get an accurate report on the situation. I just got off the phone a few minutes ago with the director of Northwestern Memorial Hospital, but what he described doesn't make any sense." Frank shook his head. "There are three victims total. Two male Homeland Security officers and a male passenger. We haven't been able to confirm what flight the man got off of yet."

"What? That should be the first thing you do, so you can quarantine the other passengers," Kate blurted.

"I know that, *Doctor*. But this passenger didn't have any identification. The man wasn't even wearing a shirt."

Kate knew right away what the signs meant. The man was likely burning up from a fever and had removed his clothes in order to cool down.

"What about video feed? There are cameras all over O'Hare," Michael said.

"Local law enforcement is checking them now. So far the man appears to have emerged out of nowhere."

"If this man has Ebola, then surely a flight attendant or pilot would have confirmed they had a very sick passenger," Kate said.

"And we have no such reports," Frank replied.

Michael cleared his throat. "So we have *no* idea where this man came from?"

"We're working on it," Frank said. "Listen," he continued. "We're following every protocol in the book, but none of this makes any sense. We're in unprecedented territory."

Kate couldn't sit still. She had so many questions, and she knew they weren't going to get anywhere with Frank. To make things even worse, she was worried about Javier. His apartment was so close to the airport.

She resisted the urge to ask to take the first flight to Chicago, knowing Michael would never allow it, especially with Ellis already in the field. She finally bit down on one of her fingernails.

Frank looked at his phone again. "Hold on," he said, palming the air in front of the camera.

"This is Doctor Frank," he said in the background.

Kate listened intently in an attempt to hear the conversation.

"Excellent, e-mail the video over ASAP," Frank said. He reemerged and faked a smile. "Good news. Doctor Roberts is on the ground and is e-mailing footage of the incident between the passenger and the two Homeland Security officers. Give me a second and I will forward it to you, Michael."

Kate stood and walked over to retrieve Michael's laptop. She returned a moment later, setting it in the middle of the mahogany conference table.

"Okay, sending now," Frank said.

Michael typed in his password and brought up his inbox. Seconds later the e-mail came through. He clicked on the link and repositioned the screen so Kate could see.

The grainy feed provided a perfect view of the entire terminal. They watched dozens of commuters hurrying to their next destination. Then an abrupt screech erupted from the middle of the crowd. The audio was crystal clear, but Kate couldn't tell if the sound was human. It sounded like an animal in distress.

Chaos ensued shortly after, and the hallway became a mass of terrified passengers screaming and running in all directions. When the passage cleared, a single man stood in front of the camera. Spasms shook his shirtless body as he walked slowly across the carpet.

As he got closer, Kate saw his face. Crusted blood surrounded a swollen mouth transformed into a suction cup. Blood oozed from his eyes. He tilted his head like a curious dog.

"What in the hell?" Kate muttered.

What they were witnessing made no sense. At that stage of infection, the victim theoretically shouldn't have the energy to move. This man was not only moving but seemed to be possessed by an invisible force. And his lips—what the hell had happened to his lips?

The man suddenly hunched over in apparent pain and clamped his bloated lips around his arm. He tore away a chunk of flesh and let out a howl that reminded Kate of some of the animals she'd heard in the remote jungles of Africa.

"My God," Michael whispered.

Kate didn't reply. She was trying to find a way to justify what they were watching. Was it possible the man had suffered brain damage? She knew of cases in which Ebola patients had gone insane and mutilated or attacked medical personnel, but that didn't explain his mouth.

She looked back at the screen just as two Homeland Security officers entered the hallway. They kept their hands on their holstered guns. Kate could hear one of them yelling, "Get on the ground!"

The man twisted his body at an odd angle, his joints clicking as he moved. His posture was grotesque, as if his body didn't fit together anymore.

Kate had never seen anyone move like that, especially not

a person with a suspected Ebola infection. She stared with morbid fascination, wondering what exactly was happening to the man in front of them. His lips and joints didn't fit with what she'd seen in the past.

They continued to watch the video in silence, Kate furiously chewing on her fingernails. She had moved to her index finger as one of the officers finally pulled his gun.

"Get on the fucking ground!"

The man snarled and lunged forward with incredible speed. With a running leap, he straddled the guard. He wrapped both legs around the officer's waist. Kate wasn't prepared for what came next. She'd never been prone to queasiness and had always thought her stomach was like a maximum-security prison, but she'd also never seen anything quite like this—nothing so barbaric.

The other officer quickly grabbed the infected man, trying to pull him off his partner. The result was a tangled mass of limbs and screams as the three fell to the ground.

Several gunshots rang out, and the infected man's body rolled onto the carpet. He shook violently, clawing at his wounds, before leaning over and vomiting black gore onto the floor.

The injured guard crawled away, clutching his neck and moaning, while the other officer tried to help him up.

More shouts echoed in the hallway as paramedics and additional security arrived. The video ended with the camera focused on the man. His twisted body was now limp, surrounded by a puddle of dark red blood.

It took Frank several seconds to gather his thoughts before he returned in front of the video feed. He very methodically reached for the Styrofoam cup of coffee and took a slow sip. He wiped his mouth and said, "Call everyone that knows anything about Ebola. I want everyone we have working on this," he said. "Everyone." Frank reached for his phone. "Shit, I have to take this." His voice was shaky.

"I'll get to work on the—" Michael began to say.

"Wait," Frank said, picking up the phone and holding out a finger. "Yes, this is Doctor Frank."

A pause.

"That's not possible. They can't already be showing—"

Another pause.

Kate bit her lip.

"But the incubation period is normally—"

Silence.

"San Nicolas?" Another pause. "What do you mean, 'everyone there is dead'?"

More silence.

"Okay, I understand, Chad. Keep this quiet until we know more."

Kate heard Michael's phone vibrate on the table. He pulled it toward him to look at the screen. She caught a glimpse of the caller ID.

Gibson/USAMRIID.

Michael ignored the call and waited for Frank to return to the screen. Moments later the deputy director dropped his own phone onto his desk and swiveled his chair back in front of his laptop camera. The deep wrinkles in his forehead were even more pronounced.

"That was Doctor Roberts again. He's at Northwestern Memorial Hospital. Both of those Homeland Security officers are showing signs of infection. Rashes, bruising, and hemorrhaging from multiple locations, and that's not all." He paused and shook his head solemnly. "Both men are showing abnormally violent behavior. They had to be restrained. A nurse and an EMT have been bitten."

Frank shook his head a second time, muttering something

to himself. "The good news is Chad thinks they found the original flight. Homeland Security boarded it an hour ago. It's a navy plane. The pilot and two navy officers were found dead—brutally murdered and apparently cannibalized."

The word paralyzed Kate with fear. There was no need to ask what any of this meant. She knew CDC's worst fears were now a reality. Ebola had not only made landfall in the United States but it had evolved into something even worse. The virus was notorious for mutating, which was what made it so deadly, but this time Kate was afraid it had made a leap they couldn't stop.

Michael's voice pulled her back to the room. "Does law enforcement think the man in the video killed the crew of the plane?"

Frank nodded. "They are checking the flight data as we speak."

"San Nicolas," Michael suddenly said. "That's one of the secret locations for USAMRIID." He looked back down at his cell phone. "Colonel Rick Gibson just called me. Shit," he muttered. "I sent Pat Ellis into the field per Gibson's request just yesterday. I figured it was a routine training mission."

Frank's eyes hardened. "Why didn't you tell me?"

"Jed, you're in LA, and USAMRIID activates the EOC for training ops all the time."

The deputy director shook his head. "Call Colonel Gibson and find out what he knows. Then let me know what the *hell* is happening."

Michael nodded and rose from his seat.

"We need to lock down that hospital," Kate said. "Isolate everyone that has come into contact with suspected cases. *Everyone.*"

"We're working on it, Doctor Lovato. Trust me," Frank replied.

"How about a sample?" Kate added with urgency. "This may be Ebola, but it has to be a different strain. I've never seen anyone that looks like a…" She peered back at Michael's laptop and considered the word on the tip of her tongue.

Monster.

She couldn't bring herself to say it.

Frank lifted a brow, as if he knew what she was thinking. "Chad Roberts is already getting samples, so you will have them in twelve hours."

"We will get started as soon as they come in," Michael replied.

It was then that she realized she was shaking. She slowly sank back in her chair, her mind drifting to Javier. She could feel her phone burning a hole in her pocket. As soon as they were done, she was going to call him and tell him to quietly get out of the city.

"Oh, and Michael," Frank said, "keep me apprised. You got that?"

"Yes, sir," Michael said. He stood and patted Kate on her shoulder. "You know what to do."

She nodded, but deep down she was terrified—deep down she wasn't sure if she did know what to do.

Beckham hesitated when he saw the Black Hawk on the tarmac. He didn't trust the Medical Corps insignia on the side or the guards standing out front with their M4s. If Major Caster had held a gun to his head, then what would stop these fuckers from doing the same?

"Let's go," one of the men yelled, waving him forward.

There was motion inside the chopper. Beckham spied

three silhouettes, one of them nearly twice as big as the others. It had to be Horn.

Beckham hurried across the concrete, shivering in the new clothes the technician had given him after the short debriefing. He decided that if Gibson was going to have him taken out back and shot, then his team would already be dead.

A flashback to the decon shower hit him before the wind from the whooshing helicopter blades. He could still see Tenor's blood churning around the floor drain. It was a painful reminder that half of his team *was* already dead.

He formed fists, his knuckles popping. Less than twenty-four hours. The amount of time it took to wipe out half of his team. Years of training—of life—all gone in an instant.

There was no controlling his anger. Noble and Caster hadn't given Beckham's team proper intel. If he had known what they were dealing with, maybe he could have saved his men.

Ducking, Beckham shielded his face from the gusts of rotor wash and moved toward the chopper. He grabbed a handhold, climbed into the craft, and took a seat. No one spoke a word. The exchange of nods was all that was needed.

Beckham's body shook from the rage growing inside of him. He sat there knowing that somewhere, halfway across the country, pairs of army officers were arriving at the homes of Tenor, Edwards, and Spinoza to feed their families lies, just like the lies he'd been fed during the debriefing a few minutes earlier.

When the chopper finally took off, Beckham broke the silence, whispering to Horn, "What did they tell you?"

Horn grunted. "Said that we encountered a group of mad scientists in Building 8 under the influence of an experimental drug."

Beckham almost laughed. They'd told him the same thing. There was no mention of Ebola or VX-99, and he knew there never would be.

"We're lucky to be alive," Riley remarked. "After seeing what they did to Chief Wright and the pilot."

"This is fucking bullshit," Horn said. Veins bulged from his forehead. "How do we know they're really flying us back to Fort Bragg?"

"If they were going to kill us, they already would have..." Beckham's voice trailed off. Now he wasn't so sure.

He blinked away the paranoid thoughts and attempted to manage his anger, but he couldn't stop seeing the haunting images of the charred bodies of his men. He'd led them through Fallujah, the Mog, and countless other missions in places most Americans didn't know existed, all without a single casualty. But it had been on American soil, deep beneath the surface, that he'd lost half his team, and now he was heading home to bury empty caskets—at least that's what he'd thought was going to happen moments earlier. His gut told him they might be flying somewhere else now.

8

Chad Roberts sat in the back seat of the cab with a sick stomach. He'd been nauseated all day. On top of that, he was exhausted. He needed a very hot cup of joe, or even better, a shot of adrenaline.

After returning home from making clinical rounds in Guinea a few days earlier, he had been looking forward to getting caught up on sleep. Instead, Deputy Director Frank had sent him straight to Chicago.

Judging by the checklist of items he still had left to work on, sleep wasn't going to happen anytime soon. Even if he could find a bed, the horrors he'd seen in the past six hours would keep him awake. The microbreak—what they were calling an *isolated outbreak*—in Chicago made the one he'd seen in Guinea look like a common cold. He could only imagine what was happening on a microscopic level. Somehow the

Ebola virus had mutated again, and this time, it had turned into something beyond his wildest fears.

Chad situated his backpack more comfortably on his legs. Pulling his breathing mask off his face, he checked his list. The most important item was already crossed off—the samples were already on their way to Atlanta on a modified jet used to transport Level 4 contagions. That was a relief. At least Deputy Director Frank could get his team working on figuring out what this thing was and how to develop a treatment, and eventually a cure.

A chirp from his phone reminded him he hadn't looked at it in fifteen minutes. One missed call and three text messages blinked across the screen.

"Shit," he muttered. Every time his phone buzzed, he worried it was a report of another case, but so far they had contained the infection to Northwestern Memorial Hospital.

With a sigh, he crammed his tablet into his bag and caught a glimpse of the driver in the rearview mirror. The metallic click from a gold ornament dangling beneath it reminded Chad of how superstitious the villagers in Guinea were.

Now the skeptical looks made sense. The driver, an immigrant from Somalia, had been eyeing Chad suspiciously. In some remote parts of Africa, Western medicine was seen as witchcraft, so it was no wonder the man had glared at Chad's CDC badge when he first got in the car. It was the same look the villagers in Guinea had given the white portable biohazard facilities that popped up outside their homes. Ironically, it was their superstition that often caused the vicious outbreaks to fizzle out. Many villagers would treat their loved ones with herbal remedies and opt not to travel to one of the major population centers for modern health care, a journey which would likely result in the outbreak spreading farther. The locals' fear of Western *witchcraft* had so far saved the world from the reaches of the Ebola virus—until now. Now the virus had popped up in one of the most populated areas in North America.

The thought was terrifying, and the sight of Northwestern Memorial Hospital was no reassurance as the car stopped outside the emergency entrance. He still couldn't believe what was happening. Not only had the virus mutated but the victims were displaying violent behavior, in some cases mutilating themselves or even feeding on their own flesh or attacking others. Many of them appeared to also be suffering from hallucinations. He'd seen that symptom before, but not at the beginning stages of infection. Typically such cases only occurred when the brain had suffered damage from lack of oxygen or internal hemorrhaging.

That was the most confusing part. The incubation period was damn near instantaneous. He'd seen this when one of the Homeland Security officers from O'Hare had bitten a nurse. She'd dropped to the floor, gripping her arm, and suddenly started seizing. In under an hour, the hemorrhaging had started. He'd never seen Ebola work so fast, and the violent behavior made no sense. It was as if the virus had possessed the victim.

He shook the thoughts from his mind and climbed out of the car, thanking the driver and handing him a twenty-dollar bill. The man hesitated, regarding it as if it might be laced with poison, before snatching it from Chad's hands.

The hospital's chief of staff, Sam Marks, waited for Chad at the entrance to the emergency room, his foot tapping nervously on the concrete. The short, bald man smiled nervously, his immaculately trimmed mustache curving around his lips.

When they'd met earlier, Sam had assured him that they were prepared to handle the microbreak. Like the cabdriver, Chad was skeptical. He'd ordered the hospital to set up an entire wing for quarantine immediately upon his arrival, but he knew right away that it was delusional to think the staff was prepared for such an event. They'd likely only been trained a handful of times on how to deal with a Level 4 virus. Northwestern was the highest-ranked hospital in the city, but even they didn't have the proper equipment to deal with such a contagious virus.

"We have everything locked down, Doctor Roberts. Just like the emergency operations plan explained."

"That's great. Help is on the way," Chad replied. He followed Sam down the hallway toward the quarantined wing of the hospital.

"Uh, when exactly do you think it will arrive?" the chief of staff asked. He sounded uneasy, much more so than when Chad had first arrived.

"Soon," he said. "In the meantime, I want to see the initial case, the man that was shot at the airport."

"Very well. This way, Doctor."

They navigated the hallways in silence until they came upon the isolation section of the hospital. A wall of glass separated them from the three infected corpses on metal gurneys. Inside, a man in a blue biohazard suit examined the bodies. It was Ted Lucas, another CDC doctor who specialized in filoviruses and had an obsession with diseases, specifically the worst kind. Chad wasn't sure what to think of him, having only worked with him a handful of times. He'd heard Ted was an adrenaline junkie, and he was rumored to take unnecessary risks in the field. If true, the man was his exact opposite; Chad prided himself on the precautions he took.

Chad pressed a button to activate the communication system. "Just got back from O'Hare."

Ted tilted his blue helmet toward them. "Any leads on this guy?" he said, pulling back the white blanket over one of the corpses. Chad could see right away it was the man from the airport. The top of his skull was missing, a result of having been shot at close range by the second batch of cops that had arrived. The victim's mouth bulged, his lips swollen and white. He would be hard to identify even with a photo.

"We think he came from a navy flight that originated from San Nicolas Island," Chad said. "If that's the case, then we should be able to locate his baggage and identification soon."

"Understood," Ted replied.

Sam stood awkwardly close to Chad, watching Ted work with an odd expression. "Have you ever seen anything like this?"

"Not quite," Chad replied. His mouth twisted to the right. "I'm pretty sure this is Ebola. But it has to be a new strain. One we have never seen."

Sam nodded, while keeping his focus on Ted. "The victims are like—"

"Zombies?" Chad said, finishing the chief of staff's sentence for him.

"I didn't want to say it earlier," Sam said. "These people are obviously alive, but my God, they're like the flesh eaters we see on TV."

"Actually, they're worse," Chad replied. "Zombies don't *think*. They aren't alive. That's why it's vital we keep this section of the hospital on lockdown until more help arrives. No one leaves. No one gets in without my approval." He watched Sam open his mouth to respond, but then something caught the man's attention down the hall.

Glass shattered in the distance. A current of anxiety rushed through Chad when he heard the screams. He knew exactly what the noises meant.

At the far end of the hall, a female patient lay on the floor, glass surrounding her twisted body. The two police officers

Sam had posted outside the isolation rooms ran toward her, their weapons drawn. "Don't move," one of them shouted.

The woman slowly rose into a crouching position, while tilting her head to the side. A curtain of hair fell over her face, making it impossible to tell which patient she was. Blood trickled down her chin onto the floor. A single ounce of bodily fluid was extremely contagious.

"Stop her!" Sam yelled. He took a step back, smacking into Chad as the woman craned her head in their direction. She pawed the hair out of her face, the broken straps of her restraints hanging loosely at her wrists. It was then Chad saw the blood oozing from her crazed eyes.

"Oh my God," Sam sputtered, his voice foundering. He backed against the glass window, where Chad could see Ted trying to get a better view.

Before the officers could fire off a shot, the woman lunged forward, the joints in her legs clicking as she burst across the floor on all fours. She moved with impressive speed, the blue of her gown blurring as she tackled the policeman closest to her. Chad had never seen anyone move like that, and he'd never heard joints snap like that either. The woman was transforming right in front of his eyes.

The second officer pulled her off his partner. He held her squirming in the air with his thick arms.

"Restrain her," Sam yelled.

Chad watched in horror as the woman frantically kicked out of the officer's grasp; a swift foot to the cop's genitals finally sent him crumpling to the ground. The second officer seized the opportunity to jam his Taser into her spine. The jolt of electricity sent her tumbling to the ground. He drew his handcuffs and reached for her flailing arms. When he finally grabbed a wrist, she reared back her head and released a black stream of projectile vomit in his face.

Stumbling, the officer pawed at the goo in his eyes. The woman wasted no time. She straddled him, wrapping her arms tightly around his back, before biting his nose off.

Chad ran for the exit. He didn't need to see any more to know what was about to happen. With the officers compromised, the entire wing would fall. He had to seal off the space. There was no saving any of these people. They had to stop the virus here, before it was too late.

When he got to the double doors he halted, realizing he'd left Ted behind.

"What are you waiting for?" Sam yelled, holding the door open with his right foot. "We can't help them!"

A sound like several balloons popping echoed down the hall as one of the officers fired his weapon. Chad flinched at the sound and then slipped through the opening, locking the door behind them. "I'm sorry, Ted," he said under his breath.

Kate could hear the CNN reporters discussing the mysterious virus on the television in the background, but she wasn't listening—not anymore. She'd stopped the moment they referred to the outbreak as "the zombie apocalypse."

The scare tactic would do nothing but incite more fear. It might boost their ratings for the evening, but the adverse effects would ripple through Chicago. Mass panic would ensue. She'd seen hot zones around the world fall apart because of news reports that were much less threatening.

She pulled her phone from her pocket, aching to hear from Javier. Where the hell was he? They were accustomed to not talking for days, but surely he'd seen her message by now.

The vibration of Michael's phone startled her back to

reality. She watched the black device rattle slowly across the table. They'd waited all evening for Colonel Gibson to call them back.

Michael snatched the phone off the table. "This is Doctor Allen," he said. "Yes, I've heard. I'm going to put you on speaker so Doctor Lovato can listen in."

Tapping the screen, he put the phone on the table and said, "Okay, can you hear us?"

"We have a hell of a situation on our hands," Gibson said. "We're in the process of deploying all of our resources to Chicago. FEMA has called up their emergency assets. The governor of Illinois has declared a state of emergency and has activated the National Guard."

"I really would like to know what the hell is going on," Michael said. "I still don't know where Doctor Ellis is."

"He's en route to Fort Bragg," Gibson replied.

"What? Why?" Kate blurted.

"What I'm about to tell you is top secret, although I'm sure the news media will get ahold of their version of the story in the coming days," Gibson said. Static crackled over the speakers, and his voice cut out. When it came back on, he said, "I'm about to board a chopper. Might be a bit shaky on reception for a few minutes."

Michael frowned and reached for the phone, pulling it closer to them.

"When USAMRIID activated the EOC two days ago, it was due to a situation at Building Eight on San Nicolas Island. I was told that one of our scientists, a Doctor Medford, was experimenting with VX-99, a chemical weapon used in Vietnam."

Michael gasped. "I thought the stockpile was destroyed!"

"Not the entire stockpile," Gibson said. "Medford seemed to believe he could use VX-99 to destroy the Ebola virus, but before he could send us the data, the facility went dark. We lost all communication with Building Eight. Normally we'd have sent in our own team, but there was simply too much at stake. We called in a Delta Force team. Your man, Doctor Ellis, was added to the mission due to protocol; I included two of my own scientists to help the operators gain access to the facility. They were supposed to get in, retrieve a sample of Medford's work, and get out. Things apparently didn't go down like that."

"Is Ellis okay?" Michael said. His voice sounded strained, deviating from his typical calm demeanor. Kate realized this was no longer a conversation between old friends.

"He's fine. Our team cleared him hours ago. He'll be back in Atlanta by the time you wake up tomorrow. The same can't be said for two of my staff. They didn't make it out, and neither did several of the Delta Force operators. I've seen the videos. Building Eight was compromised. Doctor Medford was infected with his own creation."

"How the hell did it get to Chicago?" Michael asked.

"On a layover flight. A scientist from Building Eight named Jim Pinkman was on his way here to brief me."

"I need to know what we are dealing with here," Kate interjected. "What is VX-99? What chemical did Medford use?"

"We don't know. That's why we sent Delta in to retrieve a sample."

"So we don't even know what we're dealing with?"

"No, Doctor Lovato, I'm afraid we don't. All data and records relating to VX-99 were destroyed long ago. Except it appears that Doctor Medford secured a sample of the chemical and used it in his experiments at Building Eight."

Kate felt as if she was going to throw up. How had this happened? How the hell had Dr. Medford made such a fatal error? And why had Gibson kept this a secret until now? Was he hiding something else? The events had all created a perfect cocktail, the deadliest virus the world had ever seen.

She jerked, startled, as the cell phone in her pocket vibrated. She quickly pulled it from her jeans and looked at the screen to see a text from Javier that read, *How are things at the CDC, sis? The news is scaring me.*

Kate slowly slipped the phone under the table and typed a text that read, *I'm fine. Are you okay?*

The hissing of wind crackled over the phone line. "I have to go," Gibson said. "But Doctor Allen, I need you to—"

The call dropped before the colonel could finish his sentence.

"Damn it!" Michael shouted. He slapped the table with his right palm.

Kate stared in shock at her friend and mentor. She'd never seen him lose control like this.

His voice returned to its usual cold, systematic tone. "Kate, this could be it."

"What?"

Michael's eyes narrowed, and Kate suddenly felt exposed, as if he was looking right through her.

"The extinction event. The one you wrote about in your thesis."

She shook her head. "No, we can stop it."

Her phone buzzed again, and she pulled it out of her pocket. Another text from Javier blinked across the screen. *Things are bad here. What kind of virus is this? They're saying it's turning people into zombies.*

9

April 20, 2015
DAY 3

It was 4:00 a.m., but Kate wasn't sleeping when she heard the rap on her door. Her eyes were glued to the ceiling of the small room she used for overnight stays.

The door creaked open, followed by a voice just louder than a whisper. "Kate, you awake?"

"Did we get them?" She sat up and reached for the lamp next to her bed. The light spilled over the room and illuminated Michael's exhausted features.

He nodded. "Let's go."

They passed the small break room at a brisk pace. No time for coffee.

By the time they suited up and reached the lab, her heart had started the climb to her throat. She could hardly swallow. She'd seen some horrible things in the past, but this was different. This time it had hit home. Flashbacks to patient zero at O'Hare replayed in her mind. No matter what she did, she couldn't get the gruesome images out of her head. And the call with Colonel Gibson had only added questions, not answers, about this new virus. The involvement of VX-99 deepened the mystery. Why had the scientists on San Nicolas been working with a weapon that was, by international law, not even supposed to exist? She knew little about the drug's chemical properties but had her doubts that it would actually destroy the Ebola virus.

"Ready?" Michael asked.

They stood outside the door to the BSL4 lab. Inside, the samples were already waiting in the biosafety cabinets. Kate's next task would require a clear mind and the utmost patience. A lot of people were counting on them, including her little brother. She needed to be strong for Javier—no. She *had* to be strong for Javier.

"Ready," she said, flashing a thumbs-up.

Michael keyed in his credentials, swiped his badge, and waited for the glass doors to slide open. Kate had heard the hiss a thousand times before, but this time felt different. The doors parted.

"First things first. Let's isolate the RNA," Michael said.

Kate nodded. She knew exactly what she was doing and wasn't scared of the risk of infection; she was scared of the events transpiring in Chicago, just miles from where her brother lived.

They started working at separate stations in the sterile environment. Kate used a sample marked "saliva" to isolate the virus. Next, she began the painstaking process of breaching the virus shells and separating out the RNA. The work was labor intensive, and by the time Kate finished, it was already midmorning.

"How are you doing?" Michael asked.

"Almost there," Kate replied.

He craned his head in her direction, baffled by her cryptic comment.

"Sorry," she clarified, "I'm almost finished purifying the RNA from these samples, and then I'll prep them for the sequencer."

"Good."

The purification took longer than she had thought it would, and she finished just before noon. De novo sequencing would map the entire genome of the virus. The machine was state of the art, with the ability to sequence thirty billion individual bases in a day. Ebola's genome had a relatively simple structure, with only nineteen thousand bases and just seven genes, so it wouldn't take long to get a result.

After setting up the sequencer, she joined Michael at his computer.

"Do we even know which strain Doctor Medford was working with?"

"Colonel Gibson claims they were working on a cure for the new strain," Michael replied. His voice was cold and clinical. That was always how he sounded when he was immersed in his work. "We should know by the end of the day." He finally looked away from his monitor. "Let's finish up in here, let the sequencer do its job. I want to call Jed for an update. Once the sample genomes are mapped, we can run them through the bioinformatics software and see if we can't find a match."

The program compared the sequencing results with all genomes in both the National Center for Biotechnology Information and CDC databases. Kate hoped the results would give her a better idea of what they were dealing with. "A match," she mumbled.

Her eyes connected with Michael's ever so briefly. She wanted to see if she could get a read on the man. "Do you think this is really Ebola?"

His features hardened behind his visor. "Some of the

symptoms are similar, but the behavior and some of the physiological changes don't make any sense." He shook his head and mumbled something Kate could hardly make out. "The lips. What could cause that?"

"I can't get the images of Jim Pinkman out of my head," Kate replied. She shuddered inside of her suit.

Michael reached out with a gloved hand, stopping just shy of her shoulder. "We'll figure this out, Kate."

She focused on the sequencer. The boxy machine was busy mapping the genome of the most deadly virus she had ever encountered, and the results had the potential to change the world forever.

The flight to Fort Bragg and a horrible night of sleep had provided Beckham with ample time to think. He was done with the self-pity, the feelings of failure. He was a goddamn Delta Force operator, not some grunt. He hadn't risen to the rank of master sergeant by being a weak-minded coward. He'd done so by leading. If he could have traded places with Spinoza, Edwards, or Tenor he would have.

In a heartbeat.

But Delta operators didn't get the luxury of living in a science-fiction world. Their world was war. There were no time machines or do-overs. They didn't have the luxury of second chances. The wrong decision resulted in missing limbs, death, and ruined lives. All he could do now was honor the memory of his fallen comrades and make damn sure his men *hadn't* died in vain.

Horn and Riley were waiting for him on the stoop outside his quarters. They both looked exhausted and acknowledged him with slow nods.

"How are the girls?" Beckham asked.

"Good," Horn replied. "Wife's really upset. She keeps asking what happened. I didn't know how to respond."

Beckham nodded. Sheila was a tough woman, the kind that could keep his best friend in line. Horn had hardly been able to convince his wife to let him go to the Keys for a few days, but that was before...

"Ready for this?" Horn asked.

Beckham nodded. The other operators would all be there. They would all know by now that Spinoza, Edwards, and Tenor were gone. Every single one of them had lost other brothers-in-arms. It was part of the job, part of their life.

They walked the remainder of the path in silence. Horn gave Beckham a short pat on the shoulder when they arrived and then opened the door. The sound of a blaring television greeted them. The other teams were huddled around the monitor, watching a news report. Colonel Dennis Clinton stood behind a wooden podium, his arms crossed, his face set in a stoic grimace.

Horn let the door shut quietly behind them. The metallic click prompted every head to rotate in their direction. Beckham had entered the room knowing what to expect, but when he saw the grim looks, the loss struck him even harder. He'd lost *half* of his team—half of the men he'd lived and bled with for years.

He wanted to drop to his knees, to scream at the top of his lungs. Instead, he held his head high and led his men down the aisle of leather chairs. Every step prompted a new expression of sympathy.

"Sorry about your team, Beckham," one operator said.

Another shed a tear and whispered a prayer.

There were other noises too, the faint voice of a reporter on the news. "Zombie apocalypse takes Chicago by storm..."

Beckham nearly halted in the middle of the aisle. Had he heard right?

Two other operators offered sympathetic nods as he walked by. He heard one of them say, "No way these things are real zombies." Beckham instantly picked up on the hint of reservation in the man's voice. He sounded unsure. Operators were *never* unsure.

Beckham focused on a headline scrolling across the screen, wondering exactly what the hell was going on.

SUSPECTED CASES AS FAR NORTH AS WARREN AND AS FAR SOUTH AS MONEE...

"How could it spread that fast?" Riley asked.

"They better shut that fucking airport down," Horn said.

Riley let out a controlled laugh. "They better send us in to shut down the entire fucking city."

Beckham didn't laugh. He kept his focus on the television, resisting the urge to clench his fists. He couldn't stop thinking of the debriefing and the lies they had been fed.

The solid rap of Clinton's palm on the podium pulled everyone back to the center of the room. "Listen up," he said, scanning the room with focused eyes. The room immediately went silent, a sign of respect that only a veteran commander could conjure in so little time.

"I'm sure you are all aware of the losses Team Ghost incurred yesterday morning. Staff Sergeant Carlos 'Panda' Spinoza, Sergeant Will Tenor, and Sergeant Jim Edwards were all killed in action. Funeral arrangements are pending notification of next of kin."

Beckham looked at the floor. An emptiness he hadn't felt since his mother's death filled him, as if a vacuum had suddenly sucked out his insides.

"Let's take a moment to remember our fallen brothers, men who made the ultimate sacrifice for our country," Clinton said. He bowed his head, the glare from the overhead LEDs glowing off his shiny skull. "Your service will never be forgotten." Clinton made the sign of the cross over himself and then swept his gaze across the faces of the assembled men. Beckham caught a glimpse of what he thought was grief. It was gone in the blink of an eye.

"Like so many other times in the past, we don't have time to mourn our brothers. A situation, as you are all aware, has developed in Chicago. A suspected outbreak of the Ebola virus has hit the city. Brass is saying this is unprecedented. That we should prepare for the worst. I'm going to be honest. I've never seen anything like this in my career." He looked at the television. Another headline crept across the bottom of the screen.

FEMA ARRIVES TO CHAOS.

Beckham felt his exhausted muscles tense. How the fuck was that possible? The infection had shown up in Chicago less than twenty-four hours ago. How could it be spreading so fast?

He then remembered Tenor, the confusion on his face—the fear. And then he remembered the symptoms: the vomiting, the red blotches, the bruising, and the hemorrhaging. The man had been infected for minutes, maybe less, before he started to change.

"Brass is working on contingency plans in case this thing spreads farther," Clinton said, before adding in a deeper tone, "I suspect it will." He paused and reached for the TV remote as a new line of text scrolled across the display.

"Governor Paxton has declared a state of emergency and activated the National Guard to help with evacuations," a female reporter said. "Anyone in the following counties, please make your way out of the city in a calm and—"

Clinton shut the television off and faced the teams. "Steel

yourself. This is only the beginning. For those of you that need to get caught up on sleep, I suggest doing so." He grabbed both sides of the podium, his hands forming fists as he gripped the wood. "Any questions?"

Riley raised his hand, waiting for Clinton to acknowledge him with a nod before saying, "What will our role be in all of this, sir?"

The colonel shook his head. "That's the first damn question I haven't been able to answer in my entire career. Would you believe that?"

A few of the operators chuckled nervously.

"Son, I haven't a damn clue."

By sunset the post was in chaos. Transportation aircraft roared overhead as they took off into the clouds, their rumble fading as they crossed the darkening horizon.

Beckham watched them disappear and pulled a cigarette reluctantly from Horn's pack of Camels. The burly man faked a smile, showing off a broken tooth he'd earned when an Afghani kid had thrown a brick at their team. The boy couldn't have been more than seven years old, his face a mixture of smeared dirt and blood. He was lucky Horn hadn't turned his SAW on him. Beckham had seen a trigger-happy Army Ranger kill an Iraqi teenager after a similar incident. That boy had also tossed a brick, but when he ran the soldier mowed him down.

The image would be with Beckham for the rest of his life.

The two men took a seat on the curb, watching the sky. Like the crimson sun drifting across the horizon, Beckham found his mind drifting through the violent images of his past. His mind had become a photo album of death, and he was filling it with more images every day.

"You okay, boss?" Horn asked. He took a long drag from his cigarette and held the smoke inside his lungs with his jaw clenched shut.

Beckham nodded. "Just remembering."

"I get those moments too. We all do." Horn exhaled the cloud of smoke over his shoulder and flicked the cigarette onto the concrete. He reached for another and said, "Tenor, Panda, and Edwards all knew the risks, man. And they trusted you. We all trusted you, and me and Riley, we still do. You got us out of Building Eight. If you had listened to Caster, we'd all be dead."

Beckham nodded again. This time it was more to himself, as if he was trying to justify his thoughts.

"We'd all give our lives for one another," Horn added. He hunched over, placing his hands on his knees and stretching his back.

"Why is the pain always worse when it's inflicted on one of our brothers?" Beckham ran a hand through his hair. "I mean, I'd rather take a bullet than see you hit."

Horn nodded and took a short drag from his cigarette. Exhaling the smoke through his nostrils, he said, "Because that's what it's like to be a family. I feel the same way about Tasha, Jenny, and Sheila. I'd rather burn in hell for eternity than see them suffer."

"I'd give anything to see my mom and dad again," Beckham replied.

They sat there in silence for a beat until Horn chuckled and slapped Beckham's knee. "We need to get you a girl-friend, man. You know that? You need a woman. A *real* woman." Horn laughed as he stood. "You know what my wife has always said."

Beckham knew he was trying to lighten the mood, but he couldn't seem to bring himself to laugh with his friend. "And you know what I've always said."

"You love Delta Force 'more than you could ever love any woman,'" a deep voice said mockingly behind them.

The metal door to the barracks slammed shut. Riley stood on the top step, holding a bottle of Jameson. He was laughing hysterically. Gripping his chest, Riley chuckled some more. "Do I need to remind you of Kitty's words? You know, that dancer from the Bing? She said you're the best-looking soldier she'd ever seen."

"Don't start," Beckham said. "I've had my fair share of flings and girlfriends. They never worked out because I care more about this"—he pointed to his uniform—"than some yoga instructor or smoking hot barista."

"That's not the only reason," Horn remarked. He flashed a skeptical glare at his friend and flicked the ash from his cigarette onto the ground. "You're afraid to get close to people because of your parents. You've been this way since I met you."

A pair of streetlights outside of their barracks clicked on as the last hint of sun faded away under a carpet of darkness. The darkness matched the feeling rising like a tide inside of Beckham.

"You're right, man, but it's just easier that way. I have my men to worry about. I don't need a woman. Complicates things. Can't have some girl on my mind when I'm trying to shoot bad guys."

Riley chuckled. "I like complicated women."

"You mean like that one you only thought was a girl? Now *that's* complicated!" Horn said, bursting into a deep laugh. He spied the bottle of booze in Riley's hand and said, "Give that here."

"Fuck you, man," Riley replied. "That was an honest mistake." He downed two gulps of whiskey and then handed it off.

Horn raised the bottle in the air and said, "Tonight we drink to Tenor, Edwards, and Panda." He took a long swig from the bottle and ran a sleeve across his mouth before pushing it toward Beckham. "It's the least we can do."

Beckham grabbed the bottle. "To our fallen brothers," he said. He gulped down the whiskey and felt it burn as it slid down his throat and settled in his gut. Tonight he welcomed the burn.

The three drank in silence, watching another plane take off in the distance. As the ground rumbled, Beckham knew everything was about to change—that the world was never going to be the same. What had happened in Building 8 was only the beginning. The next day was going to be a big day for the United States military.

10

Kate sat at her desk outside the BSL4 lab thinking she could hear the sound of sirens in the distance, but she knew that was impossible. Their lab wasn't just airtight, it was underground. The silence reminded her she still hadn't heard back from Javier. Her little brother was in the thick of the outbreak, and for the first time in her life she couldn't do anything to protect him.

Frantic, she checked her phone again.

No new messages.

She'd told Javier specifically the night before to send her a text first thing in the morning. It was almost 6:00 p.m. in Chicago. Something had gone wrong. She knew it.

"Kate, I just got off the phone with Pat. He's okay, but he's stranded at Fort Bragg," Michael said.

"What do you mean, '*stranded*'?"

"All military aircraft are reserved for evacuations."

"In Chicago?"

Michael shook his head. "The country."

Kate froze. There had to be some sort of mistake. "Where did you hear this?"

"Haven't you checked your e-mail?"

She shook her head and gestured toward her computer. "I've been waiting on the sequencing results. I want to get them into the bioinformatics software as soon as possible."

He nodded but didn't seem to be listening to her. His tone changed when he spoke again. There was a trace of fear.

"This thing is spreading like wildfire, Kate. Cases are popping up in Wisconsin, Iowa, even Ohio."

"But how?"

Michael ran a hand over his bald scalp. "The incubation period varies. Some people don't exhibit symptoms right away."

Kate let out a long sigh of frustration. "I don't understand."

"Neither do I, but in a few minutes I expect we will learn more. Jed Frank is hosting a nationwide conference call."

Standing, Kate eyed Michael. "I hope to God they know more than we do."

"Me too," he said walking across the lab to his station. "I'll stream the call through."

She pulled up a lab stool, dragging the rolling chair across the shiny floor. Michael sat a few feet away, pulling up the video software on his laptop.

Kate repositioned a few strands of loose hair. All of the key CDC players would be on the feed, and she looked like shit. She'd seen the worry in her features earlier that morning.

After fumbling with his computer screen, Michael managed to swivel the monitor in their direction. As they connected to the conference, she saw that the other CDC scientists shared the same exhausted look. Everyone was trying to figure out what the hell was going on.

She scanned the small facial images at the bottom of the screen. They were all there, faces she hadn't seen in months: Jim Harper, from Vermont; Angela Johnson, from Ohio; Richard Clay, from New York; and a handful of others.

Deputy Director Frank linked to the call a few minutes later. He wasted no time. "Talk to me, people. Someone tell me they know what we're dealing with."

There was no response.

"Michael, give me some good news," Frank pleaded.

"We're sequencing the genome. Should be wrapping shortly."

Frank pulled away from the screen and then leaned back in with narrowed eyebrows. "Here's what I know and the chain of events. Patient zero was a scientist named Jim Pinkman who'd been working for the Medical Corps. He arrived in O'Hare from a flight that originated at San Nicolas Island. He was part of a team working on a cure for the new strain of Ebola that's active in Guinea." Frank pursed his lips and shook his head.

"Colonel Gibson, of USAMRIID, said the lead scientist, a man named Medford, was using VX-99 to try and destroy the Ebola virus. But instead of killing the virus, the compound and virus bonded. The lab went off-line several days ago. Gibson then called in a special team that included Pat Ellis to retrieve a sample of Medford's work. That mission failed. We believe—*I* believe—that Pinkman was infected with whatever the team was working on."

"*That's* what's spreading in Chicago? Some sort of hybrid Ebola virus?" Jim Harper asked. "Are you kidding me? This is an outrage!"

"Calm down, Jim. Obviously no one knows exactly what we are dealing with. We only have theories. But whatever this is, it's spreading fast. Due to the varying incubation period and the violent behavior of the infected, we're looking at an unprecedented outbreak here, people." Frank coughed into his hand and then looked up at the monitor with a grave stare.

"Good news is it's not airborne. The first phase of the virus seems to occur minutes after infection. The symptoms are hallucinations, agonizing pain throughout the body, and itching. Some patients also exhibit extreme paranoia. The second phase is vomiting and hemorrhaging. Depending on the severity of the case, this phase onsets anywhere from within minutes to hours. What happens next is where the virus takes a strange and terrifying turn."

He blinked twice, then continued. "The final stage of infection occurs when victims engage in extreme violent behavior. There are hundreds of cases of self-mutilation and cannibalization. Even worse are the physiological changes to their bodies."

"That's science fiction," said a voice.

Dr. Richard Clay was frowning in his window of the screen. One of the older scientists on the call, the doctor had a controversial and tumultuous past with CDC.

"Lesch-Nyhan syndrome is the only disorder I'm aware of that causes such atrocious sympt—"

Frank cut him off. "I assure you this is not science fiction. Surely you have seen the videos."

Dr. Clay waved off the comment.

"As I was saying, suspected cases all exhibit violent behavior in the late stage of infection. Doctor Chad Roberts has been on the ground in Chicago since this started. He believes the Ebola virus has mutated. Our theory so far is that this mutation has something to do with VX-99."

Several outbursts erupted over the call. Kate watched as her colleagues argued back and forth. After a few seconds Frank said, "Calm down, everyone, please."

Kate used the opportunity to interject. "Whatever this is, we need to pull together all of our resources. Bickering won't solve anything."

Releasing an audible sigh, Frank narrowed his eyebrows. "Doctor Lovato is right. I know this sounds like a nightmare, and I know you are all worried about your families. That's why we need to pull together and find a way to stop this."

Kate pulled her phone from under the table. The display was blank; still nothing from Javier. She felt a wave of panic rush through her. *Focus*, she thought. *He had ample warning. He's probably on the move, evacuating with the others.*

Frank spun in his chair as an assistant walked into his room. The man whispered something in his ear. The deputy director quickly returned to the monitor wearing a mask of worry. "Shit. I have to go. I want to know the *second* someone finds something. The *second*!"

The screen fizzled and faded. Michael bowed his head toward the desk, defeated.

"This is it, Kate. I told you."

"What?"

"The extinction-level event. The virus has already spread too far. I'm not sure we can stop it."

Kate felt her phone buzz and frantically looked away from the distraught doctor. An incoming message from Javier popped onto her screen. She felt her heart race.

Couldn't make it out of the city. Will call you when I'm safe. Love you.

"My God," Kate muttered.

"What is it?" Michael asked.

"My brother, Javier. He never made it out of the city."

Michael didn't speak, but Kate knew what he was thinking. She was thinking the same thing. The likelihood of Javier making it out of Chicago was diminishing by the minute.

Kate stood and scanned the room. She couldn't think. The fear and emotional stress was overwhelming. Stumbling forward, she braced herself against the desk.

"Kate, are you okay?" Michael asked.

Taking in a deep breath, she closed her eyes. Shimmering arcs of light crossed her vision. She couldn't breathe.

"Kate—" He reached out for her. "Kate, are you okay?"

Finally she nodded and said, "Yes, I'm fine. Just got really light-headed. I need to call Javier."

"Of course," Michael said, glancing up at her with concern. "I should call my wife; she's probably worried sick."

Reaching for her phone, she swiped the screen to see an incoming call. Her heart skipped a beat. "Hello?"

"Kate. It's me, Pat."

She slouched in her chair and pointed at her phone, lipping the word *Ellis* to Michael. He acknowledged with a brief nod.

"Good to hear your voice," Kate said, trying to conceal her disappointment that it wasn't Javier. "When are you coming back here?"

"I'm not," Ellis replied. "Well, I am, but we're not staying."

Kate paused, her nostrils flaring in confusion.

"What do you mean?" she asked.

"We're being evacuated."

"What? Where to?"

"Plum Island, in New York. Colonel Rick Gibson, the commander of USAMRIID, has requested CDC send us there."

Silence washed over the line as Kate considered the ramifications of leaving now. They hadn't even finished sequencing the virus's genome yet, and then they would have to run the results through the bioinformatics software. That was just the beginning.

"Kate?" Ellis asked.

"Sorry," she said. "We can't leave. We've hardly started our work."

"Atlanta isn't safe," Ellis replied. "Plum Island apparently has BSL4 lab stations, and the military will be there to protect us."

Kate cupped her hand over the phone. "They want to evacuate us to Plum Island."

"What?" Michael mumbled.

She removed her hand. "When are you coming?"

"Tomorrow," Ellis replied.

She looked at Michael. He stood there with his arms crossed, staring back at her blankly. She remembered what he'd said earlier, that the virus had already spread too far to stop. Kate wasn't ready to accept that notion. She was ready to prove him wrong—she was ready to fight.

"We'll be ready," she said.

Chad Roberts wiped away a bead of sweat trickling down his forehead. He slowly pulled back the plastic curtain he had hidden behind. The darkness of the empty hospital room greeted him.

After escaping the isolation compartment, he'd made his way to the upper levels of the hospital. Shortly after he'd run up the stairs, all hell had broken loose. The chief of staff had vanished in the chaos.

Now Chad was alone, hiding in the dark, gripping the cold metal of a revolver he'd snagged off a dead cop.

The red glow from a bank of emergency lights flickered in the open doorway, revealing the dark hallway beyond. He peeled the plastic screen back for a better look, straining to hear any sound of footsteps.

The crack of sporadic gunfire rang out in the distance. The shots were evenly spaced and loud, likely from a shotgun. Glancing at the revolver in his shaking hand, he was reminded he was far from a weapons expert. In fact, he hardly even knew how to handle the thing.

He pulled his phone from his pocket and risked a glance away from the door to check the screen for messages.

A red bar blinked across the display.

Fuck, he thought. *Out of battery.* He had a charger in his bag. Before he reached for his gear, he peeked around the corner of the plastic curtain. The blinking backup lights flashed red over the hallway and reminded him the power was off. He had no way to charge the phone even if he wanted to.

A howl traveled through the halls. He froze. Naked feet slapped across the floor and filled the quiet hallway.

Chad gripped the revolver tighter. He slowly pulled the curtain closed again, leaving only a small gap so he could see the corridor beyond.

He fumbled with his gun as another high-pitched screech broke through the stillness.

This one was closer. Possibly even on the same floor as him.

Chad chewed on his inner lip. He slipped behind the curtain and crouched next to the air-conditioning unit. Glancing over his shoulder, he looked out the fifth-floor window. Below, he could see flashing lights from squad cars. Two military Humvees were parked on the curb, their doors still open. In the street a FEMA semitrailer had T-boned a CNN satellite truck. It was dark, but he could still see the smoke billowing out from under both hoods.

Focusing, Chad narrowed his eyes on the outlines of bodies lining the sidewalk. Puddles of blood surrounding the mangled corpses glistened under the moonlight. He pushed his face against the glass for a look at the adjacent street and gasped. It too was covered with corpses.

Footfalls from the hallway pulled Chad back to the red flickering light. He waited, the rapping growing louder with each beat of his heart. They sounded like the noise a soldier's boots made.

As he listened he heard another noise, similar to what he'd heard back in the isolation wing. It sounded like a twig bending and then snapping. The only explanation filled Chad with paralyzing fear. It was the clicking joints of one of the infected.

A bead of sweat dropped into Chad's right eye. He winced, ignoring the burn and focusing his aim on the hallway. Time moved slowly, the world frozen around him. His heart hammered at the sound of yet another snarling scream. The noise confirmed what Chad had suspected: One of the infected was making its way down the corridor. It was hunting, and he was its prey.

Chad contemplated jumping out the window. If he landed on one of the Humvees, maybe, just maybe, he could survive the fall. *Anything would beat getting torn apart by one of those things*, he thought.

When he turned back to the door, he saw it was too late. The crooked silhouette of a man stood there, the red light flickering around him like an evil halo. Every flash revealed a fresh glimpse of his twisted features: the tattered fatigues soaked in blood, a right arm hanging oddly from the socket, and finally, the blood trickling down his ghostly white face.

Chad put his thumb on the hammer, careful not to pull it back. He moved his sweaty index finger from the outside of the trigger guard to the trigger.

The man tilted his head, raising his nose into the air and sniffing for a scent.

For my scent.

Chad wanted to run, but he was captivated by the creature in front of him. It wasn't able to see him from this angle.

With one hand on the revolver and the other holding the curtain, Chad waited.

The red light flashed again, and the ex-soldier viciously licked the blood around his swollen lips, moaning in delight. Then he stopped, slowly tilting his head toward the curtain.

Chad prepared to pull back the hammer to fire, but closed his eyes instead.

Not yet.

Even if he could kill this man, others would be drawn to the sound. Shooting was his last resort.

When he opened his eyes, the man was gone. The emergency light flashed in sync with Chad's thumping heart. After a few agonizing seconds, he inched back the curtain with a free finger.

A pair of crimson eyes stared back at him. He saw with perfect clarity that the man's eyes had transformed— the irises were a sick yellowish color, and the pupils had morphed into vertical slits. They flickered as if adjusting to the light before locking onto Chad.

He pulled back the hammer with a loud click, but didn't have the chance to fire a shot before the infected man barreled into him, knocking the gun from his grip. Chad went down hard. The back of his skull bounced off the tile floor, and flashes of red broke across his vision. He thrashed his arms in the air, trying to bat the man away, but he was much stronger and had Chad pinned down.

Desperate, he punched the infected man in the side of the head. That only enraged his assailant. The man's eyes burned with hunger and rage.

Roaring with anger, he rammed his forehead into Chad's rib cage. Every bit of air exploded from Chad's lungs. The sharp pain rushed through his entire body. He saw more stars and sucked in a wild, desperate breath of air.

Swatting blindly, Chad strained to get free. His wild swings were futile. He was trapped under the sheer weight of the man and pinned by his brute strength. When his vision cleared, he saw a set of jagged yellow teeth snarling behind a pair of pale, bulging lips. They pursed in and out, making a sucking noise and then a loud pop.

The *click-clack* of chomping teeth sounded distant, but Chad could see the razor-sharp teeth as they inched toward his face. The sound intensified, the doctor's fate closing in.

Chad screamed in terror. Reaching around for his gun, he found the metal handle and swiftly jammed the barrel into the man's mouth.

"Die, you fuck!" Chad squeezed the trigger.

Click.

The revolver was empty. It was fucking empty!

The man's reptilian eyes grew wide with confusion, as if he understood how lucky he was, but a second later primal instinct took over whatever hint of humanity remained. The man clamped down on Chad's cheek, tearing a chunk of flesh free in one bite.

Screaming in agony, Chad kicked helplessly as the man fed. Red filled his vision. He blinked it away and saw a new figure standing in the doorway.

Had someone come to help him?

A jolt of adrenaline filled Chad with a brief moment of energy and hope. Swinging as hard as he could, he smashed the revolver into the man's head. The crack resonated through the room, and Chad felt some of the weight lifted. He used the opportunity to push the man off.

The soldier tumbled to the ground, but quickly jumped to all fours, shaking his injured head like he was in a daze. Bloody saliva webbed across his lips as he let out a growl.

The brief reprieve gave Chad just enough time to push

off the ground. He gripped his gushing injury, the tips of his fingers touching bone.

"Help!" he screamed. He almost didn't recognize his frantic voice as it echoed. He pivoted toward the doorway.

The emergency light flickered, revealing the man in the entrance.

Chad let out a painful gasp.

Standing there was Dr. Ted Lucas, his face covered in blood. He blinked several times and then locked onto Chad with eyes that radiated hatred...

...and *hunger*.

11

It was going on midnight, and Kate couldn't calm down. She paced nervously across the lab, chewing on the inside of her bottom lip as she waited for the bioinformatics software to look for a match and for Javier to call.

The program compared the results of the virus sequencing with all known genomes in both the NCBI and CDC databases. In minutes, she would know if they had found a match.

Kate's cell phone vibrated, startling her from her work. She dug it from her pocket and saw the call she'd been waiting for. She swiped the screen to answer.

"Javier? Are you okay?"

His reply was garbled and incomprehensible. His throat gurgled, and a guttural cough erupted over the line.

Her heart kicked harder.

"Kate..."

"Yes, I'm here. Are you okay?"

More coughs crackled in her ear. She closed her eyes, wincing at each sound. She knew what they meant.

"They're everywhere," he choked. "I feel them. Like a swarm of fire ants burrowing behind my eyes. And I'm so hungry, Kate. So hungry."

Kate brought her right hand to her face, cupping her mouth in shock. "Javier, you need to get to a hospital."

He screamed in agony.

"Javier, my God. Javier, you have to get to a hospital," she said, knowing it was already too late. Without treatment, and with Chicago in chaos, she knew he wouldn't last long.

"I have never felt so much hunger," he said in a moment of clarity. "I love you, sis. And I know if anyone can stop this virus, it's—" He wailed again, his words twisting into a snarl.

Kate whimpered, her hand falling from her lips. "Listen to me, Javier!" she shouted. "You have to find a hospital. Demand that they sedate you. Demand that—" Kate paused. She knew better than anyone that not even antiviral medicines worked on Ebola.

Tears welled in the corners of her eyes.

"I love you, Javier," she cried.

His response came in another scream that she could hardly make out. "Ahhhhhhh...love you...Stop it! Make it stop!"

Kate's stomach sank, a wave of nausea overwhelming her. She could picture her brother's face. Bloody tears streaking down his olive skin, moving into his dimples and then through the brown goatee on his chin. She could see the blood vessels around his bright blue eyes rupturing. Javier was transforming on the other end of the line, and all she could do was listen.

"Kate!" he yelled.

And then she heard nothing. The line went dead.

"No! Javier," she said frantically. "Javier!"

Kate collapsed to her knees and tossed the phone across the room. It landed in the corner with a metallic crunch.

Bursting into tears, she struggled for air. Her chest felt

tight, her heart rate elevating rapidly. The nausea intensified. Before she could react, she lurched forward and threw
up her breakfast. The acidic taste made her gag. She swiped
the remnants off her mouth and tucked her chin against her
chest, breathing deeply.

The sound of the lab doors opening startled her. Michael
was frozen in the doorway.

"Kate?" he said slowly.

Forcing herself to her feet she wiped her mouth again.
"He's infected."

"Who?"

Kate's voice softened. "Javier."

Michael extended his arms and embraced her in an abrupt
hug, his arms massaging her back. "I'm sorry," he said. "I'm
so sorry, Kate."

A chirp from a computer rang out behind them. With
tears filling her eyes, Kate leaned down to see the database
scan was complete. Two words blinked across the screen.

No match.

April 21, 2015
DAY 4

Beckham stood in the shadow of a Black Hawk, watching
another transport wing soar across the skyline. Normally,
watching the American military stretch its muscles would
give him great satisfaction. But he felt betrayed.

Used.

He'd do his duty, sure. He always did. That didn't mean
he had to like it. He couldn't stop thinking about all of the
soldiers and innocent civilians who would die before this

was over. Over the past forty-eight hours, Chicago had been reduced to a postapocalyptic wasteland. The city was teeming with the sick, and those who weren't already dead were killing one another. The perimeter the National Guard had set up around the city had quickly fallen.

The virus was spreading.

But the military was ready. The sounds and sights all around him told him they were prepared. Beckham watched a platoon of army infantrymen jog across the tarmac. They made their way to a C-130, a staff sergeant he didn't recognize barking orders at them.

"All right, Third Platoon. Check your sensitive items when we get on board. Everyone check your buddy. And Val, tighten that damn chin strap."

The sight didn't exactly restore Beckham's faith in the military, but it reminded him that he had his own men to look after. That was still his number one priority.

Throwing his pack over his shoulders, Beckham looked for his team. Riley stood a few feet away, watching in silence, his light blue eyes following the soldiers into the belly of the transport plane. The sandy brown hair sticking out of his helmet blew in the slight breeze. He scratched his cleanly shaved face as he watched. Behind that intense stare, Riley was just a kid at heart and in spirit. The team's little brother.

He patted Riley on the shoulder, and the younger operator looked up at him quizzically.

"You okay, boss?"

"Yeah. Just glad you're here, Riley."

The kid nodded, a far cry from his typical smile and laugh. He scrutinized Beckham with the same intense stare from earlier. "You sure you're okay?"

Beckham forced a half smile. "I'm good. How about you, Kid? How are *you* holding up?"

Riley's eyes flitted to the ground. It was a look Beckham had seen a hundred times before—it was the look of a man who had taken a life and was still coming to terms with it. Taking another life almost always took time to dig in. Once it did, it settled in your gut, twisting and prodding like a knife that you couldn't bat away. Only in this case Riley hadn't taken just any life—he'd taken the life of a friend.

"You did what you had to do," Beckham said. "You hear me, Kid?"

Riley swiped his nose with a sleeve. "Yeah, I hear you. That wasn't Tenor back there," he said, his tone low, as if he was trying to convince himself.

Beckham shook his head. "No, it wasn't."

Horn's loud voice boomed from inside the Black Hawk. He crouched in the open door and smacked the metal side with a paw. "That reminds me: I never said thanks for saving my ass."

Riley nodded. "You'd have done the same thing." He threw a duffel bag inside the chopper. "I still can't believe we pulled evac duty. Since when the hell did we become escorts?"

"We're whatever Command tells us we are," Beckham replied. "And it sounds like Ellis has an important team waiting for him in Atlanta. What's the status of your family, Big Horn?"

The operator jumped out of the chopper. "Brought them to base, just like you said. They'll be safer here."

"Good," Beckham replied.

Across the tarmac, the engines on the C-130 hummed to life, and all three men watched the plane lurch down the runway. Beckham shielded his eyes from the bright morning sun.

The sound of footsteps replaced the diminishing roar from the plane.

"Master Sergeant Beckham!" an energetic voice called. He didn't need to turn to know it was Ellis jogging across the tarmac.

"About time," Beckham said, grabbing the doctor's single bag.

"We almost left without you," Horn said.

Ellis paused at the doorway and watched the three operators chuckle. In a very serious tone he said, "You don't know, do you?"

Beckham tossed the doctor's bag on the floor of the bird and gave Ellis a quick once-over.

"Know what?" Horn said. He pulled his skull bandanna from around his neck and tucked it into his shirt.

"The outbreak has hit Atlanta," Ellis said quickly.

"What? How?" Riley blurted.

Beckham reached for the handle of the MP5 slung over his shoulder. The grip of the metal felt reassuring. "How did it get to Atlanta so fast? Can those things fucking drive?"

Ellis ran a nervous hand through his hair. He took off his glasses and put them in his breast pocket very methodically and then, shaking his head, said, "I don't know—by plane, possibly."

"How the hell did one of those things get on a plane?" Riley asked.

"The incubation period seems to be fluid," Ellis said. "That's how it got to Chicago in the first place. But honestly, I'm not sure how it's spreading so fast. None of this makes any sense."

"Sure it does," Beckham replied. He paused, waiting for the rumble from three Ospreys taking off farther down the tarmac to pass. Beckham loosened his grip on his weapon. "You're a scientist, right? Don't you see?"

Ellis narrowed his eyebrows. "See what?"

"Doctor Medford created the perfect virus. It doesn't kill its host, and it spreads like fire in a dry forest," Beckham said.

"I suppose you're right," Ellis said. "Which means we need to find a treatment ASAP."

"You want a treatment?" Horn lifted his machine gun. "Well, here's a cure."

Ellis's face remained stone cold. "I'm afraid you won't have enough bullets."

Grunting, Horn climbed into the aircraft and tossed his gear on the floor. "We'll see about that."

Beckham gestured at the Black Hawk with his chin. "After you, Doctor."

The first pass from the chopper's blades whooshed above them, and Beckham peered over his shoulder one more time before climbing inside the Black Hawk. Across the airfield, aircraft of all shapes and sizes waited for air traffic control to give them the green light for takeoff. Platoons and squads marched and jogged around the tarmac, filing into formations and boarding aircraft.

Fort Bragg reminded him of a forward operating base. In a way, he supposed the post had transformed into one, only this time they weren't being deployed to some godforsaken sand castle. This time, the enemy was on home turf. Beckham spit the bad taste out of his mouth as another plane took off. He paused to scan the organized chaos around them. The choke of diesel engines and the footfalls of heavy boots owned the morning. The entire post was alive with movement, preparing for a new type of war.

Kate stood hunched over a sink, her tears falling freely now. She'd retreated to the lab's bathroom to pull herself together.

She closed her swollen eyes and pictured the transformation Javier's body was going through. It wasn't hard to imagine, considering what she'd seen in the video of patient zero and what she'd heard on the conference call with Deputy Director Frank hours earlier.

Her brother would be past Phase 1 now. The alterations to his physiology would be graphic: swollen lips, receding gums, vertical pupils, hemorrhaging from every orifice. His extremities would twist and snap, his hands curling and morphing into claws.

The man Kate pictured in her mind wasn't her brother any longer. The man she pictured was a monster.

She didn't bother brushing the tears away. Like Javier, she had completely lost control of her body. Instead of hemorrhaging blood, she was hemorrhaging tears.

A double rap on the door.

"Kate, are you in there?"

It was Michael.

There was a second round of knocks.

Kate took in a deep breath and turned on the water. She didn't want to look at the image in the mirror, but she had to. She needed to see how awful she looked.

It was bad. Dark bags rimmed her swollen eyes. She was pale, and her hair was frizzled. After splashing cold water on her face, she pulled her hair back into a ponytail.

"Kate," Michael pleaded, "I need your help. We need to get everything downloaded and the data prepped for the evacuation. There isn't anything you can do for Javier now."

She opened the door and stepped into the hallway with glazed, unfocused eyes. She saw Michael standing in front of her but didn't make a move to acknowledge him.

"Kate!" Michael said. He snapped his fingers in front of

her face. "Think of your parents, your friends. They are still out there."

"I thought you said we couldn't stop this," Kate blurted without thinking.

Michael softened. "I did."

Wiping away the last of her tears, she peered into her mentor's eyes. He reached out and placed a hand on her shoulder and in a soothing, clinical voice said, "We have to try. This is our job. Millions, if not billions, of people are counting on our work."

Billions.

Kate was used to working on viruses that threatened the lives of thousands. But billions? A billion lives in her hands?

She pushed thoughts of her brother from her mind. Michael was right. The world was counting on scientists. The world was counting on their work. She had to help the living now. Her work was all that mattered. She had to stop the virus's spread before it crossed any more borders—before it reached Europe. Her parents lived in Rome. The thought of telling them about Javier made her stomach churn. She couldn't think about that now. She had to focus on finding a way to cure the infected.

They hurried back to the lab, talking as they walked. "Things are bad up top, Kate. Internet and cell-phone traffic is probably stretched to the limit."

"Only going to get worse," Kate replied.

Inside the lab, Michael rushed to his computer. "We got the PCR protocol test back. What do you make of this?"

Kate pulled up a stool. After they'd failed to find a match in the CDC or NCBI databases, they'd run a polymerase chain reaction protocol test. It was the final step to trying to match up the virus genome they'd already sequenced.

"Okay," she said, exhaling and focusing on the information in front of her. "What do we have?"

"As you know, the results showed no direct match. However, there are remarkable similarities to Ebola." Michael typed on the keyboard to load the results. "Well, I'll be damned," he said, as data scrolled across the screen.

Six of the virus's seven genes were the same as known genes of Ebola. She recognized the first three. They were used to control transcription, replication, and packaging into the new virions. But the fourth of the seven genes was different.

She pointed at the screen, knowing from memory what gene it was. "Glycoprotein on the virus shell has mutated."

Michael brought a finger to his lip. "So that explains why the hemorrhaging isn't killing the victims like it normally would."

Kate nodded as she digested the information. She spoke out loud as she considered the results. "Glycoprotein enables the Ebola virus to attach to white blood cells and spread throughout the body. The protein targets endothelial cells, which line the blood vessels. Normally that causes a chain of events that makes the cells separate from the blood-vessel walls, and it leaves a massively unstable vascular wall, permeable to blood. That's what causes the hemorrhaging."

Michael agreed. "So if the glycoprotein spike has been altered, then maybe it only links to macrophages and isn't disrupting the endothelial cells' attachment to the vascular walls as normal."

Kate nodded. "So there will be some hemorrhaging, but just enough to continue the spread of the virus, not enough to kill the host."

There was a brief pause as the two scientists reflected on the implications.

"Jesus," Michael said.

Kate spoke again. "Obviously we're dealing with a new

or modified strain here." She studied the bank of lights above, squinting as she thought. "Doctor Medford must have found a way to alter the fourth gene. It's a partial cure." She paused to think. "Shit," she mumbled. "This still doesn't make sense."

"Let's start with what we know," Michael added. His voice had returned to the clinical tone that reminded her of his expertise.

"Okay," Kate replied, trying to think clearly. "The sample from Guinea expresses a glycoprotein with a strong affinity for proteins found on the surface of the endothelial cells. The sample from Chicago does not."

"But how?" Michael asked. "And what's causing the other changes to the victims? The changes to their physiology make no sense. This new modified strain is turning victims into monsters."

Kate looked at the floor. Her brother was one of those monsters now.

"I'm sorry, Kate," Michael said, realizing his mistake.

She blinked the images away and with urgency said, "We need to put a sample of the virus in a culture dish of endothelial cells and see what happens."

"Agreed. Let's suit up."

Kate had gone to grab her bag when a loud wailing pierced the lab. Her eyes shot up to the bank of emergency lights in the corner of the room. The red lights swirled around in their glass dome.

"What the hell?" Michael said.

The sound intensified, the whine of the alarm silencing Kate's labored breathing. Her heart climbed in her throat. She rushed to her laptop just as the door to the office swung open and a research assistant burst into the room. He hunched over, his hands on his knees, panting.

"It's here," he said in between labored breaths.

"What?" Michael asked. "What's here?"

"The infection!" The young man coughed.

"What do you mean, 'it's here'?" Kate asked.

Sucking in a breath, the assistant rushed over to the television in the corner of the room. Kate had silenced it earlier. She grabbed the TV remote and clicked the volume to max. The whine of the emergency siren echoed in the room, making it impossible to hear, but she could see something was happening.

A newscaster stood on the top of a building she didn't recognize. The cameraman angled the video camera over the side of the roof. Below, a mob of people ran down the side of both streets. They streamed out of office buildings, tripping over one another and clogging the sidewalks. Cars blared their horns in the bottlenecked traffic. One driver pulled his SUV onto the curb, sending a man flying through the front window of an adjacent Starbucks.

"Where is this?" Kate asked.

"Atlanta," the assistant said, finally catching his breath. "The virus is in Atlanta. A passenger on a plane brought the infection in overnight. Atlanta, New York, Las Vegas, San Francisco. There are reports in virtually every major city," he said.

"Prep the data," Michael said, "and get ready to go. We're leaving."

12

The Black Hawk circled the glass-paneled CDC building for several minutes. Beckham patted the vest pocket that held the picture of his mom. The simple touch filled him with strength and, glancing down, he knew he was going to need it.

Atlanta was in chaos.

Reaching for a handhold, he leaned out the door to scan for a possible landing zone. He'd had ample time to plan their insertion point, but every time he thought he had a location nailed, he found a barrier.

Cars clogged the roads everywhere he looked. There wasn't a single inch of clear concrete, and there were few signs of life. Only a few panicked citizens ran through the streets. He watched them race toward a pair of abandoned Humvees surrounding the gated entry to the Arlen Specter building.

"That's our target!" Beckham yelled. The reflection of their Black Hawk flashed in the glass windows as they circled. The twelve-story building stood in the middle of a large open space of grass and walking paths. Built on a hill, the facility overlooked a road that snaked beneath it.

There was motion down there, more civilians streaming

from under the building. He lost sight of them on the second pass and focused on the Humvees outside the front gates.

"Where the fuck did the soldiers go?" Beckham muttered. "Get us closer to the ground," he yelled.

"Roger," came the voice of one of the pilots.

Beckham tightened his hold and squinted. As they descended, the runners on the ground came into focus. He spotted the missing soldiers. They were all shirtless, but there was no mistaking their ACU pants. Beckham concentrated on the pack for a better look. Even from the present altitude, he could see the men were covered in blood.

"We have infected!" Horn shouted.

Beckham's muscles twitched. He had been hoping for a secure landing, a quick in and out. Put down near the CDC building, grab Dr. Michael Allen and his team, and get the hell out of Dodge. As the chopper took them closer to the ground, he realized things weren't going to be that easy. There weren't any guards left to roll out a red carpet and let his men into the building.

"Shit," Beckham muttered. He looked to Big Horn for support. The operator hid behind his skull bandanna, his eyes the only visible feature on his face.

"Whatcha thinkin', boss?"

Beckham scanned the LZ for a safe place to deploy their rope. More of the infected darted across the ground on all fours.

Riley shouted, "Do you see that shit?"

Beckham looked for Ellis. The man sat paralyzed in the corner. "Doctor, we're going to need you on your feet."

Ellis threw up his hands. "Hell no! You're crazy if you think I'm going down there."

"We need you to get into the building," Horn grunted.

"Here, take it," Ellis replied, reaching inside his pocket

and fumbling for his key card. He held it out with a shaky hand. "That'll get you inside."

"What about the retinal scan?" Beckham asked. "Won't we need to pass that too?"

The doctor's shoulders sagged as the words sank in. He nodded slowly, tucking the key card back into his pocket.

The chopper jerked hard to the right, throwing Beckham off balance. He smashed onto the floor, sliding a few feet. A pair of strong hands grabbed his shoulders and stopped him. He looked up to see the bottom half of Horn's skull bandanna.

"What the fuck!" Beckham yelled at the pilots, grabbing Horn's right arm and pulling himself to his feet.

Before the primary pilot had a chance to respond, Beckham heard the scream of F-22s flying low over the city. He crouched and moved into the cockpit, looking through the dirty windshield. Beyond he could see three of the jets racing across the skyline.

"What the hell are they doing here?" Beckham asked, his skin tingling from a combination of awe and nerves. Nothing could put a man on high alert like the roar of F-22s flying at five hundred feet.

Turbulence shook the hovering chopper as they shrieked over top of it.

"They're going to bomb strategic locations in the city," the pilot finally said.

"You're shitting me," Beckham replied. When the man glanced at him, Beckham saw he was completely serious.

"How long do we have?"

The pilot turned back to the cockpit and cupped his headset. "They're telling all military contacts to be out of the city in thirty minutes."

Beckham felt a lump form in his throat. Shocked into

motion, he moved back into the troop compartment. "Time to move! Get on the rope, Big Horn."

"All of us?" Ellis choked. "I don't think I can do this."

"You heard the man," Riley said. He grabbed the doctor by his shirt and pulled him toward the open door.

"But we don't have biohazard suits!"

"Better hold your breath," Horn said, with what could pass as a laugh. He locked the rope into position with a metallic click.

"Nothing we can do about that now, Doctor," Beckham yelled over the whoosh of the blades. "Besides, we know this thing isn't airborne. Right?" He watched Ellis nod slowly. The man's eyes seemed detached, as if he didn't know where he was.

A voice from the cockpit pulled Beckham back to the chopper. "Where should I put you down?"

Beckham took another minute to scan the potential landing zone. Identifying an opening, he pointed to the lawn just outside the front driveway of the main entrance. "Over there!"

Seconds later they were hovering over the green space, the tree branches rocking viciously below.

Horn threw the fast rope over the side and scoped the area with his M249. Then he grabbed the line with his gloves and slid down.

Beckham watched him hit the ground and take off running for an abandoned Humvee. With a reassuring nod, Beckham slapped Riley on the back. "You're next."

Without a second of hesitation, the operator took the rope and slid down after Horn.

"Please, I don't know if I can do this again," Ellis said, his eyes pleading with Beckham to reconsider.

The distant roar of F-22s and a squadron of F-16s rumbled,

and Beckham shoved the doctor toward the door. "We need you, Doctor. Your team needs you!"

Minutes later they were running as a group across the lawn, the gusts from the helo blades swirling debris around them. Beckham shot a glance over his shoulder. The infected that had been at the gates earlier were running in the opposite direction now, chasing the helicopter. *Great*, he thought. He would take the distraction.

They halted behind a second set of Humvees parked near the building's circular drive. Beckham inched the barrel of his MP5 over the hood of a truck. The entrance looked clear, with no sign of life.

"All right, Ellis, which way?" Beckham asked.

Ellis shook nervously, his hands twitching. He jammed them in his pockets. "Through those glass doors we'll take a left, enter the stairwell, and then proceed to Lab Facility Fourteen on Sublevel D."

Beckham offered a reassuring nod and gave new orders. "Kid, you take point. Big Horn, watch our six. Doc, you're with me."

With a measured breath, he counted to three and then flashed an advance signal. Riley burst from his position with his shotgun shouldered and aimed at the front doors.

Beckham moved next. "Follow me," he said to Ellis, turning toward the entrance. They crossed the circular drive quickly, the sound of their footfalls beating against the concrete. The noise didn't bother Beckham, but the doctor's hesitation did. It was likely to get them all killed.

He would not put his men at risk if Ellis decided to go chickenshit. Beckham crouched behind a concrete ledge and watched Riley and Horn take up positions along the wall.

Beckham spied the doctor glancing nervously over his shoulder. He snapped his fingers in front of the man's face.

"Doctor Ellis, can you do this? Because we don't have much time. In less than twenty minutes, those jets are going to barbeque this city, and I do not want to be here when that happens."

Ellis emerged from his trance, and the color slowly returned to his cheeks. He swallowed and then nodded. "Yes, I can do it."

A burst of wind swept across the group. Beckham could taste the scent of burning rubber in the air. It reminded him of Iraq and half a dozen other war zones he'd been in. Plumes of dark smoke rose into the sky from locations across the city.

The sporadic sound of gunfire rang out at the same moment. The noise came from automatic rifles. Machine guns.

"Let's move," Beckham said, knowing the sound would draw any infected away.

"Contact!" Horn yelled.

Beckham saw the former soldier immediately. The man stood between them and the glass doors to the headquarters. His posture was completely off, as if his bones had been repositioned by a shitty chiropractor. Dried blood clung to the man's cheeks, forming a barrier around his swollen lips. They puckered and then made a sickening pop.

Beckham fired on instinct. He raised his MP5 and squeezed off a double burst. The first shots caught the former soldier in the chest, jolting his body backward. Bloody mist exploded from the man's open lips. The second burst hit him in the center of his forehead, and his brains peppered the concrete behind him.

"Covering fire!" Beckham yelled.

Grabbing Ellis by the collar, he yanked him toward the doors. Riley got there first. He crouched next to the entrance and swept the area beyond the shattered glass with his shotgun.

"We're clear on my side!" he yelled.

Beckham followed Riley inside. They entered an empty white lobby covered in shards of glass and bullet casings. A round central welcome desk sat empty.

"Maybe we're too late," Horn said. He lowered his bandanna and spat onto the tile floor.

"Keep moving," Beckham said.

Riley guided the team to the door at the end of the hallway. "Key card," he yelled, waving Ellis forward. The doctor ran the plastic card over the security panel a moment later. It beeped and unlocked.

Pulling on the handle, Riley moved inside the columned stairwell first. He aimed his shotgun down the stairs. "Looks clear."

"Where to, Doctor?" Beckham asked.

Ellis pointed down.

Riley moved like a ghost, hopping down two stairs at a time and landing on the balls of his feet, the sound hardly audible.

When they reached Sublevel A, Ellis paused. He wiped a bead of sweat from his forehead and looked at Beckham. "Did you hear that?"

"What?"

Beckham strained to listen but heard nothing besides the faint crack of distant gunfire.

"Why are we stopped?" Horn asked, hocking another wad of spit onto the ground.

"Ellis thought he—" Beckham paused at the sound of a metal door slamming. The sound of skittering feet followed the echo. With clenched teeth, he looked up. The noise sounded as if it was coming from all around them. Another door swung open somewhere below.

"Fuck!" Riley said. "We got contacts moving up the stairwell."

"Up top too," Horn said, shouldering his M249.

Ellis panicked. "We have to get out of here!"

With nowhere to run, Beckham locked eyes with Riley. "Clear us a path, Kid."

Riley nodded. "You got it."

He disappeared around the next corner and a deafening blast reverberated through the stairwell. Beckham yelled, "Keep them off our six, Big Horn."

"On it!"

A moment later an ear-piercing crack from an M249 rang out.

Grabbing Ellis by his shirt, Beckham pulled the man down the next flight of stairs. They passed the mangled corpse of a female scientist, still in her lab coat. There was a hole the size of a melon in the middle of her chest where Riley had shot her.

"Oh shit, oh shit!" Ellis yelled. "That's Amy. I know her!" The doctor hesitated, pulling away from Beckham's grasp.

"*Keep moving!*" Beckham yelled, grabbing the doctor's arm.

Ellis stifled a whimper and followed Beckham down the next two flights of stairs. Riley fired again, the flash from his shotgun filling the dimly lit passage with flickers of light. The scent of gunpowder lingered in the air, mixing with the smell of scorched flesh.

The doctor gagged, and Beckham yanked on his shirt before Ellis had a chance to stop and puke. Unlike in Building 8, they weren't protected by the filtered breathing apparatus of a bio suit. They were breathing 100 percent natural air. And it smelled like a war zone.

"What floor?" Beckham yelled, before pulling his scarf over his mouth and nose.

"D! We're looking for D," Ellis managed to reply.

"Riley," Beckham said. "Did you—"

Another burst from Horn's M249 cut him off.

"I heard him!" said Riley's voice, after the sound had faded.

Beckham checked the sign at the next landing.

SUBLEVEL C.

LABS 5–10.

One more floor to go, Beckham thought. He jumped over the corpse of another scientist. The poor bastard had taken the shotgun blast to the face.

Riley waited for them at the next landing, his weapon aimed down the next set of stairs. Beckham patted him on the back and then moved Ellis in between the two of them with a soft push.

"Get us in, Ellis," Beckham ordered.

Ellis pulled the card from his pocket, his hand shaking. He reached around Riley and swept it over the surface of the panel just as Horn made it to the landing. Then he pressed his right eye against the sensor.

Footfalls echoed above them.

"We've got multiple contacts," Horn said, gasping for air. He reached for a new magazine and jammed it home into his rifle. "These things are fucking fast as shit!"

The guttural screams of the infected throbbed in Beckham's ears. He cringed at the subhuman sound.

A chirp from the keypad pulled Beckham back to the door. Grabbing the handle, he nodded at Riley and slowly opened it, revealing three terrified scientists.

"Kate! Michael!" Ellis yelled.

Beckham wasted no time. He shoved the doctor through the opening and then waited for Horn and Riley to safely enter the passage. Beckham slammed the door shut behind them just as one of the infected smashed into the other side.

The impact shook the metal door, prompting several cries from the group of scientists behind him. Beckham faced them. Running his sleeve across his forehead, he took a deep breath.

"Which one of you is Doctor Michael Allen?"

A bald, middle-aged man with bushy gray eyebrows stepped forward and raised his hand. "That's me. And who are you?"

"Master Sergeant Reed Beckham, with Delta Force Team Ghost. We're here to evacuate you, and we don't have much time. What's the best way out of here?"

Dr. Allen pointed over Beckham's shoulder. "The way you came."

Kate examined their rescue team. None of them were wearing biohazard suits, and blood peppered their uniforms. It was hard to grasp that just days ago she had been busy working on a cure for the new Ebola strain ripping through western Africa. Now the country was crumbling around her, and she didn't even know what they were dealing with.

Everything had happened so fast.

She rubbed her eyes, hiding any remnant of tears. The leader, Master Sergeant Beckham, stepped forward. He pulled a sand-colored bandanna away from his mouth to reveal a face rife with exhaustion.

He was a handsome man, taller than average, with large brown eyes and a chiseled jawline. Black tactical armor and green fatigues covered most of his olive skin. He tilted up his helmet and swiped his sweaty dark hair off his forehead...

Several bangs vibrated the door, jolting the soldier into action. He pointed to the door and shouted, "Is that really the only way out of here?"

Michael nodded. "Unless any of you have other ideas?" He looked to Kate and then to Kurt, the assistant who had alerted them to the news earlier.

"There's no emergency exit?" said a young-looking soldier, the one she'd heard Beckham call Riley.

"There is, but it's not accessible," Michael replied calmly.

"What do you mean, exactly?" Beckham asked.

"He means one of them is inside," Kurt said. "A coworker, upstairs. She was infected. We locked her in the other stairwell."

"Wonderful," Horn said.

"But there's only one infected in this other stairwell?" Beckham asked.

Michael shook his head. "No, there are others now too."

"Great," Riley said. "So it's back the way we came?"

Several of the creatures smashed into the door, the echo vibrating through the metal.

Kate's world blurred, time slowing around her. She could hear the banging and the awful screams, but she couldn't move. Paralyzed, she was forced to watch helplessly as Beckham barked orders. The other soldiers moved back to the entrance, weapons at the ready. There was a hand on her shoulder and more shouting.

A pinch to her wrist brought her back to reality. She glanced up to see Beckham's intense stare. "Doctor Lovato, are you with me? I need you to get with the program."

She managed the smallest of nods and then pulled free from his grasp. "I'm with you."

Beckham held her gaze for a second. She knew he was studying her, testing her to make sure she was okay. But was she? Could she do this?

She had to. There was no other choice.

With an uncontrolled, deep breath, she joined the group of scientists. Michael stood defiantly in the center of the team, with his arms crossed. In that moment he looked fearless.

"Here's the plan," Beckham shouted over the pounding. "We're going to open this door, lay down suppressing fire, and clear a path. Then we are going to make our way back to the surface, where our ride is waiting."

"You're going to open that door?" Kurt asked, his finger shaking as he pointed. "Can't we just wait this out? We have provisions down here that will last for weeks."

Beckham shook his head. He checked his wristwatch and then in a very calm voice said, "We have thirteen minutes to get the hell out of the city before the air force drops a massive payload on Atlanta."

Kate gasped. "They can't do that. How can they do that?"

"It's what I would do if I was the president," Michael replied.

"They're going to kill millions of innocent civilians?" Kate protested.

"The bombing will be strategic," Riley remarked. "But we don't know what the targets are." He pulled a bandanna with a smiling joker face over his mouth and reloaded his shotgun.

"Any other questions?" Beckham asked.

Kate felt her heart racing. *This can't be happening*, she thought. None of this was possible—her single worst nightmare now a reality. And with Javier gone . . . She pushed the thought aside and sucked in a lungful of filtered air.

Beckham was speaking again, and Kate focused on his words, letting them ground her. "Everyone, move back to those tables. Riley, you and Horn blast anything that comes through that door. When it's clear, everyone follows us out of here. I'll cover our six as we move. Got it?" Beckham said, scanning each face individually.

Kate nodded. Their eyes connected for the briefest of moments. There was strength there, inspiration.

"Okay, let's do this," Riley shouted. He pumped his shotgun and grabbed the door handle. "On three."

Kate listened to the soldier count.

"One."

"Two."

With his shotgun in his left hand and the door handle in his right, he yelled, "Three!"

The door clicked open and he fired off an immediate blast. The loud crack echoed through the room, pulsating inside Kate's head. She moved behind a lab station next to the others and cupped her ears. Through half-open eyes, she watched the room explode into chaos.

Three of the infected burst through the door, so fast they were just a blur of lab coats and skin.

Fire erupted from the barrel of Horn's machine gun. The bullets transformed the creatures into mulch. Flesh, bone, and blood peppered the floor. Both Horn and Riley backpedaled as they fired.

When the first three corpses hit the ground, another two creatures dashed through the doorway. They made it several steps before they were cut down. And still more came, a wave of four this time.

Jumping over the other bodies, they lunged forward, making it a few inches farther than the others. The clack of snapping joints reminded Kate they were dealing with a new virus, something completely different from what the world had ever seen.

She choked on the smell of smoke and listened to bullet casings rain down on the tile floor. She cringed, gagged, and dry-heaved over the floor. Shaking Michael's hand off her shoulder, Kate looked back to the carnage. She had to see this. She *needed* to see this. If she had any hope of surviving what was to come, she needed to watch how the soldiers moved. If she was going to keep up with them, she needed to mimic their actions as best as she could.

The pile of bodies in front of the door grew. People she had known and worked with lay there in pooling blood.

In less than a minute it was over. The three soldiers reloaded their weapons, dropping their spent magazines onto the floor.

"There'll be more," Beckham said calmly. "We need to move."

Michael was the first to walk away from the table. Ellis followed him, hesitating to look at Kate. She nodded and grabbed Kurt's shirt, tugging on his collar. He cowered under the table, his eyes closed and hands cupping his ears.

"Let's go," Kate said with a final jerk.

"Don't touch any of them," Michael said as he approached the bodies. "Any fluid will carry the virus."

Beckham paused and eyed his men. "Did you guys get any in your eyes or mouth?"

Both men hesitated and then shook their heads. Riley pulled his bandanna farther up his face and then repositioned his clear sunglasses.

"If you're infected, you will know it within minutes. At least, that's the average incubation period," Michael said. He shook his head as though he wasn't certain.

Beckham checked his watch again and then stepped over the nearest corpse. "We have nine minutes before those firebombs start dropping."

Riley and Horn moved into the stairwell and disappeared around the corner. Kate followed Michael and Beckham up the stairs soon after.

Using her sleeve, Kate covered her nostrils. The smell of

scorched flesh was overwhelming. She tried to force herself to look away from the destroyed bodies of the infected but found it was impossible. Yellow eyes stared up at her, following them as they moved, like the optical illusion in a portrait hanging on a wall.

Kate tucked her nose into her armpit and reached forward to grab the back of Beckham's vest.

The team moved slowly, in single file, with Riley at the helm. When they were halfway up the second stairwell, Kate stubbed her toe on something. Blinking, she looked down to see a body, its face blown away.

"Keep moving," Beckham whispered.

She cupped her free hand over her mouth and slowly nodded, following him to the first landing. Horn waited for them there, but Riley ran ahead.

Beckham looked up at her. "You good, Doc?"

Kate nodded and checked on Michael and Kurt, who had hung back a few stairs behind her, both men breathing heavily.

Adjusting his headset, Beckham said, "Echo Four, this is Ghost. Requesting evac. Over."

Kate heard a muffled voice crackle over the channel but couldn't make out the words.

"Roger, Echo Four. We're on the move. Out," Beckham said. His eyes found Kate's once more. "Okay, bird's on the way. Let's go."

Stepping around another twisted corpse, she followed him up the next two flights of stairs.

When they reached the final landing, Beckham paused. He peered around the corner and then rested his back against the concrete wall.

"Okay," he said, glancing down at Kate and the other scientists. "Riley and Horn are going to clear the lobby. Then we move outside to the chopper."

Before Kate or the others could reply, a new sound erupted from somewhere inside the facility. Her heart kicked as Riley came bursting down the stairs.

"We need to move," he said. "Now!"

"Let's go, people!" Beckham shouted.

Horn waited for them at the final doorway leading to the lobby. Swinging the door open, he rushed through. One by one they followed his lead into the atrium. The space looked like a war zone. Broken glass lay shattered across the floor, tables were flipped, and trails of blood streaked over the tiles. To the right was the main entrance to the building, which led to the lawn—to salvation. That's where the chopper would land.

Kate kept close to Michael, Ellis, and Kurt, following Beckham across the room. Riley was positioned at the edge of the central reception desk, his gun sweeping every corner of the room, stopping on a door leading to a hallway of conference rooms and offices.

"Contacts!" he yelled.

Kate froze, and the others crashed into her, pushing her forward. She regained her balance and spun back to see what Riley was talking about.

Pressed up against the cracked glass of the door leading to the hallway were three scientists, their lips clamped to the other side.

"No," she whispered, shaking her head as one of the creatures licked the glass, smearing blood across the pane with an audible squeak.

An emergency light flickered in the hallway behind the glass and illuminated an entire group of the infected.

"*Multiple* contacts!" Riley shouted.

The group reacted to the shouts by smashing into the doors, cracking the glass further.

"Riley, keep them off our six," Beckham yelled. "Horn, take point. The rest of you, follow me."

"Moving," Horn replied. He plowed ahead like a lineman hunting a quarterback.

Michael and Kurt pushed Ellis and Kate forward. As a group, they ran after Beckham. He paused at the main entrance, slipping carefully through the broken glass doors after Horn.

The whoosh of helicopter blades thumped outside the building as the black craft descended over the lawn. Kate stopped to watch Riley as her male colleagues fled the building in Beckham's wake. The door to the conference rooms was splintering from the weight of the infected pushed up against the panes. Two of them punched through the glass with hands morphed into claws.

"Hurry! This won't hold them for long," Riley shouted. He fired twice. The first blast hit a man in the chest, sending him crashing back into the growing throng behind him. The other shot broke through the glass and punched through a man's face. His head disappeared in a red cloud of mist, and his body slumped to the ground. The group surged forward and the glass finally gave way, shattering into a thousand pieces.

Kate ran from the small army of infected, forcing her gaze away.

Cool spring air and warm sun hit her bare arms a moment later. She was on the grass now. The Black Hawk hovered one hundred feet away. It felt surreal, as if she was in a dream.

A flash of motion to her right pulled her back to the chaos. A second pack of infected were rushing from around the corner of the building. Their warped bodies spasmed and creaked as they moved. Several of them dropped to all fours and galloped like wild animals across the lawn.

Kate's heart leaped at the sight. There were so many of

them, and they were so fast. So *very* fast. Beckham fired at the new group from behind a Humvee. Michael, Ellis, and Kurt crouched behind the Delta operator.

"Run!" he screamed as he changed magazines and bolted for the chopper. Kate fought the panic in her chest, putting everything she had into making it there with him. Horn was already inside the bird, firing from a standing position. Over the gunfire she heard a panicked voice.

"Wait up!"

That was Kurt. Or was it Ellis?

She wasn't sure. Kate twisted, and her heart nearly stopped when she saw her colleagues were lagging behind. The second pack was closing in, the sight of fresh meat whipping them into a frenzy. Their croaks and angry howls grew louder.

Horn's shots dropped two of the infected, but more took their place. A former soldier dropped to the ground and used his back legs to spring into the air. He landed on Kurt and knocked him onto the grass.

"No!" Kate yelled.

She watched helplessly as the man tore into Kurt's stomach. The assistant screamed in pain, his arms thrashing. "Help me! God, somebody, please help…" His voice trailed off as the ex-soldier clamped onto his neck and ripped a hunk of meat away, silencing Kurt forever.

A wave of nausea spiked through Kate.

The other infected caught up to the first, and the entire group stopped to feed, providing Ellis and Michael an opportunity to escape. Riley was right on their tail and sprinted past them.

"Move!" Beckham yelled. He yanked on Kate's sleeve and pulled her away from the view. She ran with him to the chopper, grabbed a handhold, and pulled herself inside.

Beckham remained on the ground. Horn lowered his rifle and jumped back to the grass to join the master sergeant. They fired side by side, their rifles sweeping across the field, picking off the infected with ease.

Kate flinched each time one of them dropped. These people were her former coworkers—her friends. She lost count after a dozen. Their ragged clothing and exposed skin became a blur of wild movement.

Ellis and Riley climbed into the chopper a few moments later, but Michael had fallen behind. He was limping, his hand clutching a thigh. The first group was almost on him, only a few feet away now.

He wasn't going to make it.

Gunfire cut down three of the monsters trailing him, but the precious extra seconds weren't enough.

Kate screamed in horror as another former soldier launched into the air, tackling Michael and sinking his teeth into his right arm.

Beckham rushed forward with his weapon blazing. The bullets tore into the infected man, red blood splattering on the grass. Grabbing Michael with his free hand, the soldier dragged him to safety.

Horn cut down the rest of the pack in one sweep of his machine gun. Together, he and Beckham hoisted Michael into the chopper.

Kate rushed to his side.

"I can't go with you," Michael choked.

"Get us out of here!" Beckham yelled to the pilot.

"No!" Michael grabbed his arm. "You have to leave me. I'm infected," he said, glancing down at his bloodied bicep.

Beckham followed Michael's eyes to the wound.

The chopper pulled away from the lawn and hovered. More of the creatures streamed out of the building.

"Fuck," Beckham said, shaking his head. "You sure about this, Doctor?"

Michael nodded. "Give me a gun."

"No," Kate whimpered. "We can save you."

Michael chuckled and then winced from the pain. "You always did think you could save the world, Kate." He stood, holding his injured arm.

Beckham pulled a pistol from a holster on his leg and handed it to him.

Kate reached forward. "You don't have to do this."

For a second they locked eyes and Michael said, "You're going to get your chance to save the world, Kate. Just remember, in order to kill a monster, you will have to create one." Closing his eyes, he jumped out onto the grass below, his knees giving out as he landed.

"No!" Kate yelled. She dropped to the floor and reached down for him, but someone grabbed her and yanked her back.

"Get us out of here!" Beckham yelled.

The Black Hawk pulled away, up toward the smoke-filled skyline. The pack turned away from the chopper and surrounded Michael. The grass and tree branches whipped wildly in the wind below.

"Michael!" she yelled. He looked up and found her eyes one last time before the horde consumed him.

As the chopper sped away, the faint pop of Michael's pistol faded against the roar of jets racing toward the city.

13

Colonel Gibson choked back a cough before taking another drag. His hand shook as he brought the cigarette to his lips.

Closing his eyes, he sucked in the smoke, holding it before exhaling through his nostrils. He pressed the glowing red end into an ashtray on his desk and then leaned forward to his keyboard.

He'd listened to the audio message Dr. Medford had sent, shortly before Building 8 went dark, more than a dozen times now. Memorizing the words. Five of them stuck in his mind.

Viral weapon is too contagious.

Gibson dug inside his chest pocket for his smokes and wedged another cigarette into his mouth. He leaned closer to his computer and keyed in his security credentials so he could play Medford's encrypted message again. The doctor's soft voice spilled out of the speakers a moment later.

"Colonel Gibson, it's Isaac Medford. Got an update for you. I've finally made a breakthrough. After months of work, I was able to successfully bond VX-99 with the Ebola virus. My only fear is that the viral weapon is too contagious. I doubt anyone will be able to link it back to the United States.

I've used a highly synthesized protocol designed to make the virus look as if it was formed in nature, but a good scientist will probably be able to determine it was lab engineered. I'm sending Jim Pinkman to Fort Detrick to brief you personally."

Gibson let the cigarette sag from his lips. "My God," he muttered, remembering the call he'd made to Medford days before. The call that he'd waited on for nearly an hour before he realized no one was going to pick up at Building 8.

Now the country he loved, the country he'd fought so hard to protect over a lifetime career with the Medical Corps, was collapsing right in front of him. And no matter how anyone sold the story, he was the one to blame. He had kept the secret chemical and biological weapons program going at Building 8 and several other locations.

He'd done so to protect America against her enemies. He wasn't one of the ignorant fools who believed Russia and China had stopped developing chemical weapons back in the nineties. They had massive stockpiles of the nastiest shit known to man—stuff that could melt your eyeballs and make you cough out a lung.

Gibson watched the cigarette smoke drift around his monitor. He knew people would call him a monster. They would never understand why he'd continued the VX-99 program. His vision had been simple: to create a bioweapon that could be deployed discreetly in hot spots abroad.

Jihadist groups such as Al-Qaeda, the Taliban, and ISIS instantly came to mind. VX-99 was supposed to reduce the need to send US soldiers abroad. The program he'd developed over the years was built around that vision. He'd dreamed of a weapon that could be used on foreign soil to kill enemy targets and then fizzle out with minimal civilian casualties. It would be untraceable.

As the facts slowly surfaced, Gibson realized that Medford's creation was far more deadly and contagious than any he could have imagined. Building 8 was supposed to be a vault within a vault, a maximum-security prison for the worst contagions known to man. In the end, all it had taken was a 180-pound scientist named Jim Pinkman to carry the virus like a Christmas present out of that vault and halfway across the country, to one of America's most populated cities.

Gibson flicked the ash off the end of his cigarette and cursed. He'd only wanted to protect his beloved country. He'd never meant for any of this to happen.

But there was still hope. Gibson always left himself outs. The facility he'd had constructed at Plum Island over the past two years was that out.

Taking up his phone, he called Lieutenant Colonel Ray Jensen. The man had taken Caster's place after the massacre at Building 8.

"This is Jensen," a rough voice answered on the other end of the line.

"You got a sitrep for me on Red Ice?"

"Yes, sir. Red Ice is depleted."

With his lungs full of smoke, Gibson resisted the urge to sigh in relief. The task was finally done. All correspondence between him and Dr. Medford had been destroyed. No one could prove he had known what Medford was up to. No one could prove that it was Gibson that had ordered him to experiment with VX-99. And no one could prove that it was Gibson who had told Dr. Medford to develop the perfect bioweapon—a combination of the worst of Mother Nature and the worst of man.

"Good," Gibson replied. "And the facility at Plum Island?"

"Finished, Colonel."

Gibson nodded. Two years of hard work and planning had

gone in to Plum Island, and it had been finished at just the right time. He'd requested the appropriations under the cover of research. It was the same card every commander before him had played to get competitive congressional earmarks. And in reality, it wasn't that far from the truth. Plum Island *was* a research center, built to carry out the mission of the VX-99 program. The facility was originally meant to develop the weapon, test it on live specimens, and then manufacture the final product. Now it would serve in a different capacity. The government would use it as a research center to find and manufacture a cure for whatever Medford had created.

"Sir, are you there?" Jensen said.

"Yeah. Just checking an e-mail," Gibson lied. "Are you en route to Plum Island yet?"

"No, sir. Chopper's late."

"Understood. See you there," Gibson said, clicking off the phone before Jensen had a chance to reply. He plucked the picture of his wife and son from his desk. The image had been taken eight years ago—before his wife had died of a stroke and before his son had been killed by an IED in Iraq. It was a snapshot of happier times—times that he had meant to protect. His motivation for developing the bioweapon had been to prevent more American soldiers from bleeding out on foreign soil—young men like Specialist Nick Gibson, his son. The loss had only inspired him to work harder on a bioweapon that could be used overseas—a weapon that was untraceable, deadly, and quick, a weapon that would kill and turn the insurgents and terrorists on one another and then fade away like a ghost in the night.

"What have I done, Connie?" Gibson asked, holding the picture under the dim lighting. "What on earth have I done?"

He set the frame carefully on the desk. That photo was the last time his family had been together. He could hardly remember that day now, or how happy he'd been then. Since their funerals, he'd focused all of his effort and work on the VX-99 program.

A chirp from his watch pulled him from the painful thoughts. He turned back to his computer to reread an e-mail he never thought he'd see. The air force had been given the green light to bomb American cities. They were taking to the skies all around the country and firebombing strategic locations to stop the outbreak. Gibson knew better than anyone that no matter how many bombs were dropped, the fires had little hope of stopping the viral storm that was tearing through the world—the storm he had created.

Beckham flexed his right bicep and rubbed at a knot. Glancing up, he caught Dr. Lovato staring at him with swollen eyes. She hadn't spoken a word since they'd left a burning Atlanta, and that was over six hours ago. He'd lost track of time during the journey.

Beckham continued massaging his arm, curious now about the doctor. She looked young for a scientist, and he guessed she was in her thirties. With dark brown hair and blue eyes, she definitely was not the stereotypical virologist he imagined working for CDC. Ellis fit the description better, with his slicked-back hair and glasses.

Kate was obviously important, especially now that her boss had just been torn to shreds. Just how important she was, Beckham wasn't sure, but he knew Colonel Clinton wouldn't have authorized the mission if her team didn't possess significant value.

The main pilot's voice popped into Beckham's earpiece, and he looked away from Kate.

"New York City visual imminent. Flyby in thirty seconds."

"Copy," Beckham replied. He adjusted the strap attached to his MP5 and repositioned himself so he could get a better look. The dazzling lights of the city made the skyline glow. All looked calm. No smoke or fire that he could see. He decided to break the silence that had plagued the long flight.

"Heard anything about other cities getting bombed?" Beckham asked the pilots.

"Chicago, Minneapolis, Saint Louis, Kansas City. The list goes on."

Beckham watched Riley fidgeting in his seat. "What about Des Moines?"

"Negative. No word on Des Moines," the pilot replied.

Horn reached over and patted Riley's leg. "I'm sure your folks got out."

The kid nodded and looked out the window.

A slow and distant roar rumbled through the helicopter. Beckham knew the sound and scanned the sky for the jets.

There, heading south, into the city, were six tiny black dots, a faint blue tail of exhaust trailing a wing of F-22 Raptors. There were others too, larger planes. A fucking flight wing of other aircraft.

He scrambled to his feet and duckwalked across the metal floor for a better look. The Raptors suddenly changed course, fanning out across the city.

"Get us out of here!" Beckham yelled, realizing they were in the jets' flight path.

"Hold on."

The chopper pulled to the east, and Beckham reached out to brace himself against the window. Ellis and Kate both let out startled cries.

In the split second it took Beckham to blink, the lead Raptor swooped low. He watched in shock as missiles streaked away from the jet and zigzagged around skyscrapers. Another blink and the weapons found their targets, exploding in massive fireballs. The second wave of aircraft dropped firebombs. Flames lit up the streets, extending like a river of lava through the city.

"Oh my God!" Ellis yelled, pointing out the window.

The thump of more detonations vibrated through the chopper as more planes released their arsenals. Beckham thought of all the innocent civilians who were dying in the inferno below.

He knew better than anyone that it was likely a seventy-year-old general with a chestful of ribbons ordering the attacks, impervious to the ripple effect that came with the decision. At that point, commanders were so far removed from war they didn't really think about the average grunt or civilian. The end game was all that mattered, and in this case, it was to stop a microscopic enemy. Total annihilation was the only viable course of action for these men who had lost touch with what it meant to be human.

Another series of bombings shook the craft as the skyline lit up with orange flames.

There has to be another way, Beckham thought. His headset crackled again, and the pilot said, "I'm hearing a lot of chatter over the net here. Apparently, the president has ordered air strikes in every major city. Strategic locations only, mostly hospitals and clinics."

Kate spoke for the first time in several hours. Cupping her headset, she yelled, "They're trying to stop the spread before it blooms out of control. That will buy us time to find a cure."

Beckham regarded her with a cocked eyebrow. "How do you know that, Doctor?"

"Because that's what I would do if I was in charge."

"This is fucking insane," Riley said.

Horn took off his helmet and tossed it across the chopper. "They can't fucking do this! Those are innocent people down there!"

"They have to stop the spread," Kate said. Her voice was reserved but strong.

Shaking his head, Beckham stared at the destruction. They were flying over the ocean now, the light from a bright moon glimmering over the water below them. The juxtaposition of the burning city and the calm ocean seemed odd.

The sight of the new One World Trade Center tower put everything into perspective. A wave of crimson flames surrounded the building. New York had been hit once again, this time by a different type of enemy—an enemy Beckham wasn't sure they could stop.

The small USB drive onto which Michael had downloaded their research burned a hole in Kate's vest. She dug inside the pocket, searching for the small, metallic stick to make sure it was still there. She felt a sigh of relief when her fingers wrapped around the tiny device. Her mentor hadn't died in vain.

Kate was at her breaking point. She'd been close before— Sudan, in 2009, came to mind. A shortage of medical supplies had prevented her team from stopping a deadly malaria outbreak that claimed the lives of nearly every child in a remote village.

Those weeks had nearly pushed her over the edge, but this—this was the end of modern civilization. She'd lost Javier, she'd lost Michael, and the entire world was crashing down around her.

After the Black Hawk touched down at Plum Island, Riley quickly slid open the door. Bright white light spilled into the chopper, revealing a circular formation of white, domed buildings in the distance. The industrial floodlights showed an island transformed. The hum of generators and cough of diesel engines from construction equipment and military vehicles filled the night.

"Looks like they were ready for this," Horn said. He pulled his skull bandanna away from his mouth and spat onto the concrete.

The sight of the domed facilities pulled Kate to her feet. She hurried to the door and wedged her body between the two men for a better look.

The buildings weren't the portable Level 4 facilities used in hot zones, and at first glance she wasn't sure what to make of them. Kate didn't know much about Plum Island, but from what she could see, these buildings looked brand new.

A spotlight sweeping the dusty ground illuminated the nearest structure. She recognized the symbol above the double doors immediately. It was the insignia of the US Army Medical Research Institute of Infectious Diseases—but that didn't make any sense. For decades the Department of Agriculture had operated on Plum Island, and in 2003 the Department of Homeland Security had taken ownership.

Shoving her way past Beckham and Horn, Kate jumped down to the concrete.

"Wait up," Beckham called out.

She hesitated, the blades of the Black Hawk making a final rotation above her before slowing to a stop. She used the moment to study the buildings surrounding the tarmac. She counted a total of six white domes. All of them bore the insignia of USAMRIID.

On the tarmac, two Humvees pulled to a stop in front of them. The doors popped open, and four men in CBRN suits jumped down. Each of them held a rifle.

"It's all right," Beckham said. "Just follow their orders."

Kate nodded slowly, trying to control her breathing. She couldn't see the faces of the men behind their visors, which made her feel even worse.

One of them took five steps toward the chopper, where he stopped and raised a hand. "Everyone stay put." He swept a flashlight over Beckham's blood-soaked uniform. "Why aren't you wearing suits?"

"Command—" Beckham started to reply when the lead soldier angled his light into the operator's eyes.

"Stay put," he said in a deliberately low and calm voice. "I'm Major Sean Smith. Everyone remain calm, and we will get you through the decontamination procedures as quickly as possible. Before we start, will Doctor Michael Allen please come forward?"

Beckham shot Kate a cursory glance, locking eyes with her for a second before turning back to the officer.

"He didn't make it out of Atlanta," Beckham said grimly.

The response had no visible impact on Smith. After a short pause, he said, "Please form a single-file line and don't touch one another."

Another Humvee tore across the tarmac, skidding to a stop somewhere behind the chopper. Kate assumed their job was to make sure the Black Hawk was decontaminated.

Smith asked a series of questions about how she and the others were feeling and if they were experiencing any hallucinations or pain.

"I'm fine," Beckham replied. "We are all fine. None of us are experiencing any symptoms. None of us are infected."

"I'm asking everyone, Sergeant. Not just you," Smith replied.

Beckham held up a hand. "Okay, sir."

After they had all replied satisfactorily, Smith led them toward the first of the dome-shaped buildings.

Two armed guards stood outside, their M4s at the ready. Above them a small floodlight illuminated a USAMRIID sign.

"This is the decon facility," Smith said. "Inside you will go through a rigorous process to ensure you are not infected."

Kate raised her hand. "Where's the rest of CDC been relocated?"

"I'm afraid I don't have access to that information, Doctor...?"

"Lovato. Doctor Kate Lovato," she replied.

"I don't understand. Who's in charge of this island?" Ellis said.

"The United States Army," Smith responded without hesitating. "There's plenty of time to explain later, but for now the most important thing is ensuring you aren't infected. Please," he said, gesturing toward the building with a hand. "Doctors Lovato and Ellis will go first. Team Ghost will follow."

A cool breeze blew a strand of hair into Kate's eyes. She brushed it away and looked for Beckham's approval. He'd saved her and Ellis, and he'd done his best to save Michael and Kurt.

The man offered her a nod and then looked away. Beckham seemed skeptical. His gaze scrutinized their surroundings. Was he thinking the same thing she was—that there was more to the facility than met the eye?

She followed Major Smith toward the decon chambers, but paused at the entrance when she saw flames licking the horizon behind them. New York City was burning.

14

A lean African American officer waited on the steps outside the decontamination facility.

"Welcome to Plum Island. I'm Lieutenant Colonel Ray Jensen," he said. He reached out and shook Beckham's hand first, with a powerful grip.

The master sergeant was still shaking from the cold shower and chemicals he'd endured during decon, and the distant roar of jets and explosions echoing through the night unnerved him. He had never thought he'd hear the sounds of war on their home turf.

After brief introductions, Team Ghost followed the two Medical Corps officers away from the decontamination building, talking as they walked.

"Bombing our own cities?" Riley asked.

Smith stopped in his tracks and massaged the wedding ring on his finger. "None of you know, do you?"

Beckham cleared his throat from the rear of the group. "Know what?"

"The president has declared martial law nationwide. The Medical Corps is in charge of Operation Reaper."

"What the hell is Operation Reaper?" Riley asked.

Jensen crossed his arms and, with a stern face, said, "The fight to save the country."

"Necessary sacrifice to stop the spread of the virus," Smith added. "With strategic bombing, civilian casualties will be kept to a minimum."

"Those bombs didn't look strategic to me," Horn said.

"The virus is spreading too fast," Jensen replied. "The military is doing everything it can to limit loss of life."

Riley jumped in. "How is this thing spreading so fast?"

"Incubation period ranges from minutes to hours," Smith replied in the same calculated tone. "Once we get you to the barracks, you will receive a full briefing."

"Barracks?" Horn asked. Even in the dim light, Beckham could see the man's cheeks reddening.

"Plum Island is now on lockdown. Only evacuees with the highest level of clearance will be authorized to land here. You guys are lucky as hell. You were the last bird in before we closed the doors."

Horn immediately stepped forward. "Better check on that, because we're headed back to Fort Bragg."

Jensen shot Horn a strict glare and then said, "I need to brief the CDC doctors you evacuated earlier. Major Smith will escort you to the barracks."

"Yes, sir," Smith said. He swept a finger over his nose and watched Jensen hurry off toward another building before regarding Horn with a smirk. "You heard the man. Your orders are to head where you're told to head and stay put when you're told to stay put. No one's allowed in or out now without authorization."

Beckham watched Horn's face turn cherry red. He knew the look well. Horn was about to explode.

Taking a deep breath, Horn took a second, guarded step

toward the man. With his chest swelling, he leaned closer until he was face-to-face with the officer.

"My family is waiting at Fort Bragg, so we are *leaving*," Horn replied. "And no one is going to stop us."

"Command will have to authorize that."

Horn snorted in Smith's face, but the officer wasn't intimidated. He turned and said, "Follow me."

Beckham nodded. "Let's go, Horn."

Horn hesitated, frustration showing on his face.

"Staff Sergeant Parker Horn, that's an order," Beckham said sternly.

The operator glared at him and then reached for a cigarette in his chest pocket. "I heard you the first time." He jammed one in his mouth as they walked toward the final dome-shaped building.

A pair of armed soldiers stood guard outside. They saluted and moved aside. Smith pushed open the double steel doors to reveal men and women from every branch of the military. The personnel filled the room, some in groups talking in hushed whispers, others huddling around televisions watching the news. Beckham narrowed his eyes, taking in the view quickly. The space was a warehouse of cots and gear. It looked as if they were in this for the long haul.

"Find an empty bed and it's yours," Smith said. "There will be a briefing at twenty-three hundred." He looked at Horn one more time before leaving.

Beckham tossed the new gear bag they'd assigned him after decon onto the nearest empty cot and loosened the strap to his new MP5. He placed the weapon on the bed and then looked for Horn. The man's face was still red.

"Listen," Beckham began to say.

Horn raised a hand. "Not now, man. Not now."

Beckham wouldn't argue with Horn, not when he was

fuming. It was futile. At times like these he still wondered how the man had ever passed the intense psych evaluations required of all Delta Force operators.

"Just give him a few minutes," Riley whispered. He gestured at a crowd of marines surrounding a television. "Want to check the news?"

"Not really," Beckham replied. He walked with Riley anyway.

"He'll be all right," Riley said when they were out of earshot from Horn.

"Eventually," Beckham replied. "How are you holding up, Kid?"

Riley fidgeted with his bandanna. "Man, this shit is *fucked* up. I'm worried about my parents. They're in the dead center of this thing."

"Hopefully they made it out of Des Moines before things got really bad."

"I sent them an e-mail on day two. Told them to head to my brother's house in Arkansas. He lives in the country. Real isolated community."

"The perfect place to ride this thing out."

They maneuvered their way into the crowd of marines and found a spot to watch the news. Beckham tapped a tall man on the shoulder.

"What's CNN say?" he asked.

The young marine twisted and offered up a nod.

"It's the zombie apocalypse. Same thing they've been saying for days," the man said. "You just get here?"

"Yeah."

The man eyed Beckham's uniform again and stuck out a hand. "I'm Staff Sergeant Johnson."

"Master Sergeant Reed Beckham," he replied, shaking the man's hand.

Johnson stiffened a bit and brought his hands to the small of his back. "What brought you here, Master Sergeant—if you don't mind me asking?"

"Evac," Beckham replied. "You?"

Johnson grinned. "Security. We're here to keep those things from getting in."

Beckham regarded the man with a cocked brow. "You haven't come face-to-face with one yet, have you?"

The smile faded from the man's face. "No, Master Sergeant."

"Find me after you do. See if your attitude has changed," Beckham said. "Assuming you survive."

Johnson gulped and nodded.

The PA system barked to life before the marine could respond.

"Attention, all personnel. Please make your way to the front of the room. Colonel Gibson's briefing will begin in ten minutes."

Riley and Beckham exchanged confused looks.

"*Gibson's* here?" Riley said.

Beckham blinked, trying to make sense of the announcement. He remembered the USAMRIID symbols all over the base. Gibson was the commanding officer of the infectious diseases division. It *would* make sense for him to be here, but the rest of it didn't add up. Plum Island didn't make sense. The construction was brand new, as if it had been planned, and the mission at Building 8 had been off, the intel shaky. Was it possible Gibson's presence was just a coincidence, or was there something else going on? If he found out that the colonel *was* connected in a sinister way to the outbreak, he was going to...

Beckham's knuckles popped.

"Boss?" Riley asked. "You thinking what I'm thinking?"

Hesitating, Beckham waited for the crowd to shuffle away from the television. Riley inched closer and asked his question again in a low voice.

"Something's fucking off," Beckham replied. "I don't know how everything's connected yet, but something's definitely fucking off." He'd been an operator for over a decade. His job was to read people and situations. He was damn good at it, and he had his doubts that Plum Island and Building 8 were just a coincidence.

There was no trace of satisfaction as the revelation hit Beckham. He felt nothing but disgust. If he was right, then the virus seizing the nation was human engineered. But he knew he needed evidence for such a bold claim—evidence that had burned the moment San Nicolas Island and Building 8 were vaporized.

Beckham cursed.

"We better find Big Horn," Riley said, eyeing Beckham.

Nodding, Beckham followed Riley back to their cots. Horn was resting, his eyes fixated on a ceiling fan above.

"You ready to hear how bad things are, boss?" Horn asked.

Beckham felt a lump form in his throat. He had a feeling they were going to hear more than just what was going on outside—they were going to learn Plum Island was their new home for the foreseeable future.

The decon had gone smoothly, but Kate couldn't seem to put her mind at ease. It was swimming with questions. Nothing was adding up. Plum Island, the *virus*. None of it made any sense. She reached into the pocket of the pants they'd given her and clutched the small USB drive as she followed

Lieutenant Colonel Jensen toward one of the white, domed structures. Ellis was waiting outside.

"You all right?" Kate asked, scanning her colleague.

"I'm fine," Ellis said. He shivered.

"Doctors," Jensen said. "I'll give you a tour of your lab."

Kate stared up at the building, marked with a sign that simply read "1."

"This is where you will work and live," Jensen said. He opened the double doors and gestured for her and Ellis to go inside. "You will be assigned private rooms later. They are located on the other side of the building."

They took a metal staircase to an observation deck. At the top, a glass wall separated them from the rest of the staircase. The facility took her breath away. Designed in the shape of a hexagon, the space was unlike anything Kate had ever seen.

Below were five other compartments, all built around a central storage area. Scientists performed tests from the safety of their compartments outside, utilizing the automated robots inside the middle room.

Banks of LEDs hung from the dome ceiling, spreading an intense white glow over the space below. Everything about Building 1 was impressive, and Kate felt clean just looking at it.

"As you can see, the building is split into six compartments. We are overlooking Section 1. That's Toxicology," Jensen said, pointing. He swept his finger from room to room, identifying each space.

"Doctor Lovato," he said sternly. "You have been promoted to lead of Section 3. Your job is to figure out what we are dealing with and then find a cure. Doctor Ellis, you will assist her."

Kate nodded. She'd heard what the man said but was so

captivated by the technology she could hardly think. She couldn't get over the fact the building looked brand new—as if USAMRIID *knew* this was all going to happen.

Shaking the paranoid thought away, she said, "I'd like to get started."

"Of course, Doctor," Jensen replied. "This way."

They moved back down the staircase and took a left at the bottom of the stairs. Jensen paused to remove a key card from his pocket and then waved it over the surface of a security panel. "We'll get cards for you and Doctor Ellis shortly. We just haven't had time. Everything's been so rushed."

The door chirped and unlocked. Jensen led them into the decontamination chamber. Inside, a wall with several windows in it separated them from a series of glass cylinders. The entire space smelled like chemicals, a scent Kate had grown used to, but there was also something minty there too. It reminded her of a dentist's office.

Jensen pointed to several rows of plastic curtains. "Suits are beyond those." He checked his wristwatch and said, "I need to get going. I'm sure you know the drill. A technician will help you once you are inside."

Kate nodded. "Thank you, Lieutenant Colonel."

Ellis took a step toward Jensen, but Kate reached out and grabbed his wrist.

Jensen raised a skeptical brow and straightened his beret before leaving the room.

"What did you do that for? I had a few questions," Ellis said.

Kate held his gaze. "Something's wrong." She scanned the walls for cameras and saw one angled down at them.

Narrowing her eyes, Kate studied her colleague. It was then she realized he had no idea what was going on. The facility seemed normal to him—or, if he had any suspicions, he wasn't talking.

"Let's get to work," she said.

"Wait." Ellis reached out and patted her on her right shoulder. "I saw where this all started," he said. He took in a short breath. "Doctor Medford created something awful, Kate. Our worst nightmare."

Kate remembered Michael's final words.

In order to kill a monster, you'll have to create one.

Massaging her temples, she tried to think. What had he meant? Did he want her to create something even worse, something that could kill the virus?

"Let's suit up," Kate said. "It's time to stop talking and figure out how this thing works. We're running out of time."

Ellis ran a hand through his hair and sighed. "You're right—and you're in charge now."

The chirp of crickets and low hum of generators filled the night. Colonel Gibson walked briskly across the island, with Lieutenant Colonel Jensen at his side. Guilt ate at him with every step. With every moment that passed, the virus continued to spread. More people would die. The country was tearing itself apart, and it was *his* fault. The only thing that motivated him to keep working was the hope of finding a cure. Plum Island now housed some of the brightest scientists in the world. If anyone could find a way to stop the viral monster Dr. Medford had created, it would be someone here, under his command.

He knew the truth would eventually come out. And when it did, he would own up to his sins, but for now he had to keep going, to minimize collateral damage. To keep the ship sailing, Plum Island had to survive—for the sake of the entire human race.

With his hand shaking, Gibson stopped and reached for a cigarette as he examined the six dome-shaped buildings built in a hexagonal layout on the island. Industrial floodlights spread a glowing white carpet over the base, revealing what two years of careful planning had accomplished.

"Sir, we should keep moving," Jensen said.

The man was an invaluable asset to Gibson. He was a soldier's soldier, always completing objectives, never questioning orders. He would have been perfect to help on the VX-99 program, but Jensen was also an ethical man. His eyes had a way of deceiving him when he received difficult orders. For that reason Gibson had never brought him in on what he was doing at Building 8.

"One before we go in," Gibson finally replied, with a cigarette stuck between two fingers. He took a drag and looked out over the base. Beyond the buildings, dozens of guard towers protruded behind a two-story wall. He couldn't see the electrical fences topped with razor wire on the other side, but he knew they were there. He'd approved the layout two years ago.

He'd led the design team, which hired an architect specializing in maximum-security prisons. Gibson's request was simple: Keep people out. And while most security firms worked to keep prisoners from escaping, this architect had gone to great lengths to ensure no one would ever get inside without authorization. From the looks of it, he'd done a remarkable job.

"Sir, you're late to your briefing," Jensen said behind him.

Gibson nodded and took a drag. He was trying to buy himself more time, still unsure what he would say. He'd considered telling them the truth: that this virus was human engineered and that, at the end of the day, he was the one responsible. But morale was already failing, and he didn't particularly want to be lynched in a courtyard. Although part of him knew he deserved such a fate.

Wedging the cigarette between his lips again, he took in one long, final drag. With his eyes halfway closed, he saw a chopper flying low over the ocean toward the island.

Exhaling, he said, "You see that?"

Jensen took a step forward and narrowed his eyes. "Yes, sir, but I don't remember any authorized flights."

"Looks civilian," Gibson replied, noting a single floodlight sweeping over the water.

Jensen instantly picked up his radio. "Air Defense, this is Lieutenant Colonel Jensen, over."

"Copy, this is Air Defense. Go ahead."

"We have an unidentified helo heading westbound, en route to home turf."

The chopper hovered over the ocean on the west shore of the island. Gibson watched it closely. His hands shook nervously at his sides. He shoved them in his pockets, hoping Jensen hadn't noticed.

"Copy that— we see it and are communicating with the pilot. It's full of refugees from New York. Please advise. Over."

Jensen grunted before bringing the radio back to his mouth. In an annoyed tone, he said, "Tell them they *can't* land. We aren't taking refugees. *Over.*"

The chopper continued to hover, the lights bobbing up and down over the shoreline.

The radio clicked back on. "Sir, they say they need medical support."

Jensen shot Gibson a concerned look, but the colonel offered no trace of reassurance. Orders were clear. They couldn't risk infection.

With a sigh, Jensen brought the radio to his mouth. He

hesitated and then said, "Tell them we will shoot them down if they attempt to land."

There was another brief pause, more static joined the chirping crickets.

"Copy that, sir."

Gibson waved Jensen forward, and they continued down the path to the barracks.

For a moment he thought of the passengers and the overwhelming fear they were experiencing. There were probably kids on board, but in the end it didn't matter. They simply couldn't risk compromising Plum Island. It was far too important.

He winced when two rockets streaked away from a pair of guard towers. The first shot raced past the chopper, but the second hit it in the side. The aircraft exploded in a bright orange fireball.

"Jesus," Jensen said, raising a hand to shield his face from the heat.

Gibson dropped his cigarette and suffocated it with his boot. What he'd just witnessed was only the beginning. He tried not to think of the humans on board the aircraft as another explosion ripped through the fiery wreckage on the beach. He didn't have time for empathy right now.

"We better go, sir," Jensen urged.

With a nod, Gibson followed the man to the building.

"What the hell was that?" a panicked guard asked as they approached.

Jensen held up a hand. "A necessary precaution, soldier."

The man stood to attention when he saw the officers but kept his gaze on the fire raging in the distance. He said nothing further.

A second guard opened the doors, and Gibson walked into the room. Inside, the barracks swelled with commotion. Hundreds of uniformed men and women were talking anxiously.

"Room, atten-tion!" Jensen yelled.

The chatter quickly diminished and faded to a few hushed whispers. A female marine in the front of the crowd said, "Sir, was that an explosion?"

Gibson gave his second in command a short, approving nod.

"What you heard was a precaution," Jensen said. He kept his tone calm and measured. "There was a civilian helicopter with infected on board. They were warned not to attempt a landing before they were shot down."

Gibson pulled his hands from his pockets as Jensen moved out of the way. Grabbing the mic, Gibson repositioned it and then swept his eyes over the room with a commanding gaze. "I am Colonel Rick Gibson, commanding officer of the US Army Medical Research Institute of Infectious Diseases. Tonight, I carry a heavy burden. Tonight, I have grave news to share with you all."

The room was completely silent.

"In just four days, an outbreak of a new and deadly virus has swept our nation, spreading to every corner. It's made its way to Mexico and Canada. All of our efforts to stop the infection have failed. In a last-ditch attempt, the air force was authorized to conduct strategic bombing runs in most major cities."

He paused to let the information sink in. The room was packed with frightened soldiers and scientists—men and women who had families outside. The news was devastating, and seeing their horrified looks only intensified the guilt slowly devouring him.

Gripping the sides of the podium, he continued. "There's no easy way to say this, but you all deserve to know the truth.

Millions of innocent civilian lives have already been lost in an attempt to stop the spread of the virus, and millions more will perish in the coming days."

Chatter erupted, panicked voices ringing out from every corner of the room. Jensen stepped forward with a hand raised, and the crowd quieted.

"There is some good news," Gibson continued. "Fortunately, we find ourselves in one of the safest locations in the world. This facility is fully equipped and ready to develop, test, and manufacture a cure for the virus. And the scientists amongst you are the most capable in the world. Your job," he said looking out over the crowd, "is to find a cure."

Gibson stepped back from the podium and crossed his arms. "There are also amongst you some of the country's most experienced and most highly trained soldiers. Your job is to protect the integrity of this installation."

As he continued, he felt the strength he'd known as a commander returning. In that moment, he was the same man he'd been weeks before, the colonel who wanted nothing more than to protect America from her enemies.

"Make no mistake," he said, his voice deeper now. "You will all face tough orders. You will be forced to make hard calls, and you may be forced to kill in order to survive. Some of you have already faced such challenges and some of you have not. If we fail, this could very well be the end of the human race. This could be our extinction event."

Clearing his throat, he said, "But our country is not lost yet. I believe that in the end we will prevail. Things will not be easy, and victory will come with a high price. I hope you are all prepared to make sacrifices, for I believe this is the only way we will survive this new war."

Folding his arms, he waited for questions. A hand shot up near the back row.

"Go ahead, son."

"Master Sergeant Reed Beckham, with Delta Force Team Ghost. I'm wondering if you could tell us more about the infection and where it originated?"

Gibson squinted at the lean man in the crowd. Team Ghost, the same Delta team he'd sent to Building 8. They were here. He couldn't fucking believe it.

"The virus originated in a US lab, on US soil. We're still putting the pieces together, and we will inform everyone when we know more. Until then, I've put this installation on lockdown, and I ask you all to stay in your barracks until further notice."

Gibson stepped away from the podium, and Jensen took his place.

"Ranking officers and NCOs, take charge of your personnel. That is all," the man said before he and Gibson exited the building.

Kate stared through the glass separating her from her new office. A trio of USAMRIID scientists huddled around a monitor on the other side. They were busy trying to find a cure for the virus that had killed Michael and transformed Javier into a monster.

A sudden memory of their final moments flashed before her, and for the first time in her life, she felt a debilitating sense of anxiety. So much had happened in such a short amount of time. How could she even begin to work?

Don't start now, she thought. She had to be strong. She couldn't let them die in vain.

When she looked back through the glass, one of the scientists was looking at Kate as if she could read her thoughts.

To her surprise, the woman waved. Squinting, Kate saw a scientist even younger than herself staring back through an oversized visor. She gestured for Kate to come inside.

Taking a deep breath, she finished putting on her suit.

Ellis pulled on a pair of gloves with a snap. "You ready for this?"

She nodded and took in her first breath of filtered air. There was a minty scent to it—the same one she'd picked up on before—and she didn't hate it.

"We better get started," he said, walking past her.

He punched in the access code that Smith had given them and waited. The glass door chirped and then hissed open.

An intense white light flooded over them as they walked side by side into the first compartment. The woman who had waved approached them. Kate couldn't believe how young she looked and wondered if she was even in her thirties.

"Welcome to Plum Island. I'm Cindy Hoy, with USAMRIID," she said, looking at Kate and Ellis in turn. "I've been assigned to your division. I'm very sorry to hear about the loss of Doctor Allen."

"Thank you," Kate said. "If you could show us our stations, I'd really like to get started." Her tone was apprehensive. She cringed at the sound, hardly recognizing her own voice.

"Absolutely. Please follow me," Cindy replied, gesturing them forward.

They crossed the room to another glass door marked RESTRICTED CLEARANCE.

Cindy punched in her code and waved her card over the security panel. "Only about ten people on the island have access to this room."

The door unlocked with a metallic click, and they stepped through in single file. Inside, they approached a single round station with four monitors positioned on top. Kate could see right away that this was not the type of lab she was used to working in.

"Everything's automated, although you don't have to use the robotics to bring samples inside the lab; hence the positive-pressure suits or space suits, whatever you want to call them," Cindy said. "All samples are housed in bio cabinets." She pointed at the cylindrical glass room in the center of the building.

Kate could see the robotic arms moving back and forth inside, vials and test tubes in their mechanical claws.

Cindy pointed at the lab station. "These computers will allow you to control the robotic interfaces that will in turn conduct tests for you. The idea is to—"

"Cut down the risk of accidents," Kate said, finishing the woman's thought for her.

Cindy nodded. "That's the idea."

Ellis ran a gloved hand across the sleek surface of the desk. "I've never seen a lab like this."

"I helped with the design," Cindy replied. "My background is in virology, but I also have a degree in engineering. Odd, I know."

"Makes sense," Kate said, finally understanding why the military had hired someone so young. The woman was a rare find in a field dominated by men and rife with fossils who never seemed to retire.

Cindy dropped her hands to her sides and joined Ellis at the station, where she typed in her user name and password. A screen with the USAMRIID symbol popped up. "Before we get started, I think you should see some images of patients."

"We've seen some of them already," Kate said. She and Ellis gathered around the monitor as Cindy typed in several commands. A picture of an elderly man emerged on the screen. He lay in a hospital bed, clutching his right arm and wincing in pain.

"See anything odd about this guy?"

Ellis shook his head. "Not besides the nasty bite wound on his forearm."

"That's because he exhibited no symptoms from the injury for nearly two hours. He carried the disease to Atlanta. So did a handful of other victims."

She clicked to the next image, revealing the corpse of a middle-aged man lying on a gurney. Only the man no longer looked like a man. Cindy scrolled through the pictures, talking as she moved. "These pictures were taken during the autopsy that CDC doctor Ted Lucas performed before Chicago was overrun. We're calling this person Patient 4."

A headshot of the patient revealed the same pale, bulging lips she'd seen on the other infected.

"As you can see, the victim's lips have changed to form a sucker," Cindy said, zooming in. "If you look close enough, you'll see tiny hairlike spikes that allow the mouth to clamp onto flesh."

"How is that possible?" Ellis asked.

Cindy shook her head and continued to the next slide. The screen filled with another headshot. Patient 4's lips were held back with clamps to show bright red, receded gums and a mouthful of sharp, yellow teeth.

"It's important to point out that all victims seem to exhibit some level of intelligence, particularly when faced with their need to kill and feed. Fortunately for us, the virus does damage the frontal lobe, cutting down on a victim's ability to do things like drive cars or shoot weapons," Cindy said.

Kate crossed her arms and focused on the picture, shuddering inside her suit. "Ebola typically debilitates victims so they can't perform even the most basic of functions. In the final stages of hypotensive shock, or low blood pressure, most victims can hardly even open their eyes."

"This is different from anything you have seen in the field, Doctor Lovato," Cindy replied. "In fact, victims are able to see better than the average person. The virus has affected their eyesight. Look at this," she said as she brought up another picture.

"This is Patient 4's eye."

Kate and Ellis gasped simultaneously. The peeled-back eyelid revealed a dual membrane and a pupil that had morphed into a vertical slit reminiscent of a reptilian eye.

"How?" Ellis whispered. Then he mumbled something to himself that Kate couldn't make out.

Cindy cut to the chase. "That's why you're here." Pointing at the screen, she said, "Due to the connection with VX-99, scientists have given this strain of Ebola a new name. They are calling it X9H9, or the hemorrhage virus. But the question now is, what do you two know about the hemorrhage virus?"

Reaching for the USB drive in her pocket, Kate said, "We've already sequenced the genome of the virus and discovered the fourth gene is different from the virus that caused the outbreak in Guinea. I believe Doctor Medford found a way to modify the glycoprotein in an attempt to stop the virus from attacking all of the endothelial cells. This prevents the victim from bleeding out internally."

Cindy nodded.

"But we still don't know what is causing the other symptoms or changes. And I need to know exactly what we're dealing with before I can start work on developing a cure," Kate added. She began to speak more rapidly as she compartmentalized the task for the team.

"It's quite obvious that the virus did not mutate naturally. We now know Doctor Medford was experimenting with VX-99 chemicals. I need to know what happened in his lab. Cindy, that's your job."

"On it," she replied.

"Ellis, you're with me," Kate continued. "It's time to infect some mice with a sample of the virus."

15

April 22, 2015
DAY 5

Beckham rubbed the sleep out of his eyes and followed Horn to a long line of marines shuffling toward the mess hall. Several minutes later a cook with an underbite slopped a pile of eggs onto Beckham's tray.

"Thanks," he replied.

"Next," the man said, covering his teeth with his bottom lip.

Beckham felt an abrupt wave of empathy for the cook as he walked over to the nearest table and took a seat next to Horn. Riley joined them a few seconds later, dropping his metal tray with a loud clang.

"Jesus, man," Horn said with a mouthful of mushy food.

"Sorry," Riley replied. He looked up and said, "Hey, look who just walked in."

Beckham poked the lump of eggs, uninterested. Unless it was Gibson himself, he really didn't give a shit.

"Hey, boss. I think she's looking at you," Horn said.

Grunting, Beckham twisted around and saw Dr. Kate

Lovato standing in line. Her eyes darted away when she caught his gaze.

Riley chuckled, his laugh drawing stares from other tables.

Beckham pushed his tray aside. He waited a beat and then stood. "I'll be right back."

Walking over to the doctor, he thought of what he would say. He wasn't the type of guy to engage in small talk, but he'd felt an instant bond with Kate back in Atlanta. She had survived in the midst of the chaos.

Their connection made him uneasy. He'd learned back in Iraq to never form any emotional bond with the civilians he'd plucked from hot zones.

"Doctor Lovato," Beckham said, approaching her slowly.

She nodded. "Master Sergeant Beckham."

"Call me Reed," he said, offering his hand.

She regarded him with a cocked brow, hesitating before shaking his hand. "You can call me Kate. Thank you again for getting us out of Atlanta."

"Doing my duty, Doctor," he replied.

"Well, thanks. You saved my life," Kate replied. "Do you want to get breakfast?"

"I already have some," he said, gesturing over his shoulder to the table. Horn and Riley gawked at them, but turned away when they saw the scowl on Beckham's face.

"I meant, do you want to eat with me?" Kate said. "I only have a few minutes, but if I don't eat I'm going to fall over."

Beckham laughed. "Sure, join us after you grab some grub."

"All right."

Beckham walked back to the table. He already knew what the guys were going to say. "Don't either of you even start," he said. Sitting on the metal bench, he reached for his fork and shoveled a chunk of cold eggs into his mouth. He ignored the thoughts racing through his head. The world was falling apart around them. He didn't have time to make friends.

"Doctor Lovato's going to sit with us," Beckham said when he'd finished chewing. "So make sure you are on your best behavior." His eyes fell on Horn first and then moved to Riley. "Got it, Kid?"

The younger operator chuckled. "She's fucking hot, man," he said, turning to scan the room. "Maybe the hottest girl in here."

Beckham snapped his fingers and held Riley's gaze.

"I mean, yes, sir, Master Sergeant Beckham, sir. Best behavior. I promise."

"Damn it, Kid, I told you not to call me that," Beckham said.

Riley stifled a chuckle and went back to his food. Beckham was hardly satisfied, but he couldn't get angry at the kid's shit-eating grin. He stabbed another forkful of eggs.

A few minutes later Kate arrived with a trayful of food. She set it down and took a seat opposite Beckham.

"'Sup," Horn said.

"You did well back there," Riley added.

Kate pursed her lips but didn't reply right away. After a moment of silence, she said, "Thanks for evacuating us."

Both men nodded and continued eating. She faced Beckham. "So, do you have new orders?"

He shook his head. "Not yet."

"We're going back to Fort Bragg," Horn said.

"I thought they locked the island down," Kate replied. She opened a mini milk carton and took a drink.

"They did," Beckham said, shooting Horn an angry glare.

He held up his hands in defiance. "Hey, I'm just stating the truth. We aren't staying very long."

Horn stood and tapped Riley on the shoulder. "We better get back to the barracks."

"I'm not finished eating," Riley protested.

"Yeah, you are. Let's go, Kid," Horn said.

Riley grunted, grabbed a piece of toast, and said, "Fine."

Beckham called after them as they got up. "I'll be there shortly." He watched the two leave. Then he pushed his tray away and folded his hands on the table. "I want you to be honest with me, Doctor."

"Kate," she reminded him.

"Okay," he said, with the hint of a grin, "Kate. What are the odds we can stop the outbreak?"

"If you had asked Michael, he would have said the odds are dismal."

"But what do *you* think?"

"I think we're in a lot of trouble. The virus has spread so fast and is so contagious that it's almost impossible to stop it. Our only hope is finding a cure. But even then..." her voice trailed off, and she shook her head.

"What?" Beckham asked.

"There's still the problem of creating and distributing a cure. And what happens after that? Our economy will be in shambles. Food production will have stopped."

"You're right," Beckham said. His voice was grave and cold. "I've seen a lot of bad shit in the world, and this tops it all. But don't worry about what comes after, Kate. Worry about finding a cure, so there *is* an after."

Kate nodded. "I will. It's just..." She paused and took in a deep breath.

He considered reaching out to her and then said, "You okay?"

"I'm fine. I'm sure you've lost someone, or will have by the time this thing is over."

He nodded, painful memories of Building 8 flashing through his thoughts. Tenor's twisted face flashed through his mind.

Kate looked up, studying him for a moment. "I lost my kid brother a few days ago. And after losing Michael—" She sucked in another short breath and exhaled. "It's just been really tough to stay focused on my work."

"I'm sorry," Beckham said, knowing exactly what she was feeling, but not knowing what else to say. "Shit," he blurted. He reached for his chest pocket, remembering that he'd once again lost the picture of his mom.

"What is it?" she asked.

He shook his head and frowned. "Picture of my mom. It's a good luck charm. Just remembered it's gone, lost in decon. I used to print them off before every mission, just in case it got lost."

"I'm sorry. Maybe we can get you another one."

He nodded and changed the subject. "Things are only going to get worse, aren't they?"

"This is just the beginning," Kate continued. "But thank God for Plum Island." She glanced up at the low ceiling. "The lab has everything we need, and it's new. *Really* new. It's almost like they knew this was coming," Kate whispered.

Looking over his shoulder, Beckham skimmed the room for anyone who might be eavesdropping. Satisfied, he said, "That's because they did. Or at least I think they did." Searching her eyes, Beckham knew she was thinking exactly what he was: that there was more to the outbreak than what Gibson had told them.

"I better get back. I need to continue working," Kate said, just as a voice from the side said, "Master Sergeant Beckham."

Lieutenant Colonel Jensen had snuck up on them. He was

standing stiffly a few feet away. "Colonel Gibson needs to speak with you, ASAP."

"We're almost done here, sir," Beckham replied.

"ASAP means now, Master Sergeant."

Standing, Beckham extended his hand to Kate again and in the most polite voice he could muster, he said, "Doctor."

She narrowed her eyes ever so slightly and replied with the same restrained tone, "Master Sergeant."

A weak orange sun struggled to peek out from a column of dark storm clouds. Beckham halted outside the entrance to the barracks to scan the horizon. Squinting, he saw they weren't clouds at all, but plumes of smoke blowing away from New York.

"Never thought I'd see the day when American bombs were dropped on American cities," Beckham said.

Jensen crossed his arms and said nothing. After a moment, he said, "Colonel Gibson is waiting, Sergeant."

"Lead the way, sir," Beckham said, following Jensen down the narrow path. His suspicions about the island and about Gibson were amplified with every step. He knew everything was connected. It was obvious now that the virus tearing across the country had been developed in Building 8. But was this some sort of horrible accident, or something more sinister?

He noted the guard towers rising above the dome-shaped buildings in the distance. Everything looking brand new and stank of conspiracy.

"Pretty tight security," Beckham said.

Jensen simply nodded.

Frowning, Beckham tried a new approach. "The entire

station is pretty fucking impressive, sir, if you'll pardon my language. Never seen anything like it."

"Sure cost a pretty penny," Jensen replied.

"Looks like recent construction."

Jensen stopped outside the next building. Two guards saluted. Jensen waved his key card over a security panel and then pushed the door open.

The overwhelming scent of mint and bleach hit Beckham as soon as he stepped inside. The lobby was brightly lit and furnished with a single central desk. It sat empty, no guard or secretary in sight. A hallway veered off to the right. Jensen made his way toward it. "This way."

Their footfalls echoed off the walls as they strode down the hall. When they reached the end of the corridor, Jensen paused and knocked on an unmarked door to the right.

"It's open," called a voice from inside the room.

Jensen pulled on the handle and swung the metal door open. Beckham held his gaze for a second and then stepped past him into the dimly lit room, listening to the door as it shut behind him.

A deep voice bellowed out as soon as he entered the smoky office. "Welcome, Master Sergeant."

Beckham stiffened when he saw the light blues eyes of Colonel Gibson staring at him through a cloud of smoke. The man sat behind a large wooden desk decorated with a single metal picture frame facing away from the door.

"Take a seat," the colonel said, gesturing toward a chair in front of the desk.

"I'll stand, thank you, sir," Beckham replied. A short silence followed, and Beckham used the moment to manage all of the thoughts racing through his head.

Gibson eyed him and then stood. "Suit yourself." He turned toward a window with a view of barbed-wire fences.

"I saw your team on the list of forces here at Plum Island, and I wanted to talk to you about Building Eight."

Beckham gritted his teeth, waiting for the grilling he had expected days before. He controlled his anger with a short breath through his nostrils.

"I've read the report and watched the video. You failed to recover the sample."

"Then I'm sure you also saw what we were up against," Beckham said, keeping his voice calm and measured. "And I'm sure you saw Major Caster hold a gun to my head."

Gibson continued staring out the window. "I did. And I'm sorry for the loss of your team. All of this could have been avoided if I had known Doctor Jim Pinkman was already infected."

The response took Beckham by surprise. He narrowed his eyes at the man. "So why am I really here, sir?"

The colonel faced Beckham. The creases on his forehead looked more pronounced than they had been in the briefing.

"You're here because I need you and your men for a unique mission."

Beckham wanted to protest with a swift punch to the man's jaw, but Gibson held all of the cards. He controlled the island and all its aircraft. Beckham thought of Riley and Horn. His men came first. He had to hold strong, remain in control of his conflicting emotions.

"As you already know, I have the scientists and the research equipment I need to find a cure. But…" Gibson shook a finger.

"You need a live specimen," Beckham guessed.

"Yes. Yes, I do."

"And you want me to lead a mission to capture this live specimen."

Gibson nodded.

Beckham hated to admit it, but he *needed* the man now to get his men back to Fort Bragg. "I'll get you a live specimen, sir, but in return I'd like a favor."

Gibson shook his head. "I'm not sure you understand. This mission isn't open for negotiation. The Medical Corps has been granted full authority over Operation Reaper."

"I heard."

"You understand you report to me, then."

Beckham ran a finger over his chin. "I'm asking for a ride to Fort Bragg, sir. Give my team a chopper and you'll get your specimen inside of twenty-four hours."

The colonel just stood there, staring, his eyes burning with defiance, but there was also softness behind the anger. The man standing in front of Beckham hadn't always been such a hard-ass. Something had changed him over the years, broken him as it had Spinoza and so many other men Beckham had fought with.

A trace of empathy trickled through him as he held the colonel's gaze. It did not last. There was more to this story than Gibson was letting on, and Beckham would eventually find out the truth. He'd hoped to learn more about Gibson's connection to Plum Island, but for now he was focused on getting his men back home to Fort Bragg.

After a moment of silence, Gibson nodded. "All right, Master Sergeant. You get me a specimen, and I'll get you your ride."

Beckham really didn't like the idea of going back out there, but it was the only way. He raised a salute and said, "Deal."

Kate stood over her lab table with a stinging anger growing inside her. She welcomed the emotion, having felt so numb since they'd landed at Plum Island. For that reason she'd worked through the night, picking up where she'd left off in Atlanta.

The testing on the mice revealed only what she already knew. The virus didn't affect the endothelial cells exactly like other strains of Ebola, but the rodent models weren't exactly accurate. Mice, guinea pigs, hamsters, and rats did not always mirror the same symptoms humans exhibited, and none of the subjects she'd infected with the hemorrhage virus were displaying the same violent behavior as the infected humans.

Kate shook her head as she examined one of the mice she'd been working with all day. The creature lay curled up in the corner of a glass box.

"This isn't working. I need a specimen with closer DNA to our own," Kate muttered, looking for Cindy. The woman sat on a stool a few stations over, her visor planted against a microscope.

"Don't we have any rhesus monkeys?" Kate asked.

"Yes," she said, without looking up. "But we're about to get something better. Colonel Gibson has already authorized a mission to retrieve a live specimen and bring it back to the island."

"What?" Kate blurted.

Cindy glanced up, her lips pursing behind her visor. The woman looked confused by Kate's reaction.

"You don't have an issue with this?" Kate asked. "Do you not understand how dangerous this could be? Dealing with live samples is one thing, but an infected person demonstrating violent behavior?" Kate paused. "What if it gets loose?"

"It's a risk we have to take, Kate," Ellis said from his workstation. "Besides, I'm sure Beckham and his men will get the job done with no problem."

Kate froze. "What do you mean, 'Beckham and his men'?"

Ellis stood. "Major Smith said they're sending a special ops team into the field. I assume he meant Beckham and the others."

"Unbelievable," Kate replied. "That could be a disaster. Not to mention it breaks about a hundred laws and regulations."

Cindy let slip a laugh. "Regulations and laws? This is the end of the world, Doctor Lovato. There are no regulations or laws anymore."

Her cheeks red, Kate shot the woman an angry glare. A surge of different emotions hit her. The facility certainly *looked* secure, but she'd seen firsthand what those things were capable of. They weren't mindless, flesh-hungry zombies. They were humans—very sick humans, who were also very contagious.

Crackling from the intercom pulled the trio to the lab's observation window. Major Smith stood on the other side of the isolation glass. Kate immediately thought of protesting Gibson's decision.

Pick your battles, Kate, she thought.

"We should have a live specimen for you in the next twenty-four to thirty-six hours," he said.

"And you are seriously bringing it back here?"

Smith stood in the doorway, an incredulous look on his face. "I was under the impression you knew this, Doctor Lovato."

"Does Colonel Gibson have any idea how dangerous this is?"

"The colonel understands perfectly. And I can assure you, Doctor, that this facility is quite safe."

"I'm going on record as saying this is a terrible decision," Kate replied.

"I'll note your concern," Smith said. "And when you're done,

Colonel Gibson wants a status report." The intercom clicked off, and Smith left the room.

Kate watched him leave as a sudden roar vibrated through the lab walls. The sound was unmistakable. Somewhere above the island a military jet raced across the sky. The noise was a chilling reminder that Beckham and his men were heading into a war zone.

Sucking in a breath, she hurried back to the mouse she'd been working with all morning. It stared up at her with tiny red eyes, rolled over, and died.

16

A heavy, cold rain pounded the concrete. Soaked and tired, Beckham threw a jacket over his helmet and eyed Horn's pack of cigarettes with contempt as they waited.

"Where are these guys?" Riley asked. He sat on a stack of metal crates that bore the USAMRIID symbol on their sides.

"Don't know, but I'm starting to get pissed," Beckham replied. Loosening the strap on his rucksack, he threw it into the chopper and peered inside. A large metal cage sat in the back of the chopper, strapped tight to the wall and floor.

"Will you look at that?" Beckham muttered.

"Holy crap," Riley laughed. "That thing's big enough for a lion."

Horn ducked inside the chopper and examined the bars, pulling on them with a grunt. "Seems pretty secure."

Footsteps pulled Beckham back to the tarmac. A pair of pilots flanked by two soldiers carrying M4s and wearing white biohazard suits jogged toward the chopper. The equipment they wore made them look odd, almost as if they were astronauts.

"They came prepared," Riley said, jumping off the top

crate. He landed in a puddle. The pilots both nodded at Team Ghost before climbing into the chopper.

The two men in bio suits dropped their rucksacks and duffel bags on the pavement. Rain streaked down their visors, but Beckham could see both of them were young, barely of drinking age.

Gibson's sending me out here with rookies.

"Master Sergeant Beckham," one of the men said as he and his partner both snapped to parade rest. "I'm Specialist Preston, and this here is Specialist Wolfe. We're with the Medical Corps. Our orders are to help you obtain a live specimen of the infected."

Beckham nodded. "What about the gear? We weren't informed we would need anything specific."

"The virus is highly contagious, Master Sergeant. Lieutenant Colonel Jensen gave us these suits for you and your team."

"We didn't wear any back in Atlanta," Riley protested, staring at the specialists.

"It was Lieutenant Colonel Jensen's order. We—"

"Yeah, more orders from brass," Horn interjected.

In an effort to defuse the situation, Beckham said, "Horn, Riley, get dressed."

Both men grumbled.

Wolfe reached for a large duffel bag and unzipped it, revealing more of the suits. Beckham reached out and took one. "Remember," he said to Riley and Horn, "improvising is our specialty."

Wolfe and Preston helped Beckham and his team into their suits, ensuring they were sealed properly and the respirators were functioning. The last thing Beckham wanted was to get into the field with a faulty suit again.

Five minutes later he was staring out over the ocean and

breathing the familiar rubbery scent of plastic. The smell beat the alternative—infection. He knew how lucky they had been back in Atlanta.

The mainland shoreline came into focus as the chopper descended. Abandoned cars littered the highway. Wet clothing spilled out of open suitcases, and the gusting wind carried trash across the road. He'd seen scenes like this in Iraq, when civilians had attempted to flee the violence in their cities, but there were no charred bodies or corpses riddled with bullet holes here. The streets below were quiet, only a few limp bodies in sight.

"Any ideas on how to capture one of these things?" Riley asked.

"Yup," Wolfe said and dragged the bag in front of him across the floor. He removed a small pistol with a long barrel that looked like an air gun. "We're supposed to tranquilize one of them."

A deep voice bellowed over the channel. It was Horn, laughing hysterically. "You're going to tranquilize one of those things? You rooks have never come face-to-face with one, have you?"

Static crackled in response. Neither of the specialists replied immediately. Wolfe handed the gun to Horn. The operator took the pistol in a gloved hand and hefted the skinny weapon, turning it side to side.

"That thing will take down a rhino, Sergeant," Wolfe said.

"You sure about that?" Horn asked. "Looks like a BB gun to me. I'd prefer to use this." He reached behind him for his M249 and raised it off the floor to show the greenhorn specialists.

"Colonel Gibson wants us to bring one back alive, Sergeant," Preston said with a chuckle, "not in the form of cat food."

"How many of those do you have?" Beckham asked. He wasn't amused.

Wolfe reached back into the bag and removed four more of the guns. "One for each of us, Master Sergeant."

"We've reached Niantic, Connecticut," one of the pilots announced over the comm. "Master Sergeant Beckham, advise on insertion point."

Beckham grabbed the strap of his MP5 and crouch-walked closer to the door. As the city came into view below, he searched for an open space. He'd memorized the map of the area and quickly identified Main Street. The road ran along a thin beach and, with no contacts in sight, it looked like the perfect place to put down.

"Forget the fast ropes," Beckham said into his headset. "Land on the beach."

As the chopper descended, he began to feel the tingle of uncertainty. His idea was to have the ocean at their back; that way no one could sneak up on them. Then again, it also meant they couldn't retreat if they had to. Beckham waited for the pilot to get them low enough over the beach that they could jump down to the sand.

When they were a few feet above the ground, he flashed a thumbs-up and hopped out. He landed in the mushy sand and broke into a jog, with the muzzle of his MP5 aimed at the road beyond.

Taking point, he moved cautiously to the metal barrier lining the street. His eyes darted from side to side, scanning for any sign of contacts.

Nothing.

He flashed an advance signal. Riley and Horn ran up the beach, with the two specialists close behind.

The chopper pulled away as soon as they got to the road. In seconds it was gone, nothing but a speck on the bright horizon. Rays of distant sunlight bled through the cloud cover in the distance, an oddly beautiful sight in the gray and seemingly deserted city.

The other men huddled around him near the metal fence wrapping around the road. After they had caught their breath, Beckham said, "I'm on point. Horn, you've got left, high and low. Riley, you're right, the same. Preston, Wolfe, stay at my six between Horn and Riley and watch our asses for contacts."

Beckham glanced down at the tranquilizer gun on his belt. He grabbed the pistol and checked the cartridge before jumping over the barrier and moving onto the street.

"Let's go," he said. They fanned out across the road, taking their positions as Beckham had directed.

Besides the whistling of the wind and the rap of rain beating down on Beckham's suit, all was quiet. Nothing moved. The stillness was chilling. It reminded him of San Nicolas Island, and he wondered what infrared optics would reveal if he had them at his disposal. Would he see any sign of animals, or would he be staring at a dead landscape like the one they'd encountered on the island?

Pushing the thought aside, Beckham continued past the empty vehicles, checking each car for any stragglers. The last thing he wanted was a surprise.

"Where the fuck is everyone?" Riley asked. His voice sounded shaken, a far cry from his normal enthusiastic tone.

"Looks like a ghost town," Horn replied.

"More like a ghost port," Wolfe said.

"Keep your trap shut," Horn snarled.

A gust of wind pushed at Beckham. He wiped his visor with his sleeve and saw the Niantic River on the north side of Main Street. Hundreds of boats still covered with white winter tarps filled the marina. New boats on trailers sat unattended in the yard of a marine-supply store nearby. The ping of raindrops on aluminum filled the afternoon. In a way, the noise was oddly soothing, but Beckham knew the danger they were in.

He hesitated. They were surrounded by hundreds of places where the infected could hide, and he suddenly felt naked standing in the open.

"We need cover. Let's move," he said, waving the men toward a large warehouse in the middle of the boatyard. They took a right on Smith Avenue and passed through its intersection with Grand Street.

Beckham kept his MP5 trained on the boats to the right and swept the muzzle of the weapon back and forth, checking the houses to the left and the abandoned cars in the middle of the road.

A single plume of smoke streaming from the north side of the warehouse jolted him to a stop. He hadn't seen it before their insertion.

When the team reached the building, Beckham paused. "I'll take point. Keep combat intervals," he said. With his back to the building's white metal siding, he crouch-walked to the edge, where he balled his hand into a fist and peeked around the corner to the east.

The smoke was streaming from a smoldering pickup truck. It was obvious someone had emptied several magazines into the vehicle. Pockmarks the size of cherries peppered the exterior of the truck. The windshield was gone, shattered by the rounds, but he couldn't see any bodies inside.

Beckham looked for more cover. There wasn't much. Just two flipped boats between their position and the truck.

"Stay here," Beckham said to the specialists. He flashed a signal to Horn, who took up a post behind the boats. Riley shouldered his shotgun and followed Beckham.

With his MP5 in his left hand and the tranquilizer gun in his right, Beckham approached the vehicle cautiously. The rain beat down on his visor, the drops trailing down his small window to the world.

He waited a beat when he got to the driver's-side door. Puffs of hot breath fogged the inside of his helmet as his breathing became more labored.

Leaning down, he saw the door was cracked open just a hair, but he couldn't see anyone through the filthy window.

Riley patted him on the back and Beckham opened the door so Riley could clear the vehicle. He swept his shotgun over two empty seats and nodded. They moved quickly down the length of the truck and came to a stop at the end. Corpses were piled three deep in the bed. Someone had gone to the trouble of covering the bodies with a tarp, but naked arms and legs protruded from the stack.

"Jesus," Riley muttered.

Beckham took a step back from the truck. Another hot blast of air fogged his visor as he examined the bed.

"Everything okay, boss?" came Horn's voice over the comm.

"Stay where you are," Beckham replied.

He wiped the front of his helmet clean for a better look. There were at least a dozen bodies; all had suffered blunt force trauma and deep gashes. Self-inflicted or the result of an attack, he wasn't sure. By the looks of it, they had been dead for a while. The corpses were already decomposing.

Taking another step away from the vehicle, he heard the faint sound of raspy breathing. He spun and scanned the road. The wind hissed by as he spun again, making it impossible to hear where the sound was coming from.

"Do you hear that, Kid?" Beckham asked.

"Negative. I got nothing."

Beckham dropped to his stomach, careful not to puncture his suit, and was scanning the gaps under the cars when he saw the boy. He lay shivering on the concrete, curled up on the other side of a sedan.

"Shit. I think we have a survivor," Beckham said. "Horn, get over here." He pushed himself up and rushed over to the child with Riley. As soon as Beckham saw the boy's mouth, he halted.

"Holy shit," Riley said.

The child looked up at them, puckering his pale, bulging lips. Bloody tears streaked from his red-stained eyes. He snarled and focused yellow eyes on Beckham and then Riley.

The boy's legs—or what was left of them—were both mangled beyond recognition, as if they had gotten stuck under the blades of a lawn mower.

Beckham's stomach reeled at the grotesque sight, and he stumbled backward. How was this kid even still alive? He'd lost so much blood, the pain should have rendered him unconscious.

"Stay back," Beckham said. He kept his distance and aimed both of his weapons at the kid, waiting for the rest of the team.

Wolfe was the first to arrive. He shook his helmet. "This one won't work. Might not make the trip back." He raised his M4 and pointed at the child's head.

"No!" Beckham yelled.

The child snarled again, reaching out for the gun as if he knew what was coming.

A loud crack echoed through the afternoon, and the boy's head exploded in a spray of mist that peppered their uniforms with gore. His body slumped to the ground, twitching several times before going limp.

"What the fuck did you do that for?" Horn half shouted as he approached. He shoved Wolfe into the car.

"Hey, not fucking cool!" Wolfe replied, regaining his balance. "I was putting the kid out of his misery."

Horn raised a fist.

"Back off, Big Horn," Beckham snapped. He turned to Wolfe, who moved away.

"I was ... I'm sorry, Sergeant. We couldn't guarantee he'd survive. He was gone anyway. Why does it matter?"

The crack of lightning sounded before Beckham could respond. The boom of thunder distracted the team for a moment. Within moments the clouds had opened up. Sheets of rain washed the blood and gore away.

A deep thunder rumbled again, the noise shaking the ground. It was followed by another sound, a high-pitched croak—the same kind they'd heard back in Atlanta.

Beckham froze. The noises were coming from everywhere and nowhere. He spun and swept the area with his MP5. The other men raised their weapons, directing them across their fire zones.

"Hear that? That's why it matters," Horn said. "Those things are drawn to noise like a moth to a flame."

"Eyes on, everybody. Watch for contacts," Beckham said. He slowly moved around the car, his boots slipping on the wet surface. He steadied himself and brought his ACOG to his visor. Motion flicked across the cross hairs. He moved the sights across the boatyard, where he spotted them.

Dozens—

No.

Hundreds or more of the infected were now emerging from the boats, tossing the covers off their expensive coffins. They jumped onto the dock and took off with a speed that still amazed Beckham.

He took a step back, his mind racing. There were too many to take down. "Fall back!" he ordered.

More lightning streaked through the sky above them. Thunder shook the ground, mixing with the sounds of their footfalls as the team ran.

Beckham desperately searched for a place to make a stand. His visor fogged as his breathing became more labored. He knew they were dead if they stayed out in the open. He risked a glance over his shoulder to see that the team was right behind him.

The squawks of the infected grew louder, deeper, and desperate. Like wild animals that hadn't eaten in days, their cries were hungry. Ravenous. Another arc of lightning flashed through the sky.

"Into the warehouse!" Beckham yelled. He turned around the corner they had come from and burst back onto Smith Avenue.

"They're gaining on us!" Wolfe said.

Automatic gunfire erupted behind Beckham. He winced and chinned his comm. "Don't engage. Just run!"

Wolfe didn't hear him or chose to ignore him. The crack of his rifle rang out again, followed by the faint sound of empty brass pinging off the concrete.

Riley caught up to Beckham a few seconds later. The entrance to the warehouse was less than thirty meters away. Standing between them and the doors stood a uniformed police officer.

"Where the fuck did he come from?" Horn shouted.

For a moment Beckham thought the man was going to help them, but then he saw the officer's hands were cuffed together. It was someone's last-ditch effort to restrain the sick man.

Without hesitation, Beckham raised his MP5 and fired off a burst into the cop's chest. Gore plastered the door behind him, and he dropped to the ground, raspy groans gurgling from his throat.

The sound faded against the roar of thunder. Lightning hit the ground somewhere on the north side of town.

Riley loped up the front steps two at a time. He nudged the dead police officer's body out of the way and reached for the door's handle. As soon as he grabbed it, Beckham heard the cackling from the other side.

When the kid swung the door open, Beckham raised his MP5 and blasted the two infected waiting on the other side. They were catapulted back into the darkness. Another one came racing toward them from the right, and Beckham raised the tranquilizer pistol into the air and shot the man in the throat. The creature slumped to the floor, skidding to a stop a few feet away from Riley's boots.

Beckham moved out of the way as the rest of his team rushed through the open door. Horn slammed it behind them, locking it with a click. Riley and the specialists took up positions in the center of the room, dropping their rucksacks on the ground and bending over to catch their breath.

"Nice shooting," Riley said. "You saved my ass."

Beckham nodded and then moved over to their ticket back to Fort Bragg. The infected man looked up at them blankly, with eyes the color of roses.

"Echo One, this is Ghost One. We have the package. Request extraction. Over."

The pilot responded almost immediately. "Area is way too hot, Ghost One. Stand by for new coordinates."

Static crackled in Beckham's earpiece. He cursed their luck and shot Wolfe a glare. The asshole had informed every infected in Niantic that they were here.

"I don't like this shit," Horn said. "We don't have time to sit and wait."

The double door rattled behind them, the noise echoing through the building. Beckham's heart kicked. A thin, elderly man pressed his face against the small glass pane on the right door. His lips clamped onto the window, and a tongue flicked out, smearing dark blood in circular motions. The man pushed harder and the glass cracked, along with two of his teeth. The creature pulled back, as if in shock, and then reached up to feel the jagged shards that remained. A look of confusion and then fear raced across his features.

Beckham watched in awe, studying the monster. Everything he'd witnessed in the field led him to believe the infected were only mindless beasts with superhuman strength and speed, but this one seemed aware of his injury, of his pain.

In a fit of rage, the man smashed his fist against the door. He pounded it again and the glass shattered, raining down on the concrete floor. Another three infected joined in. Together, they rammed their shoulders against the frame. The steel shook, but it held.

"Boss," came Horn's nervous voice over the comm. "We should think about getting out of here."

"I'd have to agree with Horn," Riley added.

"No shit," Beckham replied. He scanned the room. The lobby opened up into a warehouse full of boat engines and spare parts. A metal staircase led to a second floor of offices at the far end of the space.

Sliding the tranquilizer pistol back into its sheath, Beckham moved toward the stairs. "Grab that thing," he yelled. Glancing over his shoulder, he saw Wolfe and Preston reach down and grab the sick man under his arms. They dragged his limp body across the concrete.

"Riley, clear those offices and find the best place to make a stand," Beckham said.

"Roger," Riley replied as he took off running up the steps.

The double doors shook again, more of the creatures joining the parade. Beckham knew they were running out of time. A flashback from Building 8 crept into his thoughts. He remembered the burned faces of his men and their horrific screams as Dr. Medford's staff scalded them with chemicals.

A sharp metal pole suddenly harpooned through the center of the front door, snapping Beckham from his thoughts. Beyond the broken glass, a soldier wearing only a pair of camouflage pants tugged on the rod. For the first time on the mission, Beckham felt raw fear grip him as the muscular man withdrew the pole and then jammed it back into the door. The impact shattered the lock's hardware, the knob bouncing off the floor with a metallic ping.

More thunder shook the roof. Primal screams followed, the shrieks intensifying as the creatures grew more agitated.

"Let's go!" Beckham shouted over the noise. He helped Preston and Wolfe drag the infected man up the stairs, but it was slow going. Horn and Riley took point.

"Clear!" Riley shouted a few seconds later. He moved to the railing and aimed his shotgun at the door below.

"Shoot anything that comes through there!" Beckham shouted.

Riley nodded his acknowledgment.

They had the tranquilized man halfway up the staircase when the infected finally smashed into the building. Joints creaked and snapped as they swarmed into the space like insects.

The deafening sound of gunfire exploded above them. Shotgun shells rained down on Beckham as Riley fired off calculated shots. Horn joined in with his SAW, the muzzle flashes backlighting the dim room.

Trapped at the bottom of the stairs, unable to get around Wolfe and the infected man they had captured, Preston stopped and stared up at Beckham. Terror radiated from the young soldier's eyes, pleading for help. The specialist spun, his M4 barking and cutting down the first wave of infected, but more quickly piled in. They climbed frantically over the warm corpses.

The chaos prompted another spike of adrenaline in Beckham's system. With added strength, he helped Wolfe hoist the paralyzed man to the top of the staircase. They dropped him on the metal catwalk and then joined the firefight.

The first floor of the building became a slaughterhouse, a pool of blood forming at the bottom of the staircase. There were so many corpses now that it was hard to tell where one ended and the next began. Preston was working his way up the stairs, firing as he backpedaled. He tripped on the third stair but continued to fire his rifle.

"Get out of there!" Beckham yelled.

The infected surged forward, growling in agony as the bullets riddled their sick bodies.

And still they kept coming.

Two others had jumped to the walls, skittering up the building with hands morphed into claws. The disgusting *click-clack* of their nails on the metal siding sent a chill down Beckham's spine. He couldn't stop staring at the creatures. Yes, that's what they were, he finally decided. These people were alive, but little of their humanity remained. They were...

Monsters.

"Horn, take out the climbers!" Beckham yelled.

A beat later, two bodies dropped from the ceiling, their agonized wails filling the room as they smashed onto the floor.

Beckham reached for another magazine. Even with automatic weapons, they couldn't shoot fast enough. Jamming the mag home, he aimed the barrel at the muscular former soldier who had broken down the door. The man crawled toward Preston on bloody stumps while the specialist kicked and screamed.

With the sight of his MP5 lined up on the creature's face, Beckham pulled the trigger.

Click.

The weapon jammed. Beckham slapped the bottom of the magazine with the palm of his hand and then worked the bolt to free the round. He glanced up for a brief second as the creature pounced on the specialist, punching the jagged end of its right arm through Preston's visor. Preston choked and then wailed in agony, a sound so grotesque that Beckham wanted to cover his ears.

He worked the bolt on his weapon again. The jammed round finally popped out, but it was too late. The creature was already feeding on Preston through the hole that it had torn in his suit.

Beckham fired off a burst that punched through the monster's barreled chest muscles. It tumbled off Preston and slid to join the other dead infected at the base of the stairs.

Four other creatures raced up the stairs and climbed over Preston's fresh corpse. Horn and Riley took out the first two, but the others leaped over the stairs, hit the ground, and made a mad dash toward the walls.

Beckham swung his gun in one quick arc toward the climbers, spraying the room with bullets. They were so fucking fast, a blur of flesh and tattered clothes. They moved like spiders, scrambling across the walls. He could hardly follow them with his weapon.

Riley caught one of them in the back with a blast from his shotgun. But the other man lunged from the wall to the ceiling just above the team, hanging there and releasing a shriek before he dropped to the platform.

Beckham fired off the rest of his magazine directly into the creature's midsection. The monster twitched as the bullets riddled its body and then slumped to the ground, letting out one final raspy moan.

Beckham used the moment of calm to catch his breath and survey the damage. His gaze stopped on Preston's twisted body. The man was dead. There was no doubt about it. His visor looked like a shattered egg after some alien creature had hatched from inside. Next, he looked at the tranquilized man at the top of the stairs. Horn stood over the top of him, his boot firmly planted on the man's chest.

Riley glared at Beckham, his eyes wild behind his blood-stained visor. "You think we should try Echo One again?"

Beckham chinned his comm. "Echo One, Ghost. We need extraction, ASAP." With his ears still ringing from the gunfire, Beckham could hardly hear the faint crackle of static in his earpiece. The pilot's voice drifted over the channel a moment later.

"Ghost One, Echo One. LZ is still too hot. Those things are everywhere. We have to return to home plate."

The words hit Beckham like a slap to the face. He smacked his right hand against his helmet. Had he heard right, or were his ears still ringing?

"They can't leave us out here," Wolfe stuttered.

Beckham didn't reply. He clenched his right fist, trying to think. They were surrounded.

Trapped.

"Echo One, Ghost One. We're working on a plan out of here. Just give us a few minutes."

"Ghost One, Echo One. Repeat: We cannot hold position until a safe extraction is possible. LZ is too hot, and there's no telling when it'll cool down. Closest safe extraction is about six hundred meters west of your location. Looks like a small office building. We can come down over the roof. Can you make the objective, Ghost One?"

Beckham glanced up at the second level of the warehouse. His three remaining teammates stared down from the balcony. Their bloodstained visors couldn't hide their eyes. Even Horn looked terrified.

Beckham thought about what was out there in the surrounding terrain—nothing but neighborhoods with wide-open yards around dark houses, separated by low fences. There was no way they'd make the new LZ alive.

"Ghost One, Echo One. Do you copy? Can you make the new LZ? Over."

With anger thick on his tongue, Beckham replied. "Negative, Echo One. I repeat: *Negative*. We are locked down and cannot move."

"The hell's wrong with this roof?" Horn said, aiming his M249 over his head.

Beckham nodded and chinned his comm once more. "Echo One, Ghost One. Can you come down on top of this roof? Over."

"Negative. Hostiles up top. Sorry, Ghost One. You're on your own until morning. We'll be back when we receive your all clear. Good luck."

The line cut out, and white noise surged over the channel.

Beckham looked at his team. "You heard the man. We're spending the night here. So get your ass in gear. We need to secure this AO."

"What about this guy?" Riley said, kicking the captured infected.

"Do you want to get back to Fort Bragg or what, Kid?" Horn said. He reached down and grabbed the man under his right armpit and began dragging him down the hallway that led to the offices. Riley bent down and helped him.

Wolfe crossed the platform and walked down the first two steps. He tried to squeeze past, but Beckham put up a hand to stop him.

"Is he . . ." Wolfe began.

"He's gone. I'm sorry," Beckham said. He forced himself to look away from Preston's mangled corpse and scanned the room. A rolling engine stand occupied one corner of the open space. A boat motor hung from its chains.

"Help me block up that door," Beckham said.

Together, they made their way past Preston's body and around the pile of dead infected. Beckham hurried to the motor and, with Wolfe's help, pushed it to the entrance. Kicking two corpses out of the way, they then slid the engine stand into place to hold the double doors closed.

Beckham took one last look at Preston's corpse and then clapped Wolfe on the shoulder. "Let's go," he said, climbing the stairs and leaving the carnage behind.

17

A primal screech jolted Kate awake. The sound was oddly familiar, reminiscent of noises that had kept her up at night on her first trip to the remote jungle in Congo, three years ago.

An involuntary spasm shook her body. She was so tired. What time was it? Where was she?

Another shriek followed, then rattling metal, and Kate suddenly remembered.

She shot out of the chair she'd set up outside the observation window to the animal testing area. Rubbing her eyes, she scanned the dark lab but only saw the silhouettes of frightened rhesus monkeys moving inside their cages.

Kate looked down at her watch. One hour and thirty-five minutes had passed since she'd infected the animals with the hemorrhage virus.

And now the entire lab sounded alive. Metal cages shook. Shrieks vibrated throughout the space.

Kate hit the lights. A dozen set of crimson eyes instantly gravitated to her. Blood trickled down fur and bulging lips puckered into suckers.

"My God," Kate said, bringing a hand to her mouth.

As soon as they saw her, the animals went crazy. They stuck tiny hands, twisted into claws, through the gaps in the metal bars, shaking the sides of their cages violently. A female on the bottom row tried to head-butt her way out of the cage.

Kate watched in shock. They weren't all trying to break loose. Some were tearing at their own flesh, their swollen lips clamped down on a leg or an arm as they fed.

Kate had seen enough. They were suffering, and the symptoms told her nothing more than she already knew. Under normal conditions she would apply sedatives, analgesics, or anesthetics to put the animals to sleep, but the risk of infection was simply too high.

Sitting down at the computer, she typed in her credentials and password. Next she brought up the termination screen, and with a few more commands, she implemented a procedure that would end the monkeys' suffering.

Seconds later a hissing noise filled the room. It was one of the worst parts of Kate's job, but she always forced herself to watch. Sacrificing animals was a necessary measure in viral research. A minute after the gas had filled the room, the screeches stopped. Furry bodies twitched in their cages as the rhesus monkeys struggled to breathe.

Kate picked up the phone and dialed Ellis.

A voice she hardly recognized picked up after a few rings.

"Hello?"

"Ellis, wake up. I need your help. We have some autopsies to perform."

"What time is it?" he asked, his voice groggy and slurred.

"Time to work. I'll see you in a few minutes," Kate replied and then hung up. When she turned back to the window, every monkey was dead.

April 23, 2015
DAY 6

An emergency light illuminated the clock next to Beckham with an eerie red glow. It was 0005 hours.

He'd listened to the antique piece tick for the past four hours. Sitting next to it, he was starting to wish he could smash the wood with the butt of his MP5. But then again, the sound did distract him from other thoughts—especially the thoughts of those they'd lost.

Standing, he paced over to check the door. Riley stood there with his back to the wall and his shotgun angled at the floor, waiting.

They were holed up in one of the back offices. The room was furnished with several large metal tables, blueprints of some yacht that would never see completion draped across the surfaces. The infected man they'd captured lay unconscious in the corner of the room. Horn sat on an aged leather couch next to him, his foot still pushing down on the man's chest. They had bound the man's feet and hands with heavy cords, but Beckham wasn't taking any chances. He'd assigned his friend the job of ensuring the creature didn't get loose.

Behind them a half dozen windows lined the wall overlooking a small brick building and narrow alleyway. The boatyard was beyond that. White tarps flapped on the concrete where the infected had tossed them earlier. A fire escape gave his team access to a ladder if they needed a quick exit.

The sound of clawed hands and feet scrabbling over the roof had faded hours ago. The silence was awful. He knew the creatures were still out there, waiting. The boatyard had been quiet when they arrived.

Beckham looked back at the clock. It was 0011 hours now. The warehouse was their AO for the night. He was exhausted, but he knew he couldn't let his guard down. *Fuck it, drive on*, he thought. They had to get the specimen back to Plum Island. It was their only shot at getting back to Fort Bragg.

Walking across the room, he crouched next to one of the windows and peeled back a dusty curtain. In the glow of the moon, the alley below looked empty. None of the creatures were in sight.

Relieved, he stood and moved over to the couch. The infected man's breathing was more labored now, fluid crackling in his lungs. Beckham took a knee.

"Careful," Horn said. He grunted and pressed down harder with his boot.

Nodding, Beckham swept his flashlight over the young man's body. The white beam revealed the same thing they'd seen back in Atlanta: pale, almost translucent skin with blue veins bulging, blood flowing freely from the ears, mouth, nose, and eyes.

Waving the light in front of the man's eyes, Beckham checked to see if he was conscious. There was no response. His slit-shaped pupils gazed up toward the ceiling, blank and detached.

"Still out," Horn whispered.

"Keep an eye on him," Beckham replied, standing with a groan. He walked over to Wolfe, who sat by himself in the other corner of the room.

"You doing okay?" Beckham asked. He wanted to make sure his team was ready to go at a moment's notice.

Wolfe looked up, the red glow from the emergency light illuminating his dirty visor. He stared back blankly.

Beckham sighed. He knew the expression was battle

fatigue. It had set in the moment the soldier had seen the corpse of his friend back on the stairs.

"Listen. I need you to stay focused. We can't stay here forever."

As soon as the words left his mouth, the sound of crunching glass reverberated from somewhere inside the building. Beckham froze and watched the other team members stiffen.

Another noise followed a few seconds later. This one sounded as if it was coming from the alleyway. It was a combination of frantic scraping and then shuffling, almost like a desperate animal climbing the bark of a tree to get away from a predator.

Moving back to the window, Beckham slowly pulled back the curtain, knowing exactly what was making the noise. The alleyway was dark now, the moon hidden by a dense set of clouds. He scanned the shadows for any sign of the creatures.

A blur of white suddenly flashed across the exterior brick surface of the adjacent building. It disappeared before Beckham could focus on it.

He swallowed. Hard. Cautious not to be seen, he dropped to the floor and crawled under the windows to the other side of the room. Then, standing, he gripped the shades in between his gloved fingers. The scratching grew louder, the scraping closer. Faint moonlight bled into the room.

Slowly he moved the curtain to the side. There was motion on the exterior of the building. He squinted and focused, but his mind couldn't grasp what his eyes were showing it.

Across the alley, the brick wall looked alive. Dozens of infected scaled the surface. They gripped the brick with twisted hands that resembled claws more than fingers. And they moved with inhuman speed.

The sight made Beckham's skin crawl.

"What is it, boss?" came Horn's voice.

Beckham didn't reply. His gaze was locked onto the building. The first of the group reached the edge of the rooftop. A woman dressed in tattered, bloodstained clothes stood there, sniffing. She tilted her head, finding a scent. She broke into a run across the ledge.

"Jesus," he muttered. How was that even possible? They were sick, infected with one of the deadliest viruses on the planet, but somehow it had transformed them into something stronger, faster, deadlier—the perfect human predator.

"We have contacts all over the next building," Beckham whispered into the comm. Wolfe shuffled to his feet, bracing himself against the wall. Riley stepped away from the door, his shotgun angled toward the window.

Beckham brought a finger to his visor. "Radio silence." He looked to Horn, who stood over their hostage, his boot still firmly planted against the man's chest.

The scraping sound grew louder. Beckham glanced out the window again and watched several of the infected perch on the ledge of the opposite building. They reminded him of gargoyles with the moonlight reflecting off their translucent skin. Several of them were naked, and he could see gaping wounds on their arms and legs. He focused on a man missing his chin, lips, and the bottom of his nostrils. The man lifted what was left of his nose toward the sky, sniffing with the cavernous hole in the middle of his face.

Beckham couldn't pull his gaze away from the creature. Seconds later, the rooftop was filled with the infected, and all of them were sniffing the air. Searching for prey.

They were hunting.

Beckham saw exactly what the pilot must have seen hours earlier, and now knew why he couldn't put the Black Hawk down on the roof.

Blinking, he focused on one of the creatures curled up

into a fetal position on the roof ledge. The creature scratched the concrete frantically, paying no attention to the others.

Beckham clenched his jaw shut as it suddenly tilted its head in his direction with bloodshot, crazed eyes.

Shit.

Had it seen him? He stumbled backward, nearly tripping over his own feet, his heart racing.

It saw me. Fuck. It saw me. Memories of Tenor's final moments crept into his thoughts. He couldn't imagine what the man had felt as the virus quickly took over his body.

Beckham wasn't going to let the same thing happen to him or any of his remaining men. He focused. Keeping low, he crouch-walked over to Riley.

There was another faint scuffling sound. This one came from inside the room.

Beckham almost didn't hear it at first, but when he finally made it to the door it was unmistakable. He paused, spinning to see the victim struggling under Horn's boot.

"Shit. We have a problem," Horn whispered. "Guy's waking up."

The prisoner moaned as he twisted under the weight of Horn's foot. Joints snapped and clicked, the creature fighting to get free of its bonds.

"Fucking shoot him," Riley blurted, reaching for his own gun.

Before Horn could retrieve his tranquilizer gun, the prisoner's eyes widened with awareness. He blinked, his vertical pupils fluctuating in size as he focused on the man holding him down. When he locked onto Horn, his face twisted in an agonized expression. His lips puckered and smacked.

The creature let out a deafening scream that shook the room. Horn silenced the man with a boot to the face, crushing his skull in one powerful stomp.

The poor bastard's arms twitched before going limp. Beckham held his breath, waiting for the infected across the alley to come crashing through the window.

Silence washed over them as the men prepared for another attack, their weapons angled toward the windows and door. Beckham could sense the tension in every sound. The rustle of Wolfe's suit, a muffled cough from Riley, Horn's heavy breathing—the team was petrified of the monsters hunting them.

But the monsters never came.

Beckham moved back to the window. Maybe they had moved on? The scraping had stopped.

Realizing he was still holding his breath, he exhaled and then slowly pulled back the curtains. Staring back at him through the glass was the faceless man who minutes ago had stood on the rooftop across the alley. Beckham didn't have time to think about how the creature had managed to jump across. In one rapid movement, it speared the glass with its skull and then pulled away.

A black hole was all that remained of what had once been a face. The man's lips and chin were completely gone. A mustache of teeth marks around the gaping wound made Beckham's stomach roll. Like a gigantic leech, the man pressed the swollen hole against the window.

Beckham jammed his MP5 against the glass and pulled the trigger. The rounds shattered the pane and sent the creature flying back into the night, tumbling toward the alley below.

"Run!" Beckham screamed. He heard the creature's body hit the ground. It sounded like a shotgun going off. Shattering bones always did.

The man released one final shriek of misery that sounded different from the mindless and hungry high-pitched screams of the others. There was a hint of despair in it.

A hint of humanity.

It was 3:00 a.m. when Kate and Ellis began the autopsies on the rhesus monkeys. Normally Kate would have left the job to Ellis. He had studied forensic pathology, but she wanted to get as many tissue samples to Toxicology as possible.

The work required great attention to detail, and the exhaustion from lack of sleep was slowing Kate down. She started by removing the internal organs of a female rhesus monkey and examining them delicately. There were no signs of internal hemorrhaging, as she'd suspected.

With her eyes starting to glaze over, she took a step back from the table. She placed the scalpel down and mentally checked off every task that needed to be performed. She couldn't lose her focus now, and she couldn't make a mistake.

Get a grip, Kate. You're almost there.

Ellis noticed that she had backed away from her table. "How are you doing?"

"Fine. Just needed a breather. How about you?"

"Good. I took several biopsies. Fixed them with glutaraldehyde, then embedded them in paraffin wax. Just waiting for them to dry now."

"You're faster than I am," Kate replied.

"I've done this countless times."

Kate nodded and moved back to her table.

An hour later, the samples were ready for the microscopes. Kate brought the data up on the main display. Together they huddled around the screen. They'd used a historical staining and immunohistochemistry procedure on some of the samples. The results weren't surprising.

As Kate had suspected, the morphology of the endothelial cells was mostly intact. The virus wasn't attacking the cells like other strains of Ebola.

"Confirms our theory," Ellis sighed. "The virus isn't causing massive endothelial cell death, and thus the vessel structures are surprisingly uncompromised."

"But that doesn't explain the other changes. Time to dig deeper. Let's get these to Toxicology."

Kate and Ellis spent another hour preparing the tissue slices for the technicians in Toxicology. Several of them were on standby, and Kate used the intercom to notify Compartment 1 that the samples were on their way.

"This is Rod," said a calm and clinical voice that reminded Kate of Michael.

"Good morning, Rod, this is Doctor Lovato, from Compartment 3. We have tissue samples coming your way."

"Excellent. Any specific instructions?"

"Perform a complete toxicology screening on every one of these samples. I'm looking specifically for traces of VX-99. I want to know how it works and where it shows up."

"You got it," Rod replied.

"Oh, and Rod," Kate said, "I need this back ASAP."

"Understood, Doctor."

"Thanks." Kate took her finger off the intercom and looked at Ellis. She needed some sleep. "I'm going to try and crash for a few hours."

"All right. I'll let you know if Toxicology comes back with anything before you wake up."

Kate thought of the small twin bed back in her quarters. Her body was exhausted, but her mind was on fire with worry. There was simply too much to do and so much at stake. Sighing, she changed her mind. There was no way she was going to sleep with the world burning around her, especially with Beckham and his men out risking their lives for her and everyone else on the island.

18

Beckham slammed his shoulder into the door. Every muscle in his body ached from the hour they'd spent in the stairwell, trying desperately to keep the horde of infected back.

They'd made it ten feet from their office hiding spot when they were cornered and forced to retreat to a concrete stairwell. Neither the top nor the bottom door locked. Riley and Horn held off the pack frantically trying to get in through the bottom door, while Beckham and Wolfe held off the infected on the second floor.

The growing group of creatures smashed into the door again, pushing Beckham back. Screaming with rage, he bowed his head like a lineman about to sack a quarterback and slammed into the door with his shoulder. He wasn't sure how much longer they could hold them back.

He brought his sweaty chin down on the comm. "Horn, Riley. How many do you think are down there?"

Horn's reply sounded more like a grunt. "Ugh. Five."

Beckham had no idea how many were on the other side of his door, but from the sounds of their desperate howls, he guessed there were at least half a dozen.

"We need to make a move," Riley said. He breathed

heavily over the channel. Beckham knew he was running on empty. They all were.

"Got any ideas?" Beckham replied.

"Not really," Riley said. "I guess we could try shooting our way out."

"I was hoping it wouldn't come to that," Beckham said. There was no other option. Morning was quickly approaching. They needed to get to a safe location if they were to have any hope of being evacuated. There was no way in hell they would survive another day or night out here.

With his shoulder firmly planted against the door, Beckham glanced over at Wolfe. "You good?"

The young soldier managed a nod.

"You sure?"

"Yeah. You can count on me," Wolfe replied.

Chinning his comm, Beckham said, "Okay, on the count of three, we let go of the doors and meet in the middle of the staircase. You fire the moment one of those things breaks through."

"All right," Wolfe said, nodding.

"Short, controlled bursts. Conserve ammo. Aim for the head or the heart," Beckham added.

"Got it, boss," Horn replied.

"Roger that," Riley chipped in.

Closing his eyes, Beckham calmed his breathing and focused. He kept reminding himself this was no different from firefights in Iraq or Afghanistan; these things could be killed, just like any human.

"One."

"Two."

Gripping his MP5 in his left hand, he said, "Three!"

Beckham jumped away from the door and took a careful step down the stairs, standing shoulder to shoulder with Wolfe.

The first creature hit the door at breakneck speed, stumbling and falling face first against the pavement. The moment gave Beckham the perfect view of the hallway beyond. The infected stood staring back at him, almost as if they were surprised.

He utilized the moment of confusion and fired several short bursts into the man on the ground. The bullets tore through the back of his head and he immediately went limp. The next two creatures looked down at the destroyed man's head and let out deep howls—howls so loud that Beckham could hear them over the gunfire from below.

Wolfe cut them down with his M4 in two shots. Their ruined bodies slumped to the floor. The next batch came running down the hall with amazing speed. Two of them dropped to all fours and used the momentum from their back legs to hurtle their bodies forward. The leader, a woman with crazed, rose-colored eyes, lunged through the doorway.

Beckham squeezed off a shot that caught her in the face. A curtain of black hair formed a halo around her head as she flew back into the hallway, crashing into two men behind her.

Taking two more steps backward, Beckham aimed at the creatures just as another pack came bursting into the hallway. Their hungry shrieks reverberated down the corridor.

"How we doing?" Beckham yelled.

A blast from Riley's shotgun rang in Beckham's ears, making it impossible to hear a response.

Seconds later the team stood back-to-back, their guns blazing. Never in his career had Beckham fought in such close quarters. There was nothing quite like a firefight in a space so tight and narrow. Blood and gore caked the walls as the infected grew more desperate. The insanity of the situation recharged Beckham's muscles and he fought harder, his shots precise. Calculated. He wasn't going to let his men down. Not again.

Blood splattered on Beckham's visor, throwing him off balance. He swiped it away, regained his composure, and fired the last of his magazine.

"I'm out!" He reached for another, but his hand came back empty. He instantly reached for his M9 and instead found the grip of the tranquilizer gun. With only two of the creatures left, he pulled the pistol from his belt, and with one eye closed he fired off one of the rounds at the closest one. It was just a boy.

Wolfe took out the final female infected that emerged at the top of the stairs with four rounds to her midsection. Her body spasmed as she slumped against the wall, blood smearing down the concrete.

An odd silence filled the space, ghostly trails of smoke coming from the team's gun barrels. Beckham scanned the ground. Brass casings littered the concrete, and dark red blood flowed freely down the steps, a small river making its way down to his boots. He stood in the middle of a slaughterhouse.

The sight terrified him, knowing that only a thin layer protected him from the virus that could turn him into a monster.

"We better move," Horn said. "Those things will be back."

Beckham slowly emerged from his trance. Horn was right. They needed to get to higher ground and find a place where a Black Hawk could evacuate them.

"Let's go," Riley shouted.

"Wait!" Beckham replied, remembering the boy he'd shot with the tranquilizer gun. He raced up the stairs, stepping over two dead bodies. The boy's right arm protruded from a stack three deep.

Beckham pushed the woman off of him and then nudged

the kid with his boot. His yellow, bloodstained eyes popped open, the vertical pupils blinking rapidly. The boy groaned and reached up with his one free arm, clawing limply at the air. He struggled, his lips puckering as the tranquilizer entered his system.

Beckham took a step back and watched the poor boy suffer. In a few seconds it was over. The child's eyelids closed over his reptilian eyes, and he let out one final grunt.

Nudging him with a boot, Beckham waited a few more beats and then bent down and grabbed the boy. He hoisted him over his shoulders and then joined the others at the bottom of the stairs. "Got us a new ticket to Fort Bragg."

Horn acknowledged this with a nod and then disappeared into the hallway beyond. Riley and Wolfe went next, and Beckham followed, hoping they could make it to a clear LZ before they were swarmed.

Kate twitched in her chair as the door to the research room swung open. Ellis held two mugs of steaming coffee in his hands.

"Thirsty?"

"You're a lifesaver," Kate moaned. "What time is it?"

"Nine a.m." He yawned. "Did you sleep?" He set the mugs on the table and plopped down in the chair next to her.

"A little," Kate replied. "Have you heard anything from—"

"Nope. Not yet."

Kate crossed her arms, tightening them against her chest. The room was freezing. "How about Beckham? Is he back yet?"

"Not sure, but I don't think so."

With her mind spinning, she moved on to her next question. "What's the latest on what's happening outside?"

Ellis frowned. "Colonel Gibson has placed a communications cloak over the island, so I have no idea."

Kate finished a sip from her mug and scowled. "Why would he do that?"

"I know. I don't understand either, but Major Smith tried to sell the decision as a morale thing," Ellis said. He ran a hand through his slicked-back hair and took a drink. "Things must be awful outside if he doesn't want people to know what's going on. I'm assuming the virus has made it overseas by now."

Kate resisted the urge to chew her fingernails. There was only a remote chance that other countries could have shut down their airports before it spread, preventing planes with suspected cases from landing. But there were protocols in place to prevent the spread of Level 4 contagions, and if they had been followed...

She shook the impossible idea away. Even if the virus hadn't made it to every continent yet, it would. Knowing what she did now about incubation periods and the nature of the infection, it was ludicrous to think otherwise.

"I did hear the president is dead," Ellis said nonchalantly.

Kate froze. "*What?* How?"

Ellis shook his head. "Somehow the infection made it into his bunker. The vice president is gone too."

"My God," Kate replied.

"The virus is spreading so fast," Ellis said. His voice grew lower as he spoke. "It's almost as if it was engineered." He shook his head and reached for his cup.

"What did you say? Kate said.

"Just that the virus is spreading so fast."

"No, after that."

"It seems like it was engineered to spread?"

Kate still couldn't bring herself to believe that Dr. Medford had designed the hemorrhage virus with sinister intentions. The man had done what Kate and Michael had never been able to accomplish: He'd found a way to severely restrict the destruction of the endothelial cells. It was a partial cure in its own right, but it still didn't make sense to her. *Why stop at a partial cure?* The virus was more contagious now than ever, and the prolonged life of the host had allowed it to spread across the country.

And none of this explained the transformation these people were going through. What was causing the virus to transform hosts into violent monsters?

Taking a gulp of her coffee, Kate stood and stretched. In a few hours, she would know. And hopefully then she would have some idea of how to create a cure.

Beckham grunted, hoisting the boy higher up onto his shoulders. They'd had a stroke of luck since leaving the back exit of the warehouse building. None of the creatures had spotted them, and none followed them. Clinging to the shadows, Beckham guided the team through the city streets silently and without detection.

Pausing at the edge of Grand Street, he scanned both sides of the road. Besides a few dusty vehicles, the path was empty. The only movement was from the gusts of wind that carried trash across the concrete.

With his hands supporting his cargo, he was forced to give a verbal command. "Move," he said, chinning his comm.

Footfalls pounded the concrete behind him, and he

pushed harder. The muscles in his legs groaned, burning with every motion.

They were still a block away from the extraction point, the same beach where the pilots had dropped them. According to Echo's last transmission they were on their way and would be hovering over the ocean, waiting for Ghost.

Looking toward the skyline, Beckham caught a glimpse of the morning sun. He'd never been so excited to see its beautiful crimson rays. But the feeling didn't last. The quiet streets were unnerving. There wasn't even the faint thump of helicopter blades.

Groaning, Beckham checked his watch, knowing they were close to their extraction time. If he didn't hurry, they were going to be late.

"Fuck," he mumbled. If Gibson left them out here another day, he was going to personally pay the man a visit as soon as he got back. And this time he wasn't going to hold his tongue, or his fists.

The thought gave him an extra boost of energy, and he rounded Smith Avenue anxious to see the shoreline beyond. A semitruck blocked the view, the trailer stretching across the street. Above the glistening metal, he finally saw the rotating blades of a chopper.

Our ride.

"Thank God," he mumbled, hoisting the boy onto his shoulders again.

Moving around the front of the truck, Beckham used his last bit of strength to run toward Main Street. He could see the railroad tracks now and the white sand beyond. The waves crashing across the shoreline filled his helmet with a soothing sound.

They were almost there.

Almost safe.

When he was halfway down the street, he heard a deep croaking so loud he nearly dropped his infected cargo on the concrete.

He twisted, looking for the source of the noise. Beckham strained to see through his filthy visor. Moisture fogged the inside where he'd coughed and sweated during the firefight inside the staircase. There was no way to clean it without taking it off.

"What the fuck is that?" Horn asked.

Beckham swept his gaze over the road in front of him as best he could, stopping on empty cars and then moving to a cluster of trees lining the road.

Nothing.

Riley spun a few feet away, his shotgun searching for a target. "Where is it coming from?"

Beckham shook his head. Lowering the boy to the ground, he reached for his MP5, cursing when he remembered the magazine was dry.

"Shit! One o'clock!" Riley shouted.

Beckham looked up and saw a man—a former soldier, judging by what remained of his clothing—perched on the rooftop of a three-story building. He held a severed limb in his right hand and tore away chunks of flesh in between howls.

Beckham twisted his head to the side and chinned his comm. Fighting to stay calm, he said, "Don't engage. Get to the LZ."

The whoosh of the Black Hawk's blades reminded Beckham how close they were to salvation. He reached down to grab the sick boy under his armpit. "Got to move," he whispered, in a voice so low only he could hear.

The team crossed Main Street and then carefully navigated the railroad tracks. Risking a glance behind them,

Beckham saw the infected man toss the limb off the building. Then, on all fours, the man scaled down the exterior surface of the building.

"Jesus," Beckham muttered. He found himself wondering again how that was even possible. When the man got to the street, several other infected came flying through the bottom door, deafening screeches pouring from their mouths.

Beckham could hardly hear the sound of the pilot's voice as it crackled into his earpiece.

"Ghost One, this is Echo One, en route to LZ."

The voice cut out, and Beckham watched the chopper swerve to the right.

"LZ is hot! Repeat: LZ is hot!" the main pilot suddenly yelled.

No fucking shit, Beckham thought.

The Black Hawk banked hard to the side and then hovered. In the open doorway, a crew chief grabbed the M240 door gun and fired. Red-hot 7.62-millimeter rounds tore through the air, whistling like mini missiles.

Beckham struggled to get across the sand, the boy weighing him down. When he was under the chopper, he dropped the kid and waited for the rest of the team.

Riley and Horn arrived a second later, taking up positions a few feet away. Then came Wolfe, panting heavily.

The crew chief continued to spew rounds over their heads. Infected creatures dropped to hands and feet in an attempt to bolt around the spray, but the gunner compensated quickly. The bullets cut them down one by one, splattering the beach red. The infected soldier from the roof was the last to fall. He crumpled to the ground thirty meters from the chopper, his hands reaching up toward the craft.

Beckham harbored no anger toward the creature, as he had so many other enemies. The soldier was sick, just as

Tenor had been. He had not asked for this. The virus wasn't some suicide jacket or sniper rifle that Beckham's enemies used to kill American soldiers. The real enemy was the microscopic virus inside the poor bastard's bloodstream.

The same virus inside the unconscious boy who lay curled up on the sand a few feet away. Beckham couldn't help but wonder what his role would be in finding a cure. A hand extended down above him. He looked up to see the crew chief.

"Let's go! Hoist the kid up!" the man yelled.

Nodding, Beckham reached down and grabbed the kid under his armpits. With a grunt, he lifted the child into the air. Horn helped, and together they pushed the boy toward the chopper. As soon as he was in, Beckham climbed in and collapsed with his back to the metal floor. Closing his eyes, he took in a slow breath. Filtered air had never tasted so good.

The chopper lifted into the air and Beckham let himself rest for a few minutes to gather his thoughts. Somehow they had survived and had managed to complete their mission.

His thoughts drifted to all those who had died and finally to Dr. Kate Lovato. She wasn't a damsel in distress. She didn't need saving. She had handled herself in Atlanta as a soldier would. And even though he didn't know the doctor well, his gut told him that if anyone could stop this nightmare, she could.

19

Kate rushed through the cafeteria line. She hadn't eaten in over twenty-four hours and felt as if she was about to fall over. Her stomach growled, but she had no appetite.

Grabbing a deli sandwich, yogurt, and milk that she suspected was expired, she hurried down the line. The mess hall was nearly empty now, only a few marines talking in hushed voices a few tables away.

Glancing at her watch, she saw it was only 1:00 p.m. She still had a few hours to wait for the toxicology results to come back.

As she walked toward the exit, the double doors to the facility cracked open. Three men stumbled inside.

Kate froze when she saw them.

Beckham.

"You made it," she said.

The man acknowledged her with a nod. Not exactly the response she was looking for.

"Didn't think we were going to," Beckham said. He ran a hand through his hair. "Go get some grub, guys," he said to Riley and Horn. They didn't hesitate.

"That bad?" Kate asked.

He nodded again and changed the subject. "How's the research going?"

"Slow, but we are making progress." She lifted a curious brow. "What's it like out there?"

"Hell on earth. We got you a live sample, though. The specimen's just a kid. Probably only eight or nine years old. He attacked us with another group of infected when we were trapped inside a stairwell. Compared to some of the others, the kid's in decent shape."

Kate tried to imagine what they had faced. The few hours she'd been trapped in the lab at CDC headquarters in Atlanta were bad enough, but an entire night?

"You look tired," Beckham said.

"You do too," she said.

"I am. And I'm starving." He glanced over at the buffet line.

"Where's the boy?" Kate asked.

"Gibson's men took him into one of the buildings as soon as we landed. They're probably cutting him right now." He opened his mouth as if to say more, but refrained from further comment.

The idea disturbed her more than she expected. The boy was infected, but he was still just a kid.

Beckham looked at the food line again and then hesitated, glancing back at her. "You doing okay?"

Their eyes connected, briefly. There was a kindness and strength there. She felt the same reassuring sense of safety every time she was with him. With a short nod, she managed to say, "Yes, I'm fine. Thanks."

Beckham stepped aside as the doors swung open. Ellis came rushing into the mess hall, out of breath.

"Kate, the toxicology reports came back early. You have to see these!" He panted and, in between breaths, said,

"I know...why the virus is...changing people into... monsters."

"I need to go," she whispered.

"Good luck," Beckham replied, his lips twisting to the side as if he was unsure of what else to say. With a nod, she followed Ellis out of the building, terrified of what the results were going to show.

Kate skimmed the toxicology notes as quickly as possible when they got back to the lab. She was nervous, but this was a different type of nervous—this was the nervousness she always experienced right before a major discovery.

And Toxicology had made a *major* discovery. The tissue screenings revealed traces of the VX-99. The technicians had used detergents and a variety of chemicals to digest the tissue samples. Then they used mass spectrometry and nuclear magnetic resonance spectroscopy to identify the chemical compounds of VX-99 present in the structure. Electron microscopy then revealed what Kate and Ellis had missed: Tiny nanostructures of VX-99 had attached themselves to the Ebola virus strands.

But something was still off—the chemicals weren't just solubilized in the tissues and absorbed in the cells.

Ellis nodded as she read. "The VX-99 exists in a hybrid nanostructure form."

"So we know how Doctor Medford modified the virus, but this still doesn't explain the mutation and transformation of the victim. The violent behavior, the physiology changes," Kate said. "Unless..."

"Keep reading," Cindy said. She sat next to Ellis, her hand cupped over her mouth.

Kate nodded and scrolled down to the next section, titled "Epigenetic Changes."

The two words made her pause. What the hell did they have to do with the hemorrhage virus?

She read on, digesting the information slowly.

"The VX-99 chemicals disrupt the normal cell-to-cell signaling that regulates what genes are turned on and off within cells."

"Holy shit," Ellis said. "There are twenty to twenty-five thousand human protein coding genes. Only about ninety-eight percent of those are actually active. Some of them are remnants dating back to the primordial-ooze stage of evolution. The sucker lips are reminiscent of early multicellular organisms and some more complex parasites. The vertical pupils with the double membrane could link to a number of species. And the flexible joints could relate—"

Kate held up a hand in disbelief, cutting Ellis off. She closed her eyes. She couldn't believe it. She didn't *want* to believe it. "So, Doctor Medford used VX-99 to turn on genes that harken back to previous stages in our evolution."

"It's insane," Cindy said.

"But it makes sense," Kate replied, ashamed she hadn't thought of this before. When she opened her eyes, everything was crystal clear. How could she have missed the signs? The chemicals in VX-99 reactivated the protein-coded genes that separated humans from wild animals. Ellis was right. Some of them might even date back millennia. Simply put, the chemicals turned the infected host into a predatory animal. That's what had made the weapon so deadly back in Vietnam.

Hunching over the screen, Kate read the final paragraph out loud. "Endocrine cell signaling is causing an increase in the stem cell population of dermal and bone marrow tissues."

Cindy nodded rapidly. "Fascinating. It's as if their bodies are constantly telling them they're injured, which in turn produces a constant supply of hormones that tell stem cells to proliferate and circulate in the bloodstream."

"So their glands have likely been altered as a result of VX-99 as well," Kate stated.

Ellis nodded. "Exactly—the specimens are producing more and more stem cells, which also explains their fast metabolisms."

"And," Kate said, her voice softening as she spoke, "it explains why they are hungry as hell for raw meat. It's the quickest and most digestible source of the proteins they need to keep making stem cells."

"Maybe zombies aren't science fiction after all," Ellis said. There was a hint of shock in his voice. His earlier enthusiasm had vanished.

"These aren't zombies," Kate said sternly.

She reread the three paragraphs just to reinforce what she already knew. When she finally looked away, the room was silent, and both of her colleagues sat staring at her. Their eyes pleaded for reassurance, begging her to offer a different opinion than the one they had already formed. But the facts were right in front of them. Shaking, Kate said, "Doctor Medford was never working on a cure for Ebola. He was working on a bioweapon."

"But what about the endothelial cells?" Ellis said, his voice low, as if he already knew the answer. "Maybe he was really working on a cure..."

"No," Kate said. "He was working on a weapon—a contagious, deadly, and untraceable weapon. That's why we never saw the nanoparticles loaded with VX-99. They were already filtering out of the body. If it weren't for the liver samples, Rod would never have even known."

"A weapon killed Javier and Michael," Kate whispered, almost to herself. "A weapon is killing the entire world." Her voice grew louder. "The hemorrhage virus is man-made!"

Cindy and Ellis stood, but neither said a single word.

An abrupt surge of anger washed through Kate. With her thoughts spinning in all directions, she directed that anger toward Gibson. The colonel was the engineer of more than Plum Island. He was the engineer of the hemorrhage virus. The outbreak might very well have been an accident, but the creation of the virus itself wasn't.

Kate reached for her forehead, suddenly feeling over-whelmed and light-headed. "Cindy, do you have access to any of Doctor Medford's research?"

The technician shook her head.

"But you work for USAMRIID," Ellis said. "You're telling us you don't have access to their files?"

"There are no files," Cindy replied firmly. "There never were." She shot Kate a frightened look. "I'm just as shocked as you are."

The words spoke to Kate louder than anything she had seen. She knew then with certainty that Medford had engineered the hemorrhage virus under orders from above. He'd covered his tracks to make it look as if it was actually a cure for the Ebola outbreak in Guinea. But the secret weapon had never left Building 8 inside a secure case—it had left Building 8 by accident, in human form.

The chain of events no longer mattered. All that mattered was that the hemorrhage virus wasn't from some jungle in Africa. It had been engineered in a lab on US soil—which meant it would be even more difficult to cure. And behind all of it was...

Gibson.

A man Michael had trusted. Taking in long, deep breaths,

Kate whisked away from the monitors. Overwhelmed by anger, she walked briskly toward the exit. Her mind was clear and focused now. She knew exactly what she was going to do next.

"Where are you going, Kate?" Ellis yelled after her.

"If you want to know, follow me," she replied.

Colonel Gibson walked across the small lab to peer through a thick glass panel separating the room from a holding chamber. A bank of bright oval lights hung from the ceiling on the other side, illuminating a trio of technicians strapping the limp body of a young boy to a metal gurney. They were the same type of lights that had been used to study the sole survivor of Operation Burn Bright so many years ago. They brought Gibson flashbacks of Lieutenant Brett's frail body as he twisted in the chains that bound him in the tiny cell they had kept him in for the better part of a decade.

He reminded himself why he'd reactivated the bioweapon program, as if justifying it might somehow make things seem less horrific. VX-99 was supposed to have transformed the lieutenant into a super soldier, but instead it had wiped away his humanity. Gibson's vision for the weapon had changed over the years. He'd abandoned the idea of creating a super soldier and instead had ordered Doctor Medford to create a bioweapon. VX-99 was supposed to replace the need for boots on the ground. His vision was for VX-99 to save the lives of thousands of American soldiers. Men like his son, who had died from the cowardly IEDs that insurgents used to turn young soldiers into ground beef. And best of all, the weapon would have been mostly untraceable.

No matter how he justified the past fifty years in his mind, the irony bled through. The bioweapon he'd ordered Medford to create wasn't saving American soldiers' lives—it was turning them into monsters, along with billions of innocent civilians.

The colonel closed his eyes, filled with an overwhelming guilt that tugged at his core. He'd known at the beginning of the Vietnam War that it was lost. Many would call him crazy for his actions, but in reality, he was logical. Now he was starting to wonder if this new war was lost too. Operation Reaper had failed miserably. The military had retreated from all major population zones. They were losing the country city by city.

Gibson stepped up to the glass, concentrating on the boy. His pale skin glistened under the lights, clean from the decon shower. As Gibson looked closer, he saw the symptoms of the hemorrhage virus were already reemerging. Blood oozed from under the boy's eyelids and trickled from his nose. Red blotches lined his naked arms and legs.

It was his fault that the innocent kid had transformed into a monster, he knew, but that had never been his intention. Goddamnit, he had only wanted to save lives! To protect the country he loved so dearly.

War had changed since Vietnam. Like the boy in front of him, it had evolved. America had new enemies, enemies who were merciless and brutal. Terrorist groups would stop at nothing to inflict harm on American targets. The military had done everything to take the battle to foreign soil, but the blood of too many American soldiers had already stained the sands of Iraq and the mountains of Afghanistan. VX-99 was supposed to end all of that. The bioweapon was supposed to be killing terrorists and then fizzling out before anyone knew what had happened.

Instead, Gibson was staring at a child infected with the

viral monster Dr. Medford had inadvertently created. Gritting his teeth, he looked away from the glass. It was only a matter of time before one of the scientists on the island discovered the truth. Hell, he would have told them the truth himself and explained how the virus worked if he had known. But he didn't. That's why he had sent the Delta Force team in days before to collect a sample.

Sighing, Gibson forced himself back to the window. Watching the struggling boy, his troubled mind experienced a second of intense clarity. In that moment, he knew one thing for sure. He *was* responsible for the end of the world, and he could only pray that Dr. Lovato and the other scientists would find a cure before it was too late.

Beckham moved at a half run along the concrete path leading across the island. A steady and cold drizzle beat against his bare face. He yawned, still exhausted from their mission to recover the infected child.

He stopped to take in the view of the two guard towers on the north side of the island. The concrete structures protruded out of the ground, large spotlights sweeping the shoreline beyond. A random flash of lightning lit up the skyline and illuminated the walls built around the hexagonal base. He suddenly felt like a prisoner trapped inside a maximum-security prison.

But soon that would all change. He was on his way to meet with Gibson and secure their ride back to Fort Bragg.

Thunder boomed in the distance, rattling the ground as Beckham continued walking. He approached a pair of guards standing outside the administration building with his badge at eye level.

One of them, a skinny, dark-skinned man, stepped under the light and studied it. He looked at Beckham's face and then nodded. "All clear, Master Sergeant."

Inside, another pair of guards waited. They repeated the same process. "Follow us, please, Master Sergeant," one of them said.

Beckham peered into each office as they walked. They were all empty, the lights inside them dim. When they reached the far end of the hall, the two soldiers stopped. The smaller of the two gestured toward the last door on the hall. Just then, alarmed voices rang out behind them.

The guard unstrapped his rifle. "I'll check it out," he said, nodding at the other soldier.

Beckham listened.

"I want to see Colonel Gibson!" The raised voice was familiar—female.

"Kate?" Beckham whispered. He took a step back from the door. There she was, at the other end of the hallway, arguing with the first two guards in her best *don't fuck with me right now* voice. Ellis stood behind her sheepishly.

"You're not listening, Doctor. You can't see Colonel Gibson," the guard on the left said.

"No, *you're* not listening!" Kate replied.

Beckham decided to intervene.

"I'm sorry, Doctor Lovato, but—" the soldier began to say when Beckham put his hand on the man's thick shoulder.

"Let her through," Beckham said.

The man regarded him and then backed away.

Kate and Ellis shoved past the man. Both of them were breathing hard, as if they had run the entire length of the building.

"What's this all about?" Beckham asked.

"You're about to find out," Kate replied. Her face was

flushed red. She walked briskly toward the colonel's office and entered without knocking; Beckham followed right behind her.

Inside Gibson was standing with his arms crossed, his features darkened. "Doctors," he said in a low voice.

Beckham stood in the doorway, blocking the two guards from entering.

"We know," Kate said. "Did you really think the truth wouldn't come out?"

Gibson exhaled a deep sigh that sounded like relief more than dread. Then he slowly sat down in his chair and reached for a pack of cigarettes. He jammed one in his mouth and said, "I knew you would find out."

"The hemorrhage virus is a bioweapon, a weapon that you had designed," Kate said.

Beckham stepped forward. "What's she talking about, Colonel?"

The man held up a hand. "Let her finish."

Kate glanced back at Beckham with a look of uncertainty. He gave her the shortest of nods, and she took a step closer to Gibson's desk.

"Doctor Medford created a hybrid nanostructure by bonding nanoparticles loaded with VX-99 to a genetically modified Ebola virus. At first we didn't see them. I suspect that was the point. The weapon was supposed to be untraceable. And with the endothelial cells reacting differently than they do in other strands of Ebola, I was almost convinced he had created a partial cure. I had my suspicions, but I had secretly hoped that the other scientists were right, that he was working on a cure and had created the hemorrhage virus by accident."

Catching her breath, Kate shook a finger and then continued, speaking more rapidly. "But what didn't make sense were the other changes—the sucker mouths, the distorting of the bodies, the vertical pupils, the morphed hands and feet. It wasn't until we sent samples to Toxicology that we discovered the truth. It was then we found the epigenetic changes." Her hands shook as she approached the colonel's desk.

"That weapon!" she choked. "Your weapon!" She narrowed her eyes. "It turned my brother into a monster! It killed Michael Allen, and it's rapidly killing the rest of the world!"

Beckham put a hand on Kate's left arm. She was shaking uncontrollably now.

"And you!" Kate pointed a finger at Gibson. "You were the one who ordered Doctor Medford to design it."

"I fucking knew it," Beckham said. He stood by Kate's side, supporting her as he should have done from the second they walked in the room.

"She's right, isn't she, Colonel?" Beckham said.

Gibson very calmly took the unlit cigarette from his mouth and placed it on the table. "Yes, she's right."

Silence filled the room. A lonely cricket chirped outside.

"You're right," Gibson said again. He stood and looked at them in turn. "I never meant for any of this to happen. When I sent Team Ghost to Building 8, I was trying to *stop* this from happening. Doctor Medford's last message said he had created something that was too contagious."

"But it got out," Kate said. Her breathing was steadier now.

The colonel nodded. "I ordered Doctor Medford to create a bioweapon that could be used in hot spots around the world. I wanted to end the need for American soldiers to be deployed on foreign soil. Too many of our sons have died in sandboxes that aren't worth a fucking shit. *My* son died..."

Beckham narrowed his eyes at the failing man in front of him. The colonel trailed off, his words lost. His eyes fell to the floor. The blood of so many was on his hands, including three members of Team Ghost.

Beckham felt his right fist moving at his side. He wanted to strike the colonel. God, it would feel good, but he couldn't bring himself to do it. The sobering truth was that Gibson had been motivated by the death of his only son. His justification for the bioweapon program wasn't much different from the missions of other weapons programs. The Manhattan Project had been designed to save American lives and force the Japanese to surrender. Like the atomic bomb, the virus was just another horrible weapon built for a noble purpose.

"Why?" Kate whispered. "Why didn't you tell us what we were dealing with?"

"I didn't know!" Gibson said, his voice snapping. He looked to Beckham. "That's why I sent his team into Building Eight. If I had known, I would have handed you the info on a silver platter!"

There were rapid footfalls in the hallway. Lieutenant Colonel Jensen and Major Smith burst into the room, shoving Ellis out of their way.

"What the hell is going on here?" Jensen asked.

Colonel Gibson bowed his head in defeat and in a low voice said, "Doctor Lovato can tell you."

Jensen scratched his chin and eyed Kate. After a brief pause, he said, "Well, is someone going to fill me in?"

"The hemorrhage virus is a bioweapon," she replied. "And your boss was the engineer."

The lieutenant colonel's eyes shot up to meet Gibson's. His superior nodded confidently, a final moment of strength in a career that had spanned decades. "You're in charge now," Gibson said. He held out his wrists and said, "Lock me up and destroy the fucking key."

"Sergeant Singh," Jensen said, without taking his eyes off of Gibson.

One of the guards from earlier stepped into the room. "Yes, sir?" he said.

"Take Colonel Gibson into custody."

Singh hesitated.

"That's an order, Sergeant," Jensen snapped.

Beckham scrutinized Gibson as the guard grabbed him under one arm. Flashbacks tore across his mind. The briefing on the Osprey, the pile of bodies in Building 8, and finally Tenor's terrified face as the bioweapon consumed him. In a blind fit of rage, Beckham placed his right foot forward, twisted, and threw a punch that landed squarely on Gibson's jaw.

A crack echoed through the room as the colonel collapsed. Sergeant Singh faltered, trying to catch Gibson's limp body, and both men ended up on the floor.

"That's for my men," Beckham snarled.

Gibson whimpered out a reply. "I'm sorry," he mumbled, holding his cheek. "I'm sorry for everything. I never meant for any of this to happen."

Jensen offered Beckham a nod of approval. The two men shared a moment, something passing between them that only a soldier would recognize—an understanding. Beckham had done exactly what Jensen would have liked to do.

"Get him out of here," Jensen said.

A second guard bent down and helped Singh drag the colonel out of the room. As they were leaving, Gibson paused and looked at Kate.

"Find a cure," he said. Then he looked at Beckham. "I'm sorry, but Fort Bragg is lost. I just heard an hour ago."

And then he was gone, leaving Beckham and Kate standing in shock at the news.

20

Beckham stormed out of the building, the weight of the news about Fort Bragg and the source of the outbreak tearing him apart. He rushed back to the barracks, his boots sloshing in puddles left over from the afternoon's storm. He wasn't sure how he would break the news to Horn. *How do you tell a man his family is probably dead?* He felt responsible—he had told Horn to bring his family to the post, arguing they would be safer there.

He'd learned a long time ago how to suppress these feelings—guilt and regret could destroy a soldier during war—but none of that worked right now. The end of the world had broken him. Beckham had had no one left besides his men and Horn's family. Now they were almost all gone, stripped away in a little over a week. The same darkness and dread that he'd worked so hard to shake after his mother had died had returned. But he couldn't let it consume him. He wouldn't let it consume him.

Flooded by a surge of emotion, Beckham broke into a

jog, his anger growing as he thought about Gibson and what he had done. His knuckles ached from where they had connected with the man's jaw, but goddamn, did it feel good.

As an operator, Beckham had seen the worst the human race had to offer: warlords in Africa and religious sects that kidnapped children and raised them as soldiers, dictators who crushed their opposition by murdering their opponents, terrorists who didn't care how many innocent civilians they killed. Bioweapons took evil to an entirely new and horrific level, and Beckham didn't care what the colonel's motivations had been.

He stopped outside the barracks to gather his thoughts. He still wasn't sure how he would break the news to Horn.

"You okay?" someone asked behind him. He spun to find Kate standing on the circular concrete drive outside the building, her hands in the pockets of her white trousers. She approached him slowly.

"What are you doing here?" Beckham said.

"Needed to see a friendly face—especially after what just happened back there."

"The man will burn for his crimes," Beckham replied. "I'll make sure of that."

A hollow roar shook the ground. Beckham felt it in his bones and saw several bright flashes on the horizon near the mainland.

Kate gasped at the sight. "They're bombing again?"

"What the hell's left to bomb?"

Another succession of flashes burst across the dark skyline. Deep booms followed. Beckham caught a glimpse of several jets racing away from the city, their blue exhaust trails fading into the night.

The concussions steadily increased, the ground shaking around them. Beckham felt every blast.

"How did it come to this?" Kate asked.

"Gibson," Beckham replied. "I always feared something like this would happen, that someone higher up would do something stupid and send the world to hell. I just never thought it would happen *here*."

A powerful tremor shook the pavement, and a brilliant red arc lit up the sky. Beckham shielded his eyes from the blast.

"This still seems so surreal," Kate replied. "It's chaos out there, isn't it?"

He nodded.

"Where will you go next?" Kate asked.

"I don't know," Beckham said, shaking his head. "Fort Bragg is gone. My home—" Another round of explosions cut him off. He used the moment to catch her eye and asked, "Knowing what you do now, can you stop this thing?"

Kate avoided his gaze. "I don't know."

Three flashes lit up the horizon. Kate watched them and said, "I don't know if I'm strong enough to do this."

Suppressing the dark feelings that had emerged earlier, Beckham pulled on the strength that had carried him through every difficult situation.

"You *can* do this, Kate," Beckham said, facing her. "You're stronger than you think you are. I watched you back in Atlanta. Here on the base. You are alive because of your courage and your strength. We need you."

Kate blinked and slowly nodded.

He reached forward and squeezed her hands, forcing her to hold his gaze.

"You may be our last hope," he said.

They stood there silently. Beckham finally knew what his new mission was. Protect the living—protect Kate, Ellis, Riley, and Horn.

"You're right," Kate said. "I need to get back to work."

Before he could respond, she took off running toward Building 1, leaving him to watch the world burning on the horizon.

Lieutenant Colonel Jensen spat on the concrete, wiping away a strand of chewing tobacco that had dripped down his chin. He climbed the two flights of stairs to the combat information center that looked out over the island. He still couldn't quite believe the hemorrhage virus was a bioweapon. After working with Colonel Gibson for the better part of a decade, he'd believed him when he said the work being done at Building 8 was to protect national security.

Jensen looked out over the base. He gripped the railing so hard that his knuckles turned white. Guard towers and electric fences surrounded the domed labs.

He should have known. Plum Island, Building 8—they were never built to help find a cure for Ebola; they were built to produce a bioweapon that used Ebola as a vehicle to spread. In the end, Jensen had been used too.

And now he was in charge. He needed to start thinking that way. He tucked another wad of tobacco against his gums before waving his badge over the security panel. It clicked, the door unlocked, and he left the chilly night and thoughts of conspiracy behind him.

Inside, Major Smith sat massaging the scar on his cheek, staring intensely at the feeds from security cameras around the island. The room stank of sweat and cigarette smoke.

Jensen regarded him with a nod and then moved toward the wall of communications equipment across the room. Corporal Hickman and Corporal Benzing sat there, waiting, their eyes searching him for orders.

"First things first," Jensen said. "It's time to let everyone on this island know what's going on outside." He reached toward the PA. With a push of a button, every scientist, soldier, and support staff would hear his voice.

His finger hovered over the button while he pondered all of the things he should say. Every man and woman on this island had family out there. He did too, a brother and sister in New Orleans. Last he had heard was that they were evacuating the city. That was days ago, and he knew the chances they were still alive were slim.

He punched the button to broadcast. It was time to take responsibility for the atrocities he had inadvertently helped to create.

Static cleared from the PA speakers hanging from the ceiling, and then came the muffled sound of his own breathing. He grabbed the mic and brought it to his mouth.

"All personnel, this is Lieutenant Colonel Jensen. As many of you know, Colonel Gibson has been placed under arrest for his involvement in the creation of the hemorrhage virus. I have taken command of the island. My first order is to lift the communications cloak. I know you all have family outside, and I know you are all wondering what their fate is. I will give a full briefing at 0730 hours in the mess hall."

Clicking the PA off, he said, "Corporals, see if we can figure out what's going on beyond our little island."

"On it, sir," they both said. They grabbed headsets, activating their stations with a few keystrokes.

Jensen paced behind them, waiting anxiously. Sitting in the dark for days had eaten at him, as it had everyone else. Everyone on the island was feeling the overwhelming dread of being boxed in, cut off from the outside world. This time the wait wasn't long.

Benzing pressed his headset over his ears. "Most of what

I'm picking up is automated. Emergency broadcast signals. Evacuation routes, sir."

"Same here," Hickman added. "Wait—" She scrolled her frequency dial, stopping on one of the channels she'd passed over.

"I've got something, sir," she said.

Jensen looked for Major Smith, gesturing for the man to join them. Seconds later, a panicked voice bled over the channel. The speakers crackled as white noise surged over the line.

"Does anyone copy?" asked the male voice. "Is *anyone* out there?"

"This is Plum Island, in New York—we read you, over," Hickman replied.

"Thank God," the man said. More static broke over the channel. Hickman twisted the knob slightly, and the line cleared.

"This is Marine Staff Sergeant Bell of Second Battalion, Second Marines, reporting from—" There was a pause, followed by the sound of distant gunfire.

"Shit, shit! They found us," Sergeant Bell said. "Ferguson! Where are they coming from?"

Jensen flinched as more shots rang out.

"Fuck. We need evac!" Bell said.

"Sergeant Bell, where are you? What are your coordinates?" Hickman asked.

"New York!" Bell replied.

Hickman frowned. "We need your coordinates."

Another round of gunfire cracked in the background, the deafening noise filling the CIC with the sound of war.

Before Hickman could respond, the line cut out. She glanced back at Jensen for support.

"I had no idea it was this bad," Smith said. He shook his head and walked away from the monitors.

"This is only the beginning," Jensen replied grimly. "We need to keep trying."

Hickman nodded, slowly. There was a deep sadness in her features. Hickman was young, probably only twenty-two or twenty-three years old, and Jensen knew that her training had done little to prepare her for the horrors they would face in the coming days.

"Sir, I've just intercepted several messages intended for Colonel Gibson. They're all encrypted. Looks like they were sent over the past seven days." Benzing scooted his chair closer to his computer monitor.

"Can you open them?" Jensen asked. He continued pacing behind the two officers, his eyes darting from screen to screen.

"Working on it now, sir," Benzing replied.

A few moments later the man smiled. "Got it."

Jensen swallowed and took a seat next to Benzing.

"Looks like the first two are from the deputy director of the CDC's Office of Infectious Diseases, Doctor Jed Frank."

"Bring it up," Jensen replied. He repositioned his chair to face the right-hand monitor where an image of Deputy Director Frank appeared. The video was dated 22 April. The man looked exhausted, both his eyes rimmed with purple bags.

"Colonel Gibson, we have grave news. The virus is at pandemic levels and has reached Europe, South America, and Asia. Due to the rapid speed of the infection, our initial projections were off considerably. Here is a new and more accurate depiction of what we can expect if you are unable to develop a cure in the next week."

Jensen watched as a map of the world emerged on the screen. A caption at the bottom showed the date as 22 April. Red dots illustrated the infection. The United States was already peppered with red blotches; Europe, South America, and even Asia had small clusters of the virus showing up in major cities. As the time lapse began to work, Jensen watched in shock as the entire world hemorrhaged red. No corner of the globe was safe. It all disappeared under the shroud of red dots within a two-week time frame.

"Jesus," Smith said from behind them. He was pacing back and forth nervously.

"Move on to the next one," Jensen ordered.

Benzing clicked on another video and activated it on the right-hand monitor. This was from one of the Joint Chiefs, a general named Richard Kennor. He was old, nearing seventy-five, and it showed in his wrinkled face.

"Colonel Gibson, we have deployed all of our resources to the outskirts of every metropolitan area in the nation, with the National Guard supporting active military units. Bombing runs will continue through April twenty-fifth. Hospitals and areas identified with major infections will be strategically located and eliminated. Our troops will then move in to clear out remaining cases."

Jensen swallowed a mouthful of chew, his throat catching on fire as it trickled down into his gut. He coughed, and tears filled his eyes. He'd stood by and watched the chopper full of refugees explode over the island, and he'd heard the bombs going off in New York, but he still couldn't believe that it was happening nationwide.

A sudden moment of fear paralyzed Jensen. What had Colonel Gibson done?

His staff was all staring at him, scanning his face for support or strength or God knew what. Jensen felt sick.

"Keep playing them," he mumbled, his world spinning around him as everything sank in.

The next video was dated 23 April. It was taken in what looked like a bunker. Concrete walls surrounded a small command center that appeared to be staffed by officers from all branches of the military. Deputy Director Frank emerged on the screen seconds after the video started.

"Colonel Gibson, we *need* to know the status of your work. Things are collapsing out here. The military has started retreating from major cities; their perimeters aren't holding. The infection is spreading faster than we ever imagined. Those who aren't sick are on the run. The military simply doesn't have enough troops to destroy the infected. They just keep coming."

The next videos were much of the same. The military was withdrawing and on the run. Europe, South America, Asia—it was happening everywhere.

Hearing just how grave the situation was hit Jensen harder than he had thought it would. Shit, it hit everyone in the room hard. The other three officers were quiet, waiting for his orders.

Crossing his arms, Jensen walked to the window overlooking the ocean. "I've heard enough. I want to meet with Doctor Lovato before the briefing. Hopefully she can give us some good news."

The moon vanished behind a cluster of dense clouds as he spoke. A spotlight from one of the guard towers swept the skyline, illuminating angry storm clouds rolling in. Jensen closed his eyes. The hemorrhage virus was the worst combination of man and Mother Nature, the perfect weapon, and he doubted there was anything they could do to stop it.

21

April 25, 2015
DAY 8

There was no cure. No way to bring her brother or anyone
else back.

Kate cupped her helmet in her hands and peeked through
a fort of gloved fingers at her computer monitor in the lab.
She'd worked through the night, testing several rhesus monkeys infected with the hemorrhage virus.

In the past, finding a cure would have meant simply dealing with the virus itself, but there were two problems with
the microscopic weapon tearing the world apart. The VX-99
hybrid nanoparticles had resulted in permanent epigenetic
changes in its victims. What was more, with the nanoparticles self-replicating, they were spread every time the virus
was passed to a new host.

A flashback to the creatures in Atlanta reminded Kate
that the infected were no longer people. They were monsters,
and there wasn't anything she could do to bring them back.

Ellis stood a few feet away, looking over her shoulder.
"What are we going to do?"

Kate blinked, trying to focus on her colleague. Her eyes were glazed, her vision blurry. She was tired and tense. Her thoughts were a muddled mess of theories, and they all circled back to the one she didn't want to think about.

"In order to kill a monster, you have to create one," she muttered.

"What do you mean?" Ellis said.

Pulling her gloves away from her visor, she stiffened. "Maybe Michael was right," she said. "Maybe there is no way to cure the hemorrhage virus. Maybe we need to create a monster of our own."

"I don't like where you're going with this," Ellis said. Dark bags rimmed his exhausted eyes. He brought a finger to his visor and rubbed the panel, as if he was trying to scratch a phantom itch.

"A bioweapon," Kate whispered. "If I can create a viral vector system to target the endothelial cells in the infected, then perhaps we can find a way to stop the virus after all. The best vaccine is to stop it from spreading and eradicate it altogether."

"To kill everyone infected?" Ellis stared back at her with an incredulous look. "You're talking about a weapon that will cause the victims to bleed out, right? To hemorrhage internally?"

Kate pursed her lips to respond, but instead bowed her helmet toward the floor and nodded.

"I better tell Lieutenant Colonel Jensen," Ellis said. "He wanted a progress report before the briefing."

Kate nodded, but she was hardly listening. "A monster of our own," she whispered.

Beckham sat across from Horn and watched the man's chest move up and down as he slept. He'd taken the news of Fort

Bragg much as Beckham thought he would—by punching the nearest wall. It had taken Beckham and Riley's combined effort to restrain Horn from going apeshit and waking up the entire room of sleeping soldiers.

When Horn had finally calmed down, it was close to midnight. He'd woken up several times during the night, leaning over to Beckham and asking if the news about Bragg was really true.

Beckham felt the overwhelming sadness trickle over him as he thought of Horn's two daughters and his wife. He'd told Horn they would be safer at Bragg, and now he was responsible for their fate.

But he wasn't going to give up on them yet. Maybe by some miracle they had survived and escaped Fort Bragg. If they were alive somewhere, Beckham would find them.

At 0715 hours the PA system barked to life.

"Attention, all personnel. Please report to the mess hall for briefing."

Beckham poked Horn in the arm. He grunted and shooed Beckham's hand away.

"Horn, briefing," Beckham said.

Riley jumped out of his bed a few feet away. "We're going to be late."

Beckham hesitated, knowing that Horn was not in the mood for an argument, but he wasn't going to let the man just lie there either.

"Horn, get your ass up," Beckham said sternly. "Your family could still be alive. Sitting around moping isn't going to help them."

Horn slowly sat up, running a hand through his messy hair.

"Let's go," Beckham said.

The barracks slowly emptied as the other men and women

left for the briefing. Beckham watched a group of marines file out the front entrance and wondered what news Jensen had in store for them. He knew it couldn't be good.

Horn stood, grumbling something to himself that Beckham couldn't make out.

Putting a hand on his friend's back, Beckham followed Horn out of the room in silence. There wasn't anything Beckham could say to alleviate any of the man's pain. His family was likely dead. He needed time to grieve.

The cafeteria was swollen with staff by the time they arrived. Men and women representing every branch of the military were present, and mixed in with them were the scientists that Colonel Gibson had helped collect from around the country.

Beckham scanned the crowd and found Kate near the center. Slowly, he pushed his way toward her.

The woman who turned to face him looked like a shell of her former herself. Dark bags hung under dark blue eyes.

"How are you doing?" Beckham asked.

"Hanging in there," she replied solemnly. "How about you? How's Horn?" She glanced over Beckham's shoulder to look for him.

"Not good. He took the news pretty hard. We all did."

"I'm sorry," she whispered. After a brief pause, she said, "I just found out that the hemorrhage virus has spread across the globe. My parents are in Rome."

"Shit," Beckham mumbled, his eyes falling to the floor. "Are we any closer to finding a way to stop it?"

"I think so," Kate said. "But I need more time."

Noise from the front of the mess hall pulled their attention to Lieutenant Colonel Jensen. He entered the room with Major Smith and a trio of soldiers Beckham didn't recognize.

Jensen wasted no time. He grabbed a mic and walked to

the head of the crowd. "Good morning, everyone. I'm going to cut right to the chase. As you all know I've lifted the communications cloak. For the past twelve hours, my staff has been working on figuring out what's going on outside."

After a brief pause, Jensen continued. "POTUS is dead. Every major city has been overrun by infected. The world we all knew is gone. X9H9, or what scientists are calling the hemorrhage virus, has spread all over the world. No continent has been spared. In less than eight days, the pandemic has infected over half of the world's population. Projections show that in another two weeks, over eighty-five percent of the world's population will be dead or infected."

Several gasps echoed through the room as the crowd digested the news. Jensen waited for it to sink in and then continued.

"Operation Reaper was launched to stop the spread of the virus. As you know, this meant that the military targeted high-density population zones. The mission was simple: Bomb these target areas and send in boots to clean up the mess. Unfortunately, Operation Reaper failed, and now only a handful of military installations remain active and secure."

"What about Camp Pendleton?" yelled a man somewhere behind Beckham.

"And Fort Bragg?" asked a marine a few feet away.

"Please, hold your questions," Jensen replied calmly. "We're still processing the information and will get it to COs as soon as we can."

"This is fucking bullshit! You kept us all in the dark while the world was collapsing around us!" a woman barked from the front of the crowd.

"Colonel Rick Gibson believed this was the only way to keep you all focused on finding a cure. We didn't want any distractions."

"I heard there is no cure. I heard this thing is a bio-weapon," said another voice.

Jensen clenched his jaw, sucked in a breath through his nostrils, and then raised his left hand. "What you've heard is correct," he replied. "X9H9 was designed in a lab. In one of our own labs. Colonel Gibson has been arrested for his crimes and will stand trial. I assure you. He *will* pay for—"

Chaos erupted. Angry shouts filled the room as the crowd pushed forward. Beckham grabbed Kate and pulled her away from a shouting marine.

Jensen held up his hand and shouted into the mic. "Please calm down! You are men and women of the United States Armed Forces! Stand down! That is a direct order!" A vein bulged from his forehead as he screamed into the mic.

The room instantly quieted. Beckham had never seen Jensen lose control that way. But everyone had a breaking point, and after discovering his CO was behind the virus destroying the world, Beckham couldn't blame Jensen for his outrage.

After the mess hall had quieted, Jensen continued, his voice raspy behind his tightened jaw. "Believe me, I know what you are all thinking. But in the end, it doesn't matter where this virus came from. We all still have a job to do. We may be humanity's last hope. Several of our scientists are working on a new bioweapon, one that will destroy those infected with X9H9."

"So there *is* a cure?" Riley shouted.

Jensen paused and collected himself as he searched the room. "Doctor Lovato, are you here?"

Kate raised a hand. The officer waved her forward. "Would you please explain your theory?"

Making her way through the crowd, Kate grabbed the mic. "I'm Doctor Kate Lovato, with the Centers for Disease

Control," she said, in a low, apprehensive voice. "I understand that we aren't all scientists in this room, so I am going to explain this in the simplest way I can. The hemorrhage virus was lab engineered. It's the marriage of a chemical weapon called VX-99 and the Ebola virus. Those people outside"—she pointed toward the door—"they aren't people anymore. I know this is hard to accept because I had to accept this myself when my brother turned into one of them. Those things are monsters. There is no cure. There is no bringing them back. The changes caused by VX-99 are irreversible epigenetic changes. The only way to stop this virus is..."

Kate lowered the mic and scanned the room. She found Beckham, and he offered her a reassuring nod.

She raised the mic again. "The only way to stop this virus is to kill the infected. That's what my staff and I are working on. A bioweapon that will destroy the host."

"Thank you, Doctor," Jensen said. He placed a hand on her shoulder and then took the mic.

"As you can see, we are doing everything we can to stop the outbreak. We have the most capable scientists in the world on the island, and the communications cloak has been lifted, so I will keep everyone updated as we receive information."

Jensen's words struck a chord inside Beckham. They might have shared a moment back in Gibson's office, but his gut told him not to trust the man. Not yet. He could have been kept in the dark about Gibson's work, or he could have been involved. If Beckham found out it was the latter, he was going to make sure Jensen paid the same price as his CO.

Still, Beckham couldn't help but see a decent man standing at the front of the room, a leader that the men and women of Plum Island so desperately needed. Only time would tell if Jensen lived up to his word.

Finding a cure for most diseases would take months, if not longer, but designing an experimental weapon had taken Kate only five hours. Understanding the hemorrhage virus had allowed her to design a synthesized virus of her own that she hoped would attack the endothelial cells and cause massive vascular damage to anyone infected with the hemorrhage virus.

Her synthesized virus would *only* target cells that were expressed in the proteins they had identified in the infected. Anyone exposed to the weapon who wasn't infected with the hemorrhage virus would remain healthy.

"You ready?" Ellis asked. He stood in his space suit a few feet away, hovering over a dozen samples of infected cell cultures.

"When you are," Kate replied.

"Let's see if it works."

Holding her breath, Kate used a transfer pipette to insert the synthesized virus she'd designed into the cultures. After allowing the virus to incubate for several minutes with the cells, she performed a fixation procedure to prevent the sample from deteriorating and to stabilize it for analysis under the intense beams of an electron microscope.

Each minute spent waiting for the samples to become fully fixed was agonizing. With her heart racing, Kate took one of the trays and inserted it under the microscope, then joined Ellis at the lab's main computer terminal.

She studied the spaghetti-string images of the virus on her screen. As she'd hoped, the small glycoprotein spikes that surrounded the virus strands were now attaching to the endothelial cells.

"I'll be damned," Ellis said.

Kate looked beyond the computer monitor, staring

intensely at the robotic arm inside the center room. It was waiting for her command.

All she had to do was type in a series of codes and the bot would go to work, creating the synthesized virus and preparing it for use on the boy Beckham and his men had brought back from Niantic. If she authorized this production, they could potentially have a working weapon by morning. Of course there would be more tests, but the building blocks would be in place.

Kate's fingers hovered over the keyboard as she reflected on the ramifications of her next move. This was humanity's final and most desperate attempt to prevent its own extinction.

As her mind drifted, her heart rate increased. She could feel her pulse in her head, the sound echoing inside her helmet.

She thought suddenly of Javier, and the monster he had become. He was out there somewhere, hunting with the rest of the infected. She couldn't bear to think of her brother that way.

A beat passed and she saw Michael gripping his shredded arm in the Black Hawk. She could see his final moments clearly now—she could see the fear radiating from his eyes as he took Beckham's pistol and jumped out of the Black Hawk. His last act reflected how he'd lived his life.

Courageously.

Drawing on her mentor's strength, Kate blinked and took in a long breath. Holding it in her lungs, she punched in a series of commands that authorized the robot to finish what she had started. The automated process would take hours, maybe longer, but in the morning, they would know whether her weapon would work.

A blank cursor blinked on her screen. The computer was prompting her to name the weapon. Without hesitation she typed in a single word.

VariantX9H9.

22

A loud knocking startled Kate awake.

Cracking an eye, she looked at her wristwatch.

Shit!

She'd fallen asleep inside the office at the lab facility. She sprang out of the leather chair and rushed over to the door.

Ellis and Cindy waited in the hallway. Even though she was groggy, she could see they both wore excited looks.

"What's going on?" Kate asked. "Did you find something?"

Ellis handed Kate a coffee. "You're going to need this."

"Why?" Kate replied.

"Jensen's technicians are preparing one of the infected for testing. Let's go," Ellis said.

Kate paused. She hadn't authorized that, but she should have known they wouldn't wait for her.

"Okay, show me," she said. She took the lead and hurried down the hallway.

Ellis rushed after her, speaking as he walked. "Think this is going to work?"

"I hope so," Kate replied. She paused in the middle of the corridor, suddenly remembering her request. "Did you test VariantX9H9 on a healthy batch of rhesus monkeys already?"

Ellis nodded enthusiastically. "Yup. No side effects. Since the VX-99 radically changes the proteins expressed on the cell surface, the synthesized virus only affects the endothelial cells of animals or people who are infected with the hemorrhage virus."

Kate breathed a sigh of relief and continued on.

The isolation chamber looked more heavily guarded than usual. Even from a distance Kate could see several soldiers pacing outside the white, domed building. Some of them stopped to salute Jensen and Smith as they guided Kate and her team across the concrete walkway.

Kate shielded her eyes against the blinding morning sunlight and scanned the base. "Can one of your men radio Master Sergeant Beckham and his team? I'd like him to be present for the tests."

Jensen looked confused, studying her for a moment. He turned to Smith.

"Major, can you see to Doctor Lovato's request?"

Kate wasn't sure exactly why she wanted Beckham with her when the tests were conducted, but part of her felt safer with him by her side. And if anyone deserved to see the results of her efforts, it was the man who had risked his life to make this test possible.

Inside, Jensen led them past several isolation rooms. Kate remembered them from before, but this time they weren't dark. This time bright LEDs illuminated the white, padded rooms.

Halting, Kate moved up to one of the thick, oval windows.

"I wouldn't get too close," Smith said.

A humanoid face suddenly smashed into the glass. Kate grabbed her chest and gasped, stumbling backward.

"Told you," Smith said with a nervous chuckle.

Slowly, Kate regained her composure and turned back to the window.

The infected boy from Niantic flicked the glass with a swollen tongue. His slit-like vertical pupils contracted and expanded as he tried to focus.

"I told you not to get too close," Smith said.

Kate shot the officer an angry glare and then cautiously walked up to the next steel door.

The victim, a man in his mid-thirties or forties, watched as she approached. Crusted blood surrounded his sucker lips. Fresh blood oozed from his eyes and nose. He snarled, revealing a mouthful of sharp, yellow teeth.

He lurched forward and roared with anger, pounding the pane of glass with hands distorted into claws. His long, yellow fingernails scratched down the glass.

Kate stepped back and scanned the hallway. Dozens of doors lined the corridor, all of their windows brightly lit.

"How many are there?" Kate choked.

Jensen put his hands on his hips. "Colonel Gibson requested as many as we could capture. Beckham's wasn't the only team that went out. We currently have a total of twenty infected on the island, but don't worry, these rooms were designed to hold—"

A terrifying scream cut him off.

Inside the cell, the man was head-butting the glass. The noise echoed down the hall, prompting more of the prisoners to pound on their doors.

Kate cupped her ears.

"You sure it's safe?" Ellis asked.

Jensen nodded. "Yeah."

The monster beating the glass stopped, and Kate saw a small crack in the pane. Blood dripped down the creature's forehead, and it reached up with a long, swollen tongue to lick at the fresh blood

Jensen suddenly looked unsure. "Come on," he said.

By the time they reached the end of the corridor, the entire hallway was alive with croaking and shrieks. Like the infected rhesus monkeys, the humanoid creatures had broken into a mad frenzy.

"Why aren't these people restrained?" Ellis asked.

"We've had problems keeping them restrained," Smith replied. "Their joints don't work in the same way those of uninfected humans do, so they can easily slip and twist out of straitjackets." He stopped outside the door to the main isolation room and waved his key card over the security panel. It chirped, and the doors slid open.

"This is Patient 14," Jensen said as they entered in single file.

In the observation room, Kate saw a girl who looked no older than a teenager, maybe fifteen or sixteen. It was hard to tell. The virus aged the host considerably. She lay on the ground, curled up in a fetal position. When she sensed their presence, the girl suddenly sat up, her head tilting and her nose sniffing the air like a wild animal. Her eyes flitted from Kate to the others.

The bright LEDs revealed fresh wounds on the girl's arms. Bite marks and deep gouges lined her right bicep.

Kate approached the glass with her hand covering her mouth, her heart throbbing. The effects of the hemorrhage virus were the most awful she'd ever seen.

Reaching for the observation window, Kate pressed her fingers against the cold surface. Patient 14 snarled, bending and twitching until she was on all fours.

In the blink of an eye, the girl jumped to her feet and launched her body toward the glass. She landed on her hands and feet and quickly skittered across the panel like a spider moving across a wall.

"Damn," Smith said. "Never seen one of them do that."

"I have," said a voice from the doorway.

Kate spun to see Beckham standing there, his eyes locked on the girl behind her.

"Saw the entire side of a building crawling with those things," he said coldly. "They move like insects." He jerked his chin toward the window. "Check her hands and feet. The only good thing about how they move is you can hear them coming."

"Disgusting," Smith said. "The sooner we get VariantX9H9 deployed, the better."

Jensen stepped up to the glass. The girl jumped and landed a few feet away on the floor, her back hunched and teeth snarling.

The soldier took a step back.

"I was told to report to the isolation chamber," Beckham said.

Kate nodded. "I wanted you here for this."

"For what?" Beckham replied. He walked past Cindy and Ellis, who were too focused on watching the girl to acknowledge him.

"I've completed my work," Kate said. "I've created a bioweapon of my own."

Beckham's eyes lit up. He looked back at Patient 14. She slowly crawled across the ground, her back still hunched like a lion waiting to pounce on its prey. Blood trickled from her face onto the white tile floor.

Jensen punched a red button on a control panel. White gas hissed from vents in the ceiling. The girl screeched and clawed at the chemical cloud.

"What's that?" Beckham asked.

"They are putting her out," Kate replied.

Within seconds, Patient 14 slumped to the ground, falling asleep peacefully. A trio of technicians moved into the room. They wore space suits modified with combat armor. They looked more like a SWAT team than scientists.

"Can't take too many precautions," Smith said when he saw Kate's reaction.

After restraining the girl, the technicians placed her on a metal table in the center of the room. One of them bent down and pulled a curtain of hair away from her face. Her yellow eyes stared up at the ceiling. The man held a syringe in his other hand and quickly pushed the needle into one of the blue veins bulging from the girl's forearm.

The entire team rushed back to the exit as soon as the engineered virus had been inserted. None of them looked back. They moved quickly, anxious to get out of the room.

"What happens now?" Beckham asked. He moved closer to Kate. His shoulder brushed against hers.

"We wait," Ellis said. Running a hand through his neatly combed hair, he approached the observation glass for a better look.

Kate could hear the doomsday clock ticking again in her mind and thought of her parents in Rome. She had tried to contact them using CDC's Internet servers, but they hadn't responded to her e-mails yet. She wasn't sure if they even had power in Europe anymore. Every minute that passed was another minute the infection spread closer to them, if they weren't infected already.

Behind her, the ruckus from the other holding cells echoed in the hallway. The victims were suddenly active again, beating on the doors and walls. Their enraged screams were louder. They sounded desperate.

It reminded her of something she'd seen in the forest years ago, when her team was searching for a group of western lowland gorillas in Cameroon that they believed had contracted an early form of Ebola. The journey had taken them into a very remote area, but when they had finally located the group, they weren't able to get close due to the gorillas' violent behavior. She could still remember their panicked cries. They sounded...

Primal.

Kate couldn't help but wonder if the same thing was happening in front of her, if the infected patients knew the girl had been given a dose of the synthesized VariantX9H9 bioweapon. She shook the thought away. That was impossible—but then again, this all seemed so impossible.

She waited there for two hours, watching Patient 14 twitch and kick. The technicians reentered the room periodically to check on her, sweeping flashlights over her body. Another one entered, shining his light over the girl. Then he bent down and illuminated a flow of blackish blood dripping into a puddle under the metal table. The technician stood and moved the light over the thin white blanket covering her chest. The cloth moved up and down slowly as blood gurgled from the girl's bulging lips.

Kate's stomach rolled at the sight. The virus was once again attacking the endothelial cells and causing massive internal bleeding, and it was doing so *very* fast.

A few minutes later Patient 14 took her last breaths.

One of the technicians gave a thumbs-up. A wave of nausea hit Kate like a freight train. She felt light-headed. Stumbling, she reached for the glass to brace herself. She knew exactly what she'd done. She'd created a weapon that would kill millions of people infected with the hemorrhage virus.

No.

Billions.

23

May 2, 2015
DAY 16

Jensen chomped furiously on a stick of bubble gum. He'd run out of chewing tobacco earlier that morning, and without it he was starting to get the sweats. *What shitty timing*, he thought as he looked out the observation deck window.

Somewhere out there, hundreds of aircraft were preparing to embark on Operation Depletion—the mission that would take back the United States.

The interim US president had authorized the mission after new CDC director Jed Frank explained that Dr. Lovato's weaponized virus would kill everyone infected with X9H9—and only those infected. Any survivors inside the cities who came into contact with the bioweapon would see no side effects. Tests on rhesus monkeys had proven this outcome. The new president didn't need convincing. He was desperate, and he was willing to sacrifice many to save a few.

In less than a week, what was left of the military had organized a massive counterstrike. Plum Island coordinated the manufacturing of the weapon with two secure facilities across the country. Together they had produced enough VariantX9H9 to deploy in every major metropolitan area. The technology that had manufactured the bioweapon wasn't supposed to exist, but neither was the secret weapons program at Building 8.

Jensen wasn't sure exactly how it worked, but he was told that the manufacturing process was modeled after a rapid-production system already in place for the synthetic influenza vaccines developed in 2013 and early 2014. Plum Island had been built with a manufacturing and distribution center based on this automated process. The result was a rapid development and production of VariantX9H9 that was highly lethal over a significant area.

They were just beginning coordination with allied nations, but their main focus was on American soil. Rid the cities of the infected and send in troops to clean up the rest. It was going to be messy, and he doubted there were many survivors left to save.

Jensen shuddered at the ramifications. Even if Operation Depletion did work, the country would never be the same. The population had been reduced to God knew how many people, and the economy was shattered.

The radio at the other end of the CIC blared to life. Corporal Hickman turned her dial and gave a thumbs-up. "Lieutenant Colonel, we're tapped in. Air Combat Command has fighters scrambling out of Langley. The squadron is on their way to New York. ETA fifteen minutes."

Jensen felt his blood warm. Some of the best pilots in the world were headed straight for America's favorite city, to finish what Operation Reaper had started.

"Strike teams are on standby," Major Smith said. "Beckham and his men are waiting for orders."

"Thank you, Major," Jensen said. He closed his eyes,

pushing away what felt like emotion-fueled reservations. He was asking the master sergeant to go back into the field. After all he and his team had already been through, it was yet another sacrifice.

But Jensen had his orders. General Kennor had taken over Central Command. Brass had assigned each remaining installation a bailiwick of cities to reconnoiter after the gas was deployed. Plum Island had picked up New York and a handful of other eastern cities. He was sending Master Sergeant Beckham to lead a strike team to the city after the jets dropped their payloads. Their mission was simple reconnaissance, to see how VariantX9H9 worked in the field.

The radio flickered. "Command, this is Raptor—target inbound. Request permission to engage, over."

Command responded a second later. "Roger that, Raptor. Green light to engage."

Smith joined Jensen. "Think this is going to work?"

Jensen nodded. The sun was rising over the ocean's dark waves, a crimson glow spreading a carpet of light over the water. The beautiful view felt oddly divine.

"Approaching target," Raptor said. "Stand by."

The radio chatter reminded Jensen that the pilot was seeing the exact opposite view. His jet was racing toward a postapocalyptic New York City. Jensen had seen the images. Many of the metropolis's once spectacular landmarks had been reduced to rubble.

"Weapons hot," Raptor said.

Jensen closed his eyes. He knew what came next.

Kate sat in the conference room staring at her computer, skimming the test results of VariantX9H9 to see if there was anything she had missed. Away from the safety of the island, the military was busy working too. They were dumping her bioweapon on every major city. And in just a few hours, Beckham would be deployed back to the postapocalyptic world that surrounded them.

Guilt ate at her as she sat there. She was so lucky—lucky to be protected and safe when everyone else was fighting for survival, lucky that she wasn't *out there.*

The least she could do was wish them luck. It was 10:00 a.m., and the landing strip outside the hexagonal base was teeming with activity when she got there. Groups of marines were preparing their gear outside a trio of Black Hawks. Another chopper was already lifting into the sky. Her heart skipped a beat when she saw it pull away from the island.

Was she too late? Had Beckham's team already left?

"Hey! Doctor Lovato," a voice called enthusiastically.

Kate spun to see Riley approaching. He stopped a few feet away and hoisted his huge pack onto his back with a grunt.

"You aren't coming with us, are you?"

"No, no," Kate replied, shaking her head. "I just wanted to say good luck."

Riley nodded. "That's nice of you." He pointed toward the closest Black Hawk. "Boss is over there."

Kate tried to keep up with the staff sergeant as he strode toward the chopper.

When they got to the chopper, Beckham was preparing his CBRN suit. He glanced up, a smile instantly forming on his face when he saw her.

"Kate," he said.

It was different seeing the shy side of Beckham. Back in Atlanta he'd shown no emotion. His only focus had been on saving her and the others.

"Thought I would see you off," she said. "Were you going to leave without saying good-bye?"

Beckham set the CBRN suit carefully on the ground and wiped his hands on his pants. "Of course not. We aren't leaving for another hour or so. Just doing a gear check."

Kate scanned their equipment. They looked as if they were preparing for a weeklong trip. "How long will you be gone?"

"Should only be for a few days," Beckham said. "Maybe longer. Depends on how long it takes for the bug you made to do its work."

The words made her wonder what he really thought of her work—and what he thought of her, what everyone really thought of her. Would she be seen as a savior or a monster?

"Shit," Beckham muttered. He stepped closer. "I didn't mean—"

Shaking her head, she brushed back a strand of her hair blowing in the breeze. "It's okay." She changed the subject. "What are your orders?"

"Simple," he replied. "We're supposed to serve as an extra set of eyes. Nothing more. If we're engaged, we retreat to a safe location," Beckham added. He reached into his rucksack and hoisted a pale green rectangular object that read *Front Toward Enemy* on its face. "And if we run into trouble, we've got backup this time."

"Is that a bomb of some kind?"

Beckham grinned and said, "It's a mine. Also called a claymore. If anything survived out there that shouldn't, this'll finish the job." He caught her gaze. "We'll be fine, Kate."

Fine. Safe.

The words boomed inside her mind. They no longer held the same meaning.

Riley dropped his rucksack and interjected, "Do you think we'll find survivors out there?"

Kate snapped out of her thoughts. She attempted to mask the dread she felt, the sadness that was slowly sweeping over her.

"I would say so," said a louder voice. "I'm sure there are people out there that hunkered down and stayed safe."

Horn approached from the rear, his skull bandanna already covering his mouth and nose. "There are survivors everywhere, right?" His voice was muffled slightly, but she could hear every hint of apprehension in it.

Kate remembered his family had been at Fort Bragg. She knew the likelihood they had survived was slim, but still she nodded. "Yes, that's why the new POTUS wanted to deploy VariantX9H9 as soon as possible. To save those that still remain."

Horn nodded. He and Riley walked toward their stack of gear, leaving Beckham and Kate alone.

"Good luck," she said to their backs. She didn't know what else to say, but felt like she should do more than just wish them luck. Before she could find the words, Beckham reached for her.

"Kate, I promise you everything will be fine."

In that moment she lost all control. Her breath caught, and tears filled her eyes. Everything that had happened in the past few weeks came crashing down on her. She reached forward and wrapped her arms around Beckham.

He rubbed her back gently as she sobbed into his shoulder.

"You're saving everyone," he whispered.

Kate pulled away. Tilting her head back, she locked eyes with him. "Am I?"

"Yes," Beckham said firmly. "I was wrong before," he said. "Those things aren't human. Patient 14 was no longer a person. Those things are monsters. And I would want to die if I became one too."

The rap of heavy footfalls on the concrete reminded Kate the clock was ticking. The recon teams were preparing to leave, and she was in the way.

Reluctantly, she pulled out of his grip and wiped the tears away. She didn't want Beckham or the other men to see her this way.

He searched her eyes. "You're going to make it through this."

A short nod and she wiped away a final tear. "Promise me you're coming back."

"I promise, Kate. I'll be back before you know it."

A soldier Kate didn't recognize interrupted them. "Master Sergeant Beckham, the lieutenant colonel wants to see you before you take off."

"Before you go, I have something for you," Kate said. She reached into her pocket and pulled out a small envelope, handing it to Beckham. Before he could open it, she was already walking away.

Kate listened to the Black Hawks take off in the distance. The thump of the blades slowly dissipated until they had faded completely. She watched the final chopper disappear on the horizon.

"Good luck," she whispered.

When she reached Building 4, Ellis was waiting at the entrance, flanked on both sides by guards.

"Everything okay?" he asked as she approached.

Kate had forgotten she'd been crying and wiped at her eyes. "Yes. I was told there is something we should see." She opened the door and gestured for Ellis to go first.

One of the technicians waited inside for them. Kate

recognized him as the one who had given Patient 14 the lethal dose of VariantX9H9.

"Thank you for coming, Doctors. I thought you both should see this."

Kate followed him from room to room, pausing to peer through the small oval windows above each door. The view through the glass was grotesque. The patients all lay in puddles of their own blood. But they'd seen this before, with the first round of infected they'd injected with VariantX9H9. If the second round of testing had killed all its patients as expected, she wasn't sure what she was supposed to be looking at.

"They're all dead," Ellis said. "A good sign."

"Not all of them," the tech replied.

Kate's heart fluttered when she heard the words.

The man stopped in the middle of the hallway and pointed to the door on his left. "Take a look for yourself."

Before Kate had a chance to look through the window, a man pressed his face against the glass. He stood there staring at Kate, studying her. Reptilian eyes stared back at her. Red swirled around his sclera, but they were no longer the bright rose-colored eyes she was used to seeing.

After a short scan she saw there were no signs of fresh bleeding from his eyes or nose, and the rashes on his skin looked as if they were scarring. The patient curled his fingers into a claw and scratched at the wall, growling.

"This is Patient 12," the tech said. "As you can see, he is far from dead."

Kate watched the man purse his sucker lips on the other side of the window, revealing a set of broken and jagged teeth. She didn't understand. How could this man have recovered? There had to be some sort of mistake.

"Have there been other reports of infected victims recovering?" Kate asked.

The tech quickly shook his head. "No. I just looked over the reports we got from a team in Chicago this morning. There has not been a single documented case of recovery." He paused and then very confidently said, "Ever."

"And you are sure this man was given VariantX9H9?"

He nodded. "Yes. I administered it myself, earlier this morning, when Major Smith ordered all of the remaining specimens to be put down."

Kate felt her mind spinning in all directions. There had to be something about the synthesized virus she'd engineered—but none of it made any sense. The weapon was designed to ensure the victim would bleed out quickly. So why was this man still alive?

"Maybe this guy was just—" Ellis began to say.

"Keep an eye on him, and get me a sample of his blood," Kate said, hurrying down the hallway.

"Where are you going?" Ellis shouted.

"Back to the lab."

24

Team Ghost endured the short ride to New York in silence. They didn't discuss Colonel Gibson or Kate's bioweapon. They simply sat there listening to the human engineering of the Black Hawk. Each man was still and stoic, lost in his own thoughts.

Beckham unsealed the envelope Kate had given him. A note fell out onto his lap. He picked up the piece of paper and read it under his breath.

I hope this brings you some luck.

He turned the envelope upside down, and a picture of his mom fell out. It was different from the one he normally carried, but it was her smile, her face.

"That Kate is one hell of a woman," Riley said.

"How did she know..." Beckham said, his voice trailing off. He remembered telling her about the picture in the mess hall, but nothing more.

"She asked me if I could find a pic of your mom," Riley said. "Apparently the lab still has access to the Internet."

"Damn nice of her," Horn added.

Beckham wiped away what felt like a tear. He kissed the picture and unzipped his CBRN suit, sticking the image inside his vest pocket. "Thanks, Kid," he said.

"Least I could do for keeping me alive all these years," Riley replied with a wide grin.

The chopper banked hard to the right and swept across the smoke-clogged skyline. Beckham couldn't believe his eyes. The air force had hit New York City hard.

The twisted outlines of fallen skyscrapers protruded out of a lingering cloud of smoke. Through the gaps, Beckham could make out the ruined city below. He had to clear his visor of dust just to ensure the sight was real.

It was, and it extended as far as he could see.

"Never thought I'd see one of our own cities like this," Riley said. His normally chipper voice was cold and solemn.

"Better get used to it," Horn replied.

"Stay focused," Beckham said. "This is just another mission." He said it, but couldn't deny he was having doubts now. After telling Kate they would be safe, he wasn't so sure. The destroyed city would harbor danger every step of the way: unstable buildings, gas leaks, desperate survivors, and possibly even infected.

Gripping his MP5, Beckham chinned his comm. "What's our ETA?"

One of the pilots responded after a brief crackle of static. "Five minutes. LZ is in Astoria."

"Copy," Beckham replied. They flew over Long Island Sound, moving southwest toward the city. He could see Manhattan in more detail now. Where dozens of skyscrapers stood only weeks before, now there were only piles of rubble. From the sky, the buildings looked like destroyed Lego models.

Smoke crawled across the heaps of metal and brick, hiding the street level from view. Beckham clenched his teeth and checked Riley and Horn. They were staring intensely at the same view, their visors hiding their features.

"This is Gibson's fault," Horn grunted.

"Motherfucker's going to pay," Riley added.

Beckham didn't reply. There wasn't anything he could say to lessen the shock of what waited below. It was good that they had someone to blame—it made their difficult orders easier to justify.

The chopper descended as they approached Queens. Dense smoke hung over the East River. Beckham held his breath and watched the water disappear as the smoke consumed the chopper. He mentally counted the seconds.

One.

Two.

In between counts, the Black Hawk emerged from the gray, and the outline of the Robert F. Kennedy Bridge exploded into view. The landmark had taken a missile to the midsection. Support beams sagged around the missing chunk of bridge.

Beckham flinched when he saw the girders sticking out.

"Watch out!" he yelled.

The pilots jerked the nose of the chopper toward the water and slipped under the ruined bridge, narrowly missing the jagged metal protruding under the concrete and stone.

"Change of plans," the pilot said. "Command says Astoria is too hot. Plan B is Times Square."

Beckham exchanged glances with Riley and Horn.

"Copy," he finally replied.

They pulled away from Astoria and moved over the Upper East Side. The forest of trees in Central Park jutted out of another layer of smoke haunting the district.

A few seconds later, they were hovering over the iconic Times Square. The billboards were dark, their electronic images absent. The scene made his stomach sink. Times Square was the symbol of American culture. The dark screens seemed to warn him about the country's future.

He forced himself to look toward the streets below. They were clogged with the burned-out hulls of vehicles. The charred remains of refugees who had been trying to escape the city were all that remained. Beckham had seen similar scenes in the past. Iraq and Afghanistan. These had been desperate people trying to escape with their lives.

Looking closer, he saw there was something else down there, something that Beckham couldn't quite make sense of at first. The street looked as though it was glistening and wet.

"Get us lower," he shouted.

As the chopper descended, Beckham could see the black-top was peppered with puddles of blood. Mangled bodies lay in every direction, some piled on top of one another.

"My God," Riley choked. "There have to be thousands of them."

Twisted lumps filled every city street, blood seeping from the corpses and pooling on the pavement. VariantX9H9 had worked after all. Jensen didn't need to send Beckham and his team into the field to see that. He could have simply had a pilot do a flyover.

"Get us out of here," Beckham shouted. "We need a new drop location."

Beckham kept his gaze glued on the street. There wasn't a living thing in sight—no animals or random survivors. Nothing but blood and death.

A few minutes later, they were hovering over a ten-story building that had survived the bombs. The foundation was unscathed and Beckham authorized a landing. Riley secured the rope, and they slid down to the roof.

Beckham was moving as soon as his boots hit the gravel. He swept his weapon side to side, looking for targets.

"Clear," he shouted, and waited for confirmation from Horn and Riley that their zones were good to go. It was hard to hear under the *whup-whup* of the chopper's blades. A second later, as the chopper pulled away, Horn and Riley called in a clear AO. Squinting, Beckham watched the bird ascend and race across the skyline, leaving them alone in a city that had hemorrhaged life.

Kate wasn't sure what time it was. She could hardly think. Patient 12 was driving her nuts. She simply couldn't make sense of the man's recovery.

The questions just kept coming.

Had she somehow made a mistake? They hadn't had the time for multiple tests, but those they had performed had worked perfectly. Her mind spun out of control. She was looking for a complex answer to a complex question, but maybe the answer was simple.

In that moment, it hit her.

VariantX9H9 attacked the endothelial cells that made the Ebola virus lethal. The end result was the death of the host. Except in the case of Patient 12. In the chaos of the past few weeks, she'd failed to remember that Ebola didn't have a 100 percent fatality rate. It didn't kill all of its victims. The mortality rate *was* high, but there were always survivors. And Medford had weakened the fourth gene, making the virus even less effective. So what if—

Kate gasped. The simple answer was right in front of her. Patient 12 was part of the small pool of survivors.

An anomaly, considering there were fewer than twenty patients at the facility.

Kate brought a hand to her mouth when she realized what had happened. The epigenetic changes from VX-99 remained. They were unchanged. The man was still a monster. From the observing technician's reports, Patient 12 was still fast, agile, and powerful, but he was no longer infected with Ebola. He'd recovered from the virus.

The implications were startling. Her synthesized virus was designed to attack the endothelial cells in the monster, causing massive hemorrhaging and death. That's what should have happened, but this man had survived the assault. Now he was more dangerous than ever.

Kate sprang up from the lab station and hurried across the room. She had to warn Jensen, so he could get a message to Beckham and his team. Her heart fluttered as she ran. Beckham had no idea what lurked in the smoke-clogged streets of New York. He was heading into a trap.

Beckham stood at the bottom of the fire escape he'd used to descend from the building they landed on. He tapped his helmet, cursing. His radio wasn't working. For whatever reason, the channel had cut out shortly after their insertion. He could get messages through to his team, but the connection to Plum Island had been severed.

Taking a step back, he made room for Horn and Riley, who jumped down onto the concrete. They took up position with their backs to the walls and waited for orders.

Peeking around the corner, Beckham checked the street. A street vendor's metal cart had toppled over, the contents spilled over the concrete. Beyond it were bodies and more bodies. Some were slumped against vehicles. Others were curled up on the sidewalk.

Nothing moved.

"Horn, you take point. Riley, you got our six," Beckham

said. He flashed an advance signal, and Horn jogged into the street with his rifle shouldered.

Beckham took off after him. As they moved, Beckham flicked his gaze high and low. If any infected had survived Operation Depletion, he knew threats could come from anywhere. He sidestepped around the body of a woman, her eyes wide open and wild. Her hands were twisted from rigor mortis. She'd suffered a painful death.

Keep moving, he told himself. There wasn't anything he could do for these people, but there could still be survivors.

They patrolled the street for the next fifteen minutes. The view slowly sank in. Death surrounded them. There was no escaping it.

"Regroup," Beckham said at the next corner. They met at an overturned police car and crouched into a huddle.

"Looks like we're going to get wet," Riley said. He pointed toward a gathering of storm clouds rolling in from the west. Lightning flashed on the horizon, the distant boom of thunder ringing out a few seconds later.

"Shit," Beckham muttered.

The rain fell slowly at first, but grew heavier quickly. The street rapidly turned into a river of blood that flowed into the storm drains. He'd never seen so much in his life. As he stared, he mentally calculated just how much he was looking at. Assuming each victim bled out half of the blood in their body, they would each produce about five pints. Multiply that by thousands of dead and you had a shit-ton of blood.

"Boss," Horn said. Beckham caught Horn's worried eyes. "I can't stop thinking about my family. My little girls and Sheila." He paused and looked around the corner of the car. "I keep picturing them bleeding out like that."

"Don't," Beckham said. He reached over and put a hand

on Horn's shoulder. "They could have survived. You can't lose hope, man. I haven't."

Horn gave a small nod. "I want you to know something."

Beckham looked at him.

"I don't blame you. You were right. My family was safer at Fort Bragg. If they are gone, I don't want you to blame yourself."

Beckham closed his eyes. He *had* blamed himself, and he still did, but hearing his friend absolve him lifted some of the guilt.

"I promise you, Big Horn, if they're still out there, we'll find them when this is all over—" Before Beckham could finish, Horn pulled away and angled the muzzle of his M27 toward the end of the street.

Whatever he saw, Riley saw it too.

"Contact," the kid said. He scrambled to his feet and leveled his rifle over the hood of the car.

The rain was picking up, the slap of drops hitting the concrete all around them. Beckham wiped his visor clear and focused on the road.

Three drenched figures came into view. A man and a woman holding the hands of a child who walked between them. There was more motion behind them. A man with a shotgun watched their backs. Beckham narrowed in on the lead man. He held a nasty-looking long-barreled pistol.

Beckham contemplated the team's options. This was a recon mission, but he wasn't going to leave behind survivors—especially with a kid. He twisted and whispered his orders. "Horn, Riley, stay put and cover me. I'm going to check this out."

Standing, Beckham lowered his weapon and approached the group cautiously. They stopped at the end of the block.

"Stay where you are," Beckham yelled. He watched the

man with the pistol raise the barrel, ever so slightly. *That's not good*, he thought. Beckham froze. He didn't want to scare the group.

"We're here to help," Beckham said in his calmest voice.

"Can you get us out of here?" the woman shouted. "Please! We need to get out of here."

Beckham hesitated for a beat. "Stay calm. You will have to come with us."

The woman grew frantic. She dropped the child's hand and turned to the man. "Let's go—please, let's go."

"How do we know we can trust you?" the man shouted.

"He's military," the woman said. "He can protect us from them."

Beckham raised a brow. He would ask what she meant later, when they were off the streets.

"Come on," he yelled. He twisted to run back to the squad car—and then he heard it.

It started off as a croak that slowly grew into a high-pitched screech. A second voice answered the call, releasing its own ravenous shriek.

No, Beckham thought. It wasn't possible, was it? The primal noise could only mean one thing—Kate's bug hadn't killed all of the monsters. He jerked as his earpiece crackled.

"One o'clock. On the east side of the FEMA truck," Riley said in a cool voice.

Beckham shouldered his weapon and spun back to the group of survivors. The truck was easy to spot; it was right behind them. Standing next to the hood was a single figure. A woman. He zoomed in on the curtain of black hair covering her face. Deep gouges dotted her skin, bite marks surrounding the open wounds, and he could barely make out the slits of her eyes.

This was no survivor. This was an infected.

"Run!" Beckham shouted.

The man and woman were already fleeing, pulling the child away. They disappeared into a building across the street, but the man with the shotgun held his ground. He fired off a blast at the creature, but missed. In a swift motion, she jumped on the front of the FEMA truck, landing on the hood in a crouch.

The man pumped the gun, aimed, and screamed, "Die, you bitch!" Before he could fire off a shot, a second creature burst from the glass shopwindow behind him. They rolled onto the ground, a cluster of limbs.

Beckham lined up the crosshairs of his MP5, but couldn't get a target. He shifted to his right, then his left.

Three seconds later, the man was dead, his face caved in by the barbaric blows of the monster straddling his body. Wincing, Beckham pulled the trigger and hit the creature with a burst in the back.

Blood splattered the concrete as the beast slumped to the ground.

The woman on the truck screeched, tilted her head, and extended a long, pale arm, pointing toward the squad car with a twisted hand—*toward him.* A chorus of shrieks seemed to answer her cries.

Below, another figure emerged from behind the shattered front door of a small shoe store. Down the street, an infected man came crashing out of a flower shop. More piled out of other buildings.

"Get out of there, boss," Riley yelled, his voice deep and tense.

The woman on the hood of the FEMA truck leaped onto the concrete. She broke into a sprint, zigzagging between cars before hitting the sidewalk across the street, where she dropped to all fours and bolted into the building where the survivors had fled.

Beckham hesitated. He had to save the kid. He had to save—

He blinked, watching dozens of the creatures streaming around the FEMA truck. Others scurried across the horizontal surface of the buildings to the left and right like spiders. Joints clicked and creaked. Their high-pitched squawks were indescribably terrible, a mixture of rage and pain. The street was alive with the monsters.

"Boss!" Horn yelled. "Get out of there!"

Fueled by fear, Beckham backpedaled as he fired off the rest of his magazine. Horn and Riley picked off the creatures on the walls, but there were too many. They were everywhere. Team Ghost had to retreat.

Beckham let out his own war cry as he changed magazines. He felt hopeless, knowing he couldn't save the child or the other survivors. For the third time in two weeks, he ran—away from the enemy, away from the death, away from the monsters.

Kate reached Building 4 out of breath. Her thoughts were clouded and confused. VariantX9H9 was not designed as a partial cure. It was designed to kill *everyone* infected with the virus. She'd never thought any of the victims would live.

Damn Gibson, she thought as she ran. He'd boxed her and the entire scientific community into a corner. They hadn't had the time to design a response—*she* hadn't had the time. At least he would pay for his crimes. He was locked away now, in complete isolation, waiting for the hammer to drop. When this was all over, he would answer to the entire world for his sins. She had no empathy for the man and his motivations. He deserved to burn.

When she got to Building 4, she skidded to a stop. The facility seemed eerily quiet. She stood under the radiant glow of an industrial light and scanned the entrance.

There were no guards or signs of scientists coming and going. There was only the darkness and the sporadic zap of a bug being fried as it got too close to the lights.

Looking back the way she had come, she saw a distant patrol of soldiers, their flashlight beams cutting through the night. The sight was a small relief, but still she felt a nagging doubt.

Where the hell was everyone at Building 4?

Ignoring her trepidation, she moved briskly across the hundred yards or so of darkness, where the illumination from the massive floodlights did not fall.

Climbing the steps to the entrance, she again paused. The remains of several cigarette butts littered the ground. Was it possible that the guards had taken a break without having another team replace them? Or perhaps Patient 12 had died, and now there was no longer a reason for the guards to remain.

She shook the questions away. There was only one way to find out. Removing her key card from her pocket, she waved it over the security panel. The door chirped, unlocked, and cracked open. She pulled the massive metal door open with a huff, surprised at how heavy it really was. Gasping for breath, she stepped inside the white atrium. Darkness greeted her.

Kate froze, scanning the room by what little light the open doorway provided. The hallway leading to the isolation chambers was lit only by a faint glow from an emergency light blinking at the far end.

Hesitating, Kate held the door open behind her, propping it open with her left foot. After a few seconds, her leg began to shake from the weight.

"Hello?" Kate called out.

The only reply that came was a loud bang that echoed down the corridor. Kate tried to place the noise, but she was so terrified she could hardly think.

Slowly she took a step backward. Before she could escape, her right foot slid across the wet floor. Crying out, she flailed for something to hold on to. Her hands came up empty, and she crashed to the floor with a thud.

Terrified, Kate flipped to her stomach and tried to push herself up. Her hands slid across the slippery floor and she fell forward, onto her chest.

The hair on her neck stood up when she heard the door close behind her, sealing with a metallic click. Another noise followed it. The sound was coming from the hallway. Another door had opened.

"Who's there?" she cried out.

The only reply was the sound of skittering feet.

Panicking, Kate swiveled her body in the direction of the corridor. She couldn't see anything but the faint glow of the single emergency light.

Closing her eyes, she pushed herself to her knees and spun back to the entrance. With her hands in front of her, she pawed the floor.

The sound of scurrying feet grew louder. It was closer now, and it sounded as if it was coming from above her— from the ceiling.

Frantic, Kate slid on the wet floor again. She collapsed onto something soft and knew instantly it was a body.

Gasping, she could only think of infection. Without her space suit, she suddenly felt naked. Kate held her breath and slipped into survival mode.

She scrambled across the tiles, searching the body for anything useful. A few feet away from the corpse, her fingers found the cold metal of a gun.

The sound of nails dragging across a chalkboard grew louder. It was almost on top of her now.

This isn't happening, she thought as she grabbed the rifle and pulled it to her chest. She had never fired a gun before. Didn't even really know how. She quickly found the trigger with her right hand and then ran her other hand down the length of the gun. She remembered the flashlight attachment she'd seen on the weapons.

With a soft click, a beam shot out and illuminated the dark hallway. She angled the gun across the floor, moving from side to side. The light didn't reveal any sign of life, only death.

The walls were covered in blood. The body of a guard lay sprawled out in the middle of the floor. A few feet to his right lay a technician, his legs bent in opposite directions.

A flash of movement pulled Kate away from the scene. She raised the weapon and scanned the ceiling, trying to follow the blur of skin. The stream of light caught the pale body of Patient 12 skittering across the ceiling panels.

Her blood froze when she saw the man, clinging to the ceiling upside down with claw-shaped hands and feet. He stopped when the light hit him. He sniffed the air, tilted his head, and locked onto her.

Kate froze, petrified with fear.

The creature hung there, smacking its lips together, in and out. In the blink of an eye, it released a croak and continued across the ceiling.

Kate instinctively squeezed the trigger. The gun clicked but did not fire. "Shit, shit, shit," she cried, fumbling with the rifle.

The scratching and scraping of Patient 12's nails sent another surge of fear through Kate. Her fingers crisscrossed the surface of the gun in a desperate attempt to find the safety.

Think, Kate, think. She'd seen guns before. The safety was usually on the side, just above the trigger. Her finger found the small lever, and she slid it into its unlocked position.

Falling to her back, she swung the muzzle of the gun toward the monster, following him as he crawled across the ceiling.

He was so fast.

And then he was sailing through the air, his hands extended in front of him, screaming with a rage unlike anything she'd ever heard.

Closing her eyes, she pulled back on the trigger and drowned out the terrible noise with the crack of automatic gunfire.

25

The wind howled in the distance, bringing with it the sound of the creatures. Subhuman shrieks that made Beckham's skin crawl. There were other noises too: the *click-clack* of joints popping and the scratching of claws as the creatures hunted.

Beckham peered over his shoulder but saw nothing beyond Riley and Horn's CBRN suits.

Darkness had claimed New York City, spreading a carpet of black over them. With the grid down, he was forced to use his NVGs.

His heart skipped a beat as he leaped across the narrow gap separating their building from the adjacent one. He landed with a thud but kept running, his boots pounding the concrete roof.

He heard Riley and Horn land a few seconds later. They had narrowly escaped to the rooftop, and they were on the run.

Beckham considered what had happened as he moved. From what he could see, he knew two things. One, the bioweapon Kate developed had killed the majority of the infected population. Two, the ones that had survived were different. They were smarter and more cunning. They didn't run into oncoming gunfire like their suicidal predecessors. Those who survived Kate's viral weapon were variants of the original infected.

Variants, he thought. That's what he would call them.

Beckham had never thought he would miss the days of chasing terrorists and engaging militants in firefights. At least those assholes didn't try to eat him. And they couldn't move like insects either. They usually kept both feet on the ground—much easier to shoot than these things that moved like spiders on PCP.

He skidded to a stop at the ledge of the rooftop and shouldered his rifle, trying the line to Plum Island again.

"Echo One, this is Ghost, do you copy? Over."

The response, to Beckham's surprise was almost instantaneous. "Ghost, Echo One. We are Oscar Mike, coming your way. What is your AO? Over."

Pausing, Beckham reached into his vest and withdrew a small handheld GPS. He read their coordinates and then looked over the edge.

"Roger. ETA of fifteen."

The channel faded to static.

Beckham's stomach churned when he saw the street below. Variants dashed across the tops of burned cars, jumping from vehicle to vehicle. He cursed under his breath. Fifteen minutes was a lifetime out here. They weren't going to make it two minutes if those things found them.

One of the beasts stopped below. She crouched and sniffed the air like a dog trying to pick up a scent. And she found it. Her eyes locked onto Beckham's position. He took a step away from the roof, his heart racing, bracing himself for the inevitable scream.

Nothing came.

When he peeked over the edge she was gone. Darting away with the others.

Exhaling, he scanned the flat rooftop. A billboard rose off the north end, giving them some cover. The other three sides were all exposed, save for a few stone gargoyles protruding from the ledges. It wasn't the best place to make a stand, but they'd run out of roofs.

Riley and Horn were waiting for him at the center of the rooftop. "Horn, you guard the east. Riley, you got the south side. I'll set the claymores on that billboard in case they come up that side. Then I've got the west perimeter."

"Gotcha, boss," Riley said.

"On it," Horn replied.

They fanned out. Beckham ran to the base of the billboard, dropped his rucksack, and took out the mines. The sign stood on a frame of steel that was bolted into the roof. Beckham positioned one mine to fire up the back of the billboard and the other to fire at its base, in case any Variants came up the side and tried to crawl through the support structure. When he was done, he uncoiled enough cord to reach the southwest corner of the roof, where he had placed the detonators. Then he returned to the west ledge and angled his rifle over the side, squinting.

The pack of Variants had disappeared. Maybe they'd lost the scent in the rain? Whatever happened, they were gone for now.

A small victory.

Beckham was struck by a brief moment of nostalgia, the feeling of uncertainty he'd experienced before entering Building 8 weeks earlier. He'd known something didn't feel right, but still he'd remained committed to the mission—committed until it was too late to save his men.

As he scanned the streets below, that same feeling of

doubt swept over him. Chinning his comm he said, "Any contacts?"

"Negative," Horn and Riley replied simultaneously.

Shit, where are they? Beckham studied the shadows below and the side of the building across the street.

Nothing.

Beckham walked slowly along the ledge, his weapon aimed at the rooftop just above Riley's location. The building stood only about five feet above Riley's head, and a narrow gap was all that separated the two rooftops. They'd made the jump with ease, and he could only imagine how easy it would be for one of the Variants.

Beckham looked at his wristwatch. Ten minutes to go. He didn't mind waiting in silence. He almost grinned at the idea of a violence-free evac. The thought was shameful. They had left behind survivors, including a kid. Why the fuck should he be so lucky as to get out of NYC in one piece, unscathed, as he always did? His face twisted into a frown, and he closed his eyes, hating Gibson for having caused all of this and hating himself for not being able to save the only people he'd seen who survived it.

The sound of scratching yanked him from his thoughts of self-pity.

He looked over his side of the building, but saw no motion.

"You got anything, Riley?" Beckham asked.

"Negative."

"Nothing," Horn added.

Where the fuck was that sound coming from, then? He moved along the edge of the roof. A slight breeze whistled around his helmet.

He checked his watch again.

Eight minutes left.

The scratching sound faded in the whistling of the wind.
Was he losing his nerve?

Another three minutes passed, and a soft rain began to
fall from the sky. The drops trickled down Beckham's visor,
clearing it of dust. He ran his sleeve against the panel and
did another quick scan of the rooftop and then the street.

"Still no contacts, boss," Riley said over the comm.

Two minutes left.

His heart rate spiked when he heard the bottomless howl-
ing, followed by an angry torrent of shrieks.

Beckham twisted to see a wave of Variants spilling over
the edge of the billboard. He snapped into motion before his
mind had processed what had happened. Loping forward, he
raced for the detonators and yelled, "Fire in the hole!"

Horn dove next to him, hunkering down. Riley ran for the
opposite corner and slid on his knees, covering his helmet
with his hands.

The instant the kid was in position, Beckham detonated
the mines.

A deafening explosion shook the rooftop. The tremor rattled the entire building. He clenched his jaw and looked up
as the billboard toppled over the ledge, taking with it several
thrashing Variants.

When the smoke started to clear, Beckham and Horn
stood, their weapons sweeping for hostiles.

"You okay, Kid?" Beckham shouted. His ears were ringing, but he could still hear Riley's response.

"I'm fine, boss!"

The smoke drifted away, revealing a rooftop littered with
chunks of gore. Beckham breathed a sigh of relief. Thank
God he had packed the mines.

He was clapping Horn on the back when he heard a faint
scraping.

No, he thought, *it's not possible*.

He twisted and shouldered his rifle just as a swarm of Variants climbed over the smoldering edge of the roof. Their suckers puckered in the air, popping. There were no sniffing noses or primal shrieks. The creatures knew exactly where Team Ghost was.

Gunfire erupted on both of Beckham's flanks.

He tapped his vest pocket. "I hope you're looking after us, Mom," he whispered. He centered his gun on the monsters and pulled the trigger.

Two of the Variants dropped immediately, their screams fading over the crack of Horn's M249 and the blasts from Riley's shotgun.

Beckham squeezed off calculated burst after burst, careful of his ammunition. He counted the seconds in his head until he heard the distant whoosh of a helicopter. His comm crackled, and the sweet sound of the pilot's voice filled his earpiece.

"Ghost, Echo One, approaching your AO. Over."

Beckham fired again. The rounds hit one of the Variants in the back of the head, splattering bone and brains over the ground.

"Copy. Extraction zone is hot!" Beckham yelled. "Hurry the fuck up! Extraction zone is hot!"

Riley and Horn retreated with their weapons blazing, but the Variants chasing them were so damn fast, dashing and lunging from side to side.

Beckham finished off his last magazine and then pulled his M9. With one eye closed, he followed one of the Variants as it bolted toward Riley. Holding his breath, he squeezed off a shot.

The bullet caught the man in the chin, sending him flying to the side. Riley swung his shotgun around and finished off the injured Variant before he could recover.

"Thanks," Riley shouted.

"Changing," Horn yelled. "Cover me."

Beckham turned his pistol on the final four Variants that were charging their position. "Run!" he yelled. He fired off another flurry of shots, dropping two of the creatures.

Horn held his ground, tossing his M249 to the roof and withdrawing two M9s from his back belt. Fire erupted from the barrels. A head exploded in a spray of mist.

Screaming, Horn trained his gun on the final Variant. He fired until his pistols were dry, the bullets tearing into the monster's chest, sending it flying into the night.

Beckham surveyed the rooftop and the twisted bodies of dying Variants. A few of them spasmed and kicked as they took their final breaths.

"Prepare for extraction!" he yelled. The team met in the middle of the rooftop. With their backs together, they reloaded and waited, muzzles sweeping their zones of fire for more contacts.

The ringing in Beckham's ears gave way to the thump of the Black Hawk's blades. He watched a rope drop in front of them.

Salvation.

Lowering his pistol, Beckham grabbed the rope and attached it to a clip on Horn's belt. When it was secure, he flashed a thumbs-up to the crew chief in the cargo hold above.

Riley and Beckham stepped away as Horn was pulled into the air. Neither of them heard the sound of the Variants approaching from the south. When Horn finally saw them it was too late.

"Watch out! Your six!" Horn yelled.

Two of the creatures sprang off the adjacent building and came dashing across the rooftop.

Beckham saw them just in time to squeeze off a single shot. The bullet only slowed the first man down. He snarled and kept running. Horn took him down a beat later, a round puncturing the Variant's heart.

The other creature, a woman with a screen of hair covering her eyes, lunged toward Riley. She landed on him with her feet first, knocking him to the ground with a sickening crunch.

Beckham aimed, but couldn't get a clear shot. Tossing it aside, he dove for the woman as she beat the side of Riley's helmet. Another Variant barreled into him before he could reach the woman, sending Beckham crashing to the ground.

He struggled to his back as the man punched and clawed at his head. Blood flowed from a wound in the creature's chest, squirting onto his visor. Beckham fought back, throwing punch after punch, but he couldn't see shit. Each blow scraped past the shrieking beast on top of him.

Beckham glimpsed movement to the side, where a pair of boots landed on the gravel. He recognized Horn's oversized shoes instantly.

Thrashing, Beckham did his best to deflect the torrent of punches. He was now in survival mode, trying to limit the damage.

"Help Riley!" he yelled at the top of his lungs. There was no fucking way that Beckham was going to let the kid die.

Horn's boots vanished and Beckham heard the crack of an M9. There was a second shot. Gore speckled Beckham's visor. He gasped, struggling for air, hot puffs exploding inside his helmet.

He felt the weight of the creature on top of him go limp, and with a small grunt Beckham tossed the corpse off him. Wiping his visor with the sleeve of his CBRN suit, he cleared the pane free of the chunks of brain matter.

Horn was hunched over Riley, a few feet away. Beckham quickly stumbled to his feet. The kid reached up as he approached, blood gurgling out of his mouth behind a cracked visor.

"I'm sorry, boss," Riley choked.

Beckham's heart sank when he saw Riley's battered face. He could hardly make out the young man's features.

"Take it easy, Kid," Beckham replied. He crouched next to Riley and grabbed his right hand, clutching it in his own. "We're going to get you out of here."

"Can't feel my legs," Riley said.

Beckham glanced down. The kid's right leg was ruined. A broken bone protruded from his suit just above the ankle. There was no time for a tourniquet. They had to get him to the bird first.

Riley tightened his grip on Beckham's hand. "I'm sorry," he repeated.

"Contacts incoming. Let's move, Ghost," one of the pilots said over the comm.

"Horn," Beckham yelled, motioning with a hand for the larger man to help him. Together they pulled Riley to his feet and dragged the kid over to the rope. He wailed in pain as they attached it to a clip on his belt.

A flash of movement from the south side of the building pulled Beckham's attention to another group of Variants. He could hear their claws scratching across the concrete over the whoosh of the blades. There were dozens of them, galloping across the rooftop of the adjacent building.

"Go!" Beckham yelled, giving the crew chief above a thumbs-up.

He watched as Riley's limp body was pulled toward the chopper. When the kid was halfway up, Beckham reached for another magazine and jammed it home into his M9. Horn ran to where he'd dropped his M249, reloaded it, and leveled it at the approaching creatures.

Standing shoulder to shoulder, the two operators fired. Something inside Beckham snapped in that moment. An internal machine activated. His gun became part of him. He killed without thought. He killed to avenge his fallen brothers, and he killed to protect the brother beside him. They would fight to the bitter end, to the final bullet.

Kate woke up freezing cold. Her teeth chattered as she struggled to open her eyes. With one eyelid cracked open, she saw a bank of lights hanging from the white ceiling.

Where was she? In a hospital?

Panicking, Kate tried to sit up, but her arms, feet, and hands wouldn't budge. She thrashed and twisted in protest, fear gripping her, but whatever was holding her down was tight. Lifting her head slightly, she saw white restraints strapped across her body. And then she remembered what had happened inside Building 4.

The last thing she could recall was Patient 12 lunging at her, the man's crazed eyes caught in the beam of her flashlight.

"Hey!" she screamed. "Someone get me out of here."

Squirming, she tried to get free again, but it was futile. The restraints were tight. She wasn't going anywhere.

"Help!" Kate yelled, desperation in her voice.

She froze when she heard the heavy rap of boots in the hallway. They stopped outside her door.

"Good evening, Doctor Lovato. I know you can't see me, but this is Lieutenant Colonel Jensen. I'm here with Major Smith. You are one hell of a lucky lady."

She lifted her head. Throbbing pain rippled down her

skull and neck. Closing her eyes, she clenched her jaw and waited for the pain to pass.

"Where am I?" Kate winced.

"You're in the medical ward, Building Three," Jensen replied. "I'm sorry we had to quarantine you. It's for your own safety. I'm sure you understand that."

"I feel fine," Kate said. "I'm not infected. I can't be," she said, her voice trailing off. For a moment, she felt unsure. The virus would have purged from Patient 12's body, but there was the small chance that some virions remained.

Kate felt her heart flutter and stared at the ceiling. She tried to remain calm. "When can I get out of here?"

"Soon," Jensen said. "In the meantime we need to talk to you. Operation Depletion has been an overall success," he stated. "But as you are aware, some of the infected survived. Reports are coming in right now. So far it's looking like somewhere between four and eight percent of the infected are recovering."

"That high?" Kate said, her eyes snapping back open.

"Unfortunately. The interim POTUS has authorized the mission to continue, however. Air assets are currently deploying VariantX9H9 around the country, moving from larger cities to smaller ones."

Kate felt her heart kick hard.

"Doctor Lovato, this is Major Smith."

"We are now moving into Phase Two of deploying the bioweapon, as Colonel Jensen just explained. We want to—"

"What's Phase Three?" Kate interrupted before he could finish.

Jensen's voice reemerged. "Cleanup. Once Phase Two is complete, we'll coordinate targeted air strikes and send in ground troops for the final sweep. One by one, we will clear the cities of the remaining hostiles."

Kate closed her eyes again. How many hostiles were they talking about? And how long would it take? She felt too tired to ask any more questions. Her body ached, and she just wanted to sleep.

An explosion of sounds echoed in the passage beyond. She struggled to move, to get a view of the glass window in her room.

Wheels screeching against the ground. A panicked voice said something she couldn't hear.

No.

Two panicked voices, and a third.

"Move! Get this guy into surgery ASAP!"

"Is he going to be okay?"

"You guys need to wait out here!"

Kate recognized the second voice. It was Horn. Which meant... Lifting her head despite the pain, she watched Smith and Jensen throw their backs against the wall as medical staff rushed by with a patient on a gurney. Horn and Beckham followed close behind. They were dressed in decon outfits.

"Reed!" she yelled.

The man stopped, acknowledging Jensen and Smith before meeting Kate's eyes with a confused gaze.

"Glad you're back in one piece," Jensen said.

Beckham nodded and moved to the glass, palming the surface with a clean hand still glistening wet from the showers. "Kate, what happened? Why are you in there?"

Summoning her most confident voice, she said, "I'm fine."

"She was exposed," Jensen said. "We had to quarantine her."

Beckham shook his head and he looked down the hallway. He muttered something she couldn't make out.

"Who was that?" Kate asked, terrified to hear the truth.

"Riley. He's hurt. Hurt bad," Beckham said, bowing his head as a tear coursed down his cheek, a moment of weakness finally bleeding through.

Kate felt tears welling in her eyes. She blinked them away. She needed to be strong for Beckham, as he had been for her. "I'm so sorry."

"He's going to be okay," Beckham replied, confident now. "And so are you." Lifting his chin, he narrowed his eyes. Kate struggled to keep her head up.

"We have work to do, Kate. You have work to do. There are still monsters out there."

"I know," Kate replied. "That's why I need to get out of here. I need to get back to my lab." Shaking in her restraints, Kate let her frustration show. "I'm fine!" she called, to anyone who would listen. "You can let me out of here, *now*."

Jensen shuffled to Beckham's left side. "I'm sorry, Doctor Lovato, but you know better than anyone we have protocol to follow."

"Screw protocol. I'm *fine*."

Shaking his head, Jensen stepped away from the glass. "I'll send a technician to check on you in an hour."

He put a hand on Beckham's shoulder and whispered something Kate couldn't hear. Then Jensen and Smith left, the sound of their footsteps fading down the hallway.

Beckham remained. He reached into his pocket and pulled something out.

She smiled. It was the picture of his mom.

"I'm going to put this right here," Beckham said. Reaching down, he set the image on the windowsill. "Now you have your own guardian angel. You're going to be okay," he said. "When you get better, we'll face this thing together." He turned and looked down the hallway. "They're taking the kid into surgery. I need to go."

Kate nodded. "Wait," she said. "Thank you, Reed."

"No, thank you. For giving me the strength to get through my last mission," he said, pointing at the picture. Then he rushed away, leaving Kate alone.

She stared at the image, thoughts drifting through her worried mind. She remembered Michael's final words: *In order to kill a monster, you will have to create one.*

The survivors of VariantX9H9 were those monsters now. The future wasn't set, but Kate knew they were entering a new phase of human evolution. There were two versions of the human species now. The X9H9 Variants would hunt down the human survivors in every corner of the earth. There would be no time to grieve, no time to rest. As long as they were out there, she had a job to do. She had to stop them before Michael's theory came true.

She hadn't believed him when he said that this could be the extinction event, or maybe she hadn't *wanted* to believe him. But after two weeks of watching life hemorrhage away around the globe, she realized that the extinction of the human race wasn't just a vague possibility; it was now on the horizon.

If you want to hear more about Nicholas Sansbury Smith's upcoming books, join his newsletter or follow him on social media. He just might keep you from the brink of extinction!

Newsletter: www.eepurl.com/bggNg9

Twitter: www.twitter.com/greatwaveink

Facebook: www.facebook.com/Nicholas -Sansbury-Smith-124009881117534

Website: www.nicholassansbury.com

For those who'd like to personally contact Nicholas, he would love to hear from you.

Greatwaveink@gmail.com

Acknowledgments

It's always hard for me to write this section for fear of leaving someone out. So many people had a hand in the creation of the Extinction Cycle and I know these stories would not be worth reading if I didn't have the overwhelming support of family, friends, and readers.

Before I thank those people, I wanted to give a bit of background on how the Extinction Cycle was conceived and the journey it has been on since I started writing. The story began more than five years ago, when I was still working as a planner for the state of Iowa and also during my time as a project officer for Iowa Homeland Security and Emergency Management. I had several duties throughout my tenure with the state, but my primary focus was protecting infrastructure and working on the state hazard mitigation plan. After several years of working in the disaster mitigation field, I learned of countless threats: from natural disasters to manmade weapons, and one of the most horrifying threats of all—a lab-created biological weapon.

Fast-forward to 2014, when my writing career started to take off. I was working on the Orbs series and brainstorming my next science fiction adventure. Back then, the genre was saturated with zombie books. I wanted to write something unique and different, a story that explained, scientifically, how a virus could turn men into monsters. During this time, the Ebola virus was raging through western Africa and several cases showed up in the continental United States for the first time.

After talking with my biomedical-engineer friend, Tony Melchiorri, an idea formed for a book that played on the risk the Ebola virus posed. That idea blossomed after I started researching chemical and biological weapons, many of which dated back to the Cold War. In March of 2014, I sat down to pen the first pages of *Extinction Horizon*, the first book in what would become the Extinction Cycle. Using real science and the terrifying premise of a government-made bioweapon I set out to tell my story.

The Extinction Cycle quickly found an audience. The first three novels came out in rapid succession and seemed to spark life back into the zombie craze. The audiobook, narrated by the award-winning Bronson Pinchot climbed the charts, hitting the top spot on Audible. As I released books four and five, more readers discovered the Extinction Cycle—more than three hundred thousand to date. The German translation was recently released in November 2016 and Amazon's Kindle Worlds has opened the Extinction universe to other authors.

Even more exciting, two years after I published *Extinction Horizon*, Orbit decided to purchase and rerelease the series. The copy you are reading is the newly edited and polished version. I hope you've enjoyed it.

The Extinction Cycle wouldn't exist without the help of a small army of editors, beta readers, and the support of family and friends. I also owe a great deal of gratitude to my initial editors, Aaron Sikes and Erin Elizabeth Long, as well as my good author-friend Tony Melchiorri. The trio spent countless hours on the Extinction Cycle books. Without them these stories would not be what they are. Erin also helped edit *Orbs* and *Hell Divers*. She's been with me pretty much since day one, and I appreciate her more than she knows. So, thanks Erin, Tony, and Aaron.

A special thanks goes to David Fugate, my agent, who provided valuable feedback on the early version of *Extinction Horizon* and the entire Extinction Cycle series. I'm grateful for his support and guidance.

Another special thanks goes to Blackstone Audio for their support of the audio version. Narrator Bronson Pinchot also played, and continues to play, a vital role in bringing the story to life.

They say a person is only as good as those that they surround themselves with. I've been fortunate to surround myself with talented people much smarter than myself. I've also had the support from excellent publishers like Blackstone and Orbit.

I would be remiss if I didn't also thank the people for whom I write: the readers. I've been blessed to have my work read in countries around the world by wonderful people. If you are reading this, know that I truly appreciate you for trying my stories.

To my family, friends, and everyone else who has supported me on this journey, I thank you.

extras

orbit

meet the author

NICHOLAS SANSBURY SMITH is the *USA Today* bestselling author of *Hell Divers*, the Orbs trilogy, and the Extinction Cycle. He worked for Iowa Homeland Security and Emergency Management in disaster mitigation before switching careers to focus on his one true passion: writing. When he isn't writing or daydreaming about the apocalypse, he enjoys running, biking, spending time with his family, and traveling the world. He is an Ironman triathlete and lives in Iowa with his fiancée, their dogs, and a houseful of books.

introducing

If you enjoyed
EXTINCTION HORIZON,
look out for

EXTINCTION EDGE

The Extinction Cycle

by Nicholas Sansbury Smith

A new threat will bring humanity to the edge of extinction....

The dust from Dr. Kate Lovato's bioweapon has settled. Projections put the death toll in the billions. Her weapon was supposed to be the end game, but it turned a small percentage of those infected with the hemorrhage virus into something even worse.

Survivors call them Variants. Irreversible epigenetic changes have transformed them into predators unlike any the human race has ever seen—and they are evolving.

The fractured military plans Operation Liberty—a desperate mission designed to take back the cities and destroy the Variant threat. Master Sergeant Reed Beckham agrees to lead a strike team into New York City, but first he must return to Fort Bragg to search for the only family he has left.

As Operation Liberty draws closer, Kate warns Beckham that not only will Team Ghost face their deadliest adversary yet, they may be heading into a trap...

The room erupted with applause as Dr. Kate Lovato entered the mess hall. Uniformed men and women from every branch of the military stood and clapped, cheering as she walked past.

The sound took Kate's breath away. Ever since her bio-weapon, VariantX9H9, had been deployed, she had been hailed as the "savior" of the world, the woman who had stopped the hemorrhage virus in its tracks. But there were others in the audience who glared at her with resentment. She knew what they were thinking: She wasn't a savior, she was a monster. And she felt like one. The burden of so much death rested solely on her shoulders. The weight made it difficult to breathe.

Her gaze gravitated to the commander of Plum Island, Lieutenant Colonel Ray Jensen. The African American commander narrowed his eyes as she approached. He clapped with the others, but he was sizing her up too, seeing if she was mentally fit to address the crowd. They had let her out of quarantine only a day earlier, and she was still a bit groggy.

"Good morning, everyone," Jensen said, bringing a mic to his mouth. "I think all of you know Doctor Kate Lovato, with the CDC."

More cheering rang through the room. Kate scanned the faces for someone familiar, but soon realized she was alone. Her friends were all working. Dr. Pat Ellis was in the lab, and Master Sergeant Reed Beckham and Staff Sergeant Parker Horn were in the hospital with their injured teammate, Staff Sergeant Alex Riley. The kid had come back from New York with two shattered legs. He was evidence that her weapon hadn't killed all of the monsters—a new threat had emerged in the blood-soaked streets.

The Variants.

Kate shivered at the thought. The memory of the Variant that had attacked her two days ago was fresh on her mind. She could still hear the creature's claws skittering across the ceiling. It was an experience she would never forget.

"Thank you for coming, Doctor," Jensen said. He handed Kate the mic and gestured toward a podium with the Medical Corps insignia on the front.

Kate knew what he wanted from her. He wanted her to reassure the staff on Plum Island that there was still hope, that the Variants could be defeated.

Clearing her throat, she said, "Good morning, everyone. I was told to give you all a sitrep on what's happening outside. There is good news and bad news. The good news is that Variant X9H9 is still being deployed in every major city. Ninety percent of the infected are dying. The weapon attacks their endothelial cells and causes massive internal bleeding. It's a relatively quick death."

Kate paused and scanned the crowd, focusing on a woman in the front row. She was dressed in a neatly pressed navy uniform. The officer couldn't have been more than twenty-five years old. When she saw Kate looking at her, she stiffened her back and smiled. Her eyes pleaded with Kate to say something encouraging, to tell them that things were going to be okay.

But Kate couldn't lie. She couldn't feed these people false hope. After a brief pause, she continued. "The bad news is that the other ten percent of the infected are recovering from the Ebola virus, but not the effects of VX-99. Those epigenetic changes seem to be irreversible at this point."

The word hung in the air, and nervous voices broke from the crowd. A familiar feeling of dread crept into her thoughts and caused her mind to drift. It threatened to steal her sanity, to break her.

Closing her eyes, she said, "I don't believe there is anything we can do to bring these people back." She shook her head. As she handed the mic back to Jensen, she muttered two final words: "I'm sorry."

She rushed out of the room with her eyes downcast, avoiding every single glare. No one stopped her or protested her departure. They were still digesting what she had just told them. Learning that VariantX9H9 had only delayed the inevitable was difficult to stomach, even for the most hardened of soldiers.

A Medical Corps guard opened the door, and Kate stumbled out into the blinding morning sunlight. Shielding her eyes with a hand, she looked out over the island.

Kate wasn't the type of person to leave others behind. She never ran from a fight. But the death toll from her bioweapon had taken a piece of her. The numbers were hard to fathom, with billions of losses that produced a constant ache that wouldn't go away.

She walked aimlessly across the island and paused to study the ocean, wondering what was on the other side. In the end, she'd done her job. She had stopped the spread of the virus, though she'd fallen short in eradicating the monsters. Now she could only wonder what the world looked like beyond the safety of the island.

The American military had shared the recipe for VariantX9H9 with the nation's European allies, but the strike on foreign soil had come days after the US operation. Kate hoped it hadn't been too late to save her parents, living in Italy.

Exhaling a sigh, she continued through the hexagonal campus. The white, domed buildings rose above her. She wasn't sure where she was headed; her thoughts were muddied with guilt and regrets. They drifted from Javier, her brother, to her mentor, Dr. Michael Allen. They'd been dead even before the missiles descended on Atlanta and Chicago, but if they hadn't, they would have died from VariantX9H9. From *her* bioweapon.

Kate choked on the thought.

She didn't fight the tears that streaked down her cheeks. Everyone had a breaking point, a moment where everything came crashing down. Kate had finally reached hers.

There was only one person left in the world who could make her feel better, and he was in the medical building nearby. For the first time that morning, Kate felt a sudden burst of energy. She finally knew where she was going.

Staff Sergeant Alex Riley couldn't believe his fate. He'd built a career on his speed and his ability to sneak in and out of some of the most secure locations in the world. Now he lay in a hospital bed, staring at his shattered legs and wondering if he would ever run again.

If it weren't for Beckham and Horn, he would never have made it off that rooftop. Then again, he would never have made it out of Building 8 at San Nicolas Island without them either. What were the odds?

Riley let out a sad laugh.

The noise woke Horn and Beckham. They stirred in stiff-looking chairs facing the foot of his bed.

"Feeling better?" Beckham asked.

Riley eyed his casts. "I'm happy to be alive. But my legs, man."

"They'll heal," Beckham said.

"I thought you were toast, Kid," Horn said, his voice scratchy.

"Me too," Beckham said.

"Shit. It's going to take a lot more than some crazed shithead to take me out." Riley laughed. "I would have been fine without you guys."

Horn rolled his eyes. "Right. You had the situation under *complete* control."

"Damn straight," Riley said.

The three men chuckled. It was the first time in weeks that they'd all had a good laugh. It was like old times, but they knew that things would never be the same.

A rap on the door pulled them back to the grim reality of the status quo, where old times were nothing but memories. Kate waited outside, waving from the other side of the small window in the door.

"Beckham, it's your girlfriend," Riley said, jerking his chin toward Kate.

Beckham shot him an angry glare but didn't respond. His narrowed, dark eyes were enough to silence Riley. He knew what Beckham was thinking: *Keep your trap shut or you're going to stay in that bed even longer.*

"It's open," Horn mumbled, scooting his chair to the side.

"Morning," Kate said.

Riley picked up a hint of sadness in her soft voice. He watched her walk into the room and stand a few feet away from Beckham. The shadows of the dimly lit space couldn't conceal her swollen, red eyes. It wasn't surprising, Riley thought, considering she had killed most of the world's population.

"How are you doing, Alex?" Kate asked. She hardly made eye contact with the men.

Riley forced a smile. He wasn't used to people calling him by his first name. "I'm feeling much better. The pain meds here are killer."

Kate nodded. "You can thank Colonel Gibson for that."

"How's that piece of shit doing?" Horn asked.

"He's awaiting trial," Kate said. "I noticed Lieutenant Colonel Jensen posted another guard outside his room. Must be worried about the man's safety."

Beckham stood and stretched. "I would be too, if I were him."

"There aren't enough soldiers on this island to protect Gibson from what's comin' to him." Horn snorted.

Riley shuddered. His friends were right. The colonel was partially responsible for the end of the world. He had earned a spot at the top of the list of the biggest assholes in the history of the human species.

"Any developments?" Beckham asked.

Kate shook her head. "Not really. We have reports coming in from Europe that VariantX9H9 has destroyed around ninety percent of those infected with the hemorrhage virus."

"And the ones it didn't work on?" Beckham asked.

Kate's brittle voice cracked. "Variants."

"How many do you think there are worldwide?" Riley asked.

Kate rubbed her forehead. "The last projections I put together were from old numbers, but that's all we have to go on. I estimate about seventy-five to eighty percent of the world's population has been infected with the hemorrhage virus."

Silence washed over them. No one spoke. Riley did the math in his head—if five and a half billion people had been infected, and now 10 percent of them were Variants...

"Holy shit," Riley said. "Five hundred and fifty million Variants? There's one of those things for every three human survivors." He let out a low whistle.

Kate cupped her hands over her head. "You don't need to remind me."

"Sorry," Riley said. He reached for a pillow and propped it behind his back, wincing in pain.

"You did what you had to do, Kate," Beckham said. He stood and put a hand on her shoulder. "You saved the human race."

Kate glanced up, tears sparkling in her eyes. "I stalled the inevitable."

"What's that mean?" Riley asked. "We all know the world will never be the same. But even after we kill all of those things, we'll still have people left to rebuild society, the economy, food production..."

Riley searched Kate's face for confirmation, but she pivoted away to stare out the window. She parted the blinds with a finger, letting the sun leak through. "The human race might be the next species on the extinction list after all," she said, with her back still to Riley, Horn, and Beckham.

Sandra Hickman and Ralph Benzing looked exhausted. They sat in front of a wall of communications equipment in the command center, quietly skimming the channels for intel.

Lieutenant Colonel Ray Jensen paced behind them anxiously. Both communications officers were in the twelfth hour of their shift, and he could tell that the coffee was finally starting to wear off.

Chatter was coming in from around the country. Jen-

sen hadn't even started filtering the info streaming in from
Europe. There was so much to process, but his priority was
Plum Island and keeping his people safe. There was also a
larger mission—a mission that Central Command was still
piecing together.

"Here we go," Benzing said, cupping his hands over his
headset. "I'm picking something up."

Jensen chewed the inside of his lip. The phantom taste of
tobacco made his stomach growl. Four days without it and
he was already going through withdrawals. Digging into his
pocket, he felt for a piece of chewing gum.

"Patch it over the speakers," Jensen said, preparing himself for the worst. He'd never been much of a deep thinker;
taking things too seriously caused unnecessary stress. Now
that he was acting commander of one of humanity's last
strongholds, all of that had changed. The fate of so many
rested in his hands. Every single soul on the island was
invaluable. Whatever Command was cooking up was likely
to put many of his own in harm's way, and he wasn't looking
forward to it.

"It's an automated message," Hickman said. "I'm picking
it up on several frequencies."

"Switching," Benzing said. "Mine just cut out."

The speakers coughed static and then went silent for several seconds.

"What happened?" Jensen asked. He leaned over Benzing's
shoulder as a voice suddenly crackled from the speakers.

"This is General Richard Kennor, broadcasting from
Offutt Air Force Base. This mission might be the most
important in the history of the United States military. Our
species has been divided. Operation Depletion was a success, but now we face a new enemy. I have seen with my
own eyes what these creatures are capable of. Our brave men

and women in the armed services are vastly outnumbered. But we have something these monsters do not." He paused for a moment and then said, "We have the weapons of the twenty-first century."

Goose bumps popped up on Jensen's skin as the general's voice grew louder. That was the effect legendary commanders had on those under their command. They could convince young men to run into enemy fire and politicians to fund wars based on lies.

"With these weapons at our disposal, I am confident that we *will* retake our streets. America will once again be a free nation," Kennor said.

There was a break in the transmission. The general came back online a moment later. "In ninety-six hours we will embark on Operation Liberty, a massive coordinated attack that will send our remaining troops into every major city to destroy the enemy. Stand by for specific orders to be relayed to individual bases and outposts in the coming hours."

Jensen caught Hickman's worried gaze. He stood strong, his arms folded. Managing his emotions was key to reassuring those under his command. With more at stake than ever before, it was imperative he retain his composure.

Giving Hickman a strong nod, Jensen walked to the observation window. "Get Major Smith on the line. Tell him to get here ASAP. We have a war to plan."

Beckham shoveled a spoonful of slop into his mouth. He wasn't even sure what he was eating. It tasted a bit like fish but had the texture of chicken. He forced the food down and looked over at Kate.

She cringed. "What is this?"

"Better get used to it," Beckham said in between bites. "We're going to be eating reserve supplies. Riley was right when he mentioned food production. The world economy has shut down, which means..."

Kate answered with an exaggerated sigh. "No more hamburgers."

Beckham chuckled. "I thought you were going to say 'no more margaritas' or something."

"We still have tequila," she said with a wink.

Beckham held his spoon in front of his lips and ran his tongue along the roof of his mouth as he studied the doctor. She wasn't exactly his type, definitely not the kind of woman that he normally dated—when he dated, anyway, he reminded himself. The last woman he'd dated had been a yoga instructor. That had ended when he walked in on her banging a college football player half his age.

He'd have kicked the guy's ass if he had cared enough. Beckham had always been loyal to his team first. He had yet to meet a woman who could hang with him on a ten-mile run or three-mile swim. And that was okay. His career had taken precedence over finding a partner. His men were his family.

But he couldn't deny there was something about Kate. She carried herself in a graceful way. Strong, intelligent, and striking, she was the type of woman his mother would have wanted him to marry. He shook his head. There was no place for those thoughts in this new world. Everyone was dead or dying outside the safety of their little island. He refused to be the asshole who made a move on a woman at such a vulnerable time. But he couldn't deny he was attracted to her. More than that, he cared about her. Looking at Kate made him realize, for the first time in a very long time, that he *could* care.

Horn walked briskly toward their table. His eyebrows were scrunched together, his strawberry-blond hair sticking out in all directions as if he'd been running his hands over his skull.

"What's wrong?" Beckham asked.

"Lieutenant Colonel Jensen and Major Smith want to see us," Horn said. He turned to Kate. "Wants to see you too."

Kate finished off her plastic cup of juice and raised a brow. "About what?"

"Sounds like Central Command is planning something big."

Beckham dropped his spoon into the mush on his tray. He had known another operation was in the works. If he were in charge, he'd be planning one himself.

Kate and Beckham stood at the same time, grabbing their trays and following Horn between the packed tables. Several uniformed men and women glanced up from their food as they walked by. For once they weren't looking at him or Horn. They were looking at Kate.

"There goes the savior of the world," an African American marine sneered. Beckham recognized him from weeks before. He paused in his tracks and took a step back, shooting the man an angry glare.

"You have a problem, Johnson?" Beckham asked. His nostrils flared.

"No," Johnson said. "Sorry."

Beckham nodded and held the man's gaze for several seconds before following Kate and Horn outside. When they reached the door, she leaned over and whispered, "Thank you, Master Sergeant."